"I worry about you," Belle whispered to Falcon. "Whenever you're away, I pray for you constantly."

"You refused to become my wife, Belle. How can you worry like one?"

They slid together off the horse; they had arrived at his camp, in the familiar small clearing. The ground was softened with a thick carpet of leaves and a stream that flowed into the Wateree River provided clear, sweet water. It was a fine home for him, but it was no place for Belle.

"I'll build you a fine house," he promised as he set her on her feet. "Just as soon as the war is over."

"I'd not even thought of a house," Belle replied, twisting her hair atop her head to keep the long curls out of his way. When he stepped back, she shrugged off her gown, then turned to help him peel off his shirt. She laid her palms on his chest and felt his heart beating far more steadily than her own. "Here we can see the stars, and hear the song of the stream."

"You are very easy to please," Falcon murmured against her throat.

"No, sir. I am not. You're the only man I've ever allowed to try."

He ran his fingertips over her smooth shoulders. "I have pleased you, haven't I, Belle?"

"Always," Belle promised against his lips, and she was so lost in him she didn't see a single star overhead, or hear the musical trill of the stream. . . .

BOOK YOUR PLACE ON OUR WEBSITE AND MAKE THE READING CONNECTION!

We've created a customized website just for our very special readers, where you can get the inside scoop on everything that's going on with Zebra, Pinnacle and Kensington books.

When you come online, you'll have the exciting opportunity to:

- View covers of upcoming books
- Read sample chapters
- Learn about our future publishing schedule (listed by publication month *and author*)
- Find out when your favorite authors will be visiting a city near you
- Search for and order backlist books from our online catalog
- Check out author bios and background information
- Send e-mail to your favorite authors
- Meet the Kensington staff online
- Join us in weekly chats with authors, readers and other guests
- Get writing guidelines
- AND MUCH MORE!

Visit our website at
http://www.zebrabooks.com

WILD LEGACY

Phoebe Conn

Zebra Books
Kensington Publishing Corp.
http://www.zebrabooks.com

ZEBRA BOOKS are published by

Kensington Publishing Corp.
850 Third Avenue
New York, NY 10022

First Printing: January, 1999
10 9 8 7 6 5 4 3 2 1

Printed in the United States of America

'Tis love that
makes me bold and resolute,
Love that can find a way
where path there's none,
Of all the gods, the most
invincible.

—Euripides
(480-406 BC)

One

Summer, 1780
Williamsburg, Virginia

Belle Barclay replaced the worn volume of Thomas Gray's poetry in the bookcase. Then, seeking something more to soothe the restlessness that had kept her awake well past midnight, she ran her fingertips along the spines of the two dozen other books on the same shelf. The house was silent, and the ruffled hem of her nightgown brushed across the pine floor with a soft whisper. She had lit only the lamp on her father's desk; surrounded by deep shadows, she moved with a languid ease that belied her inner turmoil.

She swept her blond curls aside with a graceful flip of her hand before bending down to peruse the next shelf. A book bound in red leather caught her eye. The title was only vaguely familiar, but when she carried it to the desk and read the first page, she recalled the tale in such vivid detail she had no desire to read it a second time. Disappointed, she had just returned the book to its place when she heard the back door open and close.

Panic surged down her spine, but she forced herself to think despite the fierce pounding of her heart. There were no Revolutionary War battles being fought nearby, but there were enough local Loyalists who wished the Barclays harm to justify her fright. Determined to defend her sleeping family, she fought to remain calm. Her step was silent as she padded around the desk on bare feet, but her hands were shaking so badly as she removed the pistol from the top drawer that she bumped it loudly against the highly polished mahogany. The noise echoed in her ears with an alarming wail until she realized it could not possibly have carried past the partially open door.

Whoever had entered the house would have seen the light in the study, so she didn't bother to douse it before stepping into the shadows beside the door. From this vantage point, she had a clear view of the hall, enabling her to see the intruder easily a second or two before he caught sight of her. Her mouth had gone dry. A cough hovered at the back of her throat, and she swallowed hard to dispel it.

Her elder brother, Beau, was a privateer away at sea, but he wore boots and moved with a confident stride she would have recognized instantly. Unlike a man returning home to a warm welcome, this fellow was creeping down the hall with a step so light the only sound was an occasional creak of the floorboards. The Barclays had far too many beloved relatives, dear friends, and goodmen working for them for Belle to risk firing at a shadow, but should she recognize danger rather than a familiar face, she was ready to do what she must. She cocked the heavy pistol and raised it with both hands, then drew in a deep breath and held it; her lungs had nearly burst before a man stepped into the ray of light thrown past the open door.

He was an Indian brave, and an exceedingly handsome one. His long ebony hair fell over his shoulders in careless disarray, and his worn buckskins were edged with tattered fringe. He was tall, with a lean, muscular build his soft deerskin clothing revealed in sensuous detail. As their eyes met, his dark glance lit with recognition, and the slow smile that spread over his well-shaped lips slurred into a rakish grin.

He reached out to brush Belle's pistol aside. "If you're standing guard, I like your uniform."

"Damn you, Falcon, you gave me an awful fright." After dropping the pistol to her side, Belle brushed her cousin's cheek with a light kiss. Then, embarrassed that she had revealed just how dearly she loved him, she turned away. Excited to see him, but relieved beyond measure that he hadn't been an enemy she would have had to shoot, her breathing relaxed to its normal easy rhythm as she circled the desk to replace the weapon in the drawer.

Falcon followed Belle into the study. He grabbed the crystal decanter of brandy sitting on the corner of his uncle's desk, raised it to his lips, and took a long swig. He returned the ornate bottle to its silver tray with deliberate care, but needed two tries to insert the delicate stopper. He wiped his mouth on his sleeve, but his wide grin remained. Eager to claim a passionate welcome, he waited for Belle to return to his side, then drew her into his arms.

As Falcon's mouth covered hers in a bruising kiss, Belle reacted with shocked dismay. She slammed her palms against his chest to push him away but he was far too strong a young man to be bothered by such an ineffectual protest and hugged her all the more tightly. Caught in his embrace and nearly smothered by his ardor, Belle grew dizzy. The experience was exhilarating rather than unpleasant, and in the next instant she relaxed against him with a grateful sigh.

Swiftly lost in the wonder of him, her response grew as ardent as his. She slid her arms around his waist and clung to him as he deepened his kiss to explore her mouth with a lazy insistence that demanded total surrender. Thrilled by his forceful affection, she rubbed against him as he moved his hands down over her hips to mold her supple form to the hard planes of his.

Wanting still more, Falcon grasped Belle's waist. She was tall, but so slender he lifted her easily and sat her atop the desk. He shoved her linen gown up out of his way and stepped between her legs. All the while his lips never left hers, and he moaned way in the back of his throat as he slipped his hands beneath her gown to caress the soft fullness of her bare breasts with a sweet sense of wonder.

Belle's heart pounded with passion rather than fear. She had grown up with Falcon, and that he finally wanted her with the same desperate desire that she could no longer hide was the most extraordinary happenstance of her life. His kiss was flavored with brandy and his hair scented with the smoky residue of a dozen campfires, but he was the only man she would ever love.

Unwilling to waste a precious second of this glorious night, she leaned into his touch. Wanting the same sweet sample of his bare skin that he had of hers, she slid her hands under his loose-fitting shirt to caress his back. He often went bare-chested in summer, and his deeply bronzed skin held a fiery warmth. It sang beneath her fingertips, calling to her as seductively as his passionate kiss.

She cuddled against his face as he nibbled her earlobe with playful bites, then pressed his lips to the rapidly throbbing pulse in her throat. His callused hands were rough, but his touch was gently adoring. He cupped her breasts in his palms and stroked her nipples into tight buds with his thumbs. Wild yet tender, Falcon was the magical lover Belle had always dreamed he would be. They relied on taste and touch in the darkened room, but their gestures had the smoothness of lovers long parted and at last reunited with great joy.

When Falcon drew away to loosen his belt, Belle realized she was about to lose her virginity on the top of her father's desk, but it seemed so utterly right she didn't voice even a hint of doubt. All she wanted was for Falcon to speak of the love that bathed his kisses in splendor. She had waited much too long to miss hearing the words now when she needed them most.

What Falcon craved was something far more primitive.

He yanked Belle forward and slid his hand between her legs to part the triangle of golden curls. Gliding his fingers along her cleft, he felt her fiery inner heat. Satisfied she was ready for him, he began to probe for the source of her slippery wetness with the smooth tip of his hardened shaft. He merely teased her at first, then pushed forward to delve deeper.

Falcon's mouth covered hers, but Belle gasped and recoiled at the first sharp stab of pain. She grabbed a handful of his hair and yanked his head back to force him to meet her gaze. His lashes veiled his eyes, but passion had made them bright.

"Say you love me first," she coaxed in an anxious whisper.

Poised to drive deep within her, Falcon had a firm grip on Belle's waist. He wanted her so badly he couldn't read the question in her eyes. All he saw were her kiss-swollen lips and a cascade of tousled blond curls. If what she wanted were pretty promises, he would gladly give them while he still could.

"Love you," he mumbled in a brandy-scented slur.

That garbled vow was a far cry from the tender declaration of affection Belle had hoped to hear. Suddenly the cause of his disappointing lack of eloquence was painfully clear and she cursed the fact she had not noticed his sorry state when she had first recognized their prowler as her cousin. "You're drunk," she cried.

As Belle choked on tears, she blamed herself for wantonly encouraging Falcon's desire without once questioning his sincerity. Mortified by how pathetically eager she had been for his love, she gave him a mighty shove that sent him stumbling backwards. She jumped down off the edge of the desk and fled the study before Falcon had regained his balance. She raced up two flights of stairs to the third floor, ran past her sister, Dominique's, room, and plunged into her own.

She closed and locked her door and wept with a bitter fury. That Falcon had to be drunk before he wanted her was so insulting she wanted to die. Thank God she had not been too proud to ask him to speak of love, or she might have given herself to him and then discovered he was so drunk she had to help him up the stairs to bed.

Clearly, the sip of her father's brandy had not been his first that night. Would she have been his first woman, or the second, or even the third? "My God," she shuddered. She had never even suspected fate could be so cruel, but as she began to pace, she doubted Falcon's memories of the night would be nearly as clear as her own.

Astonished, and then completely befuddled by the violent change in Belle's mood, Falcon pulled his pants back into place and started after her, but when she tore up the stairs as though she were being pursued by demons, he gave up the effort and entered his own room on the second floor. He was thoroughly disgusted with her for teasing him so shamelessly and then balking at the last moment. So what if he had been drinking? He was sober enough to have pleased her if she had only given him the chance. He yanked off his buckskins, flung them aside, and sprawled across his bed.

Then he remembered the silken sweetness of Belle's flesh, and moaned with frustrated desire. He ran his hand down the flatness of his belly, and still needing the taste of rapture she had denied him, moved lower to satisfy the longings she had aroused. With that blessed release came the first good night's sleep he had had in weeks, but Belle taunted him even in his dreams.

When Falcon awoke in his own bed the next morning, he rubbed his eyes and sat up slowly. He savored the blissful calm of home, then lay back down to enjoy another few minutes' sleep. As he closed his eyes, the sight of Belle fleeing up the stairs filled his mind's eye and he groaned with the very same agonizing disappointment he had felt at the time. Then, recalling the wildly amorous encounter that had preceded her panicked departure, he began to laugh.

Wide awake now, he left his bed and went to the window. The tobacco was growing tall in fields that stretched as far as the eye could see, and if the war didn't come to Virginia, it would be another good harvest. The fact that the routine hadn't changed at home was comforting, but he knew he had changed, and definitely not for the better. He had seen too many good men die, and killed far too many of the enemy, to remain untouched. The shocking eagerness with which he had approached Belle had certainly proven that.

She deserved better than a rough coupling on a desktop and he was ashamed of himself now. After cleaning up and dressing in a fresh set of buckskins, he went out to the garden and picked the largest bouquet he could hold and carried it into the sitting room where Belle was seated with her mother, his mother, and Dominique. He winked at Dominique as he came through the door, kissed his mother and Aunt Arielle, then knelt down on one knee in front of Belle and handed her the flowers.

"I'd stopped at the Raleigh Tavern, and wasn't all that sober when I got home last night." He paused, knowing she would understand the true meaning of his vaguely worded apology while the others in the room would not. "I was rude to you, and I'm very sorry. Will you forgive me?"

Belle tried to focus on the beautiful bouquet rather than Falcon's grin, which she considered much too wide. Apparently he regarded the regrettable incident as merely unfortunate, but she was deeply wounded. She inhaled the luscious fragrance of the gardenias and roses nestled among the camellias, but their sweetness failed to erase her lingering sense of shame. She pushed the floral tribute back into his hands.

"Give these to your mother. I'm glad you're home, but please excuse me, I need some air." She rose, and without once looking at Falcon directly, left the room.

The damning realization that Belle was not about to simply dismiss what had occurred between them last night filled Falcon with a chill of dread. She could be stubborn when she set her mind to it, and it looked as though that was precisely how she had chosen to behave. A mountain of roses would not win forgiveness from Belle's lips when she was in that mood, and his happiness at being home evaporated in a cloud of regret. He grew awkward, and struggled to his feet without a bit of his usual manly grace.

"I should have brought flowers for you all," he apologized, and placed the bouquet on his mother's lap.

Falcon was usually as adept at masking his emotions as Hunter, his Seneca father, but that morning his mother saw his torment clearly etched on the finely drawn features which proclaimed his mixed blood. Easily imagining the problem with Belle which had caused his distress, she rose and went to the door. "Please come and take these flowers and put them in a vase, Dominique. They're so lovely I don't want them to go to waste."

Ordinarily, her Aunt Alanna was soft-spoken, but Dominique heard a definite ring of authority and feared that rather than a polite request, she had just been given a direct order. Reluctant to obey, she pretended not to understand. "Am I being asked to leave?"

"You've always been a bright girl," her mother complimented. A French woman who had been born in Acadia, Arielle's voice still held the soft accent of her native language. "Please do as your Aunt Alanna asked."

Disappointed at being excluded, Dominique left her chair, but paused to run her hand down Falcon's fringed sleeve. "Courage," she whispered, and then, taking the lovely flowers from her aunt, she swept out of the room in a colorful blur of coral satin.

Alanna closed the door behind her niece and leaned back against it to prevent Falcon from leaving as well. "Lord knows, you are more your father's son than mine, but if you were too drunk to behave as a gentleman should, and insulted Belle, you are in real trouble, again. This family has had more than enough scandalous romantic liaisons to permit another to flourish under our own roof. Now, you're going to tell your Aunt Arielle and me precisely what took place between you and Belle last night. If it matches the stricken look that crossed your face when she walked out, I won't wait for your father to take a horsewhip to you. I'll do it myself."

Falcon had never lied to his mother, but he did not see how he was going to tell her the truth now. He licked his lips and tried to find a way to even begin the story he knew he would have to censor drastically as much for Belle's sake as his own. The silence grew strained before he finally cleared his throat and spoke.

"It was late when I got home. The house was dark except for the lamp in the study. I've no idea what Belle was doing there, but I stopped to say hello. I had a drink of Uncle Byron's brandy, and—"

Falcon wiped his sweaty palms on his pant legs but it didn't erase the memory of the creamy smoothness of Belle's skin. He still thought of her as a pretty child, but she had been all woman last night. A very passionate woman, he recalled in much too painful detail. His guilt compounding, he crossed his arms over his chest and shifted his weight from one moccasined foot to the other.

"Well, I was in such a good mood, I kissed her good night. She dashed upstairs, so I feared I'd offended her. That's why I wanted to apologize." He had described the encounter as being as innocent as he possibly could, but when he caught the disgusted glance passing between his mother and aunt, he knew they hadn't believed a word of it. He covered a nervous cough, and tried again. "We were only together a few minutes."

His story sounded ridiculous even in his own ears but Falcon sincerely doubted he and Belle had been together long at the pace he was moving. Not even the James River was that swift, but it had been long enough for him to dip into the moist, hot sweetness of her. He winced. "Belle and I have always been close," he offered, his voice trailing off to a whisper.

Arielle left her chair and came within a step of her nephew. As attractive as her daughters, she was delightfully feminine and extremely perceptive. She had never seen Falcon blush, but even as deeply tanned as he was, there was a definite burgundy tinge to his cheeks. She could not recall ever seeing a man look so pathetically guilty; protective of her daughter, she pressed him for more details of what had transpired between them.

"I have the impression there's more to this than you described. Would you care to begin again?"

Falcon turned toward his mother for help, but she looked as deeply offended as his aunt. "No, ma'am. I thought it was just a friendly kiss. Belle obviously mistook it for more."

Alanna scoffed aloud. "If there were even a hint of truth to your tale, after a single kiss Belle would have bade you a good night rather than run upstairs, and you would have had no need to apologize to her this morning. From the great bunch of flowers you carried in here, it's clear you have a very guilty conscience."

Caught in his own web, Falcon fought to break free. "I kissed her. She ran off. I wanted to do what was right."

"Like the rest of the men in this family, you may know what's right, but when it comes to women, that doesn't mean you always do it," Alanna countered.

"Please," Arielle cajoled, "rather than torture Falcon with his relatives' mistakes, let's concentrate on solving today's problem. Besides, the Barclay men, and Hunter as well, have always behaved admirably."

Clearly unimpressed by that statement, Alanna cocked a brow, forcing Arielle to make a mild concession. "I suppose it's all in your point of view. The French expect men to have passionate natures; it's a great pity the English do not." In a gesture Dominique often copied, she reached out to touch Falcon's sleeve.

"Belle has adored you since you were children. She tagged along after you while Dominique preferred to remain with me and play with her dolls. You taught Belle how to fish, climb trees, and hunt with a bow and arrow."

Falcon smiled at the memory of those far more innocent days, but being reminded of how Belle had always looked up to him made him feel even worse and he had not thought that possible. His chest tightened, creating a painful ache. "I think I ought to be having this conversation with Belle."

"Yes, you should," Arielle agreed. "You've been home so seldom the last few years, perhaps you've not noticed that Belle is no longer a child who's happy to trail in your shadow. She's a lovely young woman, and she's never shown the slightest bit of interest in any man but you. I think you took advantage of that fact last night. An apology won't be nearly enough, Falcon. You owe my daughter a proposal."

Falcon could already feel the horsewhip biting into his back. His aunt was right. He had taken advantage of Belle's affection for him, but a forced marriage was harsh punishment. Still unwilling to admit to more than a kiss, he tried another argument. "How can I offer marriage when none of us is certain we'll survive the war? I don't want to risk leaving Belle a widow."

Arielle promptly dismissed that objection. "I lost my first husband, but I'd not trade a minute of the joy we shared to be spared the pain of his death. Bernard's love will always be a part of me. We'd all be devastated if anything happened to you, but Belle would mourn you forever whether you were her husband, or simply her cousin."

Alanna stepped aside and opened the door. "We'll not begin planning the wedding until Belle says she'll have you, but you'd best offer marriage before your father hears news of this and uses his fists to insist that you must."

Falcon nodded, and considering himself lucky to have escaped any further interrogation, strode from the room. When he found Dominique waiting for him just outside the back door, he flashed a quick grin, but the seriousness of her expression stopped him cold. "Don't you start on me, too," he warned.

Dominique took his arm and walked with him to make certain they would not be overheard. "This concerns a whole lot more than a kiss doesn't it, Falcon?"

Falcon patted her hand, then slipped out of her grasp. "That's going to remain between Belle and me. Now excuse me, I've got to find her."

"She's probably down by the river."

Falcon already knew that, and turned away with a wave. He and Belle used to get up early and go fishing together. She had never been squeamish about slipping worms on her hook the way other girls were. They had sat on the dock and waited for the sun to come up on more mornings than he could count. She had been his best friend and the silence of dawn had never been lonely with her by his side.

He had always thought she was awfully pretty, but he had been more impressed by the fact that she would hike up her dress and climb trees even easier than he could. She wore lace-trimmed caps, but they were always askew, and more often than not she had small twigs and dried leaves caught in her fair curls. He had thought her a swell friend, but usually had not even remembered that she was a girl.

She had turned thirteen and he had been sixteen the year the war had begun. Wanting to fight with the Virginia militia, he had grown up fast, while she had remained at home to linger over the last joys of childhood. Well, after last night, there was no mistaking the fact that Belle was most definitely a grown woman. She had always been so independent he knew she wouldn't take to the idea of marriage any more than he had. At least he hoped she wouldn't. The only trick would be in convincing her to tell her mother that.

Belle hadn't spent more than a few anguished minutes at the docks before going on to the Scott plantation, which bordered the Barclays' on the south. Falcon's elder brother, Christian, had married Liana Scott, but that had worsened rather than healed the twenty-year rift between the two families. When the colonies had declared their independence, Ian Scott, a staunch Loyalist, had freed their slaves and taken his wife and two sons home to England to wait out the war.

The land surrounding the once-prosperous plantation lay fallow, but Liana went home every week to check the house, so Belle didn't feel as though she were trespassing when she crossed over onto Scott land. She followed the trail along the river, and while sorely tempted to keep on walking clear to Florida, she turned off on the path leading up to the house. A Georgian mansion as imposing as her own home, she thought it a shame it had stood vacant so long, but today she was glad for a place to be alone.

She sat down at the top of the marble steps and looped her arms around her knees. The day was beautiful, warm and bright. A ladybug landed on her hand, and she shooed it away.

When she had come downstairs that morning, she had actually believed she could pretend the day was like all others. Then Falcon had walked into the sitting room carrying half the garden in his arms and the pretense had not only become absurd, but impossible. He never stayed home for long, and she would strive to avoid him, but she did not want to be home the next time he returned.

There were hospitals in desperate need of nurses to care for injured soldiers so she could provide service to others, but her heart would never mend. Not after last night, it wouldn't. She wiped her eyes on her apron and took a deep breath, but when Falcon came around the corner of the house, she was so sick at heart she quickly looked away.

"How did you find me?"

Shocked by the pain he had glimpsed in her eyes, Falcon drew to a halt several steps away. "I'm a scout," he reminded her proudly. "I could track you down anywhere."

Still not looking his way, Belle smoothed the damp wrinkles from her apron. "Why would you want to?"

Grateful she was speaking to him, Falcon sat down on the bottom step and turned toward her. He could see she had been crying, and it had made her blue eyes all the more vivid. "I won't give you the sorry excuse that I was drunk last night," he began with the sincerity he wished he had shown in their last conversation, "because I was still responsible for my actions."

Belle could barely stifle her anger. He had been drinking, so nothing that happened had mattered to him, while every caress had been precious to her. *That wasn't fair!* "The last thing I want to hear are excuses. Please go away."

"No, not until you hear me out."

Belle got up, walked right on by him, and started down toward the river. Not about to leave things in the dreadful mess they were, Falcon refused to let her escape him again and went after her. "You may have gotten away from me last night, but there's no use trying to outrun me now," he called. In a few quick strides he caught up with her. He reached out to catch her elbow and turn her back toward him but the instant his hand brushed her arm, a jolt of pleasure shot clear through him.

"My God," he moaned, but he didn't release her. He

couldn't. Why hadn't he noticed how long her lashes were, or the way the pretty pout to her lips invited kisses? Why hadn't he noticed that his best friend had become a desirable woman long before now? Dominique had taken his arm, but he hadn't felt anything even approaching the excitement that filled him now.

"I had intended to do a better job of apologizing for last night, but now that I've found you, the only thing I regret is that you stopped me."

Astounded by that remark, Belle could only watch as he lowered his head. She knew he was going to kiss her, and even fearing she would be no more than a casual diversion to him, she couldn't turn away. His lips met hers in a tentative caress, but as the tip of his tongue traced her lower lip, she opened her mouth to welcome his kiss as wantonly as she had last night. The same delicious magic flowed through him as before, and Belle drank it in before finally finding the courage to pull away.

"No, stop," she begged. She took a step backward, but he moved forward and the distance between them remained much too close. "Please, let's not repeat last night's near-tragic mistake."

Falcon groaned in frustration. "My only mistake was having too much to drink before I got home, not what happened between us after I got there."

Belle turned her back on him, but he was standing so close she could still feel his heat radiating clear through her. "The last time you were home, you didn't kiss me like that. Apparently I didn't appeal to you until you saw me through a haze of spirits."

Falcon had not kept count of how many women he had slept with during the course of the war, and while he had certainly enjoyed every one, none had ever affected him as strongly as Belle. He wanted to hold her and never let go, but left his arms hanging limp at his sides. "I don't even remember the last time I was home, but I'm sorry if I dis-

appointed you. I don't want you doubting me, Belle, so I'll
make you a promise I intend to keep. I won't touch liquor
ever again," he swore.

Belle chanced a glance over her shoulder, and when she
found Falcon's expression as pained as her own, she turned
back toward him. "Had you been sober last night, what
would you have said when I asked you to say that you loved
me?"

Falcon reached out to touch a curl that peeked from beneath her snowy cap. It was the color of sunshine and he
remembered how beautiful her hair had looked last night
tumbling loose over her shoulders. "I wanted you so badly,
I would have said anything you wanted to hear." Too late,
he realized how awful his confession had sounded. "What
I mean is—" He saw Belle raise her hand, but knowing he
deserved it, didn't try to dodge the resounding slap she
whipped across his cheek.

"You bastard!"

Again she tried to run away, but Falcon was too quick
for her and caught her around the waist. He pulled her back
against his chest and crossing his arms over her bosom,
held her wrists so she couldn't scratch or hit him again.
"Do you have any idea what I do when I'm away?"

"It's enough that I know what you do when you're
home!"

Falcon knew he deserved that insult, too, but he kept
after her. "Listen to me! I don't serve with the regular militia anymore. I fight with guerilla bands that strike the British from ambush. We steal supply wagons, weapons,
ammunition. When I'm not doing that, I take my rifle, get
as close as I can to the enemy's camp, and start shooting
the officers. I'm the best marksman in Virginia, and I can
shoot a man in the heart from 200 yards. If I'm just as
dangerous when I get home, I can't help it."

Belle closed her eyes, but she couldn't shut out his stirring words, or the fiery warmth of his embrace. She leaned

her head back against his shoulder, and remembering last
night, wondered why he thought he was the only one who
could be described as *wild*.

Two

Fearing Belle was about to bolt again, Falcon hung on to her tight. He leaned over her shoulder and savored the delicious sensation as he rubbed his cheek against hers. He had only a light beard, but he was very glad he had taken the time to shave that morning. The touch of her skin felt so incredibly good, and she smelled sweeter than the flowers he had gathered for her.

"I wish you'd kept the bouquet," he whispered in her ear.

She had longed for an expression of love, not an apology. "I couldn't accept it when it was offered for the wrong reason."

She was dressed in an indigo gown whose bodice dipped low to offer a tantalizing glimpse of the fullness of her breasts. Fully enjoying the delectable sight, Falcon moved his left arm down to encircle her narrow waist. He then had a free hand to pull off her cap. He flung away her combs, and fragrant with the piquant scent of lemons, her long curls tumbled over her shoulders in waves that reflected the sun's bright sparkle.

Falcon had never dreamed just holding a woman could be so pleasant. This was his dear Belle, though, and that made all the difference. "I've thought of you so often, Belle."

Because he was never out of her thoughts, Belle wanted to believe him, but she had been all too quick to accept his affection last night, and had become far more cautious as a result. "Would you have come looking for me this morning if I hadn't been in the study last night?" she inquired softly. "Would you have still said you thought of me if you weren't burdened by guilt?"

Falcon had already admitted he would say whatever it took to please her, and he was disgusted with himself for being so tactless. "I'm cold sober, so there's no reason to doubt my words. I'm sorry you had to prompt me last night. I should have said that I love you a long time ago."

Belle closed her eyes to savor his vow, but was it spontaneous, she agonized, or had she merely coaxed it from his lips a second time? Sadly, she feared she had. Apparently he had not loved her until they had chanced to cross paths while he was at a weak moment. "Perhaps I should have waited up for you in the study last year."

Tightening his hold on her waist, Falcon yanked her around to face him. There wasn't a trace of affection in his expression now. "Don't laugh at me, Belle. I'll readily admit I didn't behave as a gentleman should, but are you going to forgive me, or am I going to hear about it every single time you're cross with me for the rest of our lives?"

His eyes had narrowed to menacing slits, and it was all too easy for Belle to imagine him picking off British officers with a cold precision. He had been eager to make love to her last night, but wouldn't any warm and willing woman have inspired the same response in a weary soldier? Again, the answer was all too clear. Overcome with sadness, she shook her head.

"No, I think we'd both be better off if we forgot last night ever happened." She forced a smile, but it trembled on her lips. She offered her hand. "Agreed?"

For a long moment, Falcon simply regarded Belle with a forbidding stare, but then, overcoming his anger, he at last took her hand and drew her close. He didn't want to make another costly mistake, and phrased his proposal with the care it deserved. "Will you do me the honor of becoming my wife?"

Belle drew in a sharp breath for there was nothing she wanted more, but not like this. "You've apologized, Falcon. You needn't offer marriage, too."

While his initial reaction was immense relief, his heart was swiftly flooded with numbing disappointment. He had never proposed to another woman, and it had not even occurred to him that Belle might turn him down. He took it as a grave insult.

"What you're really saying is no, isn't it? Why? If you hadn't stopped me when you did, I'd have no choice about marrying you."

Before the war, Falcon had been easygoing rather than hot-tempered, but Belle refused to make any allowance for what he must have suffered when he had just made it abundantly clear he was thinking only of himself. She yanked her hand from his and stepped back. "But I did stop you, and I want us *both* to have a choice."

Falcon was half a foot taller than Belle, and when he moved close she was forced to crane her neck to look up at him. "You've forgotten something," he insisted darkly. "I may have had too much to drink last night, but you knew precisely what you were doing. You were all over me. How can you pretend what happened between us doesn't matter?"

He had tied his hair at his nape that morning, but when he had kissed her last night it had been loose, and spilled over her face with the sensuous warmth of black velvet. Recalling an even more provocative caress with an embarrassment laced with the moist heat of desire, Belle fought her traitorous body's shameless cravings and squared her shoulders.

"I do care," she assured him proudly, "far too much to accept a proposal given out of a noble sense of duty or guilt if you believe you've tarnished my honor."

Falcon responded with a rude laugh. "I did a hell of a lot more than tarnish it, Belle."

His rebuke was an arrogant boast rather than an expression of regret, but she couldn't deny its truth. As memories of his intimate touch became increasingly vivid, her face grew hot with a bright blush. "Yes, I suppose so, but there will be no consequences, so neither of us has to suffer."

Still enchanted by his elusive cousin, Falcon raised his hand to caress her feather-soft cheek. His mind might have been clouded by liquor last night, but he had a clear memory of how it had felt to nudge against the fragile barrier that had prevented them from becoming one. In another instant the tender flesh would have torn and he would have buried himself deep within her heated core. There would have been consequences aplenty then.

If only she hadn't stopped him.

"You weren't suffering last night, and neither was I. Far from it." He stopped there rather than insult her by telling her she'd been a better lover than all the other women he had ever had put together.

What Belle saw in his dark gaze was a promise of many more such luscious nights, but he was wrong. She had suffered an unbearable anguish when she had discovered brandy was fueling his desire rather than love. "There's no rush."

She had been so agreeable in the darkened study, and Falcon wished she would show him the same sweetness today. He ached with wanting her and tried not to sound as annoyed as he felt with her maddening distance. "What do you mean?"

Belle toyed with the fringe on his sleeve, letting it dance through her fingers as she replied, "The next time you come home, ask again, and because you've given up drinking, there will be no mistaking your motives."

That softly voiced taunt was more than Falcon could bear

calmly. "Didn't you just give me your hand to promise last night would be forgotten?"

Even frowning, Falcon was the handsomest man Belle had ever seen, but it still hurt to look at him and she dropped her glance. "Yes, but that doesn't mean I didn't learn a valuable lesson I intend to remember."

Searching for a way to reach her, Falcon gazed off toward the river. When they were children, she had chased him along the muddy shore and the patter of her bare feet had echoed the rhythm of her laughter. All his childhood memories included her, and they were all happy. The war had dimmed those carefree years, but they came back to him now in such acute detail he could actually taste the wild blackberries they had picked and tossed into each other's mouths. His expression relaxed into a sad smile.

With a light tap of his index finger, he tilted Belle's chin to force her to look up at him. "If this is the last time I'm able to come home, will you please remember that I swore I loved you, and asked you to marry me?"

Belle's heart skipped a beat. She had been up late last night, as she had on so many others, because she was worried sick about him. The Scott house beckoned invitingly and part of her longed to take him inside and find the softest feather bed. An equally compelling voice argued that she ought to make absolutely certain that he truly loved her before she lost herself in him again. She sighed sadly as she made the only choice her pride allowed.

"Please help me find my combs." She plucked her cap from the grass, and waited for him to fetch the tortoiseshell combs from where he had tossed them.

Discouraged that he had been unable to persuade Belle to his point of view, Falcon was quick to blame her rather than his own lack of eloquence. "You were a stubborn little girl. You know that? We spent most of our time together but you fought me every inch of the way. I'd hoped that you'd changed."

He looked as depressed as Belle felt, but that only served to strengthen her resolve. She wound her curls into a thick coil she secured with her combs, then replaced her cap with a careless tug to restore the modest appearance she knew she no longer deserved. She turned away and started toward the path home.

"You're the stubborn one," she called over her shoulder.

Falcon watched her a moment. She didn't walk with Dominique's seductive sway, but with a long, sure stride that reminded him again of the saucy little girl who had been closer than his shadow. "Wait," he shouted, but she didn't slow her pace and he had to sprint to catch up with her. He was too angry to take her hand, and rather than argue, didn't speak as they walked home. It wasn't until he saw his aunt and mother standing on the front porch, their arms crossed over their bosoms, their expressions as suspicious as when he had left them, that he realized he and Belle should have agreed on what they wished to say.

"What did you tell them?" Belle whispered anxiously.

Still smarting from her rejection, Falcon was tempted to threaten her with the truth and force her to accept his proposal, but he successfully suppressed the bitter impulse. He just shook his head to warn her to be silent, and greeted the curious women with a solemn shrug. "She turned me down," he told them.

"What?" Belle cried. She had been positive Falcon's proposal had been prompted by guilt-laden remorse rather than love, but now it was painfully clear he had merely been following orders. She had not even imagined she could feel any worse, but suddenly she did. She scorched Falcon with a searing glance, then turned the full fury of her anger on her mother and aunt.

"Did you two force Falcon to propose to me? Is it completely beyond your comprehension that he might have wanted me on his own?"

Aghast that Falcon had lacked the sense to relate his results in private, Arielle tried her best to soothe her daughter's wholly justifiable outrage. "After his halting explanation of what occurred between you two last night, it was merely a strongly worded suggestion, Belle. Please don't be insulted. We want what's best for you."

Belle had a very good idea of what her mother and aunt must believe, and because the truth was almost as bad, she didn't care to offer a denial before brushing by them and entering the house.

Dismayed he had inadvertently made a bad situation even worse, Falcon started after Belle, but his mother quickly stepped in front of him to block the door.

"Let her go," Alanna urged. "She's too angry to listen to anything you might have to say. After dinner, I want you to move your things over to Christian's house," she directed firmly. "That way, there can't possibly be a repeat of last night's regrettable incident."

His brother's house stood no more than fifty yards away, so what his mother asked was no hardship, but Falcon was deeply insulted all the same. "Don't you trust me anymore?"

Alanna dared not look at Arielle, but she was positive she had her support. "Let's just say it will be better for all concerned if you and your lovely female cousins aren't under the same roof."

Falcon had helped to build Christian's house. He had made bricks from clay they had dug from the banks of the James River, and stoked the fires to bake them. The timbers had been cut from forests on their land and he had labored to lay the pine floors and carve the fine walnut paneling. It was a beautiful house with a magnificent view of the river, but Christian and Liana had a daughter and two little boys, and his sister, Johanna, and her husband, David, who shared the fine home, had two small sons of their own.

Falcon loved his niece and nephews, but he didn't want

to live in a house filled with rambunctious children. "I'd rather sleep in the stable," he replied sullenly.

Alanna shook her head. It had been months since they had seen Falcon, and she didn't want to chase him away, but she truly believed the family honor was at stake. "Sleep wherever you like as long as it isn't in this house."

Falcon sent his aunt a questioning glance, but Arielle looked away rather than take his side. He knew better than to waste his breath arguing with them. It was almost time for the noon meal, and he rested his shoulder against the house.

"I want to talk to Father before I agree to anything."

Rather than own slaves, the Barclays employed free men, and Hunter supervised their work in the fields. "He should come up to the house soon," Alanna assured him.

"I'll wait for him here." Falcon wanted to see his brother and sister too, but they would have to wait. Certain he had also learned a valuable lesson, he spent the time while he waited for his father rehearsing how best to describe what he had done. No, he corrected himself, *almost done.* He closed his eyes, and the memory of Belle's delicious kiss instantly seeped through him. A low moan escaped his lips. When his father called his name, he jumped in surprise.

"Have you taken to sleeping on your feet?" Hunter asked as he came up the steps.

"No, but there are times I wish I could." Falcon straightened up, stepped into his father's embrace, and hugged him with unaccustomed fervor before backing away. Hunter's ebony hair had begun to gray at the temples, but if anything, the lighter shade served to enhance his handsome appearance. His buckskins showed off a build as trim as his son's, and his dark eyes sparkled with a bright inner light.

Falcon knew what he wished to say, but had difficulty getting started. His only hope was that his father recalled his own youthful romantic adventures fondly enough to be sympathetic. He again described his midnight encounter with Belle in innocuous terms, but as his father's stare grew increasingly cold, he knew he wasn't fooled any more than his mother and aunt had been. After recounting how swiftly Belle had rejected his proposal, he lowered his voice to a whisper.

"We didn't make love," he swore, "although I sure wish now that we had."

Hunter cocked his head and studied his younger son's defiant expression with an intense gaze. Even with the vague description Falcon had provided, Hunter understood he and Belle had shared a dangerously passionate tryst. Painful memories of the one time he had made love to Christian's mother made it difficult for him to be objective. "Belle deserves more than a few kisses at midnight," he scolded.

"I agree, but now Mother doesn't even trust me to sleep in the same house with her."

Hunter folded his arms across his chest and nodded. "I don't trust you, either."

Hurt by his father's scorn, Falcon made another stab at winning his support. "I've stopped drinking."

"Good. Have you begun thinking?"

Falcon supposed he deserved that, but it was still difficult to accept. "I only have a few days," he explained. "I don't want to be treated like a criminal."

"Then stop behaving like one," Hunter replied. "It may not be such bad luck that Belle turned you down. This will give you the time to court her in a more courteous fashion. If you can manage it."

Falcon was beginning to feel as though he had fallen into an abandoned well. Each time he tried to better his situation, he only succeeded in getting himself more deeply mired in the watery muck at the bottom. "Look—" he began again.

With the speed that still made Hunter a formidable foe, he slammed his son back against the side of the house. Falcon's head bounced off the bricks. "No, you look,"

Hunter ordered in a threatening snarl. "You and Belle will make the perfect pair. I've no doubt that she loves you, but last night you must have insulted her very badly if she refused your proposal today. How do you behave with other women if you treat your own precious cousin so rudely?"

Falcon would have come right back at any other man who had manhandled him that brutally, but he had too much respect for his father to fight him. He yanked his buckskins back into place, but there was nothing he could do about the sharp pain in the back of his head. "Women have always liked me," he replied as soon as he had caught his breath, "and that's because I treat them as well as you treat Mother. I know how all this sounds—"

Hunter came close to bouncing Falcon off the wall a second time, but caught himself at the last instant. "I know from bitter experience just how quickly a woman's passions can change. You may never have another chance to win Belle for your wife. Don't waste it."

Sick of taking everyone's abuse, Falcon was too angry to keep sacrificing himself to protect Belle. "It would never have gone past the first kiss had Belle not wanted me, too. She wanted me!"

Shocked by the vehemence of Falcon's tone, Hunter backed away. "Yes, and she was sober. Never forget that." He gestured toward the door. "We need discuss this no further. You're too thin. Come, let's have dinner with the others."

Falcon had lost his appetite. He had expected a respite from danger when he had come home, but he had stumbled into more peril than he faced from the British. "Is Uncle Byron home?"

"Yes. Are you afraid of what he'll say about this?"

Falcon had always admired his uncle. Byron had attended the Continental Congress, which had declared war on Great Britain, and was widely respected by the men who supported the Patriot cause. He was also a generous uncle who had never made any distinction between his cousin Alanna's children and his own.

"Yes, and with good reason."

"You have far more reason to fear me," Hunter warned, and led the way inside.

Still doubting he could eat, Falcon followed his father into the dining room. His brother, Christian, was apparently unaware of the trouble he was in and wore a ready grin as he came forward to greet him. Christian's wife, Liana, was smiling prettily, and their five-year-old daughter, Liberty, ran to meet him. He caught the lively red-haired girl in his arms and lifted her high. Only a quarter Seneca, she was the image of her mother, but the laughing child Falcon saw in his mind was Belle. He hugged Liberty tightly, then set her down and she dashed back to her mother's side.

His sister, Johanna, and her husband were there, too, but his nephews had been left at home in the servants' care. Falcon hugged her and shook David's hand. He moved on to his uncle, but it was plain from Byron's good-natured smile that he had not been told anything yet. Falcon shook his hand, then his cousin Jean's, who at sixteen was nearly as tall as his father. He was a studious lad who planned to follow his father into Congress.

Falcon nodded to Dominique and feeling relieved that Belle had deigned to join them, included his whole family in the warmest smile he could manage. "It's good to be home." As a chorus they cheered him and replied how good it was to see him.

As everyone began to move to their places at the long table, Falcon quickly decided against taking his usual chair between his mother and Dominique. Instead, he cut around the end of the table to take Beau's empty seat across from Belle. Her mother occupied the place at the end of the table, and Arielle appeared, like his mother, to be making an attempt to pretend nothing out of the ordinary had occurred.

Falcon caught Belle's gaze and held it. When she smiled

slightly, he realized she was more provoked with her mother and aunt than with him over the proposal issue. That was an enormous relief, but he still felt far from content at the way they had parted. Things had gone so badly he was ready to go, but he knew he ought not to leave without at least attempting to make a better impression on Belle. He just wished he knew how to go about it.

With twelve adults and Liberty, the table was crowded; as Falcon ran a silent tally, he hoped he was the only one who had noticed they had assembled an unlucky number. "I miss Beau," he offered as soon as Byron had completed the blessing.

"Yes, we all do," Arielle replied, "but I imagine he is having far too exciting a time to miss us."

Johanna had dark hair and eyes like her brothers, but her fair mother's sweet prettiness. "Let's not talk about Beau when Falcon's home," she begged. "You must have had some adventures since the last time you were here, Falcon. Won't you please tell us about them?"

"My tales would only spoil the meal," he responded, but the whole table urged him to continue and finally he gave a report. "Since General Clinton captured Charleston in May, the Patriots in South Carolina have suffered terribly. Their homes have been torched, their livestock slaughtered, their crops ruined. Great numbers of people have been herded into prison camps, but the meaner the British are, the more determined we've become to defeat them."

In the early days of the war, Christian had fought with the Virginia militia, but now that he had three children, he had chosen to remain at home. As their plates were being served, he hoped aloud that Charleston would soon be liberated. "The British must be stopped before they reach Virginia," he vowed.

"Yes, we all hope for that," Byron agreed. "Now please, we've read enough accounts of the war in the *Virginia Gazette* to understand the situation without relying on Falcon's description. Let's enjoy this delicious meal without any further mention of the war."

"You can't mean that," Belle argued. "What other subject even compares with it? Everyone is well. The tobacco crop should be excellent. Now, why don't we turn our thoughts to helping the good people of South Carolina? Are there enough volunteers to care for the wounded, Falcon?"

Falcon had a mouthful of the savory layered chicken and pastry dish that was one of his favorites among his aunt's recipes and he had to raise his hand to plead for a moment to swallow before answering. "I'm out in the countryside, Belle. I don't really know, but I imagine there is always a need for help in tending the wounded."

Rather than pursue her interest in volunteering with the whole family present, Belle simply nodded, but she found the idea increasingly appealing. In Acadia, her mother had been known as a *sage-femme*. When she had come to Virginia, she had continued to practice her healing arts and had passed on a treasury of herbal cures to her daughters. There was obviously a need for trained healers in South Carolina, and Belle was eager to go. She glanced toward her mother.

"Don't even think about it," Arielle whispered.

Belle smiled, but she had no intention of abandoning the idea. Her mother may have forced Falcon to propose, but she could not keep her at home when it was far too painful to remain. She had missed Falcon terribly while he had been away, but her loneliness did not even begin to compare with the wretched disappointment she felt today. He was so close, but now she doubted she could trust anything he said, as sincere, and his nearness was agony. She toyed with her chicken, but didn't raise a single morsel to her mouth.

After the first few awkward bites, Falcon had found the chicken so delicious he asked for seconds, but he wasn't so absorbed in the food that he missed his aunt's warning. That Belle might consider traveling to South Carolina to tend wounded soldiers was not an idea he would encourage, either. He glanced down the table at Dominique and found her laughing at an amusing observation of King George III her father had made. She was a consummate flirt, but he had never even been tempted by her seductive ways.

Seduction wasn't the word to describe what had happened between him and Belle. That had been a glorious mutual surrender. He watched Belle take a sip of wine. Her gesture was graceful, and as the crystal goblet touched her lips, he was filled with a longing to kiss her that was so strong he had to look away. He had refused a glass of wine, but was sorely tempted to ask for one now. He had meant his promise to Belle, however, and knew better than to break it right in front of her.

He sat back in his chair and listened to the conversations taking place around him. At Belle's urging, the discussion had continued to be centered on the war, but each person had his or her own view. The loss of Charleston was lamented deeply, but none had lost faith in the United States' ability to prevail. He felt Belle watching him, and turned back toward her with a smile. He had caught her studying him with a serious gaze, and hoped he had not displayed such poor table manners that he had given her a new cause to refuse him.

He apologized just in case. "I've been eating my meals squatting beside a campfire for so long, I've almost forgotten how to use a fork."

"Nonsense," Arielle assured him. "I'm positive you can still behave as a gentleman." A smile crossed her lips, but failed to brighten her gaze.

Falcon couldn't bring himself to thank her for a comment he had taken as a warning rather than a compliment. He looked across the table at Belle, and wondered if he might touch her without the others noticing. He extended his leg, slipped his foot under her dark blue skirt and lace-trimmed petticoats, then ran the side of his moccasin up her calf.

She sat up with a start, and he had a difficult time swallowing the laugh that would have alerted everyone to his mischief. Belle sent him a furious glare, but the flattering blush in her cheeks was so pretty he forgave her.

Finally allowing himself to relax enough to enjoy being home, he gave his attention to his other companions. For a few blissful moments, the familiar scene held a perfection he knew he would remember with great fondness while he was away. Then Dominique caught his eye, and raised her wine goblet in a silent toast. He did not feel like a returning hero though and could barely nod an acknowledgment.

Dominique was an elegant beauty who belonged with a man who shared her extravagant tastes. Flirtatious and sweet, she deserved to be pampered by a doting husband, while what he wanted was a woman who cared so deeply for others she wished to discuss the war and worried about the wounded. He was appalled he had disappointed Belle so badly she had turned him down, and he was ashamed he had not thought to propose on his own. With sudden insight he realized why his father had been so angry with him, and feared what Belle deserved was a better man than he would ever be.

He felt for the lump swelling on the back of his head, and his fingers came away covered with blood. He grabbed his napkin to wipe his hand, then carried it with him as he lurched to his feet. "Excuse me," he begged, and unable to explain his urgent need to get away, he left the room with unseemly haste.

Three

A wrinkle of dismay crossed Byron Barclay's brow. "What's happened to Falcon?" he asked. When he received a perplexing mixture of puzzled and averted glances from the others gathered at his table rather than an explanation for his nephew's hurried departure, he raised his voice. "Is he hiding something from us? Has he been wounded?"

"No," Hunter answered. "Or perhaps yes *and* no, since you asked two questions."

Becoming annoyed, Byron attempted to sort out what he took as a deliberately evasive reply. "Yes, he's hiding something, but no, he hasn't been hurt?"

"Let's discuss Falcon later, my darling," Arielle suggested with convincing firmness. "Please be assured his health isn't troubling him. Now would anyone like more chicken? I do believe it's especially good today."

Possessing a keen interest in Falcon's peculiar behavior, Dominique leaned toward her father and whispered, "Falcon and Belle are, well, interested in each other."

Shocked by such an unexpected development, Byron raised his brows, but when Dominique nodded to assure him her comment was true, he sent an accusing glance toward Hunter. Twenty-six years earlier, the Seneca brave had seduced Byron's sister, Melissa, who had hurriedly wed Ian Scott. Tragically, she had died giving birth to Hunter's son, Christian. Nearly a year later, Hunter had wed Byron's

cousin, Alanna Barclay. They had raised Christian and together had had Johanna and Falcon.

Six years ago, in a move that had completely baffled them
all, Christian had begun pursuing Ian and Rebecca Scott's
daughter, Liana. In a fit of bitter rage, Ian had disowned
Liana and abandoned her on the Barclays' doorstep. While
she and Christian were happily married, no one would ever
compliment him on the manner in which he had won his
bride.

Appalled that Falcon appeared to be following in Hunter
and Christian's scandalous footsteps, and with his own
sweet Belle, Byron threw down his napkin and started to
rise. "I must speak with Falcon at once."

Belle could only imagine what Dominique had confided,
but because her father's reaction was such a poor one, she
feared it had been dreadful and leaped from her chair. "Finish your meal," she offered helpfully. "I'll call him."

She left the dining room before her father could forbid
her to go, and raced on out the front door. She had seen
the troubled look fill Falcon's eyes just before he had left
the table and thought he would seek the river for solace
just as she had that morning. She found him down at the
dock, and was pleased her intuition had proved correct.

Falcon recognized the sound of Belle's footsteps as she
ran across the weathered wood, and turned to face her. Not
realizing he still held the bloody napkin, he waited for her
to come close. "I know it was rude of me to leave. I'm
sorry."

Alarmed by the bright red splotches on the square of
white linen, Belle rushed forward. "Have you been hurt?"

"What? No." Falcon wadded up the stained napkin and
jammed it into his pocket. "It's nothing. I just hit my head."

"When? On what?"

It was fear that had brought her close, and while her
concern was touching, Falcon was positive he wasn't worthy
of it. "It's nothing," he protested, but she started to walk

around him, searching for the wound, and he had to turn on his heel to stay ahead of her. "I don't need your help, Belle, and after last night, you ought to be smart enough to stay clear of me."

There weren't any bloodstains on his buckskins, but Belle doubted he was fine. She did not understand how he could have been fondling her under the table one minute, and then become this coldly forbidding stranger the next. "You must have been hit harder than you thought because you're not making any sense," she scolded. "Now bend down so I can take a good look at you."

Falcon was reluctant to agree, but thinking this might be the last time she would ever want to touch him, he knelt down on one knee. He took her hand and held it to the back of his head. "There, you can feel the lump, but it's stopped bleeding. Don't bother asking how I got it because I won't tell you."

They were so close that Belle longed to press his cheek against her bosom and simply hold him. When he released her hand, it was a struggle to simply stroke his hair lightly and step back. She would have sworn she had seen the full gamut of his emotions since last night, but as he rose, his expression took on a depth of anguish that frightened her.

"My father wants to see you, but you needn't face him alone. You weren't alone last night, and that's when the trouble began. It's as much my fault as yours, and I won't allow anyone to blame you."

The defiant tilt of her chin made it plain she was adamant about protecting him, but Falcon couldn't accept such a sacrifice and shook his head emphatically. Although he was the eldest and had instigated their childhood pranks, Belle had always defended him when they were caught. Their parents had never wanted to punish her harshly, so on more than one occasion he had escaped with a light scolding rather than the stern reprimand he had deserved. She was a treasure, but he had thought only of fulfilling his own needs last night, and of getting out of a forced marriage this morning. He could not forgive himself for being so selfish.

"No, stay out of it," he warned. His sorrow deepening, he looked off toward the river. "I'd rather die than hurt you, but last night, well, I just wanted a woman, any woman, and you happened to be there. You had the good sense to stop me, and showed even better judgment in refusing my proposal today. I'll always be grateful to you for being so much wiser than I.

"I'll talk with your father, but I won't admit any more than I did with our mothers, and then I'm riding back to South Carolina. You've seen what has to be the worst side of any man, and I can't expect you to forgive me for treating you like a woman I'd pay for her favors."

Belle could not accept that crude dismissal of what they had shared. Until the moment she had asked for words of devotion, she had felt loved and cherished rather than merely used. Tears welled up in her eyes. "In wasn't like that, Falcon, not at all."

Falcon discounted her opinion with a rude laugh and began backing away. "How would you know, Belle? You've never been with a whore, and I've been with plenty." He watched an anguished light fill her tearful gaze and while he longed to hold and comfort her, he feared all his tender promises would sound like another awkward attempt to win forgiveness for the inexcusable liberties he had taken. Unable to bear the heartache he had caused her, he left her standing on the dock alone looking very young and afraid. As he approached the house, he cursed himself with every step for placing her in such a miserable situation.

He prayed he could fool his uncle as easily as he had fooled Belle, but his whole body ached with the pain of hurting her, and he doubted he could speak at all. He stepped into the dining room and waved to his uncle, but then waited in the study for him to finish eating. Bathed in warm sunshine, the book-lined room invited the serious discussions that often took place there, but Falcon recalled last night's seductive shadows and felt sick to his stomach. He sank down into one of the red wing chairs and closed his eyes. He had fallen asleep by the time his uncle joined him.

Byron shook Falcon's shoulder. "Would you like a brandy?"

Embarrassed to have drifted off, Falcon quickly straightened up. "No, thank you. I've given up spirits."

"Really?" Byron poured himself a splash of his favorite drink and sat down at his desk to enjoy it. "Beau was more Christian's friend than yours," he mused thoughtfully, "and Jean was too young to keep up with you, but as I recall, you and Belle were inseparable. I want your word that you won't push your former closeness into more than it ought to be."

Falcon returned his uncle's level stare as he repeated his demand in his mind. All he had needed was one more push, or thrust, and they would be planning the wedding. Because his earlier attempts to defend himself had gone so poorly, he was content for the moment simply to agree. "You have it."

On Falcon's infrequent visits home, their conversations had centered on the war. As Byron regarded the young man more closely, he noted his weight loss and another change that was far more disturbing. Falcon didn't just appear weary; he looked past caring. During the French and Indian War, Byron had seen that same fearlessness reflected in Hunter's eyes. The Seneca brave had fought with a stoic exhilaration, yet whenever their eyes had met, Byron had been grateful they were allies for it had been terrifyingly plain that Hunter would show an enemy no mercy.

Unlike Hunter, Falcon had not been raised as a Seneca warrior, but he had grown to manhood with a rifle in his hand. "You've served long enough," Byron advised. "Don't go back."

Falcon thought his uncle daft. "Stay home, but stay away from Belle?" He could still feel the angelic sweetness of her caress. "That's impossible."

Belle and Dominique were pretty and popular, and Byron was positive if the war had not gone on so long, by this time they would both be happily married and have children of their own. Falcon wasn't the husband he would have selected for Belle, but she had always been too strong-willed to accept his choice anyway. She and Falcon were related, but only as second cousins, so there was no real barrier to the match.

"Then stay and marry her," he suggested.

"She's already turned me down," Falcon replied, "and with good reason." He sat forward slightly. "If you've no more to say, I'd like to start back for South Carolina while there's still plenty of light."

Byron had not meant to chase Falcon away from his own home, and immediately began to argue. "You can't want to leave when you only arrived home last night."

"I know, but I shouldn't have come." Falcon rose with a weary stretch. "It's better for all of us if I don't stay."

"Wait a minute," Byron cautioned. "I can't believe Belle turned you down. Give her a few days to get used to having you home again, and her answer will surely be different."

Falcon leaned against the edge of the desk. "No, she made a wise choice, and I'll not try to influence her to change it."

"Sit down," Byron urged, but Falcon shook his head and remained standing. "I couldn't love you more if you were my own son," Byron swore convincingly. "You look exhausted. Don't leave home until you've had a chance to rest and eat plenty of good food. You'll not only be doing yourself a favor, but the men with whom you serve as well."

Falcon responded with a rueful laugh. "I'll be doing the

family an even greater favor by leaving." He waited as Byron left his chair and came around to the front of the desk. They were standing right where he and Belle had been last night. Guilt made Falcon's skin crawl, and he wanted out of the study so badly he began inching toward the door. "Thank you for all you've done for me over the years. You've been the best of uncles."

Falcon offered his hand, and Byron took it. "Be careful," he begged. "We don't want to lose you."

Falcon doubted it would be much of a loss, but nodded, and left before his uncle grew maudlin. He knew he ought to tell his mother and father good-bye, but didn't feel up to hearing any more of their questions or advice. He went to his room to gather up the few things he had brought home, then left by the back door. He went down to the stable, where a groom had brushed his sorrel gelding's coat to a burnished copper. When the handsome horse saw Falcon he tossed his white mane and snickered a greeting.

Falcon thanked the groom, then saddled his mount himself. He was proud of the fine horse he had named Rusty Nails, but he had quickly dropped the reference to color and begun calling him Nails. He was just leading Nails to the door when Belle appeared. She was out of breath, her face flushed, and so lovely he had to turn away. "Just let me go, Belle."

Belle ran her hand over the sorrel's rump as she circled him. At seventeen hands, Nails was of an impressive size, but playful; she didn't fear being kicked as she followed Falcon. She reached out to touch his sleeve before he could put his foot in the stirrup.

"Kiss me good-bye," she begged.

"Belle—" Falcon spoke her name in a soft sigh, but the feeble protest was lost when she stepped into his arms. He couldn't refuse the affection he craved so badly, and he slid his arms around her waist. He lowered his mouth to hers for a kiss he meant to be no more than a gentle caress but the instant their lips met, he was lost in a haze of desire.

Her taste was delicious, her whole body so soft and sweet; one kiss blurred into a half-dozen before he found the strength to push her away. Her gaze was as dazed as his, but Falcon knew he had made the best decision for them both. He mounted with a haste he would have used in battle, then galloped out of the stable, determined to stay out of her life.

Belle ran to the wide doorway and watched him ride away. She had always missed him when he was away, but now as he disappeared in the dust-cloaked distance, she was overcome with a sorrow so profound it approached the painful loss of death. Unmindful of the groom's curious stare, she wept openly, certain she had done everything wrong and yet unable to imagine how she might have set things right. When Dominique found her half an hour later, she had not moved.

Dominique handed her sister a lace handkerchief and urged her to dry her tears. "Whatever is wrong with you?" she asked. "Both you and Falcon are behaving strangely, and I want to know why. Aunt Alanna made me leave the sitting room right after you rushed out so all I have are suspicions without the necessary facts. Come, let's find a quiet spot to sit and talk. I want you to tell me what happened from the very beginning, and don't leave out a single delicious detail."

The very last thing Belle wanted to do was confide in Dominique, but she let herself be led to a bench down by the river. Once there, she offered only a brief sketch of what had happened in the study. "We just kissed," she lied. "Then this morning Mother and Alanna forced Falcon to propose to me. It was a wretched situation for us both, and quite naturally I refused."

From what Dominique could recall, Falcon had looked more embarrassed than burdened with guilt when he had presented Belle with the beautiful bouquet and vague apology. "That doesn't make any sense," she chided. "There's got to be more to this if they demanded he propose, and I insist that you tell me everything."

They often discussed their beaus, but Belle had never had more than a passing interest in any man except Falcon and had had no reason to keep secrets. She blotted the last of her tears on Dominique's now soggy handkerchief. "No, not this time, Dominique. I want these memories to be solely mine."

Dominique studied her sister's downcast expression and leapt to the only possible conclusion. Shocked, she reached out to take her hand. "My God, Belle, did you make love with him?"

Belle looked out over the river. A bright green dragonfly dipped low on the water. She envied him his iridescent wings and wished she could escape her pain in the churning river's mist. In her view, she and Falcon had most definitely made love, but she knew Dominique wasn't referring to the tantalizing exchange of fevered kisses that had led them to the brink of intimacy, but to the act itself.

"No, but I do love him and would have had I not realized at the last instant that he'd been drinking and wasn't himself. Now stop pestering me. I feel awful about this whole mess, and Falcon's gone back to the war."

Stunned by Belle's somber declaration of love, Dominique relaxed her pose and leaned back against the bench. "I won't deny that I love Falcon, too, but it's not in the way you mean. It's with the same sweet sisterly warmth I love Beau, Jean, and Christian. Falcon treats me as a sister, but I've always known you meant much more to him."

Belle longed to believe she had inspired Falcon's ardor, but his comment about whores had dashed any such naive hopes. "He said he had just wanted a woman, any woman. I was convenient."

Disgusted with her cousin, Dominique's expression filled

with revulsion. "What an awful thing for him to say. It doesn't even sound like Falcon."

Belle studied her sister's face before replying. Dominique had a more vivacious personality and far more flirtatious ways, but their features were strikingly similar. Like their mother, their blue eyes held a hint of green, and their profiles had a cameo's elegant perfection. They also had Arielle's pale blond hair, but had inherited their father's charming curls.

"No, it doesn't," Belle agreed, "and I didn't want to believe him either, but he swears it's the truth." She closed her eyes and sighed sadly. "I'm so afraid he's not coming back."

If Belle's shocking portrayal of Falcon's flippant excuse for his behavior was correct, Dominique did not understand why she would even want him to. Knowing such a bitter comment would be no comfort, she held her tongue until another far more appealing possibility presented itself. The blissfully romantic thought made her smile. "If I truly loved a man, as you love Falcon, then I would make love to him even if he were drunk, and I'd accept his proposal no matter what had prompted him to give it."

"Dominique!"

Dominique could see she had shocked her sister, but wouldn't hesitate to stoop to deception in the name of love. "I'm serious, Belle. If my beau had too much to drink and were in an amorous mood, I'd make certain that by dawn he would be so desperately in love with me he could not wait to make me his wife."

Belle took note of the triumphant gleam dancing in Dominique's eyes, and did not doubt the confident beauty's ability to succeed. "Yes, you would," she agreed, "but I don't recall your ever being in love. So many men have called on you, brought you expensive gifts, and sworn their devotion. While you've always been gracious, you've never expressed any particular fondness for any of them. You've broken their hearts, and one by one, they've all drifted away."

Embarrassed by Belle's summation of her romantic involvements, which truly had all been brief and quite innocent, Dominique hated to think of herself as merely being fickle. Perhaps she had been spoiled by the admiration she had always received without having to do more than smile. She had certainly enjoyed the company of each of her suitors, but had longed for something more than pretty presents and adoring sighs. Despite Belle's current sorrow, she envied her her love for Falcon and wished she had felt more than a vague sense of disappointment with her beaus.

"There was one man," she recalled wistfully. "You might have been too young to remember Sean O'Keefe. He was a British officer, and looked absolutely magnificent in his uniform, but he only pursued me to be near Liana and when his true purpose became clear, he left and didn't return. Besides, I have my pride, and wouldn't have spoken with him even if he had."

"I do remember him," Belle replied. "He was tall and dark and quite handsome."

"Yes, that's him. He kissed me a time or two, and there was definitely something special about him, or at least I thought there was at the time. Perhaps it was only the danger of being courted by a British officer while all the men here were plotting rebellion. I wonder if he's still alive."

Falcon had described how easily he shot British officers, but Belle thought better of relaying such distressing news when Sean could easily have been one of his victims. "If he is, he might be in Charleston."

"Yes, he just might." Dominique seldom allowed herself to think of Sean, and then it was always with regret. She was silent a long while, but when she at last turned to Belle, her tone had dropped to a more serious level. "I caught only a fragment of the conversation at your end of the table, but didn't you ask Falcon about the need for volunteers to tend the wounded?"

"Yes. I didn't want to be here the next time Falcon came home, and going on a mission of mercy would make an excellent excuse to leave. Now my main concern is that Falcon won't be coming home."

Belle's sorrow was so deep, her love obviously sincere, that Dominique didn't hesitate to offer what she considered a brilliant suggestion. "Then let's go after him."

"What?"

Dominique laughed at her sister's dismay. "The men in our family have all served to further the cause of the United States, but what have we done? Nothing but provide amusing company for the young men who have a few days to spend with us between battles. They're grateful for any woman's company, and I never trust their compliments to be sincere. Why don't we go to South Carolina and tend the wounded? It would give you the chance to straighten out things with Falcon, and if I can locate Sean, perhaps we could meet."

Belle shook her head in disbelief. "You make it sound as though you're planning the entertainment for a picnic when the trip would be dangerous, and when we arrive in South Carolina we'll undoubtedly find men are dying every day, or living in such terrible agony they're in desperate need of care. If you left a hospital to meet a British officer, both sides would accuse you of spying. Are you eager to hang?"

"Spying? I hadn't even thought of that." Dominique looked sincerely pained, but her expression quickly brightened. "You're right. Attempting to contact Sean in the middle of a war is a stupid idea, but volunteering to tend wounded soldiers certainly isn't. Mother has taught us a great deal. I know we could ease suffering, and we aren't making any contribution to the war sitting here."

"No, we're not, but from the harshness of Mother's response when I mentioned it, we're unlikely to be given permission to go."

"Christian's fought with the militia. Beau's at sea. Falcon is undoubtedly the best scout fighting with the Patriots, and Jean's helping with Father's commitments to Congress. And here we sit, forced to bide our time, hoping a couple of brave men will survive the war and offer marriage. Frankly, I'm sick of being nothing more than a beautiful diversion when I have the skills and talent to heal."

Dominique rose and unconsciously primping, smoothed out the folds of her skirt. "Let's just go, Belle. Let's gather up some clothes made of simple homespun fabrics so we won't draw attention to ourselves, and just go. I swear, Falcon's visit is the most exciting thing to happen here in weeks, and he's already gone."

Belle broke into a slow smile as she considered Dominique's plea. She had grown up trailing after Falcon, and the prospect of seeing him again held enormous appeal. Dominique might wear more lace and perfume than she did, but beneath the polished guise of a fragile beauty, she had resilience and strength. Their parents had instilled courage in them as well as their sons, but Belle feared no matter how eloquently they stressed their humanitarian desires they would never be permitted to tend wounded.

"I think we'll have to keep our plans a secret," Belle said, "or we'll risk being locked in our rooms. I doubt we could overtake Falcon, but he taught me how to track, and we might be able to follow his trail. If I asked Hunter what route Falcon had taken, I'll bet he would draw me a map."

Dominique reached out to take Belle's hands to pull her to her feet, and danced in place. "What an adventure! I can't wait. We'll need food. Come on, let's go back up to the house and make a list—otherwise, I'm afraid we'll forget something essential."

"Yes, we have to be very careful about this, or we'll be stopped before we leave or soon after." Belle had absolutely no idea what she could say to Falcon when they overtook him, but for the moment, she pushed that concern aside. "You're right, Dominique. Too little has been expected of us, and now that we've thought of a way to make a contribution, we ought to do it."

"Yes, we must. Can you think of an excuse for us to leave the house early tomorrow morning?"

"I often fish. I have old clothes I usually wear, and you can borrow a simple gown from Johanna and say you're planning to join me. We can take a lunch, and tell everyone we're hoping to make a day of it. We won't be missed until late afternoon, and by then, we'll have been traveling a good ten hours."

"Hunter will come after us," Dominique warned. "And if you ask for a map, he'll know right where to look."

Belle nodded, and quickly discarded the idea. "Father has maps he marks to follow the progress of the war. I'll copy one." Her mind racing to find other ways to ease their journey, she forced herself to take a deep breath and remain calm. "We'll have to take some of Mother's herbs, but not enough for her to miss them tomorrow."

Dominique drew Belle to a halt. "When we reach the house, ask Mother for advice. I'll go up to her room and take what I can. We'll need barberry root bark to treat wounds, white willow bark for fevers, and what else should we have?"

"Comfrey powder is good for wounds, and what about chamomile? It's an excellent treatment for both fever and wounds."

"Yes, I'll get that, too. Try and keep her talking ten minutes at the very least. That will give me the time to select the medicines we need and rearrange her supplies so she won't notice anything is missing."

"I'll try."

"No," Dominique scolded. "You'll have to do better than that. Falcon's broken your heart and ridden off to war. Cry if you must, but once you ask for her advice, I know she'll have plenty to say."

Belle was well aware of the fact that their mother was a woman of strong opinions, but she did not realize how strong until they were seated together in the sitting room where the morning had begun. Christian and Liana had taken Liberty and gone home, as had Johanna and David, so once Dominique had excused herself, Belle was left with her mother and aunt. Sensing Belle's reluctance to confide in Arielle with her there, Alanna made a discreet exit.

"This has been the worst day of my life," Belle began, and she did not have to resort to theatrics to summon tears.

Arielle moved to take a place at her daughter's side on the settee. With windows on the west, the cheerful yellow room was a bright refuge on lazy summer afternoons. This was their first opportunity to talk since Falcon had tactlessly blurted out the result of his proposal, and she welcomed it. "I'm sorry for contributing to it, Belle, but I don't understand why you rejected Falcon's proposal when I know you love him."

"Had he proposed when he brought me the bouquet this morning and said that he loved me with all his heart, I would have been overjoyed and said yes. But that's not what happened."

Arielle gave her daughter a comforting hug. "Your father is very concerned about him, Belle. War does terrible things to men, and while we all believe independence is worth the tragic human cost, that doesn't mean we won't suffer while paying it. If you and Falcon are destined to be together, and I truly believe that you are, then you'll eventually work out whatever problems prevented your becoming engaged today."

Belle clung to that hope. "I wish I could believe you."

"My predictions seldom prove wrong. The real question, however, is whether or not you believe in Falcon."

In the space of a day the handsome Indian had been passionate, aloof, sarcastic, withdrawn, and yet, so dear to her that Belle had no doubts. "Yes, I believe in him. He's so much a part of me, I feel lost when he's away."

"I doubt he'll be able to stay away long this time. Too much was left unresolved between you."

Belle knew that was true in her mind if not in his, and nodded to encourage her mother to continue providing helpful advice. When Dominique joined them for tea, she hoped she could recall even half of it. Her sister winked at her, and she had difficulty hiding her excitement. She could not wait to see Falcon again. The hazards of the journey and the dangers of war seemed slight compared to that joy, and she fought not to smile so widely that she'd inadvertently alert her mother to their plan.

Belle knew it was foolish, but believed with all her heart that Falcon's love was worth the risk. She prayed that the next time they were together there would be no doubts, nor apologies, but only more of the heavenly bliss she had found in his arms.

Four

At supper that evening, the table was still set with the same extravagant care as it had been earlier in the day but only Belle, Dominique, their brother, Jean, their parents, and Hunter and Alanna were gathered in the dining room. Except for special occasions, Christian and Liana and Johanna and David dined with their children in their own home; as Byron surveyed the smaller group, he wished they were present again so that Falcon's absence would not be so painfully obvious. He had repeatedly recalled his conversation with the troubled young man, but considering the importance of the subject could see no way it might have gone better.

He still felt guilty, however, and feared he was to blame for Falcon's hurried departure. Before bringing the blessing to a close, he added a plea for Falcon's continued protection from harm but it did little to ease his aching conscience. "This may not be the most appropriate time to discuss Falcon's visit, but I do want everyone to know that I encouraged him to stay. Regrettably, he refused."

The mention of Falcon's name made Belle exquisitely uncomfortable, and she was grateful she couldn't see Dominique's expression. She was so excited by the prospect of following Falcon she could barely take a sip of the thick vegetable soup they had been served. Her spoon rattled against the edge of her bowl in a frantic tattoo, and she had to set it aside and break off a piece of the half ryemeal, half cornmeal bread known as rye-an'-injun. She added butter and chewed with deliberate care so as not to choke. The empty chair opposite her mocked her dreams cruelly, and she felt her mother's gaze as plainly as the heat from an open oven and did not dare glance her way.

Arielle noted Belle's bright blush, but after their conversation that afternoon she considered her daughter's embarrassed reaction perfectly normal. "Like you, I do wish he had stayed longer, but I trust Falcon and Belle to work out their differences on his next visit. He is a fine young man, but clearly the war has given him experience far beyond his years. We must all pray that we will soon win our independence so that Falcon, and all the young men fighting for our country, can come home and resume leading peaceful lives."

"We all want peace, Mother," Jean agreed, "but I would like to fight in at least one battle."

"That is only because you have no idea of what a battle really is," Hunter warned. "Death is not always swift, and the screams of dying men can echo in your memory forever."

Alanna saw Belle recoil with dread and kicked her husband's shin under the table. "Please, the horrors of war are well known. Can we talk about something else? I fear none of us will be able to digest this delicious meal."

Hunter caught Byron's eye and held it. "My son is his own man. Do not blame yourself for chasing him away."

"Thank you. I'll try not to," Byron replied without conviction.

Dominique waited until everyone had taken several spoonfuls of soup before speaking in a soft, casual tone. As always, her voice held a hint of enticing intimacy. "Belle and I were thinking of going fishing tomorrow. Do you want to come with us, Jean?"

"And have you scare away all the fish with your constant

giggles?" Jean teased. "No, thank you. I have work to do here for Father."

Dominique held her breath, waiting for someone to object or at least notice that she had never shown any interest in fishing before that evening, but no one did. "Belle knows of several fine places along the river where we might have a pleasant picnic. Then if we do more giggling than fishing as Jean predicts, we'll at least have had a lovely day."

As the eldest, Dominique frequently attempted to advise Belle, usually completely without success. But after Belle's tragic misunderstanding with Falcon, Arielle thought the suggestion of a picnic a wonderfully thoughtful gesture. "What a splendid idea. I'll ask Cook to pack you something special. Enjoy yourselves and if you catch fish for our supper, fine. If not, we'll dine on something equally good."

Dominique broke off a bite of bread, but before it reached her lips, she noticed just how closely Hunter was observing her. Alanna and her father were cousins, so the Indian was merely a cousin by marriage, but all Byron's children called him Uncle. His dark eyes seemed to stare right through her, but she refused to behave as though she felt guilty for planning to run away.

"Is something wrong, Uncle?" she asked. "If you know of a good place to fish, we'd welcome the suggestion."

"Do you plan to go fishing in your satin and silk?" Hunter asked, amused by the thought of the elegant young woman baiting a hook.

Dominique frowned slightly, as though sincerely troubled by his remark. "I'd not thought about my clothes, but you're right, Uncle. There's nothing in my wardrobe that will do. Do you think Johanna might lend me one of her linen gowns?"

Shocked by that question, Arielle replied before Hunter could. "Really, my darling, Johanna's clothes are as lovely as yours. We'll find something appropriate for you here. Just be certain both of you wear your caps pulled down low. That way you won't come home as freckled as the field hands."

Belle needed a swallow of wine to wash down another bite of bread, then finally overcame her near-suffocating excitement to join in the conversation. "Perhaps I have something for you to wear, Dominique. Come up to my room with me after supper."

Dominique smiled at Hunter before thanking her sister. He frequently wore a disapproving frown around her, but he was never hostile. She knew he considered her a flirt, which she could not deny. She had never doubted that he loved her every bit as much as he loved Belle and Jean, however. She thought of Sean O'Keefe then. She had certainly flirted outrageously with him, but that had been just prior to the outbreak of the rebellion when the British officer had rightly suspected her family of disloyalty to the king. The danger their involvement entailed had not been the only attraction, though, or she was certain his memory would not have lingered to this very day.

As the conversation drifted to other subjects, Belle had to force herself to finish her soup. She had never had to keep such a delicious secret from her family, and it was all she could do not to blurt out the plan she and Dominique had devised. It would be promptly denounced as absurd and forbidden, so she kept it locked in her heart, but she did not draw a relaxed breath until the meal ended after bowls of blackberries in cream. As soon as she and Dominique had reached her room, she quickly shut the door and began to pace.

"They didn't seem in the least bit suspicious," she said.

Dominique perched herself on the edge of the bed. Her room was decorated in a pale pink as delicate as dawn, while Belle's was a sky blue that very nearly matched their eyes. Dominique thought her sister's room pretty, but she preferred her own and seldom spent any time in Belle's.

"No. Why should they be? Haven't we always been perfectly obedient daughters?"

Last night's late encounter with Falcon was still too vivid
a memory for Belle to agree. "Not always," she confessed,
but refused to add the incriminating details. "I'm eager to
leave, but that doesn't mean I'm not frightened. Not about
the journey, really, because we ride well enough to reach
South Carolina without mishap, but I can't predict Falcon's
reaction. What if he's furious rather than thrilled to see
me?"

Dominique had never cared deeply enough about a man
to agonize over his reaction to anything she did, but Belle's
torment was etched so plainly in her anguished expression
she readily understood her pain. "Let's worry about Falcon
after we get there," she proposed. "Tending the wounded
is such a worthy goal; let's concentrate on that rather than
him for the time being. What we need to do now is look
as though we're preparing for a picnic while we gather everything we need for an extended trip. That means we have
to take only the essentials with us, like Mother's herbs and
a change of lingerie. Our hairbrushes, of course," she
quickly added. "It might be wise to have more than a single
pair of shoes."

Belle raised her hands to her temples. "I'm not going to
be able to sleep at all tonight," she moaned. She had had
little sleep the night before, either, but would not delay their
plan until she was well rested.

"We'll need money," she recalled. "Not so much as to
invite robbery, but some at least. I do expect we'll be paid
for tending the wounded, but what if it isn't enough to cover
our lodgings?"

Dominique gestured toward the desk. "Bring your sav-
ings and I'll bring mine. Where's that list we began this
afternoon? We had food and clothes, but not money, and
we mustn't forget anything else because once we leave the
house, we can't return or we'll surely be caught."

Belle had just opened one of the small drawers in her desk to retrieve the list she had hidden when she was interrupted by a knock at the door. She sent Dominique a pleading glance, then hurried to answer it. Her mother stood in the hall holding a simple blue and white gown folded over her arm. Belle recognized it instantly as one of her Aunt Alanna's. She opened the door wide and gestured for her to come in.

"Will this do, Dominique?" Arielle asked. "Alanna had intended to pass it on to one of Cook's daughters, but you could certainly wear it to go fishing first."

Dominique slid off the bed and came forward to take the cotton gown. She held it up and smiled. "Yes. This is perfect. Please thank Aunt Alanna for me if I don't see her before we leave in the morning. I didn't mean to insult anyone when I mentioned borrowing a gown from Johanna. After all, she has her mother's taste in clothes and prefers cotton and linen to satin and lace. I hope it didn't sound as though I believed she went around in rags."

Dominique was an exquisite creature, but unfortunately, she never quite saw the world as clearly as her mother did. Belle had a far more practical nature, but Arielle never discounted Dominique's remarkable gift for painting even the most mundane aspects of her life with wildly dramatic strokes. "Well, I'm afraid it sounded as though you considered her everyday gowns only good enough to wear for fishing, but because Johanna wasn't there, and neither Hunter nor Alanna will ever repeat your remark, no harm was done."

"Oh dear. I didn't mean to be tactless."

Because it was one of Dominique's most common failings, Arielle did not scold her again. "Just be more careful about your comments in the future. Cook will have your picnic basket prepared before she goes to bed. Now don't you two stay up too late."

Belle walked her mother to the door. "We won't," she

promised. "The best time to fish is just after dawn." She held her breath until her mother had started down the stairs, but Dominique's eyes were lit with a wicked light. "The way you look, one would think you're the one hoping to catch up with a sweetheart. I thought you agreed attempting to see Sean O'Keefe would not only be foolish but dangerous. Have you changed your mind?"

Dominique shook her head and again pointed to the desk. "Of course not. Now find the list," she reminded her sister. "We're not finished and I don't want to risk leaving anything important behind. As for Sean, your comment about being hanged as a spy was enough to banish thoughts of seeing him from my mind. Now let's see—food, clothes, money. What else should we take?"

"Fishing gear," Belle added in neat script. "With it we can feed ourselves the whole way so it would be valuable even if we didn't have to take it to make our trip believable."

"Yes, of course. Don't forget a tinderbox for flint and steel as I'd not want to eat the fish raw."

Belle made a note of it. "A small sewing kit," she added. "We're sure to rip our skirts riding through tall brush."

The sisters went over the list several times and added a Bible, soap and towels, and several pairs of stockings. Dominique reviewed the list, and unable to think of anything more, took her sister's hands in a fond clasp. "I know what we're doing is right, Belle, and not simply for Falcon's sake, but our own. When we've found work in a hospital, we'll write to Mother and Father and let them know we're well and happy. I know they'll be angry with us for leaving, but I can't help but hope they'll also be proud of us for wanting to be of service in such troubled times."

Belle managed a nod, but as soon as Dominique had crossed the hall to her own room, she began to shake. She clutched her arms and told herself again and again that what they were doing was right. The memory of the sorrow that had filled Falcon's eyes as he had kissed her good-bye had convinced her her place was with him. She let no other thought intrude as she gathered the few belongings she intended to take. She would have to wait until her parents had gone to bed to copy one of her father's maps, but she would trace a path to Falcon, and pray with every step of the way that he would also view what she was doing as right.

Belle slept fitfully that night, for whenever she fell asleep she was jarred awake by the sheer audacity of what she and Dominique were about to undertake. If pursuing Falcon proved to be a fool's errand, she would have no one to blame but herself. But if it brought him back into her arms, then the risk would have been well worth it.

She was up and dressed in a pale blue muslin gown more than an hour before dawn. Her trip downstairs after midnight had prompted her to fetch a lantern from the back porch rather than rely on a candlestick when she feared she would be shaking so badly she would spew tallow all over her clothes. Her belongings were packed in a single leather bag she would lash behind her saddle. Chilly, she grabbed a warm woolen shawl and wrapped it around her shoulders. Leaving her bag to pick up on the way out, she took the lantern and tiptoed down the hall to Dominique's room.

Jean was a sound sleeper so she doubted he would awaken, but if he did, she would simply provide their brother with a gentle reminder of their fishing trip and send him back to bed. She rapped lightly at Dominique's door, then let herself in. She had fully expected to have to wake her sister, but Dominique was not only up and dressed, she had made her bed.

"Ready?" Dominique picked up her bag and came to the door. "I've taken care to be quiet, and I've not heard a peep from Jean. Let's hope we can slip by everyone else as easily." She noticed Belle's shawl then, and quickly fetched one of her own. She scanned her room with an anxious glance, then blew out the candle on the dresser and was ready to go.

Belle picked up her bag as they passed her room, then held the lantern aloft to light their way. They hesitated at the second floor landing, but it was much too early for either their parents or Falcon's to be awake and stirring. Belle tugged on Dominique's sleeve, and the pair made their way on down the stairs and out the back door.

The rhythmic chirping of crickets ruffled the cool night air, and the most ambitious of the English sparrows nesting near the house had already begun to trill their familiar greeting to the dawn. As they neared the kitchen, a mockingbird called loudly, startling them both, but they hurried inside without wasting the breath to scold it. As promised, their picnic basket sat on the pantry table, but a day's rations of ham, cheese, bread, and cider wouldn't be nearly enough to sustain them on their journey.

Dominique plucked a string of dried apples from its hook on the wall. "I know we'll be able to gather berries along the way, but we ought to have something in reserve for the day we can't find any."

"My God," Belle moaned. "I almost left without a pan to fry the fish." She hurriedly sorted through the utensils and found an iron skillet just the right size for the two of them. Taking care not to create a rattling clatter, she removed it from the stack of pans. "We can cook beans in this too, and cornmeal. Fill a small bag with each, please, while I fetch some more ham from the smokehouse."

Dominique picked up one of the cook's aprons and spread it on the table. She set the iron skillet in the center, then rummaged around for cloth to hold the provisions Belle had requested. She had loved to help in the kitchen as a child, but it had been years since she had worked there and she had to search for everything far longer than she would have liked. As soon as Belle returned with the ham, she knotted the corners of the apron to make a sturdy sack.

"I put in a knife and cooking spoon," she whispered, "but we'll have to stop at the scullery for plates and utensils." She peeked out at the sky, but it was still a dull gray with no hint of the coming dawn. "We should have started gathering everything earlier."

"Have you had second thoughts?" Belle asked anxiously.

"No, of course not. I just don't want to ride for two days and find we've already run out of everything."

"We won't run out of fish, nor berries," Belle promised. She picked up the picnic basket, then had to shift hands to carry her satchel and lantern. "I know we can do this, Dominique. Falcon taught me everything Hunter taught him, and he travels the countryside without worrying he won't be able to provide for himself."

Dominique struggled to carry the bundle of foodstuffs through the door, then bent down to pick up her bag. "I shall hold that thought whenever we lack for anything."

Belle turned back toward her. "If you've changed your mind, say so now. I'd prefer to go alone than listen to you complain the whole way to South Carolina."

Startled by the vehemence of her sister's tone, Dominique came to a sudden halt, but did not drop her burden. "There's nothing for me here," she replied with fierce determination. "Have you forgotten that this was my idea to begin with? Now let's hurry to the barn before the stableboys begin work and notice how much we're taking."

"I'm scared witless," Belle confessed, "but I won't turn back."

"Neither will I," Dominique insisted. When they reached the scullery, she made a quick trip inside for plates and utensils that would never be missed, then the sisters stayed on the path that ran past the carriage house and smithy to the stable.

Belle placed the lantern beside the double doors before

laying the rest of the things she had been carrying in the dirt. It took two hands to pull open one of the heavy doors, then she quickly brought the lantern inside. Both she and Dominique owned prize mares they rode often, but now she wondered if they were the best choice.

"We've dressed in simple clothing to appear inconspicuous, but I didn't think how much attention fine mounts will attract. They are such beautiful bays, and I fear everyone will remember seeing them even if they forget us."

Dominique brushed that worry aside. "They're beauties because their reddish hides are kept glowing with constant grooming. Let's just toss a bit of dust on them as we ride along and tangle their manes so they don't look nearly so sleek and pampered. Besides, I thought you meant to guide us through the countryside rather than along the main roads. With luck, no one will see us after we take the ferry across the James River."

It was easy to argue that they had been blessed with good luck from the day they were born, but Belle did not want to rely upon luck now. "Your idea's a good one," she said instead. "We'll just let Baby Dee and Ladybug get so sweaty and dirty they can pass without notice as easily as we."

Dominique's lips formed a pretty pout. "That will be the real challenge, won't it? To pretend that we're humble serving girls on an errand rather than respectable young ladies who expect to have their commands obeyed. It will be like acting a part in a play," she enthused.

"Hush, and saddle Baby Dee. At least we know how to care for our mounts ourselves, and that's a blessing. A side-saddle may be fine for a jaunt into town, but for a trip this long, we'd be better off riding astride."

As they were growing up, Byron Barclay had been a superb teacher who never excluded his daughters from the skills he taught his sons. If they showed no interest he excused them, but not until he was satisfied they need not be dependent on any man. Belle had been more appreciative of the lessons, but as they saddled their pets, Dominique handled the task just as effortlessly.

It took careful planning to secure all they wished to bring to their mount's saddles, but with Dominique carrying the picnic basket and Belle the fishing gear they had found in the stable, they were at last ready to go. Belle doused the lantern, and leaving it behind, the sisters rode their horses down the soft dirt path to the river. The sky had just begun to lighten with a faint blush, and they could find their way along the familiar path without mishap, but each sent a longing glance toward home when she thought the other wasn't looking.

At noon, Arielle went out the front door and looked down toward the river. It was a lovely day, warm and clear. A perfect day for a picnic, and yet by midmorning she had begun to feel uneasy.

Byron walked up behind his wife and slipped his arms around her waist to pull her close. "Pretty day," he murmured as he nuzzled her throat.

Arielle slid her hands over his. "Yes, it is, but I didn't really expect the girls to be away so long."

Byron drank in his wife's subtle perfume. A delicious blend of wildflowers, it was among her most effective potions and never failed to stir his desire. "Why not? Belle has always been happiest with a fishing pole in her hands."

Arielle relaxed against him, but she was worried still. "Perhaps it was only Falcon's company which made fishing such a pleasant pastime. I've seen her standing alone on the docks, gazing out at the river so often these last few years. I should have guessed her thoughts were of him. I don't think he knew how much she missed him."

"Surely he must now."

Comforted by her husband's embrace, Arielle remembered the strained beginning of their own romance. Adversaries in Acadia, neither his British friends nor her dear Acadian neighbors had approved of their friendship; but regardless of the dire opinions of others, they could not have ignored the joy love offered them. She had lost everything she had once held dear, but did not regret her choice. She and Byron had been happy together for more than twenty years and she prayed they would have at least another twenty to celebrate their love.

"Perhaps I'm more upset about Falcon's visit than I thought," she murmured, "but I do wish the girls would hurry home."

"They are high-spirited creatures, but what possible harm could befall them, Arielle? They know the riverbank as well as this porch, and ride as confidently as Jean. Should they encounter even the slightest problem, our neighbors on the river would offer their help most willingly. Now come inside and let's dine with no further mention of our daughters. Think how sad Hunter and Alanna must be that Falcon left again so quickly."

"Oh, how thoughtless of me," Arielle sighed. "I blamed Dominique for that failing only last night, but truly, I am no better." She took Byron's hand as they went inside, and did her best to keep the dinner conversation light rather than burden Hunter and Alanna with her foolish worries when their concern was rightly with Falcon, who had left to fight in the war.

Byron had been sincere in his attempts to lift his wife's spirits at noon, but when their daughters were not home by three, his confidence that the day would be as ordinary as he had supposed was badly shaken. The afternoon was sultry and he could easily imagine Dominique and Belle napping on a grassy riverbank, but he wanted them home. Leaving his study, he paused at the door of the sitting room where Arielle and Alanna were sipping lemonade and doing their embroidery with lazy stitches.

"I thought I'd ride up the river and meet the girls on their way home."

Arielle knew all of her husband's expressions and while he was smiling, she saw the tension he was attempting to hide in the taut muscles along his jaw. "I'm trying not to worry," she replied, "but thank you for going to find them."

Alanna had not realized it was so late. "They're probably dangling their feet in the river and paying no more attention to the time than I am. I do want them to enjoy their idle hours, but I can barely recall being as young as your girls."

"That's odd," Byron said. "I remember those years vividly. You were already married to Hunter and raising Christian at Belle's age, and by Dominique's, you had given birth to both Johanna and Falcon. There are days when I think it's good our daughters have enjoyed so many carefree years, and then others when I pray they have not missed a chance for marriage and family."

"The war can't last forever," Alanna assured him.

Because he had been among the first to agitate for freedom from Great Britain, Byron felt responsible for every life lost in the cause he held so dear. "No. It can't, but our girls need the joys of peace as much as the men fighting." He came into the room to kiss his wife good-bye, then hurried away before the conversation became any more maudlin.

He followed the fresh tracks on the path bordering the river, but when he came to the spot where he had taught his children to fish, the marsh grass was high and untrampled. Disappointed not to have found his daughters quickly, he went on, but at the next shady spot there was no sign they had stopped there either. Recalling a mention of pretty places for a picnic, he thought they might have ridden farther than usual, but when the sun dipped low toward the river and he still had not found them, he was forced to return home alone.

He left his horse at the stable for one of the boys to tend

and sprinted up to the house. One look at his wife's anxious expression and his heart fell. "I thought they might have ridden inland and come home by a different route, but obviously they aren't here."

"No, and now I'm sorry I didn't beg you to go out looking for them at noon."

Having overheard their conversation from the parlor, Hunter and Alanna entered the hall. "I'll leave at first light," he promised. "They won't be difficult to track."

Arielle clutched Byron's hand tightly. "They should not have to be tracked," she cried. "They were just going fishing, so they would have stayed beside the river. How could they possibly have gotten lost?"

"They are not lost," Hunter said. "They must not want to be found."

Arielle stared up at her husband. "I don't understand. Why would they hide from us?"

Alanna saw Byron shake his head, and offered her own explanation. "Belle asked about tending wounded yesterday. You discouraged her interest, but could that be where she and Dominique have gone?"

Arielle's eyes widened in fright. "Oh, no, they wouldn't have tried to reach South Carolina on their own, would they?"

"Perhaps they mean to overtake Falcon," Hunter suggested. "Do not worry, I will stop them before they have gone far. I should have known Dominique did not really want to fish."

Arielle clung to her husband. "But that means they lied to us, and they've never done that. Can't you go after them tonight? What if they haven't gone after Falcon? What if they've been kidnapped?"

Hunter cocked his head, throwing the question to Byron, who did not want to believe the Loyalists in Virginia could be so mean. Then again, there might be other men, deserters

from either side who would kidnap his pretty daughters simply for sport and use them very badly.

"We can't wait for first light," he announced suddenly.
"I tracked them a long way up the river. I thought they
were just wandering, but they must have been making for
the ferry. We can ride a long way tonight, cross the river
as soon as the ferry begins to operate, and overtake them
by noon. Grab whatever you must, Hunter, and let's go."

Alanna came forward to encircle Arielle's waist as the
men left without telling them good-bye. "Come, let's have
some supper and decide upon an appropriate punishment
when the girls come home tomorrow."

Arielle pulled away. "I can't eat," she sobbed. "I just
can't believe they would lie to us and take such an awful
risk. How could they even dream they could make it to
South Carolina unharmed? How could they have even considered making such a long and dangerous trip?"

Alanna followed Arielle into the parlor and encouraged
her to at least have a cup of her own soothing herbal tea,
but in her heart she knew once Belle had fallen in love
with an Indian brave, no risk was too extreme.

Five

Knowing just how swiftly Hunter would track them, Belle and Dominique kept up a brisk pace all morning. They stopped to rest and ate a bit of ham and cheese while they waited for the ferry, but as soon as they had crossed the James River, they angled southwest. Skirting the plantations bordering the river, they used the well-worn trails alongside the tobacco fields to hide their tracks.

Refusing to give in to fatigue, they stretched what little was left of their endurance to ride past the last cultivated field and escape into the shadowed forest that lay beyond. Once shielded by the trees, they rode until their mares were so tired they could not in good conscience ask them to continue. Belle slid out of her saddle, then led the way into a stand of oaks bordering a narrow stream.

"This is as good a place to camp as any," she called to her sister.

Dominique followed, and after dismounting, she struggled to remove the gear she had slung over Baby Dee's rump, then hauled off the saddle and blanket. She stroked the mare's neck and led her to the stream. "We should have brought rope to tie them tonight," she said, as Belle brought Ladybug up beside them.

"Rope," Belle repeated numbly. "Yes. We'll find some tomorrow, or braid grass to make our own, but the horses are as exhausted as we are and won't stray tonight."

"I'm so tired I couldn't even braid my hair, let alone grass," Dominique replied. She knelt to scoop up a handful of water. "I can't remember ever feeling so dirty. We wanted the mares covered in a layer of dust, but not us. Do you think it's safe to bathe here?"

There was perhaps an hour of daylight left, and Belle surveyed the land surrounding their campsite with a weary gaze. Dotted with oak, birch, and pine, it offered a tranquil sense of security, but she was still on her guard. "We haven't seen anyone for hours, but it might be a good idea to wait until after dark to bathe. I'll build a fire as soon as we gather firewood, but I don't have the energy left to cook."

"Neither do I," Dominique agreed. "Cold ham and bread will be fine." She left her mare grazing near the stream and walked back to where they had unloaded their belongings. Not caring if she got grass stains on her aunt's gown, she lay down on her back, flung her arms wide, and stared up at the canopy of leaves overhead.

"Do you think Falcon could have come this far yesterday?"

Belle stretched out beside Dominique. "No. He left in the afternoon, so he must have stopped long before this." She closed her eyes and moaned softly. "I knew traveling this far on horseback was going to be difficult, but I never dreamed it would be exhausting. I'll get up in a minute to see about the fire."

"Yes, do," Dominique murmured sleepily.

Belle closed her eyes for what she believed would be just a moment, but she dozed off, and when she awoke, dawn had already spilled over the forest floor and turned the night air into a pale golden haze. Terrified they would be caught and herded back home like stray sheep, she sat up, pulled her wrinkled cap into place, and leaned over to shake Dominique awake.

"We've overslept," she cried. "Wake up. It's time to go."

Dominique lay curled on her side. She needed a moment to recall why she was sleeping on damp grass, then pushed herself up into a sitting position. "What happened last night?" she asked through a lazy yawn. "I don't remember a thing."

Stiff after sleeping on the ground, Belle rose shakily and stretched her arms above her head, but she still felt sore and began to massage her neck. "Nothing. We were going to build a fire, bathe, and eat a cold supper, but we fell asleep where we first lay down to rest."

"I've got to take a bath," Dominique complained. "I can't ride another mile as sticky as this."

Belle didn't want to take the time, but when Dominique stumbled off toward the stream, she followed. As predicted, their mares were grazing no more than fifteen feet away. Belle swerved to run her hand over Ladybug's rump, then hurried on to catch up with Dominique.

"Hunter will be relentless," she worried aloud. She kicked off her shoes and sat down to remove her stockings. "His stallion is stronger than our mares, and he'll probably not carry anything heavier than a knife. That means the distance between us will shrink with every passing hour. He's got to know where we're going, but he can't know the route. If we make it erratic, it may compound his problems enough for us to retain the advantage."

Dominique shucked off her gown, petticoats, and lingerie with great haste, then waded out into the stream. The water was icy cold, and the rocky stream-bed slippery, but she was too desperate to wash herself clean to be bothered by such slight discomforts. "I forgot to bring the soap and towels," she exclaimed. "Will you please run back and get them?"

Belle weaved slightly as she rose, but wanting soap and a towel for herself, did her sister's bidding without complaint. "How very spoiled we are," she remarked as she returned to the water's edge. We don't even heat the water for our baths. We just step in when they're ready."

Dominique leaned over to take the bar of soap from Belle's hand. "That was precisely my complaint yesterday. All that's been expected of us is that we sit and look pretty. We're encouraged to read widely, but never voice an original thought in front of anyone but the family." She began to scrub herself off with a vigorous rhythm. "When we're so pampered and weak, how are we ever to survive the ordeal of childbirth?"

Belle dropped the last of her petticoats on the grass. She unlaced her corset, yanked off her chemise, and stepped out of her drawers. She stuck a toe in the stream and shivered. "Our Aunt Melissa didn't," she reminded her.

That was such a sobering thought, Dominique could not let it pass. "Do you think of her often?" she asked. "After all, she paid a terrible price for loving Hunter."

The water was so cold that Belle's teeth began to chatter as soon as she had stepped in, but she had a ready reply. "I like to think she was punished for not loving him, but no, I seldom think of her." She shared Dominique's soap and washed with a frantic thoroughness before stepping out on the grass. The sisters had bathed together since childhood and although Belle was slightly taller, they had figures so similar they could wear each other's clothes. Neither felt the slightest twinge of embarrassment as they dried off.

It was Dominique who went to fetch their clean linen drawers, but both sisters dressed with a haste that would have shocked and amazed their mother. They ate ham, cheese, and bread while repacking their gear, and were in the saddle within half an hour of waking. They were not nearly as energetic as they had been the previous morning, but surviving the first night on their own, even if they had done it poorly, had given them the courage to go on.

* * *

Byron felt sick clear through. As a young man he had fought the French, and not been this frightened. Hunter's expression was serene, as though he were setting out to track a stag rather than two beautiful and defenseless young women. They had arrived at the ferry before the owner that morning and had to wait for the first crossing, but the moment the man appeared, Byron offered to reward him if his memory were good.

"My daughters are blond, and riding a pair of matched bays. I think they may have come this way. Did you have any passengers who fit that description yesterday?"

After years of working on the river, Simon Farquhar's back had acquired a permanent stoop and his deep-set eyes a perpetual squint. He peered up at Byron, taking note of the quiet elegance of his gray suit and proud beauty of his black stallion. He caught the distinct odor of wealth on the crisp morning air and hoped he could recall enough to satisfy the inquisitive gentleman.

"Most of my passengers are simple folk traveling to and from settlements in the Ohio Valley," he began. "Families, mostly, and single men hoping for better than they've left."

Byron nodded appreciatively. "Yes. I'm sure you tote more than your share of chickens and mules, but I'm looking for two pretty young women. You'd not have forgotten had you seen them."

"I was just getting to them, sir," Simon argued. "They weren't like the usual traveler, so I'd have noticed them even if they had not been pretty."

"They did cross here then?" Byron pressed.

"Aye, that they did, around noon I think it was. Shy creatures they were, too. Barely looked up as they paid the fare."

Surprised the girls would strike anyone as demure, Byron shot Hunter a questioning glance, and the Indian edged his mount forward. The sorrel horse was Rusty Nails' sire and also a magnificent beast. "Do you remember their gowns? Were they red, green?" he asked.

Simon pursed his lips thoughtfully and stamped his right foot as though hoping to jog his memory. He tried not to stare at the Indian, but he had never seen another with such a fine horse, or traveling with a gentleman. "Blue," he announced suddenly. "One was dressed in blue, and the other had a gown with blue stripes. I remember the pair because they had such pretty hands. They had the pale, dainty hands of fine ladies."

Byron doubted Simon had been close enough to that many fine ladies to observe their hands, but the clothes sounded right, and Belle and Dominique had inherited their mother's delicate hands and graceful gestures. "Did you see where they went when they left the ferry?"

"That I did not," Simon replied, "but I could watch for them and send word to you if they come back across."

Positive that if his daughters recrossed the river they would be on their way home, Byron shook his head. "Thank you, but that won't be necessary." He tipped the ferryman for his help, paid for two fares, then dismounted and led his horse onto the flat-bottomed boat.

Hunter slipped from his saddle and followed Byron to the rail, but waited until the ferry got underway before he spoke. "It's clear your girls were not kidnapped, and they were smart to act shy."

"Smart?" Byron scoffed. "They've been incredibly stupid. How could they have done this to us?"

Hunter gazed out over the river. He would have preferred to swim across with his mount, and felt uneasy on the wide wooden boat. "They have done nothing to you," he argued persuasively. "They wanted something you and Arielle could not give."

"That's impossible. They lack for nothing."

Hunter had learned long ago that while he and Bryon might have lengthy conversations, they did not always understand each other. He tried again. "They are as pretty as the roses in your garden, and smell as sweet, but they are too bright to be content without a purpose, and you can not give them that."

Insulted by that peculiar opinion, Byron drew in a deep breath and released it in a weary sigh. He relied on Hunter for a great deal, but never for advice on how to run his family. "What purpose should a woman have other than to pursue an interest in literature and the arts and create a happy life for her family?"

Hunter waited for Byron to answer his own question, and when he was unable to, the Seneca brave prompted him. "They are part of your family, but must long for families of their own. Why else would a young woman want to tend wounded soldiers? Wouldn't she rather have a baby to mind?"

At last understanding Hunter's point, Byron nodded thoughtfully. "I want that for them, too. Should I have forced Falcon to wed Belle?"

That was a much more difficult question, and Hunter took a long time to answer. "No, for neither of them would have been happy. Falcon would always have felt that he had no choice in the marriage, and Belle would have suffered the endless doubt that Falcon might not really love her. I would not wish that sorry fate on anyone, let alone my son and your daughter. Does it trouble you that they are kin?"

Byron wondered if Hunter weren't attempting a diplomatic approach to asking if he objected to Belle marrying his son. When he and his brother, Elliott, had brought Hunter home back in 1754, they had never imagined the brave would become part of their family. He had merely been an able scout they had admired. His sister, Melissa, had admired Hunter even more and Christian had been born as a result.

"Had Belle fallen in love with Christian I could not have borne it," he confessed honestly. "But they are first cousins and I could have objected on those grounds. As for Falcon, well, he has always had a special fondness for Belle and been so protective of her that I know he'll make a fine husband. If we can find her and bring her home."

Hunter pretended a rapt interest in the river. "Had Falcon wanted Dominique, I could not have borne that, so we are both lucky he and Belle chose wisely."

Each Sunday the family attended the Bruton Parish Church in Williamsburg, and before returning home, Byron visited the graves of his father, brother, and sister. He frequently brought flowers, but the beauty of the blossoms never completely dissolved his sorrow at the sad errand. Even after all these years he still missed his brother and sister terribly.

"Dominique is so much like Melissa it frightens me at times" Byron confessed softly. "Arielle didn't know Melissa, and Alanna is such a dear soul she has never drawn the comparison in my presence, but it's unmistakable. It would not surprise me to find this trip is her doing."

The ferry had reached the opposite shore before Hunter had to comment but it was all he could do not to see Melissa whenever Dominique entered the room. Everything about his niece reminded him of the subtle seduction that had broken his heart and cost Melissa her life. Forcing away those tragic thoughts, he led his horse off the ferry. The road ahead was little more than a rutted wagon trail but too heavily trafficked for him to track the Barclay girls.

"They may have traveled the road a ways so that anyone watching from the river would be confused, but they would soon turn south." He drew himself into his saddle with an easy stretch, then pointed to the grassy edge of the trail. "Watch for any sign of riders leaving the path before a crossroads. They have come a long way in a single day, and must have stopped for the night soon."

"The ferryman said they crossed around noon."

"Yes, but that does not mean they rode much farther."

Convinced the pair had not, Hunter kept a sharp eye on the flat expanse of wire grass brushing the sides of the road. As the sun rose at their backs, the blue lobelia and lupines graced the landscape with a dreamlike azure cast. There were plantations on this side of the river, too, and in the distance tobacco fields of the same distinctive verdant beauty as their own beckoned invitingly.

"Do they have friends on this side of the river where they might have passed the night?" Hunter asked.

Byron knew every tobacco farmer in Virginia, but that did not mean he enjoyed every man's company, entertained them in his home, or visited in theirs. "No, we're too far from home to see any of these people except at Publick Times when the town is full. It would only be a waste of time to stop at each plantation to ask for them."

Deeply troubled, he added another worry. "I don't want it to become common knowledge that my daughters are missing. That's why I didn't give the ferryman my name. You know as well as I do that there are unscrupulous men who would waste no time in searching for them, but who would not turn them over without expecting, or demanding, to be paid handsomely."

Sorry that was true, Hunter merely nodded. When they had ridden an hour without sighting a fresh trail breaking away to the south, the Seneca brave drew his mount to a halt and Byron stopped with him. "We didn't think to follow the path alongside the river. Perhaps they used it rather than come inland."

"No, not if they didn't want to be seen," Byron argued, "but they might have veered south the instant they left the ferry and ridden through the fields." He removed his cocked hat and wiped his forehead on his sleeve. While touched with gray, at fifty-one his blond curls were still thick. "I thought we'd find them before now."

"So did I," Hunter agreed. "There's a trading post up

ahead. We can get something to eat and ask if anyone there saw them."

Byron struggled to fight back his rising panic. "I'm not hungry, but it will be worth the time to stop if they were seen nearby. They can't simply have vanished after leaving the ferry."

"They may have used the plantation roads yesterday but skirted the houses. If no one has seen them at the trading post, I want you to go home. I'll ride south and get ahead of them if I must, but I'll find them more quickly on my own."

Byron knew Hunter could travel faster alone, but while that might be the wisest alternative, he could not accept it. "I can't go home without them, Hunter. They're too precious to me and I could never face Arielle without them."

Hunter did not confide his latest worry to Byron, but it had just occurred to him that they were not tracking two gently-bred girls, but a pair in which one possessed Falcon's skills. Falcon had taken great pride in teaching Belle his father's lessons, and Hunter had only laughed at the time. Now he knew just how dangerous it had been to teach Belle how to move through the forest with the stealth of a Seneca brave.

He hesitated to give Byron advice, but he doubted they would find anything at the trading post except tasteless food and potent ale. As a young man, he had worked in a trading post on the Mohawk River. It was where he had learned to speak fluent English, and perhaps more importantly, how to use his fists to reduce another man to a quivering, sobbing wretch.

The last stop for travelers bound inland, this small outpost was built of pine logs and held all manner of useful items from pots and pans to sacks of cornmeal. The musty odor of the squat building reminded Hunter of days he would rather forget; he sampled very little of the watery stew offered by the proprietor's wife, and none of the ale. Byron again asked about two young women traveling alone, but received only shrugs from the proprietor, Jason May.

"I can't recall when I've seen women traveling alone," Jason declared in a booming voice that echoed off the brass pots dangling just above his head. "These are treacherous times, and no lady worthy of the name would travel the roads without an escort."

"I agree," Byron assured him. He toyed briefly with the idea of describing Dominique and Belle as servants rather than his daughters, but again unwilling to inspire a search by men he did not know, he tipped Mr. May, downed a pint of ale, and walked outside with Hunter. "You know what we'll need better than I do. What should we purchase before we move on?"

"I have been thinking," Hunter began in a hushed whisper.

Byron leaned close. "Of what?"

"We may have to go farther south than I thought to find the girls. While I would never deliberately lead you into one, it is possible we might encounter a British patrol. Your name alone will get you hanged."

"I'm not fool enough to give it!"

Hunter sent his friend a glance that readily conveyed his understanding of that obvious fact. "You are too well known, Byron, and if any of the British forces who have served in Williamsburg were to see you, they would not even ask your name before knotting a rope. To my shame, the Seneca are fighting with the British, so if I am found near their lines I can say I came to volunteer." He paused a moment to allow Byron time to consider the wisdom of his words.

"The Patriots can not afford to lose you," Hunter stressed. "You must go home. Tell Arielle I will find her daughters and bring them home soon."

Byron had been so concerned about the safety of his girls that he had not once considered the danger to himself in prowling the countryside between Williamsburg and

Charleston. He took a step away, and then turned back. "I'd gladly give my life to save theirs, but that's not really the choice here."

"No. It is not."

Byron wanted to argue, but Hunter's advice was too wise to dispute. "What will you do?"

"Cut south, and either get ahead of them to stop them from going on, or cross their trail and overtake them. Belle must be using what Falcon taught her, and I failed to consider that."

"So did I." Byron did not want to go, but had to accept that he must. "I know you will treat my daughters as though they were your own."

Hunter nodded. "Belle may be very clever, but she will tire and make mistakes. I'll catch them."

"Do you need to buy supplies?" Byron offered, ready to pay for them.

"There is better food in the forest than here." He watched Byron mount his horse and managed a smile for him. "Hurry, and you can be home before dark." As Hunter approached his own stallion, he had already forgotten his old friend and begun stalking his daughters.

Traveling over the grassy forest floor and then along the banks of the Nottoway River, Belle and Dominique made nearly twenty miles on their second day. They had seen no one, and while they had again ridden as far as their weary mounts and they could stand, neither felt secure. They unsaddled their mares, let them drink from the river, then led them back into the sheltering trees to graze.

"I'm going to catch us some fish for supper," Belle announced confidently. "You build the fire."

"That seems fair," Dominique replied. She gathered a heap of fallen branches, then opened the tinderbox. She had never actually lit a fire by herself, but had seen it done often enough to believe it consisted of little more that strik-ing a spark and standing back as the wood began to ignite. She had worked for half an hour with steel and flint and was near tears of frustrated rage before she remembered the servants saved all the worn handkerchiefs, linen under-wear, and sheets for tinder.

Lacking any spare bits of linen, she raked up a mound of dried leaves and after several more fruitless attempts to ignite a blaze, succeeded in striking a spark that caught the serrated edge of a crisp oak leaf. She blew on the tiny curl of smoke, and a flame danced into life. She shouted with glee, then kept adding leaves until the smallest of the branches began to burn. Enormously pleased with herself, she sat back to enjoy the fire's crackling warmth.

Belle had had to search for a worm to bait her hook, but once she found one, she quickly got a strike. She flipped the bass out on the riverbank, removed the hook while the fish was still twitching, and reused the mangled worm. It took a while longer to catch the second bass, but the third and fourth came easily. She cleaned the fish at the water's edge, then threaded her line through the gills to carry her catch back to camp. She found Dominique seated beside an ample fire, braiding long strands of grass into a crude rope.

"Did you have any trouble with the fire?" Belle asked.

"No, none at all," Dominique assured her with a relaxed smile.

"Good. It won't take me a minute to fashion a rack."

Dominique watched as Belle gathered four notched sticks. She drove them into the ground to form the corner posts of the rack, laid two sticks in the notches to link them together, then laid several more sticks across those to form a grid to hold the fish. "How did you learn to do that?" she inquired.

"Falcon taught me," Belle boasted proudly. "On more

than one occasion we roasted part of our catch to feed ourselves, and brought the rest home."

Dominique couldn't help but notice how her sister's gaze
had brightened when she spoke of their cousin. "What else
did he teach you?" she teased in a sultry whisper.

Belle laid the fish upon the rack, and stood back to watch
them roast. "All manner of useful things," she replied absently, "like how to follow bees back to their hive, or hunt
with a bow and arrow."

"That wasn't what I meant," Dominique scolded. "I want
to know what really happened in the study the other night."

Belle's gaze didn't leave the fire. "I've already told you
I won't share what happened."

Dominique laid the grass rope aside and rose. "We have
brothers so we both know how a man looks nude. I can't
remember ever seeing Falcon without his clothes, though.
Do you?"

"He goes without a shirt all summer."

Her fatigue forgotten, Dominique circled the fire. "You
know that's not what I meant. Besides, it's been several
summers since he was home. I do remember his skin was
deeply tanned, and his hair was a glossy black mane. He
and Christian never have seemed as civilized as Beau and
Jean."

"Civilized?" Belle turned the word over in her mind.
Both of Hunter's sons possessed a wildness that set them
apart from the Barclay brothers but that wasn't all she loved
about Falcon. "Beau's a privateer. That's about as uncivi-
lized as a man can get."

"We're not talking about Beau," Dominique reminded
her. "We're talking about Falcon. How does he kiss? Is he
clumsy, or tentative and sweet?" When Belle didn't glance
her way, Dominique moved closer. "Maybe he's had more
practice than I thought. Does he use his tongue in a slow,
deep curl?"

Losing patience, Belle grew harsh. "There was a time

Beau called you Demonique," she chided. "Hush about Falcon, or I'll start calling you that, too."

Dominique knew precisely why she had prompted such a vociferous reaction and began to gloat. "Ah, so he does know how to kiss better than the boys in Williamsburg."

Belle used the cooking spoon to turn the fish to roast the other side. "The boys are soldiers now, and you ought to refer to them as *men*."

Her curiosity apparently satisfied, Dominique sat down and continued working on the rope. "There's absolutely no difference between the two, Belle. Lord knows, I've watched enough grow up to testify to that. Men might be a little taller, or more muscular, but their minds are on exactly the same thing as boys: how fast they can move from a tender kiss to licking a woman's breast. And that's just for a start." She grabbed up another handful of grass and began working it into her braid.

"Ask Falcon when you see him if you don't believe me," she added.

It was the reference to licking breasts that chilled Belle clear to the marrow. That Belle might be describing her own experience with Falcon rather than guessing at her sister's seemed a likely possibility, but she did not want to believe it had ever happened. She did not know what she would do if it had.

"I want you to tell me the truth, Dominique," Belle insisted.

Surprised by that request, Dominique looked up. "I always do."

"Good. Then you'll tell me if Falcon has ever kissed you, or wanted more, won't you?"

Dominique tossed the rope aside and stood. "What kind of a question is that?"

Belle stared at her older sister. After the day's long ride, Dominique's curls were tangled and her gown stained, but the fire lit her face with a taunting glow. They looked so much alike, and yet their personalities could not have been more different. Dominique amused herself with a multitude of men, while Belle had always loved only one.

"Tell me the truth," Belle ordered again, her voice low and threatening.

"The fish are burning."

"Is that your answer?"

Dominique rolled her eyes. "I think maybe I was eleven, so he would have been ten. It was on Christmas Eve, and everyone was kissing everyone else. Does that satisfy you? I told you I love him like a brother, Belle. Is that all you think of me? Did you think I'd been meeting Falcon out in the barn each time he came home and that we just pretended nothing was going on? Maybe I have kissed more than my share of men, but Falcon was a child the last time I kissed him and so was I. Now let's eat those poor fish before they're reduced to charcoal."

Belle slid the roasted bass off onto their plates and sat down close enough to her sister to share the last of the cider, but it took her a long time to apologize. "I'm sorry," she finally offered. "It's just that Falcon bragged about being with other women, and I couldn't bear it if you'd been among them."

"Well, neither could I!" Dominique exclaimed. "Now I'm too tired to fight with you again tonight, so let's just finish eating and go to sleep."

Belle didn't argue, but she took the time to braid her own rope to tether Ladybug. She burned the rack she had built, and in the morning covered the cold ashes left from their fire with dirt and leaves so that no one passing through the forest would ever suspect anyone had spent the night there. Then, almost able to feel Hunter's breath on their necks, the sisters left in a great hurry.

Six

On the third day of their journey, the August weather was sweltering and Belle and Dominique were elated when they reached the Meherrin River around noon. They removed their shoes and stockings and hiked up their skirts to ride Ladybug and Baby Dee across, then dismounted and splashed their arms and faces with cool water. After ripping off her cap, Dominique knelt down and dipped her hair in the river. When she sat up, she flung her sopping curls this way and that to create a cool breeze, then just let them drip down over her shoulders and onto her bodice.

Belle kept a close watch on the opposite side of the river as she pulled on her stockings. "Hunter may be no more than an hour or two behind us," she warned. "Put on your shoes and let's go."

Dominique left her shoes at her side. "What if everyone's so angry with us for running off that Hunter hasn't bothered to come after us? It's something to consider."

"Not seriously," Belle argued. She rose and brushed the bits of dried grass from her skirt. It was so hot she wished they could have ridden on wearing only their chemises. She had insisted on haste, but now had to take an extra minute. "I'm taking off my corset," she proposed. "I'm thin enough without it to still fit in my gown, and so are you."

Delighted with the idea of removing the tightly laced garment, Dominique nearly danced with joy. They had worn only lightly boned corsets, but on horseback on a hot day, even delicately embroidered brocade had grown increasingly uncomfortable. They had to remove their gowns first but did so with such haste that they were undressed and dressed again in less than five minutes.

"Let's ride along in the shallow water for a while to hide our tracks, then we'll double back," Belle suggested, and again led the way. Ladybug splashed along, apparently content to travel through the water until Belle chose a patch of rocky shore that would hide their tracks. They angled west, reentered the forest, and were on North Carolina soil before sundown. They had crossed an occasional hunting trail, but relying on Belle's carefully drawn map, had avoided settlements and again seen no one in their travels.

"Would Hunter ride through the night?" Dominique asked as they made camp.

"He might, but I doubt it. There's too great a chance that he would ride right on by us if he did. Still, I don't think we ought to risk lighting a fire. Let's just eat cheese and ham."

They had seen blackberry vines growing wild and thick early in the afternoon but Belle had refused to stop long enough to pick more than a mouthful. "I wish we had some more of those luscious berries," Dominique said. "I should have filled my skirt with them and we could have had a feast tonight. All I see growing here are wood violets, and they're too pretty to eat."

"Let's pray we're not reduced to eating flowers before we reach South Carolina," Belle replied. Although four years younger, she felt responsible for Dominique's welfare in addition to her own. "We'll pick the first berries we sight tomorrow. Will that make you happy?"

"It might," Dominique mused wistfully. She fiddled with the ribbon ties on her shoes. "I doubt Hunter expected us to get this far. We ought to be proud of ourselves, Belle. Not one of our friends would even contemplate such an adventure, let alone actually pursue it. I should have brought a diary and pen and ink to record it."

Belle cut several slices of ham and pushed the plate toward her sister. She was positive they had forgotten more important items, but knew they were both over-tired and made an effort to be civil. "I imagine they might ask us to write letters for the wounded, so you should have access to paper and ink as soon as we reach a hospital."

Despite the fact that they had eaten very little that day, Dominique still craved berries and took only a tiny bite of ham. "I hope we won't have to write to anyone with the dreadful news that their beloved son or husband has died. They wouldn't expect that of us, would they, Belle?"

Belle unwrapped the last of the rye-an'-injun bread and broke off half for Dominique. "I believe that sad duty falls to the officers, but I hope we can be of service."

"Well, of course we can," Dominique vowed. "Were we not in such a great rush, we could have gathered more herbs. I hope we'll have enough to at least get started. Not that we'll have to tend every wounded man ourselves, but it worries me that we won't be able to do enough."

Because Dominique was not given to introspection, Belle was surprised she was so deeply concerned, but let the remark pass unchallenged. "I imagine you'll make most of the men feel better simply by whispering their names in that husky drawl of yours."

Dominique responded with a delighted smile. "I suppose flirting could be considered care, if it served to lift a man's spirits."

At that point, Belle was more worried about keeping her own spirits high. She unpacked their map and pointed to a wavy line. "This is the Roanoke River. We should cross it tomorrow, and I want to ride downstream again before swinging back west. There will just be creeks to ford for a while after that and we'll have to make certain to water the mares and refill the cider jugs at every one."

Dominique smoothed out the creases and studied the map a long moment before tracing their route with her fingertip. Embarrassed by the dirt beneath her nail, she hurriedly removed it. "Do you really believe we've come that far?" she asked. "Not that I haven't felt every single mile."

"The rivers provide such good reference points, I know exactly how far we've come." Belle refolded the map and slipped it back into her bag. "I feel as though I've crawled the whole way. Let's get to sleep." She doubted she would ever enjoy sleeping on the ground, but had discovered her shawl made a passable pillow and rolled it up into a soft ball.

Dominique hadn't finished eating. Because they had so little in the way of provisions, she broke her bread into tiny chunks to make the meal last. "Aren't there some Indian tribes in North Carolina?"

"Oh, Lord," Belle moaned. "All we need is more Indians on our trail."

"No, I'm serious. There must be some living in these lovely woods."

The woods truly were lovely, thick with hardwoods and pine, fragrant with the last blooms of the blue-violet wisteria, and splashed with bright yellow wildflowers; but Belle missed the orderly fields of home. "I believe the Cherokee prefer to live in the mountains and we're staying well east of those."

Dominique still wished they had picked some berries, but refrained from making another complaint. She thought about brushing her hair, but lacked the energy to begin such an arduous task so late in the day. Had they been at home, the family would just be sitting down to supper, and that melancholy thought brought a mist of tears to her eyes. She missed everyone terribly, but did not want Hunter to find them any more than Belle did. When she finally lay down to sleep, she said a brief prayer for the continued strength and cunning to elude him.

* * *

In the following days, Hunter came tantalizingly close to catching Belle and Dominique, but they continued to elude him. They were traveling faster than he had anticipated, using streams to hide their trail and erasing all evidence of their campsite each morning. His first attempt to get ahead of them and block their way failed, and just when he was about to make another, he came dangerously close to riding into a British encampment. He left his stallion tethered to a low branch of a red cedar and crept close to make certain they hadn't caught the girls, but there was no sign of them.

The mere sight of the red-coated soldiers brought a bitter taste to his mouth, but he watched as the group was met by another of equal size traveling from the east. He dared not move close enough to overhear their words, but from the gestures he observed, drew the conclusion they were also on their way south. Knowing that the troops might be between him and Byron's daughters brought a cold fury to his heart, but he could circle past them that night and continue the chase. The problem would be bringing the girls back through their lines; he did not want to take any risk with their lives.

He lingered to run a quick tally, but lost count when a third detachment of troops arrived. It was led by an officer clad in the splendid attire of the Coldstream Guards, but it was not only the distinctive uniform Hunter recognized. It had been several years since he had last seen the man, but he remembered him clearly. His name was O'Keefe, and he had tried and failed to prove that Hunter's son, Christian, was behind a series of pamphlets ridiculing the actions of King George III and Parliament. Ordinarily, Hunter could not think of the hilarious flyers without laughing, but he had to stifle the impulse now.

O'Keefe had been unable to charge Christian with sedition, nor lure Liana away, but the whole family had counted him an enemy even before the armed rebellion had begun. Hunter chose to simply watch and wait, but as soon as night fell, he hurried on toward the girls. He now had to watch his back, and gave up all hope of posing as a volunteer should he be caught because O'Keefe would order his execution even faster than he would Byron's.

Belle and Dominique were well aware they would have to avoid British troops to enter Charleston, but did not consider them an imminent danger so far inland. They had been traveling more than a week, and by now the hot August sun and the rigors of the trail had burned away all trace of the soft prettiness which had graced their features when they had left home. Their once-attractive gowns hung loose from their shoulders, and with no time to brush and style their curls, they wore them coiled in a tight knot beneath their tattered caps.

They seldom spoke during the day, and at night exchanged little more than a few hushed whispers before going to sleep on the softest ground they could find. They awoke before dawn, and after eating whatever remained of the berries they had gathered the previous afternoon, quickly got underway. They caught and roasted fish for supper when they could, and cooked beans and cornmeal when they weren't near a stream. They slept, too exhausted to dream, and began each new day with the hope the end of their journey was near.

On their tenth day on the trail, they stopped to pick huckleberries, and soon their fingers were stained blue with the juice. They ate almost as many as they saved, but soon filled the bottom of their picnic basket with the tasty fruit. Their spirits were buoyed by the sweet song of a meadowlark when in the space of a heartbeat, they were surrounded by a British patrol. Belle's heart lodged firmly in her throat, but as always, Dominique's face brightened at the sight of men.

"Good afternoon" Dominique directed her comment to the young lieutenant. He was not unattractive, but his eyes were a forbidding gray that lacked any hint of warmth. He sat astride a dapple-gray gelding with a rigid posture more suitable to a military parade than traversing the countryside. They had deliberately avoided settlements to minimize the risk of being seen, but she hoped in their disheveled state they could pass for a farmer's daughters and not arouse his curiosity.

"I do believe the huckleberries are as sweet as they have ever been. Would you and your men like to have some?" She raised their basket invitingly.

Lieutenant Leland Beck shook his head. He hated everything about America, with the possible exception of the young women. This pair did have bright blue eyes peering out of their dirt-smudged complexions, but from what he could see of their figures in their faded gowns, little else to recommend them. Then he noticed their mounts tethered nearby and the packs on their backs made him suspicious.

"Where are you from, and where are you bound?" he asked crossly.

As frightened as she had ever been, Dominique exchanged a quick glance with Belle, who appeared to have been struck dumb. A bee buzzed close to the basket and she shooed it away. "We are from Virginia, sir, and because we've a talent for healing, we've come south to be of service to the wounded."

"And what possible service could such a filthy pair be?" the lieutenant asked, sending his men into peals of coarse, snorting laughter.

Unused to such an obnoxious lack of manners, Belle was sufficiently insulted to find her voice and argue. "The journey has been hard," she stressed. "It's very rude of you to laugh at women on an errand of mercy."

Taken aback by that charge, Leland nodded slightly. "I meant you no disrespect, miss, but in your present state, I believe you'd frighten more men than you'd cure."

Ignoring that discouraging comment, Dominique smiled prettily at the sergeant and was tickled when he began to blush. She might lack proper grooming and a fine gown for the moment, but she was pleased to find she still possessed a talent for turning men's brains to butter. "We'd not tend a soul without bathing and washing our clothes first," she promised, "but you and your men all look healthy, Lieutenant—?" She paused, waiting for him to provide his name.

"Leland Beck," he announced clearly. He could not argue with her assessment of his troops, but he still thought there was something peculiar about the two young women. "You're sisters?" he asked.

"Yes, sir, we are," Dominique replied sweetly.

"And what did your parents say about your wish to serve the wounded? Weren't they terrified that you two might become casualties yourselves?"

Belle smiled weakly and waited for Dominique, who was far more imaginative, to provide a believable answer. As could be expected, Dominique did not disappoint her. "We're orphans," she replied with a pitiful catch in her voice, "and needed no one's permission."

"Orphans?" Leland repeated. "How convenient."

"What an awful thing to say," Dominique challenged, her tone instantly turning harsh. "We loved our parents dearly, and do not pass a single day without praying for the repose of their souls. It was our beloved mother who taught us all we know about healing, and she would want us to share our knowledge with all who are in need."

The sergeant leaned over and whispered just a shade too loudly, "They might just as easily be whores, sir, but there's a need for them, too."

Neither Belle nor Dominique had ever imagined they might have to defend their honor to a British officer, but they recoiled with disgust when they realized they would have to. "I'll not dignify such wretched speculation with a response, but if you'll provide directions to the nearest field hospital, we'll be on our way," Belle announced. She locked arms with Dominique and hoped these soldiers had more important things to do than question them. She could feel Dominique shaking, and stood as proudly as she could on trembling legs.

The pair spoke with the cultured language of fine ladies even if they did not look the part, and that discrepancy disturbed Leland Beck so badly he doubted anything they had told him was true. He stared at them long and hard, then gave the sergeant a terse order. "Search their things."

Belle's first thought was of the map and she grew faint with fear. If they were accused of being spies, they would have no way to defend themselves, but then she realized any traveler could rightfully claim need of a map. Hers was merely a sketch, not a detailed drawing which would be of help to the military, and she had not added the notations of battles her father had made on the original. Still, she had no way of knowing what a surly British officer might imagine and couldn't stop her heart from racing.

Forgetting the map, Dominique breathed a silent prayer of thanksgiving that she had not kept a diary, for surely she would have made clear their desire to aid the Patriots rather than the British. "We've little other than a change of undergarments and our herbs," she volunteered, "and I daresay you've seen both long before this."

The lieutenant had to admire the girls' spirit, but he was not satisfied as to their intentions until the sergeant brought him a handful of what looked to him like dried daisies. "And pray tell, ladies, what might these be?"

"That's chamomile, sir," Belle responded quickly, still praying the sergeant would not uncover her map. "It makes a fine poultice to aid healing, and you must know that it also makes a soothing tea for all digestive complaints."

Sorry he had not caught them in a lie, the lieutenant nodded wearily. "Yes, of course. My mother was fond of giving me chamomile tea for stomachaches."

"She sounds like a wise woman," Dominique complimented with another pretty smile, but she hoped to herself that her son was as well. She had known a great many British officers before the war, and unlike this belligerent fool, they had been gentlemen who had treated her well. She could feel Belle's distress as acutely as her own, and wished they had anticipated and rehearsed how to deal with such a dangerous encounter. Hoping to seem unconcerned, she tossed a couple of berries into her mouth and watched the sergeant's blush deepen several shades.

"Shall I search the rest of their gear, sir?" the sergeant asked. "I don't know one herb from another myself."

"Don't you dare make a mess of our things," Belle scolded. "Herbs must be treated tenderly, or they'll lose their power to heal."

The sergeant shrugged helplessly. "What do you say, sir? I'd not want to destroy their precious herbs when the men wounded at Camden are in such great need of medicines."

"Are there wounded nearby?" Belle asked, not really believing how terribly their plan had gone awry but after insisting they had set out from Virginia on an errand of mercy, she could scarcely ignore the mention of wounded although she had no intention of actually tending British regulars. "Please don't waste another minute of our time if there are. Just give us directions so that we might find them as quickly as possible."

Lieutenant Beck leaned forward in his saddle. "They're a two-day ride from here and because you might meet units of General Gates's militia still fleeing the battle, we'll provide you with an escort."

Dominique was no more eager than Belle to ride into a British camp, and sought the most obvious way to avoid it.

"How very kind of you, but aren't you and your men needed elsewhere to fight?" she asked.

Amused by her question, the lieutenant finally flashed a predatory grin. "Not after the beating we gave the militia in Camden. It will be weeks before Gates can gather enough men to challenge us again. Of course, first he'll have to stop running himself."

That sarcastic comment was met with more whoops from the soldiers, but neither Dominique nor Belle allowed her expression to betray her dismay. The battle must have taken place after they had left home or they would have heard news of it, but knowing the lieutenant would exaggerate any British victory, they doubted the accuracy of his report. They waited, feigning an outward calm while each prayed that the soldiers would choke on their gross laughter.

Lieutenant Beck nodded toward the sisters' mounts. "Ride toward the front of the line with me, ladies. That will spare you another layer of dust."

"How thoughtful of you," Dominique replied, but she was appalled by the insult. She took the chamomile from the sergeant, but as she did so she slid her blue-tinged fingertips across his wrist in a saucy caress. He turned bright red all the way to the roots of his hair, convincing her he would be as easy to manipulate as the boys at home.

She added the stalks of chamomile to the basket of huckleberries and carried it over to the horses. She waited for Belle to mount Ladybug, and then handed her the basket to hold while she pulled herself up into Baby Dee's saddle. "Don't say a word," she ordered in a hoarse whisper. "We'll go with them now, and escape just as quickly as we can."

Belle had no argument with that plan, and smiled sweetly as she handed the basket back to Dominique. She then took up a position beside the loathsome lieutenant for what she feared would be an uncomfortably long ride to a place she had absolutely no desire to go.

* * *

They camped that night at the banks of the Great Pee Dee River. Disgusted with the lieutenant's abusive descriptions, the sisters approached him right after supper. "If we could borrow a couple of clean shirts to wear," Dominique proposed, "we'll launder our garments in the river and hang them up to dry tonight. After we bathe and don clean clothes tomorrow morning, I do believe you'll change your opinion of us."

Unwilling to lend his own clothing to women he did not trust to be anything more than enterprising strumpets, Leland Beck ordered his sergeant to locate the necessary spare clothing. Badly embarrassed that the young women had overheard his remark about their possible profession, the sergeant immediately unpacked a worn but clean shirt of his own, and passed among the other men with an urgent plea for another. Rather than the lack of interest the lieutenant had shown, the soldiers argued over which of them would be allowed the honor of lending one until the sergeant was forced to make the choice to avoid fisticuffs.

When the sergeant brought her the shirts, Dominique rewarded him with another delighted smile. He was perhaps twenty-five, with sandy hair and close-set eyes of a pale, clear blue. His ears stuck out from his head at an unfortunate angle, but despite his earlier remark he had become so eager to be of service she could not help but be touched. "Thank you for your kindness, sergeant. May I ask your name?"

Flattered beyond all reasonable expectation, the sergeant stumbled over the pronunciation. "It's Thomas, Thomas Danby, miss." He whipped off his hat and bowed from the waist.

Dominique clutched the clean shirts to her breast. "We've not introduced ourselves, have we?" She glanced at her sister and after briefly considering giving aliases, decided their own names would do with the addition of their Loyalist neighbor's surname. Because Ian Scott had taken his family to England, she knew he could not dispute her claim.

"I'm Dominique Scott, and this is my sister, Belle. We're very pleased to meet you, Sergeant Danby."

Belle took Dominique's elbow to lead her away. "Scott?" she whispered anxiously. "What an imaginative choice."

Dominique turned back to wave at the sergeant. "It's as good as any Tory name. Now let's just hope we've enough soap left to wash everything clean."

Belle knew Dominique was doing what she felt she must to keep them safe, but she wished she had not gone about it in her usual flirtatious manner. "Why don't you ask your dear friend, Sergeant Danby, if he doesn't have some we can use?"

Dominique caught the faintly disapproving edge to her sister's question but felt no need to defend herself. "I will if we need more than we have."

They moved upriver to take advantage of a thick clump of foliage, which made an effective screen, and hastily removed their gowns. Belle peered around the bushes to make certain they hadn't been followed before she removed her petticoats. Next she untied the drawstring at the neckline of her chemise and let it fall. She quickly donned the borrowed shirt, then slipped off her stockings and drawers.

"I could have lived my whole life without having to spend the night camped with British troops," she mumbled under her breath.

"Do you honestly believe that I'm looking forward to it?" Dominique asked. "I keep telling myself that we can't turn away from wounded men, but with any luck, we'll be able to escape before we have to." She stripped as hurriedly as Belle, and wearing only the sergeant's shirt with the sleeves rolled above her elbows, knelt down at the water's edge and began scrubbing her gown. The blue stripes had faded to the shade of robin's eggs and would soon disappear altogether.

The ruffled hems of her petticoats were badly tattered but she rubbed soap into them just as furiously. She did take more time with her lace trimmed cap, chemise, and drawers, and took care to rinse them thoroughly. She spread her clean garments out over the shrubbery to dry, but thinking her soiled stockings weren't worth the effort to wash, left them knotted in a ball at the shore.

"Will you watch while I bathe?" she asked Belle. "Then I'll stand guard for you."

"Just a minute. Let me finish my clothes." Belle's back was beginning to ache from bending over and she had to sit up a moment. "I don't even think I can sleep tonight," she confided softly. "Should we try to run away? After all, once we reach a field hospital, it might be even more difficult than it will be to escape from here."

"They've tethered Ladybug and Baby Dee with their horses," Dominique reminded her. "Surely they'll post a guard. After all, if there are militia in the area, they wouldn't want to risk being shot while they slept."

"I doubt the militia would shoot a sleeping man."

"Belle! That's not really the issue." Tired of waiting for her sister to complete her washing, Dominique bent down to get a glimpse of the camp through the leaves. The soldiers were still seated around the campfire, and laughing amongst themselves rather than looking their way. She moved upstream and cast off the shirt. She had already begun soaping her hair when she remembered a towel. The night was warm, and her curls would soon dry on their own so she decided against asking Belle to fetch one, but made a mental note not to forget one again.

In the course of their journey they had learned how to bathe with efficiency and haste, but she would never learn to love cold water and quickly returned to the river bank. She shook like a wet puppy, squeezed as much moisture as she could from her hair, and then again donned the sergeant's shirt. "If there's no way to avoid reaching the field hospital, we can always say we need to gather more herbs. Then we just won't return."

"Yes, that's a good plan." Finished with her laundry, Belle spread it out next to Dominique's, then laid the shirt on a dry rock. She also washed her hair first, then scrubbed herself clean with a brisk rhythm. She turned toward the shore as she left the river and caught a glimpse of the lieutenant standing not twenty feet away. He was shaded by the pines, but she saw him clearly before he darted out of sight.

She grabbed her shirt, jammed her arms into the sleeves, and buttoned it as she crossed the distance between them. She was too angry to think, but when she reached the tree where she knew she had seen him, he had already fled. "Bastard," she mouthed under her breath. She returned to Dominique's side.

"The lieutenant was watching us," she reported. "We were so worried about his men following us, but he was the only one who did."

Dominique searched the surrounding trees without sighting anyone. "You don't mean it!"

"I most certainly do. I saw him as I came out of the river, but he ran off before I could confront him. We're sure to defeat the British if their officers have no more honor than that."

Dominique clapped her hand over her sister's mouth. "We're on the same side," she scolded. "You mustn't forget that for a second. We're sweet little Tory girls who want nothing more than to see America again ruled by the king!" Certain she had made her point, she dropped her hands. "This may even work to our advantage. I know we've lost weight, but I doubt he's seen any women as pretty as we are for a good long time."

"Wonderful," Belle exclaimed. "Do you want to be his whore?"

Dominique straightened up proudly and managed to look surprisingly genteel for a young woman clad in a borrowed shirt. "No. I do not and it will not come to that, either. Now let's get what sleep we can and keep our wits about us tomorrow. Maybe the militia hasn't fled at all. If they attack this patrol tomorrow, we'll be rescued right away."

"If we aren't shot dead in the initial exchange of gunfire," Belle warned darkly. "Oh, I'm sorry. I'm just so tired and frightened I don't know how much more of this I can stand."

Dominique stared at her baby sister. "Think how much Falcon has stood, and it won't seem bad at all."

Thoroughly shamed, Belle followed Dominique to the spot where they had left their belongings. They were well apart from the soldiers, but she had seen a hunger in the lieutenant's eyes that marred her dreams. Spying on them as they bathed had been a thoroughly reprehensible act, and she had every intention of telling him so at her first opportunity.

Seven

In the morning, Belle donned her clean lingerie and shook out her gown in a futile attempt to smooth the wrinkles. Like Dominique's, her gown had also been bleached by the sun and the once pale blue muslin was now closer to dove gray. Grateful it was at least clean once more, Belle slipped it on and shuffled her feet impatiently as Dominique laced it up the back.

"I don't believe there's anything lower than a man who'll spy on a woman while she's bathing. I'll not trust anything the lieutenant says," Belle murmured fretfully.

"It will be difficult to challenge him when we're not speaking the truth ourselves," Dominique declared softly. "Then again, this may be precisely the time to confront him, as women with something to hide would surely avoid trouble. By courting it, we'll appear not only righteous, but innocent as well."

"Yes. That's the way I'll look at it." Belle had brushed out her hair, but left the long curls flowing free. Her cap had worn as sheer as lace, and as she turned it in her hands, she had little hope of using it for anything other than a handkerchief. "We can't pretend it didn't happen, and even if you didn't see him, I'm positive that I did. He was nearly drooling, too. Do you want to come with me?"

"I wouldn't miss it," Dominique cried. She came with a dancing step that made her long curls bounce against her shoulder blades and followed Belle to where the lieutenant stood drinking his morning cup of tea. Freshly shaven and neatly attired, he looked the part of an officer even if they now knew he lacked the character necessary for such a responsibility.

"We'd like to speak with you," Belle announced clearly.

Leland Beck had not really expected much in the way of improvement from the sisters, but as he swung around to face them, he nearly dribbled hot tea down the front of his uniform. They were regarding him with hostile stares, but it did not detract from the loveliness of their features. Once relieved of the accumulated grime of the trail, they were obviously ladies, and exceptionally beautiful ones. He had noted only the bright blue of their eyes the previous day, but now saw the thickness of their long, dark lashes. Their hair was a sun-streaked blond, and the lush fullness of their lips held a subtle rose tint. Unable to trust his voice not to break, he inclined his head slightly to encourage Belle to speak her piece.

"Alone," Belle insisted. She gestured toward a secluded spot several paces away from the soldiers, and when Leland nodded, she and Dominique led the way. When Belle turned to face him, she did not mince words.

"The British officers of our acquaintance have all been honorable men," she began, "so it pained us greatly to discover that you are not."

Reacting to the harshness of her tone, Leland discounted Belle's prettiness and raked her with an insolent glance. "I've no idea what prompted your insult, but I'll advise you now not to repeat it."

"Oh, but I will repeat it," Belle countered, "and loudly if you invade our privacy a second time. I do hope you enjoyed what you saw last night, but don't spy on us ever again or I'll tell your troops just how unprincipled you truly are."

Leland stared down at the sisters, his disgust as plain as

theirs. "Frankly, neither of you is worth a second look," he replied in a caustic whisper. "Now have your breakfast and be ready to ride in ten minutes. We've a long way to travel today, and I'll make no allowances for the two of you."

"And we shall make none for you, sir," Belle responded proudly. She walked away, and Dominique went with her, but Dominique could not resist sending a parting glance over her shoulder. The lieutenant was watching them with what she considered a malevolent stare, but believing that was an improvement over the leer Belle had described, she regarded the conversation a success.

Hunter had picked up the girls' trail shortly before they had been overtaken by the British patrol. At first he had hoped the cluster of hoof prints obliterating their mares' tracks might have belonged to a unit of the Colonial militia traveling in the area, but when they had made camp, he had crept close enough to identify the troops by their uniforms. After they had ridden out the next morning, he found Dominique's shredded stockings by the river and wondered whether she had simply forgotten them or left them behind as a clue to their whereabouts.

He scooped up a drink from the river and let the cool water trickle slowly down his throat. He had promised Byron that he would bring his daughters home, but he had not anticipated their falling into British hands. He would follow and keep an eye on them, and with luck, he might lure them away, but as he mounted his stallion, he had very little hope of success.

Already accustomed to riding the whole day, Belle and Dominique did not utter a single word of complaint when the lieutenant pressed his men to travel further than he had in the past. Camden lay approximately fifty miles west of the Great Pee Dee River, and they made more than half that distance the first day. In the evening, the sisters again sat apart, but shared the troops' rations.

Sergeant Danby sent them frequent smiles, as did the other soldiers, but apparently under orders, none approached them wanting to chat. Knowing they would have to tell nothing but lies if anyone did, they weren't a bit sorry to have no one but themselves for company. "I came to find Falcon," Belle whispered, "but I might as well have stayed home if we're trapped in Camden."

"The plan to gather herbs is a good one," Dominique offered reassuringly. "We'll be gone perhaps an hour the first time, maybe three the next. Then we'll simply disappear as easily as we did from home. We have experience fending for ourselves now, Belle, and we can put it to good use. Falcon will be proud of you. You'll see."

Belle glanced up to find Leland Beck watching them. At least they were fully clothed this time, but she did not like having their privacy violated a second time under any circumstances. "I hope they're not more men like Lieutenant Beck in Camden," she revealed softly, "as it would make our stay even more difficult."

"There will be good men there, too," Dominique reminded her. "Maybe all the wounded will have recovered by the time we arrive and we'll be able to travel to a camp closer to Charleston. Let's hope that's the case."

Belle had yet to have an opportunity to dispose of her map and finally confided her worry in Dominique. "I can't walk up to their fire and burn it, and while I could bury it, I don't want to be without it if we do get away."

"When we get away," Dominique stressed. "Why would they search our gear a second time? Just leave the map where it is and we'll have a use for it. I didn't sleep well last night. Did you?"

"I haven't slept well since we left home. I heard something moving through the underbrush. Perhaps it was a raccoon or opossum, but I couldn't be certain it wasn't Lieutenant Beck sneaking up on us in the darkness."

"He wouldn't dare," Dominique argued.

"If he would watch us bathe, I'd not put it past him." She hated the man and all he stood for. Fatigued from the tension of having British companions as much as the length of the day, she was filled with a painful longing for the love she had tasted too briefly. "Do you suppose Falcon could be near here? He's probably no more than a day or two ahead of us, and he might have reached Camden in time to fight."

"Is Camden on your map?"

"Yes. But it's much farther west than I intended for us to go."

"Then Falcon would probably not have gone there, either. Keep your wits about you, Belle. This isn't the time to be daydreaming about Falcon when a single slip might reveal who we are. We ought to embroider our tale a bit should anyone ask more questions than Beck. Let's say we're from Norfolk, and that our father was a captain who was lost at sea. Then our poor mother died of a broken heart. That's believable, don't you think?"

"I don't think we ought to say they're dead. That's like wishing that they were."

"It is not, and besides I've already done it. James is a good name for a father. What do you want to name Mother?"

Not eager to comply with Dominique's request, Belle was about to argue, then decided the damage had already been done when the lie had first been told to Beck. "Our names are French, so shouldn't she have a French name as well? Perhaps Marie?"

"Perfect." Dominique was very pleased with their efforts and encouraged Belle to continue. "What about Father's ship? Do you have a name for her?"

Belle looked up at the sky. The stars were just beginning

to appear, and she took comfort in the fact she had seen the very same lovely patterns at home. *"Summer Sky,"* she murmured to herself, and then to Dominique. "Our dear father would have navigated by the stars and adored the long summer nights."

"Oh, yes. He was wonderfully romantic." Dominique reached for her shawl. "It's no wonder Mother pined away without him. Now let's go to sleep as we're sure to need all of our strength tomorrow."

Hovering between sleep and fleeting wakefulness, Belle felt rather than saw someone watching them. She sat up and clutched her shawl, but no one was stirring in the camp. The fire had burned down low and cast flickering shadows across the sleeping men. The man standing guard added more wood, then walked the perimeter of the small encampment with a slow, shuffling stride.

An owl hooted in the distance, and crickets whose sound was identical to those beneath her window at home chirped in noisy profusion. She reached out to warn Dominique, but her sister was already sleeping soundly. Not wanting to wake her without a good reason, she withdrew her hand. She waited, fearing the lieutenant was spying on them again, his cold gray eyes menacing them from the shadows but in the darkness she had no proof.

Belle had every reason to be nervous and yet she forced herself to lie back down and wait for sleep to come. There was a soft, rustling sound in the trees—the wind perhaps, or opossums hungry for tender leaves on a warm night. The longer she listened, the more alive the forest became with soft whispers and faint moans. Several of the soldiers snored, and their rattling rhythms mixed with the forest creatures' calls. She counted the stars, and gradually her tension drained away. At last she breathed a weary sigh, and surrendered to the night.

* * *

Camden was the oldest inland community in South Carolina. Founded on the eastern bank of the Wateree River in 1733 by the trader Joseph Kershaw, it had been occupied by the British since June. Lord Cornwallis had taken Mr. Kershaw's beautiful new mansion for his headquarters. Rather than escorting them to the elegant Greek Revival structure, Lieutenant Beck took his charges across the now scarred cotton fields to a farmhouse surrounded by rows of tents set up to quarter the wounded. Eager to be rid of the troublesome girls, he grabbed the arm of the first physician he saw and gladly handed them over.

Stephen Perry was a robust young man with pale brows and bright green eyes. Although balding, he had long since given up the practice of wearing wigs. In his shirtsleeves, he wore a weary frown and an apron speckled with dried blood. "You've come at a good time," he greeted them. "Those we couldn't save have all died, and those still too weak to leave their cots will be grateful for any kindness. I hope the sight of a missing arm or leg won't sicken you."

Neither Belle nor Dominique had given any thought to how severe the soldiers' battle injuries might be. They exchanged a frightened glance and assured him it would not. "We've brought our own herbs, sir, and can speed the healing of most wounds."

The doctor hesitated a long moment as he pondered the wisdom of their offer, but after asking them a few questions he shrugged away his doubts. "Your remedies won't harm them so go ahead, but should any of the soldiers refuse your attentions, don't force their acceptance."

"No, certainly not," Belle assured him.

"Come with me then, and I'll get you a couple of aprons. We've relieved the farmer of his home for the time being, but I'm using the parlor for my surgery, and have the weakest of my patients quartered inside. I imagine we can find a tent for you, though."

"A tent will be more than adequate," Belle replied. She

and Dominique waited at the back door while the doctor went to fetch their aprons. "I think it's a good thing we did not arrive sooner as I could not have borne watching him amputate limbs."

"Oh, please," Dominique moaned. She gagged at the thought of having to carry a severed arm outside by the lifeless fingertips. Most of the time she was grateful to be blessed with such a vivid imagination, but it did not serve her well now. She glanced around the side of the small wooden house and was relieved not to find a tangled heap of rotting limbs. They had observed their mother tending cuts and scrapes and any number of minor illnesses but never a bullet wound or a bloody stump.

"I'm afraid I'm beginning to feel sick already," she whispered.

"I've felt sick to my stomach ever since we met Lieutenant Beck," Belle replied. When Dr. Perry returned with the aprons and squares of cotton to serve as kerchiefs, she managed a smile as she donned hers, but it was faint.

"Come on inside," Perry invited. "Our surgeons' mates are exhausted, and if you can relieve a couple for a shift, they can get some much needed sleep. I'll not expect you to do anything more than observe the wounded and make certain they rest comfortably today. A sweet smile will do wonders for most of them."

Belle hoped that under the circumstances, finding a pleasant expression would not be an impossible task, and followed him inside. After gazing out over the long rows of tents surrounding the farmhouse, Dominique gathered the courage to go up the steps, too. The sickly sweet odor of death assailed the sisters as they came through the door, and when they were shown into the farmer's bedroom, now crowded with cots, the first thing they did was to throw open the windows to clear away the stale air.

Eight men were quartered there. One was a gray-haired veteran who had lost his right leg above the knee, and the others were all as young or younger than Sergeant Danby. They suffered from a gruesome collection of wounds that had left them unconscious, or semiconscious at best. Draped with soiled sheets, they were a pitiful sight indeed.

"Who's doing the laundry?" Belle asked the physician.

"I have men doing what they can," he replied.

"Well, obviously it isn't nearly enough," Dominique countered. "I'll start water boiling if it isn't already, and see that these men have a change of linen as quickly as it can be arranged." She had thought tending wounded men would involve little more than dispensing herbal remedies. Faced with the harsh reality of the situation, she was eager to escape in what was surely a worthwhile and necessary task.

Rather than being insulted, the British surgeon broke into a wide smile. "Bless you, my dear, for we've sorely needed a woman to run the laundry."

"Will you be all right here?" Dominique asked her sister.

Belle felt fully competent to watch the men sleep, and nodded. "Yes. Go ahead, I'll get along fine." Dr. Perry left with Dominique, and Belle went to the closest window to draw a deep breath of fresh air. She rested her hands on the sill and leaned out until she felt strong enough to survey her patients more closely.

Two had chest wounds and were wrapped in such thick bandages she doubted they could move should they wake, but she paused a few minutes to hold each man's hand in a loving clasp. Had Falcon been severely wounded she would have wanted someone to tend him with more than merely adequate care, and keeping that thought in mind, she walked among the others and caressed their stubbled cheeks and spoke encouragingly. She returned to the window often, however.

Falcon had described how brutally the British had treated the good citizens of South Carolina, but now seeing the evidence in the ravaged fields, she understood a great deal more than she had then. She wondered if the farmer who had owned this modest home had been shuffled off to a prison camp, and supposed that he had. When he was able to return, she doubted he would be able to rid the dwelling of the stench of war, and hoped he would burn it to the ground and build another.

Dominique found the young men responsible for the laundry lounging beside their kettles rather than stoking the fires beneath them, while a small mountain of dirty sheets lay beside them untouched. "This is a fine way to treat your wounded," she scolded. "Would you want to lay wrapped in filthy sheets? I think not. Now get to work to boil the water. There's plenty of sunlight left to dry as many sheets as you can wash before supper."

The men scrambled to their feet, and believing Dominique must actually possess the authority that rang so clearly in her voice, got to work. She circled them with an anxious stride, cajoling here, prodding there, until the lines they had strung were drooping with freshly laundered sheets, then deciding what they required were more lines, she set them to work stringing more.

Dominique didn't see Belle until suppertime when she carried her plate inside. "I've already eaten," she whispered, for truly she had not believed she could swallow a bite inside that little room. "How are you getting along?"

Belle sat down on the windowsill to eat what looked more like vegetable soup than stew. "None of my patients has given me a bit of trouble. In fact, none has been awake more than a minute or two and then I've given them a drink of water and a few kind words and they've gone right back to sleep. We'll have to change their dressings before we can apply a poultice or salve and I don't wish to disturb them. How did things go with the laundry?"

Dominique described her progress, then apologized. "Just give me a day or two to get used to being here, then I'll stay with you. Dr. Perry found us a tent, and I've put our belongings inside. The cots are none too comfortable, but should be better than sleeping on the ground. We're at the end of the row, nearest the house."

"Have you seen anything more of Lieutenant Beck?"

"No, thank God, but he would not be quartered near the wounded. This is the perfect place to hide, Belle, as no one is around who is not either too badly injured or too tired to take note of us. We can come and go as we please, too, so it will not be impossible to get away."

"Hush," Belle warned. "One of these men may overhear. They all look asleep, but some could just be resting with their eyes closed."

"Yes, of course. I'll be more careful."

Dominique remained with her sister until a surgeon's mate arrived to watch the men for the night. Their tent was barely tall enough to permit them to stand in the center, but wanting only a place to lie down, they weren't bothered by the lack of space and hurried to undress. Dominique kept her fears she might not find the courage to tend the wounded to herself, and Belle hid her guilt over tending their enemies rather than their own brave men, but neither spent a comfortable night.

Hunter lost all hope of rescuing Belle and Dominique when they entered Camden. From what he had been able to observe on the trail, the girls weren't prisoners. He wondered what story they had told, but knowing Dominique's flair for the dramatic, he assumed it had been colorful. They had been taken to a field hospital rather than a prison camp, so obviously they had succeeded in their desire to nurse the wounded, but he considered it a catastrophe that they would be serving the wrong army.

He had met too many pompous British officers before the war to fear the pair were in any real danger from their lot, but he was badly torn about leaving them. He turned toward home with a heavy heart, sorry that he had to abandon his pretty nieces, but after being away for nearly two weeks, he felt he owed their parents a report. Then perhaps he would return and watch over them from afar, but for tonight, he could do no more that include them in his prayers.

Belle and Dominique were drawn into the hospital's routine so smoothly that within a few days' time they were trusted to supply far better care than the hastily trained surgeons' mates. Several of the men Belle had first tended recovered sufficiently to leave the farmhouse for the surrounding tents, and the burden of care for those remaining no longer overwhelmed her. After the treatment she recommended proved to be more efficacious than that which Perry was able to provide from his medical stores, the surgeon allowed her to tend several of the men on her own.

Once Dominique had organized the laundry to run more efficiently, she joined Belle in caring for the wounded still lodged in the house; her smiles were worth as much as her herbal salves. She did indeed write a few letters, but fearing she would only betray herself with a diary, made no personal record of her days. She was kept so busy that there was no time to plot an escape, but with the wounded growing stronger every day and their need for constant care diminishing, she hoped it would soon be possible.

Fear prevented them from growing overly fond of their charges, and whenever they left the farmhouse, they wore their white cotton kerchieves pulled low not only to shade their faces, but also to discourage the attentions of the other men in the camp. They never saw Lord Cornwallis, nor did they wish to, but the knowledge that so formidable an enemy was nearby was a constant torment. As Dominique had once proposed, they were indeed playing parts, but because they believed them to be temporary, they played them with admirable compassion.

Then one evening, soldiers rode up to the farmhouse in

a ramshackle wagon and in a great commotion of shouts and curses, demanded immediate attention for a fallen officer. Dominique was at the door in an instant to silence the unruly crowd. Before calling for a physician, she walked around to peer into the bed of the wagon to observe the man's injuries. When she recognized him, she grew faint and had to grab for the warped side of the cart to remain on her feet.

A scant three weeks earlier she had actually wanted to see Sean O'Keefe again, but not here where one word from him would send them straight to a prison camp, if not worse. Then she realized in his present state he was unlikely to give them away. He had been shot in the left shoulder, and not only was his red coat marred with a dark stain, his white breeches were also drenched in blood. She backed away as the soldiers lowered the tailgate and began to lift Sean.

"Be careful," she cried. "Where was he shot? Was there another battle nearby?"

"No, ma'am," one of the soldiers called out. "A Colonial rogue shot him from ambush. The bastards aim for the officers, then flee. We caught only a glimpse of a sorrel hide as he rode off, but we'll not let him get away."

Hunter had a sorrel stallion and Dominique's first thought was of him; then she remembered Falcon rode a similar mount. "Watch his head," she warned as they carried Sean up the steps. She had never witnessed any of Dr. Perry's surgery, nor did she wish to, but she followed Sean right into the parlor where Dr. Perry met them. He had made an operating table out of long planks propped upon barrels but it provided a steadier surface than the farmer's dining room table.

As soon as Sean was placed on the makeshift table, Perry began shouting orders and promptly cleared the soldiers from the room. One of his mates was there to assist him, but Dominique hovered at the foot of the table. "Do you think he'll survive?" she asked breathlessly.

Perry tossed Sean's bloody coat on the floor and ripped open his badly stained shirt. After a quick examination of the wound, he looked up. "The bullet went right through so that saves me the trouble of digging it out. It looks high enough to have missed his lungs, but he's lost a great deal of blood. Do you know him?"

Dominique hesitated to admit that she did. She and Belle were supposedly Tories, and would quite naturally be acquainted with British officers. On the other hand, she dared not admit that she knew Sean for fear he would come looking for her the instant he was well enough to walk. "I'm not sure," she finally replied. "He resembles someone I once knew, but it's been years since I've seen him."

Perry worked quickly to free the wound in Sean's shoulder of fibers from his coat and shirt, then bound it tightly to stem the flow of blood. "Well, this is Sean O'Keefe. Was that the man's name?"

At that moment, Dominique felt that denying it would be tantamount to wishing him dead. "Yes, but I've never seen him so pale."

"As far as I know, this is the first time he's been shot and it's no wonder he looks a tad peaked. I want to make certain we've got the bleeding stopped. Are you too tired to watch him for a while?"

"No. Where do you want to put him?"

"We'll clean up this mess and leave him right here. It's unlikely he's strong enough to roll off the table."

Dominique moved to the end of the table and pulled off Sean's boots with a gentle tug. The mate then disposed of his breeches, but his linen drawers were also soaked with blood and he removed those, too. Working there, Dominique had become inured to the sight of naked men, but none had been Sean and her hands shook as she went to fetch warm water to wash the bloodstains from his body. She was relieved when the mate took the bowl from her hands and saw to the chore himself before covering Sean with a sheet.

"Will you give me your honest opinion on his chances?" Dominique whispered to Perry.

The surgeon shook his head regretfully. "They're not good. I'll send Belle over with your supper, but I doubt you'll have a long wait."

Devastated by that news, Dominique was ashamed for thinking of the danger to herself when Sean was barely clinging to life. She leaned close and stroked his hair lightly. A rich brown, it was still as thick, but had grayed at the temples. She wondered if he had married and perhaps fathered children since she had last seen him.

His face was thinner, but no less handsome; she was certain he must have been popular wherever he had been posted. The night was warm, but his skin felt too cool to the touch, and she quickly brought him a blanket and tucked it around him gently as though he were a sleeping child. She checked his bandage every few minutes, but it remained unstained by seeping blood. From what she had seen, Dr. Perry was an excellent surgeon, but he could not make up for lost blood, so it was possible Sean had already been past saving when he had arrived.

If these were the last hours he would spend on the Earth, she would not leave him. She reached under the blanket for his hand, but he didn't return her fond squeeze. He had touched her heart as no other man ever had, but there would be no opportunity to confess that now. Even if there were a chance to reveal that cherished secret, she would not. Had he been well, he would only have laughed, and perhaps rudely reminded her that he had only called on her to be close to Liana. She had merely been a temporary diversion, as so many men had been for her, but she was very sorry it could not have been more.

What if he had loved her? she agonized. With their countries at war, they would never have found a way to be together. But he had not loved her, and the tender feelings seeing him now evoked made no sense. But still, she felt an intense desire for more than the brief, chaste acquaintance they had had years ago.

There was ham that night, undoubtedly stolen from the farmer whose house they occupied, but before Belle could apologize for that fact, she recognized Dominique's patient and nearly dropped her plate. "My God," she whispered. "Did he see you?"

Dominique shook her head and replied in the same hushed tone. "He's too weak to even open his eyes, let alone recognize anyone."

"What are you going to do?"

"Wait here with him. Perhaps kiss him good-bye before he dies."

Dominique had never shown such devotion to another man, but Belle readily believed that wistful comment. Just the sight of Sean O'Keefe terrified her, and she did not understand how Dominique could bear to tend him, let alone be so calm. "How was he injured?"

Dominique replied without glancing up from her patient. "He was shot from ambush by a man on a sorrel horse. Do you have any idea who that might have been?"

Doubting her sister would have any appetite, Belle set her supper aside. "It's a tactic Falcon might have used, but he's not the only one. It could have been another man entirely."

"Yes, it might have been Hunter. Which is every bit as bad as Falcon." Dominique pressed Sean's fingers but his hand remained limp in hers. "Sean can't do us any harm now. If you don't mind, I'd rather be alone with him."

Belle would have preferred to dance with the devil. "And if he wakes?"

Dominique would not allow herself that hope. "He won't, but even if by some miracle he does, after all these years he might not even remember me."

"You remembered him, didn't you?" Belle's voice had a gritty edge of fear. "Maybe we ought to leave tonight."

Dominique understood Belle's concern, but she thought it misplaced when Sean was too weak even to utter a moan. "I won't leave him," she stressed, "not while he's so close to death. If he survives, we'll surely have to flee, but not tonight, Belle."

Belle wanted to scream with frustration. "I hope we're not making a dreadful mistake," she argued.

Dominique at last met her glance and gave a slight smile. "It doesn't matter that Sean's a British officer tonight, Belle. He's simply a badly wounded man who needs a friend and I'll not leave him."

Falcon had called her stubborn, but Belle saw the resolute glint in Dominique's eye and knew no argument she could possibly give would sway her. Feeling not only defeated but betrayed, she left to go to their tent where she would pray for their safety, and not waste a single word on Sean O'Keefe when his survival could so easily mean the end of theirs.

Eight

Dominique had been up since dawn, and had Sean been lying in a bed rather than stretched out on hard wooden planks, she would have climbed right in with him. Seated beside him, her whole body ached with a numbing fatigue her mind refused to acknowledge. She propped her elbows on the edge of the plank table and studied Sean's face with renewed fascination. The laugh lines at the corners of his eyes were deeper and she remembered he had had a warm, rolling laugh that had enticed her into the merriment. It was one of the many things she had missed when he had stopped calling on her.

Fearing his breathing had grown more shallow, she leaned forward slightly. Was he slipping away? she anguished. She thought of dear Belle, who saw the danger Sean posed so clearly, but her own feelings defied such neat classification. She and Sean had told each other flattering lies, and even knowing he had never been sincere, she could not forget how delighted she had been by his attentions.

Until she had met him, her callers had all been boys, but he had been a grown man and made her long for his delicious kiss. She jumped as Dr. Perry tapped her shoulder, then was badly embarrassed that she appeared to have been neglecting her patient when just the opposite was true. She had been lost in him.

"I'm so sorry," Stephen murmured. "I didn't mean to

startle you." He peeled back the edge of the blanket covering Sean's shoulder to check his bandage and appeared more perplexed than gratified. "I'd be pleased that he's no longer bleeding if I didn't fear there's simply very little blood left in him. At least he's in no pain."

"Isn't there something more we can do for him?" Dominique asked.

"He's warm and safe. That will have to do. Go on to bed. I'll sit with him a while."

"No," Dominique refused emphatically. "He'll do much better with me."

Stephen laughed at her fervor. "I agree. Any man would prefer to awaken with you by his side, but, dear lady, Sean is unlikely to wake."

Dominique's spirits fell even lower at that sorry prediction. "Then it won't matter who's here, will it?"

In the brief time Stephen Perry had known Dominique, he had become completely enchanted by her. He admired her sister too, but Dominique's appeal went far beyond a mere talent for healing. So late at night he knew he would not be overheard, and revealed a hint of his feelings in a playful jest.

"If I believed Sean were going to survive, I'd be very jealous of the attention you're showing him."

Shocked by the tastelessness of the physician's remark, Dominique dared not look up at him. Thus far, they had exchanged only comments about the running of the hospital and the care of the patients. She was positive neither her words nor actions could possibly be regarded as flirtatious, and yet he was blatantly flirting with her. At another time and place she would have been flattered, but not now. Tears welled up in her eyes.

"Please," she begged, "Sean was a dear friend once, and I can't bear to hear you dismiss him so lightly. It's very cruel."

Appalled that he had made such a tactless error, Stephen

began to back away. "Please forgive me. This obviously isn't the time to talk. I'll check on Sean again later."

Dominique nodded and let him go without further comment. She took Sean's hand and laced her fingers in his. "He doesn't understand how tough you are, does he? I imagine you'd have to be shot half a dozen times to give up on life. We made an awful mess of things the first time we met, and I daresay they can be no better now, but I would be happy just knowing there is someone like you alive in the world. Please don't leave us yet."

Lured from the depths of his dreams by the sadness in her voice, Sean's eyes fluttered slightly, then opened. He looked up at Dominique, his gaze dulled by pain, and yet after a long moment, he attempted to say her name. Too weak to speak, he could only mouth the word, but she understood.

"Oh, you can hear me, can't you?" she asked. "I'll stay right here with you, Sean, and in the morning, perhaps you'll be strong enough to speak."

Sean's eyes were the light brown flecked with gold described as hazel, but they appeared pure amber in the dim light. He felt Dominique's hand on his and although he tried, doubted he had managed even faint pressure in return. He saw the tears spilling over her lashes, and wanted to hold her in his arms but all he could do was stare. He believed her to be no more than a trick of his imagination, and assumed he must be dying.

He had not realized her image was still so clear in his heart, but he was grateful for her comforting touch as he lost consciousness again. He did not stir until long after the sun was high in the sky the next morning and then his shoulder was such a burning torment he could not recall a thing that had happened since he had been shot. A surgeon's mate sat dozing by his side, and while he could not speak above a hoarse whisper, his curse was sufficiently foul to wake him.

While Dr. Perry was amazed Sean O'Keefe had survived the night, he hid his dismay as he spoke with him. Feigning a confidence he did not truly feel, he expressed a hope for the officer's complete recovery. He moved him into the bedroom, placed him on a cot next to one of the windows, and prescribed heavy doses of laudanum for his pain. He sent word to Dominique that her friend was much improved, but the physician was still so embarrassed by his clumsy handling of their last conversation he was relieved when she slept past noon.

Unlike Dominique, Belle had no convenient excuse to allow her to miss work but she avoided Sean by keeping her back to him whenever she had a reason to visit a patient in the bedroom. He dozed fitfully, and posed no threat for the moment, but just knowing he was there filled her with dread.

As soon as Dominique was awake, she hid from Sean by again supervising the laundry, but she couldn't elude Belle. The work detail assigned to the laundry was chopping firewood, and knowing they would not be overheard, Belle pressed her sister for a solution to their latest dilemma.

"Have you any plan at all?" Belle asked. "I certainly did not wish the man dead, although it would have been better for us, but what are we going to do now? I doubt he'd remember me, so if I'm the one charged with his care you may be able to escape his notice a few more days, but the minute he sees you, we're going to be in very grave trouble indeed."

Dominique kicked a soiled sheet into the next pile to be laundered and raised her fingertips to her temples. "I'm too tired to think right now, Belle. Give me a couple of days—then I'll give the problem my full attention."

"We may not have that long!" Belle scolded. "We've nearly depleted our store of herbs, and that's an excellent reason to replenish them. Let's tell Dr. Perry we must search for more this very afternoon. You know he'll believe us."

"Yes. He would, but I'm simply too tired to go today. Now see to the injured, and leave me to handle this filthy linen."

Belle's stomach was churning painfully. "I swear I can feel the noose tightening about my neck. Does the danger Sean poses merely excite you?"

Dominique regarded her sister with a weary stare. "I sat up the whole night, expecting each breath he drew to be his last. I'm too exhausted to become excited about anything."

"We've absolutely no choice about this," Belle warned.

"I know," Dominique agreed through a wide yawn. She turned and began to sort another bundle of stained sheets. Unable to face either Sean or Belle, she concentrated on forming manageable heaps so the wash would at least get done even if she failed to accomplish anything else.

Belle knew precisely what they had to do, but seeing she was making no progress with Dominique, she shook her head sadly and walked away. She prayed Dominique really was just too tired to think clearly, but she would not allow her to use that excuse after today.

As she crossed the yard, the eerie sensation of being watched gave her a sudden chill. She stopped in mid-stride and turned in an attempt to catch the culprit. There were wounded lounging near their tents and other men following the routine necessary to keep the camp running, but none was looking her way. Fearing it was merely guilt that was troubling her, she went back to the farmhouse intent upon doing what she could for everyone but Sean.

Falcon had left Nails tethered in the woods, and crept up over the rutted landscape to get close enough to observe the British soldiers moving about Camden. The imposing white house being used for their headquarters seemed completely out of place on the edge of the wilderness, but he supposed it suited their grandiose schemes. At least he had culled Sean O'Keefe from their insufferable ranks. He had never been so happy to have a British officer in his sights, and hoped the bastard had broken his neck in the fall from his horse.

Despite his hatred of the enemy, he dared not fire when he was so vastly outnumbered, and his attention wandered to the tents housing the wounded. From the looks of it, a good many soldiers had survived the recent battle there, which was a great shame when Baron De Kalb had lost his life fighting with the militia. Falcon felt guilty for not having been there, but he would do his part now to keep the British from growing comfortable with their victory. He watched, waiting for a patrol to be dispatched with the intention of following and creating still more havoc.

Bored with the inactivity in the camp, the young women circling the tubs of boiling laundry caught his eye. He would have quickly dismissed them had he not realized from the expansiveness of their gestures that they were arguing. He hoped they were debating how best to scald the most British regulars and laughed to himself until something about them struck him as hauntingly familiar. He did not recognize their clothes, and kerchieves hid their hair, but the grace of their motions tugged at his memory until he could not help but compare them to his cousins.

He had not imagined there was another pair like Belle and Dominique in all the world. Perhaps if there had not been two of them he would not have noticed the similarities, but these women moved with the casual elegance of a country dance and created a poignant longing for home. He took care not to become so absorbed in their antics that he grew careless, and surveyed the surrounding terrain with an anxious glance to prevent anyone from ambushing him as he so often did others. Satisfied he was safe, he remained longer than he had intended, but each comparison he drew made him increasingly uneasy.

He supposed there were other women with lithe figures and volatile natures that would encourage the argument he was observing with such keen interest. He wondered if they had been residents of Camden before the British occupation, or merely camp followers. If they were the latter, perhaps they were arguing over an officer they both admired. He doubted it had been Sean O'Keefe. Physically the man was not unattractive, but he had the soul of a viper and would doubtless be as faithless with this pair as he had once been to Dominique.

One of the women turned away, the argument apparently over, and as she walked toward the adjacent farmhouse her long, sure stride was identical to the one his temper had prompted from Belle on the banks of the James River. He knew he could not possibly be observing her and Dominique. That made no sense at all. They were at home in Virginia, or at least he assumed they must be.

He stayed low to the ground as he returned to Nails, but that was out of habit rather than caution when his mind was so full of Belle. He had a camp deep in the woods where British patrols never ventured, but as he rode there he could not quite convince himself it was merely guilt that had made him see Belle and Dominique rather than two strangers. What if they actually had been there? he asked himself, and before nightfall he returned to Camden and again kept watch to discover where they slept.

He also scanned the camp for sentries, but there were none posted near the hospital. The wounded men could not leave their tents for a midnight stroll, but still not dismissing some unexpected danger, he moved with a panther's stealth as he circled around behind the farmhouse and approached the girls' tent. Although it was late, a lantern lit inside silhouetted the winsome pair against the tautly stretched white canvas. While the light would enable him to identify the occupants quickly, if they were not Belle and Dominique, he did not want them to glance up, see an Indian, and begin shrieking as though they feared being murdered.

He waited, hoping they would soon fall asleep, but instead, one left the tent and hurried into the farmhouse. He saw only her shadow as she passed by, and heard the gentle rustle of her skirts, but even that faint hint of her was familiar. He inched closer to the tent, taking care to move with a soundless step. One flap was raised to serve as a door, but when he at last came close enough to peer inside, it was all he could do not to yell so loudly he would have awakened the whole camp.

He quickly ducked inside and yanked down the flap. Belle was seated on her cot, brushing her hair, and as she turned toward him Falcon clamped his hand over her mouth before she could utter a sound. "What in God's name are you doing here?" he whispered in her ear.

Belle's heart was thundering so violently in her ears she scarcely heard his question. At once thrilled and terrified, she placed her hand on his wrist and tugged gently to coax him to release her. She could have replied then, but the expression on his face was so menacing she did not even know where to begin. She wanted to throw her arms around his neck and kiss him until he swore he would never leave her again, but clearly he was in no mood to accept such an affectionate welcome.

Falcon dug his fingers into Belle's shoulders and shook her. "Tell me," he urged in an insistent whisper.

Belle swallowed hard. "I tried to follow you," she finally answered.

Falcon was so angry he had great difficulty keeping his voice low. "Did you really expect to find me in a British camp?"

Belle shook her head. "This wasn't our choice, but theirs. We were on the way to Charleston."

A quick glance around the tent convinced Falcon they had brought little more than what they had on their backs.

He could not even believe they had been so stupid. "Come with me, and don't make a sound." He took Belle's hand as they left the tent, and after skirting the farmhouse, he led her out across the field. She tripped once and nearly fell but the instant he caught her and set her back on her feet he started off again at a pace close to a run. He did not stop until he had reached the edge of the woods and even there he did not feel safe.

"Do they have any idea who you are?" he asked, his voice slightly louder but no less harsh.

Belle had known Falcon might not be pleased to see her, but she had hoped after his initial dismay he would understand why she had followed him and be glad. She tried to hold onto that hope as she repeated the story she and Dominique had made up about their background. "Dr. Perry doesn't really care who we are now that we've proven our worth in his hospital. That's where Dominique is right now. She went to check on Sean O'Keefe. Did you shoot him?" She held her breath, already knowing the answer, and wondering if he would lie.

"I was sure I'd killed the son of a bitch. Don't tell me Dominique is trying to keep him alive."

Even when Falcon spoke in a whisper, Belle felt singed by his rage. He had warned her at home that he had changed, and he proved it with every angry word. She drew in a deep breath for courage. "We planned to leave before he is well enough to cause us trouble."

"Is that what you were arguing about this afternoon?"

"Were you watching us?" Belle had been infuriated with Lieutenant Beck for spying on them, and while she knew Falcon's motives must surely have been different, she did not want to believe the two men were anything alike. "I sensed I was being watched. It must have been you."

"I didn't want to believe it was you." Falcon turned away and stared up at the sky. "I told myself it couldn't possibly be you two, but all the while I knew from the way you moved that it could be no one else. Didn't you understand anything I said about the war, Belle?"

His buckskins were a pale gold in the moonlight, and his hair an ebony slash through his broad shoulders. Even separated by several feet, she felt his strength and the smoldering heat of his anger. Words of love would have no meaning for him now, and yet she could not lie.

"Yes. I understood it all, although I didn't really grasp how awful it was until we got here and saw how many wounded there were. I simply wanted to be with you."

Falcon swore in the Seneca tongue to spare her the sound of the vile names he thought she deserved. Still livid, he turned back to face her. "What did you expect to do? Were you going to tag along after me as you did as a child? Perhaps load my rifle for me while I did my best to kill Sean O'Keefe and all the rest of his contemptible kind?"

Even knowing Falcon had developed a temper, Belle had never expected him to be this furiously angry with her. She was as badly shaken as she had been on the ride to Camden, but fought to remain calm enough to reason with him. "Dominique and I were hoping to tend wounded men from the Colonial militia. I didn't expect to travel with you on raids, Falcon, but I had hoped to be able to see you more often than I had at home. I was so afraid you weren't coming back, you see, and I couldn't accept that."

Nothing Belle said made any sense to Falcon. He wanted her to be safe at home, not here where her presence merely compounded his problems. Knowing that at any moment a stray bullet might end her life was even worse torture. He had always believed her to be the sensible sort, not as reckless as he. "You can't have told your parents what you intended to do or they'd have stopped you."

That taunt hurt Belle badly because she knew just how greatly she and Dominique must have disappointed them. "No. We didn't confide in them. We just ran away the day after you left home." Belle was tempted to remind him that had he not taught her how to survive in the wilderness, they would never have dared to follow him. Then she realized he would not be pleased by the way she had put her knowledge into practice, and kept still.

Falcon had known Belle was independent, but he had not considered her willful. "You used to respect their opinions, and mine. How could you have even imagined that I would be glad to see you here when the danger is so great?"

Belle had mistakenly believed that on Falcon's last visit home he had hurt her as badly as he possibly could, but she had been wrong. Cut to the marrow by that abusive question, she realized her devotion had been completely misplaced. She lashed out to repay him for this new and painful insult.

"I knew you liked being with women, so I thought it might as well be me. Obviously that was a very stupid mistake, but I'll not make another where you're concerned."

Falcon could have strangled her in that instant, and clenched his hands tightly at his sides to control the brutish impulse. "The British are as thick as swarming bees here in South Carolina, and you thought I would have time to entertain women?"

"No. Just me," Belle answered. "Go away and forget you saw us. We've gotten along very well on our own and—"

"You are British prisoners!" Falcon hissed. "How could you have done any worse?"

Filtered through the trees, moonlight fell in uneven splotches across Falcon's face, making his expression more frightening than if he had been wearing war paint and feathers. Tired of defending herself, Belle took a step backwards, then, fighting tears, turned and ran toward the camp. Soft lights glowing in the farmhouse windows beckoned invitingly, and she raced over the field, terrified to think she would feel far more safe in a British hospital than with the Indian brave she had always adored.

* * *

Hoping to find Dominique, Stephen Perry glanced in the bedroom and found her by Sean O'Keefe's side. This time he took care to confine their discussion to medicine. "I waited for you to change his dressing. Normally I would use a bread and milk poultice with the second bandage. I suppose you'd prefer chamomile?"

Dominique had two excellent reasons for that choice. "Why, yes, I would. I believe there's enough left for Sean, but then Belle and I will need to gather more of the herb."

"Bring what you have."

Because their supplies were used there, they had left their basket of herbs in the farmhouse kitchen, and Dominique quickly returned with a strong infusion she had brewed earlier. She soaked a clean cloth in it and waited for Dr. Perry to complete removing Sean's first bandage. She then draped the poultice over his shoulder to cover both the entry and exit wounds. She was so intent upon the process, she did not notice Sean's eyes were open until she stepped back.

"You weren't a dream after all," Sean murmured in a husky whisper.

Dominique frowned slightly, imploring him to be still. "He looks much better tonight, Doctor."

"Hello, Sean," Stephen said. "I won't ask how you're feeling as I'm sure it isn't good. Just give us a minute to wrap your shoulder again, and we'll let you go back to sleep."

Sean grimaced as Stephen began to work. "Hurry up," he begged.

"Take his hand," Stephen urged. "That's sure to make him feel better."

Dominique moved around to the other side of the cot to grasp Sean's right hand. He was still weak, but this time responded with a gentle clasp. She tried to smile, but couldn't. He was staring up at her, studying her with an intensity that unnerved her completely.

"Be still, Sean," she warned, hoping he would understand her meaning while Dr. Perry would assume she was encouraging him to help him with his task. She began to tremble, and Sean clutched her hand more tightly. She remembered how strong he had been, but now hoped he would be too weak to leave his bed for a good long while.

As soon as he was finished, Stephen stepped back. He picked up the bandages he had discarded, and nodded toward the door. "I'll bring you more laudanum so you can go back to sleep."

"Wait," Sean pleaded softly.

Stephen responded with a knowing smile. "I'll let you talk with her for five minutes, but not a second more."

"I won't tire him," Dominique promised, but she held her breath until the physician had left the room. The other men quartered there were sleeping soundly, but she knelt beside Sean's cot so he alone would hear.

"I want so much for you to get well," she insisted. "Please believe me."

Sean closed his eyes for a moment, then tried to smile. "Have you cut your hair?"

Dominique released his hand to remove her kerchief. She shook out her curls and they spilled down over her shoulders in a radiant cascade. "There. I'm pleased to see you still have your hair, too." She combed it back from his temple with a gentle caress. "I'm so sorry you were hurt."

"So am I." Sean started to laugh, then caught himself when a fiery surge of pain shot down his left side.

Dominique saw the agony flash across his expression and reached for his hand. "Please, You must rest. Don't try and say anything more."

Sean looked away, but held her hand long after Dr. Perry had brought the laudanum, and he had fallen asleep.

Before leaving the room, Dominique checked on the other injured men. She knew their names now, and had heard their stories of home. They were sweet boys, really, and impossible to regard as the enemy now that she knew them as individuals. She paused at Sean's cot for a last good night, and brushed his lips with a tender kiss.

Her chest felt tight as she approached the tent she shared with Belle and she hoped her sister was already asleep because she did not feel up to arguing again. She raised the tent flap and stepped inside, but she was astonished to find Belle seated on the canvas flooring. She was weeping huge tears, and covering her mouth with both hands to muffle her pathetic sobs.

Dominique immediately knelt beside her. "Oh, Belle, I'm so sorry. I told Dr. Perry we'd have to gather herbs and he didn't seem in the least bit suspicious. We'll leave in a day or so. I promise we will."

Embarrassed to be found in such a miserable state, Belle dried her eyes on her apron. "I've been such a stupid fool," she sobbed.

"No, not at all," Dominique assured her. "Sean was awake again tonight, but he's so dazed by laudanum he can't think clearly enough to wonder why I'm here. We'll be safe another day or two, and that will be plenty of time to get away."

Belle didn't even know where she wanted to go anymore. "Falcon's here," she revealed, and in a halting whisper she described just how thoroughly wretched he had made her feel. "This whole trip was utterly pointless," she declared. "I thought love was worth the sacrifice, but he doesn't even know the meaning of the word."

Her eyes again filled with tears as she looked up at her sister. "How can I go home and tell everyone Falcon didn't want me?"

"Belle, that can't possibly be true!"

"You didn't hear him or you'd know I mean less to him than the beads on his moccasins. I'm nothing. Nothing at all."

Dominique had never seen Belle so badly upset, and she seriously debated asking Stephen Perry for some laudanum for her, but at the last minute realized she would have no way to explain why her sister was in such dire straits. "Falcon must have been shocked to discover us here. Give him a few days to accept the fact. If he came to speak with you once, he'll do so again."

Belle shook her head and wrapped her arms around her knees. "He's probably ten miles from here by now. I'm sorry, Dominique. I've gotten you in such an awful mess, and it was all for nothing."

Dominique took a firm hold on her sister's shoulders. "Stop that this instant," she hissed. "Coming after Falcon was my idea in the first place so I'd never blame you for the way the trip's turned out. Besides, I've gotten to see Sean, even if it wasn't the way I expected to, either. Now we're going to have to keep our wits about us, Belle. Let's work as we usually do in the morning. In the afternoon, we'll go out to pick chamomile, and that will be the last anyone here will ever see of us."

Belle wished they had left that day so she would not have had to suffer through an awful scene with Falcon, but she could not find any joy now that Dominique had agreed to go. "I can't go home," she repeated numbly.

Dominique hugged her tightly. "Oh, Belle, you've not done anything shameful. Everyone will understand that you had to follow your heart. I'll insist it was all my doing anyway." She stood and hauled Belle to her feet.

"Now let's just go to sleep and try to make everyone think tomorrow is no different from any of the other days we've spent here. If Dr. Perry sees you crying in the morning, he'll pester you to tell him why and what can you possibly say? I don't think a lovers' quarrel will be a convincing excuse."

Belle slumped down on the edge of her cot. "It wasn't a quarrel," she stressed. "It was the end."

Dominique stroked Belle's hair with the same tenderness she had shown Sean. "Falcon has always loved you, and no matter what he said tonight, he loves you still."

Belle wrung her hands. "He isn't Falcon anymore. He's someone else, Dominique." She hated him for changing, for abandoning her after he had shown her such a small sample of how glorious love could be. She drew in a ragged breath and released an anguished sigh. When she looked up at Dominique, she could barely see her through her tears.

"He is the one who shot Sean, and he was thoroughly infuriated to learn he isn't dead."

Dominique wasn't surprised by that announcement, but when she stopped to think how easily Falcon had slipped into camp to speak with Belle, she was terrified. "Do you think he might sneak into the hospital?" she asked. "I know he wouldn't risk shooting Sean again, but it would take only an instant to slit a wounded man's throat."

"Oh, my God," Belle moaned, the possibility too awful to bear.

"I'm sorry. I didn't mean to upset you again. It would be cowardly to attack a wounded man and I'm sure Falcon would never stoop that low."

"He isn't Falcon anymore," Belle stressed. "Have Dr. Perry post a guard at the hospital, or sit with Sean yourself, but don't leave him alone tonight. He isn't safe."

"Thank you." Dominique leaned down to kiss her sister's cheek, then dashed back to the farmhouse. On the way, she realized she could not admit how she had learned Sean was in danger without revealing Belle had spoken with Falcon. Because that would endanger all three of them, it was another secret she would have to keep.

The surgeon's mate who was on duty after Stephen had retired was a competent lad she would have trusted on any other night, but telling him only that she was worried about Sean, she sat beside her former beau and prayed until dawn that Falcon was as badly confused as Belle, and would have no appetite for vengeance.

Nine

Falcon ran down to the river but the water's icy chill had no effect on his blazing temper. He scooped up great globs of mud and hurled them downstream, venting his torment. He had left home heavily burdened by the anguish he had caused Belle, but that pain was slight compared to this agony. That she could calmly sit in a nest of the king's vipers ripped at his soul.

His thoughts a furious blur, a long while passed before he could move beyond the horror of finding her there to the nettlesome task of deciding what to do about it. Leaving her in a British camp was not an option. After such a heated argument, he knew better than to approach her a second time tonight, but he would not let another night pass without rescuing her. If she refused to listen to reason, then he would just pick her up and carry her off.

There was Dominique to consider as well, however, and while he was strong, he knew he could not carry two squirming females off into the woods without attracting the attention of the British sentries. He washed his hands in the river, then splashed water on his face. He had been sent to Camden to kill, not to rescue young women who should have been smart enough to stay at home but his primary mission would have little value if he could not save them.

He threw back his head, and knowing the British would not be able to distinguish his voice from a wolf's, let out a long, feral moan. But tomorrow night, he vowed to smother his cries in Belle's tender flesh. He made his way back to his camp and stretched out on the leaves he had gathered for a bed, but his dreams were dark, and his anger renewed by the dawn.

After being up all night again, Dominique slept until noon. When she finally entered the farmhouse, Stephen Perry thrust a spoon and bowl of broth into her hands. "Sean won't eat unless you feed him. Make certain that he finishes every last spoonful. Officers always make the most demanding patients, and he's no exception. Insist that he behaves himself with you and maybe he'll give my mates less trouble."

Dominique was alarmed to hear Sean was alert enough to eat, but unable to refuse Stephen's request, she carried the bowl into the bedroom. Lieutenant Beck was leaning over Sean's cot, speaking in a hushed voice. Frightened her ruse was over, her hands shook so badly the broth sloshed in wild waves in the bowl. She glanced back toward the door, but before she could flee, Leland Beck straightened up and saw her.

"Good afternoon, Miss Scott. I'll get out of your way so you can give the colonel his dinner."

The lieutenant's expression was merely curious rather than threatening, prompting Dominique to wonder what Sean had just told him. "Good afternoon," she replied as calmly as she could. The lieutenant nodded politely, but as he passed by her, his expression filled with disdain. He raked her with an insolent glance, his eyes lingering on the soft swell of her bosom. He may have claimed she and Belle weren't worth a second look, but obviously he had not meant it. Sickened by that silent insult, she hurried on to Sean. He was still pale, but with his cheeks shadowed by a second day's growth of dark stubble, he was infinitely more menacing.

Dominique felt torn, for while she believed she may well have saved Sean's life by keeping a watch on him last night, she feared every hour she and Belle remained there increased the risk to their own lives. She sat down in the chair beside him and dipped the spoon into the broth. "I'm glad to see you're well enough to eat," she told him, and then jammed a spoonful of the clear soup into his mouth when he opened it to reply. He sputtered slightly, but swallowed.

"Delicious, isn't it?" she asked.

Sean still had one good arm, and while he lacked much in the way of strength, it was enough to block her next attempt to feed him. "Wait," he ordered gruffly. "Beck said he provided you and Belle with an escort here. 'The Scott sisters,' he called you. Somehow I don't believe Ian would be pleased that you're claiming him as kin."

Cheered that he had not greeted her with a threat, Dominique managed a slight smile. "First you must eat, and then we'll talk," she insisted.

"Promise?"

Dominique rolled her eyes. She knew precisely what value he would assign her word, and did not give it. She raised another spoonful of broth to his lips and he opened his mouth obediently. "Neither of us is in any position to bargain at present," she whispered. "So I propose we simply concentrate on making you well."

"Ian would be touched by your concern for me," Sean responded smugly.

"Just eat!"

Sean swallowed the rest of the nearly tasteless broth without further complaint, but the instant Dominique set the empty bowl on the floor, he reached out to grab her wrist. He did not ask the most obvious question aloud, but the sharp angle of his brow spoke it clearly. He tightened his grasp and waited.

Sean was still so weak that Dominique could have easily broken his hold, but she chose to relax instead. She looked out the window and wondered if Falcon were lurking nearby. She did not actually owe Sean an explanation, and she could not provide one that even hinted at Falcon's involvement, but desperately needing his sympathetic silence, she gave the truth the same clever spin she had used the first time they had met.

"Belle and I were restless at home. We wished to tend wounded, and came south believing we could be of service. I like to think that we have been."

Dominique exhibited a serenity she had lacked in their earlier acquaintance. Sean assumed maturity had imparted a new seriousness to her manner, but if anything, it made her even more desirable. She was a woman now, rather than a luscious child, and he wished he felt well enough to fully appreciate the change. Disgusted that just sipping soup had tired him, he closed his eyes for a minute. When he opened them, he longed for far more than his damaged body would allow.

"Kiss me," he said.

It was an order rather than a request, but Dominique leaned over him to comply. When her lips met his, she felt an unnatural warmth and grew alarmed. Intimidated by his grasp, she had been concentrating on the conversation so intently she had not felt the heat in his hand before now.

"You're feverish," she worried aloud. "I'll change your dressing and brew some special tea."

"Poison?" he asked, only half in jest.

Dominique shook her head. "If I'd wanted you dead, Sean, you'd already be in the ground." She peeled his fingers off her wrist and went to fetch the last of the chamomile infusion to make another poultice. She removed his bandage and found his shoulder swollen and inflamed.

She worked quickly to spare him pain, but each time her fingertips brushed his skin, she felt him flinch.

"This may hurt a bit now, but it will speed the healing and you'll feel better soon."

Sean had nearly bitten through his lip to keep from crying out. "I hope so."

"We keep tea made from the bark of the white willow brewing constantly. I'll bring you some, and don't worry, I'll add honey to improve its taste." She soon returned with a battered tin cup and raised his head so he could sip it easily. "Try and sleep now without the laudanum if you can," she encouraged. "I'm going out for more herbs, and I'll give you another cup of tea as soon as I return."

Fatigue and the warm tea had dulled the sharp edges of Sean's mood and he closed his eyes without making another pointed comment. Dominique touched his hair lightly, then withdrew. "We need more chamomile," she announced loudly enough for both Belle and Dr. Perry to overhear. Busy with an amputee, the physician waved her away.

Belle had been folding bandages, but laid them aside. "Let's saddle our horses then, and gather some."

Dominique led the way out the back door, but they found Lieutenant Beck standing just outside. "If you've somewhere to go, Colonel O'Keefe instructed me to provide you with an escort," he said.

He looked inordinately pleased about the assignment and considering the haste with which he had abandoned them there, Dominique thought his change of heart odd. Unless, of course, Sean had prompted it. "That won't be necessary," she replied. "We're just going out to search for herbs. We won't be away from camp long."

The lieutenant moved to block their way. "That's far too dangerous an errand for you to run alone, ladies. While British regulars would never attack defenseless women, Colonial troops are unfettered by scruples. Now, either my men and I accompany you, or you will not be permitted to leave camp."

Leland Beck was obviously in control of the situation, but Belle could not hide her disgust. "I would hate to take a man of your unique abilities away from his other duties, Lieutenant. If you have a musket we could borrow, we'll gladly defend ourselves."

The lieutenant appeared to give her request serious thought, but then shook his head. "I know you could probably defend yourself with that lively tongue of yours, Miss Scott, but Colonel O'Keefe is very worried about your sister. Let's hurry. I don't want any of the wounded to suffer from lack of attention for too long."

"Neither do we," Dominique assured him. They brought along the picnic basket to hold whatever they might find, but neither young woman could keep her mind on the task. This was to have been a brief excursion designed to allay Dr. Perry's suspicions, if he held any, as to their loyalty. Their second trip was to have been their escape, but stymied on their first, each was desperately disappointed.

As they neared the edge of the woods, Belle fully expected Falcon to shoot Lieutenant Beck. She certainly did not like the officer, but the prospect of his losing his life at any moment was a terrible strain. She prayed Falcon would wait for another target, but it was difficult to seek medicinal herbs while anticipating the bloodshed he could so easily cause. She and Dominique dismounted to pick some sprigs of peppermint, but the lieutenant was never more than a few steps away, preventing them from modifying their escape plan.

Horribly distracted by his presence, they returned to Camden with only a few of the herbs they had hoped to find, but it was enough to justify the trip in Dr. Perry's eyes, even if they had failed miserably in their own. Dominique gave Sean a second cup of white willow bark tea, but he sipped it slowly, and she was sincerely worried that he might still be too weak to survive his wound. His safety was also a continuing concern, but she had yet to invent a plausible excuse for him to have a guard An armed soldier would only endanger Falcon's life should he come for Sean, and that possibility tormented her, too.

Once they had returned to their tent, Belle released her frustrations in a strangled hiss. "You can't keep sitting up all night with Sean and working most of the day," she complained, "or you'll exhaust yourself and end up on a cot with the wounded."

Dominique had barely touched her dinner, but she was too tired to have much appetite. She knew Belle was right, but could see no alternative. "My health can't be a priority," she replied. "I really believed we could just ride out of here, but with Lieutenant Beck tagging along after us everywhere we go, that's not going to be possible. We could just sneak away on foot in the dead of night, but I'd hate to abandon Baby Dee and Ladybug."

"We may have to," Belle countered. "No, wait," she begged. "What if we were to set all the horses loose?"

"After we'd saddled our own?"

"Yes," Belle enthused. "That would surely create enough confusion to allow us to get away. Let's do it tonight."

Dominique grabbed for that hope, and then just as quickly discarded it. She wanted to leave as badly as Belle, but not yet. "I'm worried about Sean. He was feverish this afternoon."

Belle made an effort to hold her temper, but was only partially successful. "He's a British officer, Dominique. We can't trust him to do anything other than betray us."

Dominique rose from her cot and placed her hands in the small of her back as she stretched lazily. "He could have done that yesterday, but didn't."

"Perhaps he's toying with us the way a cat delights in tormenting a mouse, He'll bat us around with his paws until he grows bored, and then we'll be swallowed without so much as a burp."

Despite Belle's vivid metaphor, Dominique did not want to believe that Sean could be so cruel. "It's also possible he still has feelings for me."

"Do you want him to?" Belle chided. "Do you want him to beg you to stay with him? Why do you think he told Lieutenant Beck to keep an eye on us? Was that the action of a loving, trusting man?"

"He has no reason to trust us, Belle, but he's been badly hurt and may not be thinking all that clearly." Dominique waited a moment and then added, "Like Falcon, I'm sure he's shocked and surprised, and doesn't know quite what to make of us being here."

Belle had thought of little else all day. "That's why we need to move on now," she stressed, "before either of them turns vicious."

Dominique understood that her sister was still recoiling from her latest bitter encounter with Falcon, but she trusted her cousin not to turn on them. Sean, however, posed another problem entirely. "I'm going to check on Sean, but I won't wait up with him all night. Now that I've had time to consider the matter fully, I know Falcon wouldn't harm him while he's as weak as a babe."

Sick of arguing about Sean, when Dominique returned to the farmhouse, Belle fetched a bucket of warm water to wash, then sat on her cot in her chemise. She did not know which was worse, the prospect of Falcon bursting into their tent a second time, or that he might have already ridden as far as he could go in the opposite direction. Worn out by worry, she lay down and closed her eyes, but Falcon soon interrupted her dreams.

Falcon knelt beside the cot and ran his hand down Belle's back, then leaned close to kiss her cheek. "Belle," he coaxed, "wake up. We need to talk."

Belle had left the lantern burning for Dominique and she

could make out Falcon's expression clearly. The fierce strain anger had lent his features was gone, and a slow smile curled across his lips. This was the man she loved, but still wary, she sat up slowly.

"You ought not to be here," she scolded.

"Neither should you," Falcon replied. "Where's Dominique?"

"Where she always is: tending Sean."

Falcon heard the note of jealousy in her complaint and wondered if she missed her sister's company or envied her devotion. "Do you want him for yourself?" he asked.

Sickened by his question, Belle glanced away. She had never wanted any man but Falcon, but could not forget how eager he had been to escape her on his last visit home. *And she had pursued him!* she agonized. "I hope Sean dies an agonizing death," she finally replied, "and soon."

He knew without having to ask that she would have told Dominique that he had shot Sean, but he did not regard it as a breach of trust. He would have bragged about it to Dominique himself had he had the chance. "Come with me," he urged, but Belle shrank back slightly and that hurt him badly. "Are you afraid of me now? Have I ruined everything between us?"

The pain of that possibility filled his expression with such utter desperation that Belle reached out to caress his cheek. She loved him so dearly, but he had given her an awful fright. "I didn't think you wanted anything between us."

Falcon knew he had given her good 'cause for that sorry opinion, but hoped to change it. "You have always been a challenge, Belle." He slid his hand around her neck to draw her close for a kiss he made very light and endearing until he was confident she wanted more as badly as he.

"Come with me," he repeated in a softer tone. "It's too dangerous for us here." He rose and offered his hand to help Belle to her feet.

She reached for her shawl and stepped into her shoes. "I'll just wear my chemise. If anyone stops us I'll say I was going to the river to bathe."

"And what excuse should I give?"

"You're so clever, they wouldn't even see you."

"The soldiers are too lazy to watch the river. We'll be as safe there as we were at home on the banks of the James." He raised the tent flap and peered out. He heard crickets aplenty, but no male voices carried on the warm night air. He reached back for Belle's hand, then left camp by a different route than he had used the previous night. Once they reached the river, he followed the narrow trail skirting the shore a long way upstream, then angled into the woods. Too hungry for Belle to take her all the way to his camp, he turned and drew her into his arms.

Belle's first thought was that Falcon could not make up his mind about her from one day to the next while her love for him never wavered. Her second thought was that his kiss was so delicious she did not care how fickle he might be. She leaned into his embrace, slid her hands under his shirt, and hugged him tight. He was lean and tough, and she took comfort in his strength rather than demand the touching promises she had once craved.

Falcon released Belle just long enough to rip off his shirt, then threw it down to provide her with a soft bed. He tossed away her shawl, and then drew her back into his arms. "You are already mine," he breathed against her lips. It was an arrogant vow, but the only one he would give. He wound his fingers in her hair. Touched by the moonlight, the curls shone like spun gold.

He kissed her hard, and then deeply. He traced the delicate bow of her lips with the tip of his tongue, teasing her until she thrust her tongue into his mouth in a passionate plea for more. He sucked her tongue, and lifted her off her feet. Her shoes fell to the leaves, and when he set her down, he untied the bow at the neckline of her chemise. He

stepped back, and needing no encouragement, she shrugge
it off. The linen garment pooled at her feet, but she quickl
stepped out of it and back into his arms.

Falcon uttered a low, satisfied groan as the lush fullnes
of Belle's breasts melted into the hard planes of his ches
He ran his hands down her back, then cupped her buttock
to enjoy the silken smoothness of their gentle swell. H
ground his hips against hers, forcefully proving how badl
he wanted her, then captured her mouth for another kis
that blurred into another, and another.

Belle's whole body ached with wanting him, the tips o
her breasts were exquisitely sensitive, and she felt hersel
growing wet with desire. When Falcon leaned down t
suckle, she slid her hands through his hair, and with a grace
ful dip encouraged him to drop down with her and stretc
out on his shirt. She could hold him so much more easil
now that she did not have to fight to remain on her feet.

Falcon's mouth was still at her breast, but he ran his han
up her thigh, parting her legs and separating her tender fold
with a gentle sweetness that made her cry out for more
His fingertips dipped, circled, and teased, creating the mos
delicious sensation she had ever known. The glorious feel
ing grew, spreading like the petals of an opening rose, an
she bent her knee, encouraging him to give still more.

Belle's own scent was more seductive than the fines
French perfume, and Falcon burned with the need to sample
her taste. He trailed kisses over the smooth flatness of he
stomach, then parted the triangle of curls and sent the ti
of his tongue across the bud nestled at the top of her cleft
He felt her shivering response, but knew it could not possibly be revulsion and took far more, lapping up her essence
until her soft, mewing cries became breathless gasps.

He unfastened his belt with one hand, shoved his buckskins aside, and moved up over her. Propping himself on
his elbows, he slid the tip of his manhood through her
crease, retracing the path he had just blazed with his lips.

He coaxed lightly, probed gently, and then with a savage lunge, thrust deep into her heated core, and lay still. He felt her pain as surely as he had her pleasure, but waited now for it to wane.

He kissed her eyelids, her earlobes, and then her trembling lips. "I am sorry to be the one to hurt you," he murmured in a husky whisper, "but I could not have stood it had it been another man."

Belle could not even imagine such a possibility. She grabbed a handful of his hair to pull his mouth to hers and kissed him with an enthusiasm that erased whatever fears he may have had as to her reaction. He began to move with an easy motion that created soft flutterings deep within her. She relaxed in his arms, needing all he could give, and floated into it on passion's wings.

The pain soon blurred into a numbing warmth, which gradually swelled to the pleasure he had taught her to expect. She clung to him, mirroring his thrusts to pull him down even deeper, until lost in him, she was filled with a sparkling burst of joy that enveloped him in the same glorious splendor. She had followed him for love, but knew this night would leave them forever changed.

She whispered in his ear, "I swear I love you more than life, Falcon."

The brave rose up slightly. "No. Never more than life, for I could not bear to lose you." He smothered her pretty promises with lavish kisses and made love to her again. Then, when the sky began to lighten, he took her down to the river to wash away all evidence of their passion. He felt her watching him as he bathed, too, but shook his head.

"I can't keep you with me a minute longer. Tell Dominique you are leaving tonight. I'll come for the both of you. Be ready."

Belle shook the leaves off her chemise and pulled it on over her head. "We'll need horses. Is there a way to take Ladybug and Baby Dee?"

Falcon responded with a derisive snort. "I could steal horses from a British camp at noon. Don't worry. I'll have your pets." He walked part of the way with her, then, after a last lingering kiss, disappeared into the woods and left her to find her way back to her tent alone.

A thin layer of fog brushed the ground, making it difficult for Belle to follow the main path from the river, but she stayed close enough to prevent anyone from tracing the route of her late-night excursion. She held her breath, half expecting to find Lieutenant Beck waiting for her, but there was no one standing guard by their tent. Dominique had sworn she would not sit up with Sean again, but her cot was empty.

Not really caring what her sister did after having spent such a reckless and wonderful night with Falcon, Belle lay down to catch what sleep she could before morning. She stretched and with a mischievous smile, wondered what it would be like to make love with Falcon in a feather bed.

Dominique's night had been anything but blissful. Sean was in agony, and while she had every confidence her chamomile poultices were healing his wound, he had no such belief. Dr. Perry had prescribed increased doses of laudanum, but Sean had refused them.

"I can't even move my arm," Sean complained.

"It's only been a few days since you were shot," Dominique reminded him. "You were lucky not to have bled to death before you got here. You need to rest. Why won't you take the laudanum?"

Sean's eyes were clouded with pain, but his words were clear. "Perry wants me unconscious so he can cut off my arm."

Dominique sat back slightly. "Is that what has you so upset? Are you afraid you're in danger of losing your arm?"

She was holding another cup of willow bark tea, and

when Sean reached for her hand it spilled all over her apron. "Don't laugh at me," he cried. "I'd rather be dead than lose my arm. I'll give you everything I own, but you've got to promise me you'll not let him do it."

Ignoring her wet apron, Dominique grasped Sean's right hand in both of hers and leaned close. If the inflammation in his shoulder spread, amputating his arm would never save him. He was too weak to survive the procedure even if it would and she knew Dr. Perry would never put him through such an agonizing ordeal when it would surely kill him.

"Listen to me," she urged calmly. "You're so tired you're not thinking clearly, and what you need is rest. You needn't promise me anything to watch over you. I want to do it. Now, my poultices can only do so much. You've got to do the rest by getting enough sleep so your body can heal itself. I won't let anyone harm you while you're asleep.

"I'll fetch some more tea, and then some laudanum so that you can finally get to sleep. I can't bear to see you in so much pain, Sean. Take it for me if you won't do it for yourself."

Sean had been healthy his whole life, and until now, never wounded. He knew he was behaving very badly, but he couldn't help it. He was sick and frightened and in so much pain he couldn't reason clearly. "You mustn't leave me."

Dominique reached out to stroke his hair. "It's nearly dawn, and I'm so tired, I can't stay awake much longer, but I'll sleep right here beside you. Now you must promise me to drink the tea and take the laudanum." When, after a lengthy pause, he finally responded with a slight nod, she went into the kitchen and found Stephen Perry discussing another critically ill patient with one of his mates.

"Would it be all right if I moved one of the extra cots next to Sean so I can get some sleep? He's terrified you're going to amputate his arm the minute he swallows the laudanum."

Worn out himself, Stephen had no patience for such foolishness. "I'm going to assume that's his fever talking rather than his sincere opinion of my professional competence, but frankly, his chances for survival have never been good. Sleep beside him if you like, but don't be surprised if he dies before morning."

Dominique stared at the surgeon with open disgust. "Are you still jealous of him?" she asked. "I want you to understand this, Doctor. I have absolutely no interest in you, and if we lost every single man in the camp I would still have no interest in you. Now, I intend to see that Sean O'Keefe not only survives the night, but makes a full recovery."

Badly embarrassed that she would make such a personal comment in front of a third party, Stephen shooed the mate out of the room. "That wasn't necessary," he argued. "I've done all I can for Sean, Just as I have for everyone else. As for you, well, I think I've been exceedingly generous when neither you nor your sister arrived with any letters of recommendation. For all I know, you could be spying for the Colonial army!"

Dominique refused to allow the terror that comment caused to show in her face. With forced calm, she refilled the cup with tea, poured out a small glass of laudanum, and replaced the cork in the tincture of opium with a careless slap. "If I were a spy," she announced clearly, "I'd be sleeping with Lord Cornwallis rather than trying to keep Sean alive. Now I'll thank you not to bother either of us before noon tomorrow."

She went back into the bedroom to care for Sean, then moved an empty cot so close to his she could hold his hand while she slept. "You must trust me," she whispered. "You'll soon be well." She heard him mumble something about trust, but too tired to care what it was, she closed her eyes and went to sleep.

Ten

Sean made such slight improvement during the day that Belle had scant hope Dominique would leave him that night. By evening she had given up on logical appeals and was reduced to shamelessly playing on her sister's emotions, but Dominique stubbornly refused to think past a few critical hours to what lay beyond. At her wits' end, Belle was near tears as they shared a hurried supper in their tent.

"I can't ask Falcon to keep taking the risk of entering camp," Belle implored. "If you won't leave with us tonight, then give me a date when you will and I'll tell him to return for us then."

Dominique tapped her fork against the side of her tin plate in an agitated rhythm. "Don't you think I'd like to have the assurance that we would be gone in a day or two? I just don't want to leave Sean, not knowing whether he lived or died. I'd like to say I'll be ready to go tomorrow, or the next night, but I don't want to make plans I can't keep."

Belle felt sick with disappointment and fear, for she had little hope Falcon would accept a delay calmly. How could he when she was so tortured over it? "Sean has friends who would recognize us," she worried aloud. "What if one of them appears? Do you think Sean would defend us if we were accused of being spies?"

"If he lives," Dominique replied, "I hope that he would."

"What if he doesn't? I want out of here *now*." Belle was so badly frightened even her skin tingled with dread. "I don't understand why Falcon and I don't mean more to you than Sean O'Keefe."

"You do!" Dominique cried, but the sadness in Belle's eyes was proof she wasn't believed. "I want you to leave with Falcon tonight, and I'll follow when I can."

Belle shook her head. "I won't even consider leaving you behind. How could you possibly explain my disappearance? Even if you said I'd run off with my lover—" She paused, stunned to realize how great a secret she had just revealed. Refusing to give Dominique the opportunity to ponder her error, she rushed on. "With me gone, your commitment to the British cause would no longer be trusted."

"Perhaps not, but you and Falcon would be safe." Dominique had caught Belle's inadvertent confession, but knowing how dearly she loved Falcon, let it pass. "I've got to get back to Sean." She rose, and then leaned down to kiss her sister's cheek.

"I want you and Falcon to go without a shred of guilt or worry. We'll all be together again soon." She ducked out of the tent before Belle could respond, but she had made the only choice her conscience would allow and had no regrets.

Belle's tears splashed onto her plate, but with a shuddering sob, she stilled them. She wished she had agreed to meet Falcon at the river because now there was no reason for him to come to her tent. She blamed herself for the mess they were all in, but that did not change it. Too nervous to sit still, and too frightened to walk around the camp, she followed Dominique up to the farmhouse and did what she could to ease the suffering of the injured. But it did little to help her prepare for what she feared would be another horrible scene with Falcon.

* * *

After midnight, Falcon left Nails tethered at the edge of the woods and made his way to his cousins' tent. When he found Belle fully clothed but alone, he began to swear. "Where's Dominique? Must I pull her from O'Keefe's arms?"

Belle grabbed his hand. "We can't talk here. Let's go."

Falcon led her back to Nails. Recognizing her scent, the horse greeted her with a soft snicker, and Belle ran her hand down his neck in a gentle caress. The handsome horse was another stirring reminder of all she had left behind in Virginia, and she feared her chances for returning home anytime soon were very poor.

"I wanted to be certain you were safe before I fetched your mounts," Falcon told her. "Now where's Dominique?"

Belle steeled herself for what would surely be a furious reaction. "I begged her to come with us, but she needs more time." Eager to embrace him, Belle moved close, but as she reached out, Falcon backed away and all she caught was a handful of swaying fringe.

Falcon swore a bitter oath as he pulled free of her grasp. "I've already been here too long, and so have you," he complained. "We must go tonight."

Badly disappointed that he could not spare a few seconds for the affection she craved, Belle dropped her arms to her sides and shrugged helplessly. "We can't take her by force."

"Why not? Tell her I need to speak with her. Bring her here and I won't have to strike her hard to knock her unconscious. By the time she awakes, we'll be a long way from Camden."

Belle knew Falcon would take care not to hurt Dominique badly, and she was tempted, but then thought of how angry she would be should Dominique separate her from Falcon in such an underhanded fashion. "No. Even if we don't agree with her, we ought to respect her wishes. Can you give us a week, and return for us then?"

"You'd rather stay with her than go with me?" Falcon asked with an accusing sneer.

"I have no choice!" Belle countered in a pleading whisper. "If I lcavc with you tonight, I'll never forgive myself should anything happen to Dominique. And if I stay, and lose you, I'll surely die of a broken heart. I'm only asking for a week, Falcon. If you can't come back for us then, we'll get away on our own."

Falcon stared down at Belle. The moonlight graced her features with an innocent sweetness, but she possessed a will of iron. He could not fault her courage, and admired it, but her plan was ridiculous. "You wouldn't travel three miles before another British patrol found you."

"Your father didn't find us and he must surely have searched. We didn't know there were British soldiers so far from Charleston, but now we do, and we won't make another careless mistake."

Sick of arguing, Falcon moved close and pulled Belle into his arms. He lowered his head to kiss her, but there was no tenderness in his manner that night. He tightened his hold on her arms and weighed his need to have her against her insulting loyalty to Dominique.

"Dominique chose Sean over you. Why can't you choose me?"

Belle rested her cheek against his shoulder and wished his words had been as soft as his buckskins. "If only it were that simple. If it were, I'd leave without looking back, but nothing is simple here. Clearly we ought not to be here in the first place, but it would be very wrong to leave Dominique behind. I beg you, please don't ask me to do it."

She did not seem to realize he could take her away by force as easily as he could have taken Dominique, but Falcon was loath to do it. He wanted her to come with him willingly. "A week," he finally agreed, "and I expect you to thank me for being so generous."

Relieved beyond measure that he had responded with understanding rather than hostility, Belle hugged him more tightly. "That seems fair," she murmured softly.

"Not here," Falcon replied. He released her only long enough to leap upon Nails, then pulled her right up behind him. He took her back to his camp where, safe from all intruders, they lost themselves in each other in what neither wanted to be the last time. When he brought her back to the edge of the forest at dawn, he lingered, watching her cross the field until she disappeared in the pearl gray mist.

Each time they parted, Belle pulled away a larger piece of his heart and he felt the resulting ache more deeply. He was also desperately sorry he had not shot Sean O'Keefe in the head. He wheeled Nails around in a tight circle, then rode away, intent upon killing as many of the British scourge as he possibly could before the week was out.

For three days, Sean hovered in a twilight of feverish pain, but on the fourth morning, he awoke before Dominique, and his head was clear. His shoulder throbbed with a dull ache, but he could stand it, and to his amazement, he actually felt hungry. His memories of the last week were no more than a hazy blur, but he did know Dominique had been with him the whole time.

Of all the women he had met since arriving in the Colonies, she was the very last one he would have expected to show such tender devotion. She had poured tea down his throat when he had been too ill to raise his head and she had applied poultices to his shoulder even after he had begged her to let him die in peace.

Even now, she lay stretched out on a cot pulled close to his. Her kerchief had slipped off while she slept, and Sean caught a flaxen curl and rubbed it between his finger and thumb. Soft as silk, the shiny strands spilled over his palm;

bored without her company, he gave a fierce yank to wake her.

"You're a poor nurse," he scolded. "Get me something to eat."

"Sean?" Startled by his rude summons, Dominique was so grateful to hear him speak in a rational tone she quickly pulled her hair from his hand and rolled off her cot. She leaned down to touch his forehead and was elated to find his skin cool. "Thank God, you're yourself again. I'll bring you some porridge."

Sean grimaced in disgust. "I'd rather have a slice of roast beef."

"I doubt I can find one, but—"

Sean's eyes narrowed to menacing slits. "You'll bring me exactly what I want, or I'll let everyone know who the Scott sisters really are."

Dominique's joy at finding Sean alert dissolved instantly. "I saved your life," she murmured numbly.

Amused by her consternation, the film of tears brightening the vivid blue of her eyes left him unmoved. "Thank you, but if you think that entitles you to some special consideration on my part, you are badly mistaken. Now fetch my breakfast, and be quick about it."

The vile taste of hatred rose in Dominique's throat, but she did not know whom she despised more, Sean for being such an arrogant ass or herself for expecting gratitude. Hurting Belle and Falcon by staying with him now seemed the very worst of follies, and she cursed under her breath all the way out to the kitchen.

One of the surgeon's mates was stirring a pot of porridge, but she knew better than to offer it to Sean. "Colonel O'Keefe is awake and asking for roast beef. I'll keep the lumps out of the porridge if you'll go find him some."

Perplexed by that order, the young man reluctantly handed over the long-handled spoon. "I'd be lucky to find him a piece of chicken," he replied, "but I'll see what I can do."

"Thank you." Dominique swirled the bubbling porridge. "The colonel will be ever so grateful." She gritted her teeth as she wondered what Sean would demand next. The fact that she could have spent even a second of her time praying for his recovery struck her as lunacy now. Why had she ever cared whether or not such a despicable swine succumbed to his wound? How could she have made such a horrible mistake?

Had she envied Belle's love for Falcon so badly that she had imagined there had been more to her brief acquaintance with Sean than had ever existed? How could she have been such a pathetic fool? Had she been betrayed by pride? Had she remembered Sean fondly when his only distinction was that he was the one man who had not fallen to his knees and begged for her affection?

She whipped the porridge around the pot, bashing the lumps and hating Sean more with each passing second. When Belle entered the kitchen, she blurted out her sorrow. "I've made a terrible mistake, and I owe you an apology."

Surprised to find her sister cooking, Belle gathered the stack of bowls and prepared to distribute their patients' breakfast. "I can't imagine why. You've worked harder than anyone here."

Dominique spoke through clenched teeth as she beat another lump from the porridge. "Yes, that's certainly true, but it was for all the wrong reasons. Sean's finally lucid, and the bastard's feeling well enough to treat me like his personal slave. How could I have been so stupid as to have cared whether he lived or died?"

Balancing the stack of empty bowls, Belle made a quick trip down the hall to peek into the bedroom. She saw Sean speaking with Dr. Perry, and hurried back to Dominique. "Isn't this good news?" she asked. "It should make our plans all the easier to carry out."

"I'm not sure I can survive three more days here."

"Good, then we'll have no arguments this time. Now start filling these bowls. We've patients waiting for breakfast."

"I've not even had time to comb my hair!"

"They'll be too hungry to care," Belle teased, but she could at last see their escape becoming a reality and could barely contain her joy.

What Dominique could barely contain was her disgust, both with herself and Sean O'Keefe. When the surgeon's mate returned with a hunk of beef which had already been simmered to make broth, Dominique slapped it on a plate, cut it into tiny pieces, and carried it to her obnoxious patient. "I've found breakfast for you," she greeted him sweetly, "but I'm afraid you may find the meat too tiring to consume."

"I'll be the judge of that," he replied. He had felt her constant presence when he had been too ill to see clearly, but after taking a bite of beef, he finally noted just how disheveled and fatigued she looked. "Haven't you another gown? It looks as though you've slept in that one."

"What an astute observation." Dominique guided another sliver of beef to his mouth. "You don't look your best, either, Colonel, but because you've been seriously ill, I'm making allowances for you. Because I've not left your bedside, I suggest you do the same for me."

Sean swallowed the stringy morsel and wondered if he would not have enjoyed the porridge more. "Don't push me, Dominique."

"Push you?" she asked. "I've no idea what you mean, Colonel. I've not had the opportunity to congratulate you on your promotion. I'm sure it was well deserved, but frankly, I fully expected a man with your remarkable abilities to have become a general by now."

Stung by her biting wit, Sean swore. "My God. You want me to turn you in, don't you?"

"It couldn't be any worse than waiting on you."

Dominique knew better than to taunt him, but she just couldn't keep still. She slid another piece of beef into his mouth and glanced out the window rather than watch him chew. The barren field did not provide an entertaining view, but it was still better than her surly companion's accusing stare.

"You'll continue to take excellent care of me," Sean whispered, "or I'll have Lieutenant Beck arrest Belle."

Dominique found it difficult to believe she had actually been terrified Falcon might slit this insufferable idiot's throat, when it now struck her as a great pity that he had not. "Belle is no more guilty of a crime than I am. If you betrayed her, would you be able to look yourself in the mirror when you shave?"

Sean swallowed and smiled. "Easily."

Dominique jabbed her fork into the next bite, but as she steered it toward Sean's mouth, he caught her wrist. "Am I going too fast?"

Sean hated being trapped flat on his back, but he was not about to accept Dominique's insolence. "No, on the contrary, you're too slow. Make more effort to please me, Miss Scott, or I'll make you very, very sorry."

"You already have," Dominique assured him. He glared at her, but after a couple more bites, shook his head and closed his eyes. "I ought to change your bandage," she said, although it would be difficult to restrain the impulse to pour salt in his wound.

"Later," Sean mumbled, and worn out by the slight exertion eating required, he drifted off to sleep.

Dominique waited a moment, then realized he wouldn't bother her for another hour or two. Even knowing it was stupid to bait him, she thought it was what he deserved. She did not want to trap Belle with her tongue, however, and prayed for the patience to remain civil.

She heated water and took it to her tent to wash her hair and bathe. The day was already hot, and she wished for one of the pretty summer gowns she had at home. Her aunt's dress was worn, if not yet threadbare, and she was sick of wearing it. Having no choice, she pulled it on over clean lingerie and stepped outside the tent to dry her hair in the sun. Before long, Sergeant Danby appeared. They had exchanged a wave a time or two in passing, but Dominique had not spoken with the earnest young man since their arrival in Camden.

"We'll be moving out in a day or two," he said, as he walked up to her. "Not that you and your sister will miss us much, but, well, I will miss you."

"Why, Sergeant, what a sweet thing to say. Do you expect another battle soon?" Too late, Dominique realized she ought not to have asked. Lord knew, she and Belle had no way to pass on any vital information that might come their way, but she did not want to be accused of collecting it.

Danby scuffed the toe of his boot in the dirt. "We're going up the Wateree River to invade North Carolina, but so many men are down with the fever I doubt we'll be ready to fight any time soon."

Dominique felt her heart lurch, for if Cornwallis's troops were victorious in North Carolina, they would surely march right on into Virginia. She shook her head and pretended to have more interest in her damp curls than his announcement. "Both my sister and I have appreciated your kindness, Sergeant. We'll pray for your safety."

Never having dreamed she would include him in her prayers, Thomas Danby's smile spread over his face with the ease of butter on a hot muffin. "Thank you. I sure wouldn't mind getting wounded if I could have you for a nurse."

Dominique startled the young man with a quick kiss on the cheek. "You just concentrate on staying healthy, Sergeant."

Thomas began to shuffle backwards, his whole face lit

with a scarlet blush. "I'll pray for you, too, Miss Scott, and maybe we'll see each other again."

Dominique smiled and waved, then rushed back into her tent. She had not come to Camden to spy. She and Belle had not even wanted to visit the town, let alone care for British wounded there. Falcon wouldn't be back for three days, but when he did arrive, she would insist Belle relay Sergeant Danby's news. The Colonial militia might already have deduced Cornwallis's plans, and it might be too late to warn them if they were unaware of them, but she could not simply pretend she had not heard what she had.

Afraid she had left Sean unattended for too long, she coiled her curls atop her head and covered them with her kerchief. She knotted her apron at her waist, and ready for work, reentered the farmhouse. She did not dare tell Belle what she had learned while anyone else could overhear her reaction, but holding in another secret merely added an additional layer to her terror.

Sean was still asleep, and she sat down to write a letter for one of the young men who had been wounded in the chest. If not showing rapid improvement, he was at least holding his own; she was pleased to be able to help him describe his injuries for his family, but refused to allow him to discount them as minor. He was too weak to argue, but as they discussed how best to reveal the truth, she noticed Sean was awake and watching them. Ignoring his silent summons, she did not rush the dictation but completed it at a leisurely pace, then handed the letter to one of the surgeon's mates to include with those being sent home to England. Only then did she swing by Sean's cot with a cup of willow bark tea.

Shoving her cot aside, she pulled up a chair and continued in the same bold tone as she had used when she'd left him. "You've lost weight, and I'm afraid food is in such short supply here that I won't be able to find you more beef. There's some bean soup simmering on the stove, though. Do you feel hungry again?"

She kept her attention focused on the cup rather than Sean's face as she gave him the tea, but he wasn't as docile as the other patients. They would swallow whatever she brought them, while he might easily take a perverse delight in spitting everything she served him right back out into her apron. She held her breath until he sipped the drink without protest.

"I want out of here," he murmured.

"Nothing would please me more than to see you leave," Dominique assured him, "but you're far too weak to make any travel plans."

"Yes. I know. That's why you're going to make them for me."

Dominique sat back and gripped the tin cup with both hands. "I'm sure Dr. Perry would be far more helpful in that regard."

Sean tried to flex his left arm and winced when the pain tore all the way to his toes. He needed a long moment to catch his breath. "My arm's useless, and I'm no good to anyone like this."

"You weren't expected to live," Dominique confided softly. "Give your body time to heal. It's much too soon to regard yourself as an invalid. Would you like to send a letter to your family, or perhaps you now have a wife?"

Sean's gaze darkened slightly, but he responded, if reluctantly. "I've no family, nor a wife, but there is a woman I've missed."

Willing to take dictation for an entire novel if it would distract him from issuing vile threats, Dominique excused herself to fetch more paper, pen, and ink. When she returned to her chair at his bedside, she crossed her legs and propped a Bible, the only book handy, on her lap. It made a convenient, if unconventional, desk, and she set the small jar of ink on the windowsill.

Even seated right beside the window, she didn't feel a hint of breeze, but it was her companion, not the heat, which was the main source of her discomfort. The sheet covering Sean had slipped nearly to his waist, but she had seen so many bare chests of late, it didn't strike her as immodest. Dark curls spread over his chest and nipples, but narrowed to a thin line as they reached his flat belly. The folds in the wrinkled sheet hid his navel, but she had seen him nude the night he had been brought to the hospital, and several times since. She had not forgotten a single detail of his well-muscled frame, either.

Believing the fact that Sean was such a handsome man had gotten her into her current predicament was enough to still her thoughts before they turned erotic, but when she finally met Sean's gaze, his sly smile made her wonder what he had been thinking. His beard grew low on his cheeks, and she no longer found it unattractive despite his lack of humanity.

"Well, what's her name?" she asked, and dipped her pen into the ink.

"Just begin with, My darling."

Dominique nodded, then paused with her pen in midair. "First, I need to say you're dictating the letter as I'm assuming she'll immediately know the handwriting isn't yours."

Sean frowned slightly. "No. I'm afraid I've been rather lax in my correspondence, and I've never written to her." When Dominique shot him a disapproving glance, he turned surly. "I've been occupied with fighting a war. Not that I need to excuse my behavior to you. Now just write and don't criticize a single word."

Dominique raised her brows. "I haven't said a thing."

"Well, don't give me that look again. I feel guilty enough without your adding to it."

"That's difficult to imagine." Still believing an explanation was necessary, Dominique began by identifying herself as a field hospital volunteer, and then on the next line, wrote his salutation. "Then what?"

"Will she believe me if I say I've been thinking of her, even if I haven't written?"

While Dominique had offered to transcribe his letter, she had not expected to have to help him compose it and the hint of doubt in his voice prompted a shrug. "Probably. If she loves you, she'll be inclined to believe anything you say."

"How can you be so certain?"

Dominique knew he was far too clever a man to ask such a foolish question, but gave him an answer anyway. "Perhaps you've forgotten, but I'm also a woman, and I know just how easily we can be misled." She smiled knowingly and hoped he would take her remark as a not-at-all-subtle reminder of just how blatantly he had lied to her. "I'd suggest that you speak from the heart, but I doubt that you have one."

Sean reached over and laid his hand on her knee.

Dominique pushed it away, but he put it right back. "What do you think you're doing?"

"Whatever I please," he cautioned. "Should I call Lieutenant Beck to help me?"

Sean was much too weak to demand more than a feeble grasp of her thigh, but Dominique could very easily imagine him sending that same wandering hand up under her skirt, or down her bodice. Worse yet, he might insist she perform intimate favors for him. Sickened, she had difficulty catching her breath, but her choices were clear. She could either stop him now and accept the consequences, or give in inch by inch until there was nothing left of her soul.

"Take your hand off me," she ordered so softly only Sean could hear.

Defying her, Sean dug his fingers into her thigh, but then just as quickly he released her and laid his hand on his chest. He stared up at her, his glance hard and the curve of his well-shaped lips turning cruel. "Tonight," he promised, "and don't try and give me laudanum to make me forget."

Dominique decided right then that no matter how adoring he made his letter sound, she would add a footnote to alert the poor object of his fickle affections to the fact that he was a thoroughly unprincipled rogue. "I can scarcely wait," she replied, clearly unenthused. "Now let's finish this up. Your bandage needs to be changed."

"Do you provide all the men with such affectionate care?"

"Every last one. Now what is it you want to say?"

"Hmm. It's difficult to think about her when your beauty is so distracting."

Dominique knew she was too thin, and her once-beautiful complexion was splashed with freckles. Beauty, indeed! She sat back in her chair. "I had this absurd notion that you would have changed—for the better, of course. If this unfortunate woman knows you're a rake, then say anything to fill the page. If, by some remarkable happenstance, she believes you to be an honorable man, then you would do her a great service by not writing to her at all."

Sean slid his hand down under his sheet. "She knows me exceedingly well."

"Ah, she's your mistress. Why didn't you say so?"

"Would it matter?"

"Of course. You should be completely honest with her."

Sean almost laughed, but caught himself before he took too deep a breath and caused himself more pain. "It would be a novel approach. She should enjoy that for a change. All right. Let's say that I've been shot, and may become a hopeless cripple."

Exasperated with him, Dominique sighed deeply. "Can't you even approach the truth at a closer range?"

"Can't you?" Sean challenged. "Look at me! I'm too weak to leave this cot. There's not much I can do, except—"

He closed his eyes and left the sentence hanging. It took a moment, but Dominique finally noticed he was moving his hand beneath the sheet. "What is it you're doing?" she hissed.

Sean's expression had turned dreamy as he looked up. "I want to be certain I can still please her."

"This is no time for such an experiment!" Dominique was smart enough not to slide her hand down his arm to his hand where he would undoubtedly catch hold of her fingers and make her finish the job. Instead she grabbed his elbow to bring his hand back to her thigh. "There. Hold onto me if you must grab something. Now we've got to have more than, 'My darling'."

"I was so close," Sean complained sadly, but then he began to knead her thigh. "God, you feel so good."

Dominique looked around quickly to make certain the other patients in the room hadn't caught the husky note of desire in Sean's voice. Fortunately, the afternoon was so warm they were all dozing. "I don't believe you really want to write to this woman."

"Oh, but I do. Let's just say that I've been shot, but not even the specter of death could erase her lovely face from my memory."

"Really? That's rather good, Sean. She should be deeply flattered." Dominique's handwriting was replete with graceful feminine swirls, but she took special care to make each word flow with gently curving strokes. "That's a promising beginning," she added, then cautioned herself to remember not a single word would be sincere.

"Good." Sean rubbed his thumb in a small circle on her thigh. "We've been apart far too long, but I've not forgotten the honeyed-sweetness of her kiss, nor—"

"Just a minute, don't get ahead of me." At first outraged by his possessive hold on her leg, Dominique was finding his more gentle touch increasingly difficult to ignore. She doubled her efforts to produce beautiful writing, and completed his second sentence. "Yes, and . . . ?"

Sean's voice was still seductive. "How the sunlight gifts her fair curls with a silvery glow."

"She's blond? I thought you preferred redheads," Dominique remarked without glancing his way.

"That was a long time ago, Dominique. A great deal has happened since then."

"None of it good, I imagine." Dominique reviewed what he had dictated thus far. "You've praised her lovely face, honeyed kiss, and fair curls. What about her figure? Is she such a voluptuous woman you dare not refer to it?"

"No. She's as slender as a moonbeam."

"Why, Sean, that's truly poetic." Dominique added the phrase to the letter. His hand was still now, merely resting on her thigh, but she felt the heat of his touch all the way through her faded gown and layers of petticoats. It was an effort not to squirm out of his reach, but she did not want him pleasuring himself again, which she was certain he had done merely to embarrass her. Her emotions in a riotous jumble, she had to force herself to meet his glance.

"If you're tired, we can finish this later," she offered.

"No. I want to complete it now. Just tell her how sorry I am that we met at such an inopportune time, but now I hope love can be our only concern."

His tone was surprisingly gentle, and for a brief instant Dominique wondered if perhaps he had truly fallen in love. Just as quickly, she reminded herself that he was undoubtedly manipulating the poor woman's feelings as blatantly as he had her own. "Do you feel up to signing it?" she asked.

"I can try."

Dominique was glad to have an excuse to shift her position, and give him something else to do with his hand. She dipped the pen in the ink, handed it to him, and turned the Bible and sheet of stationery toward him. "Hurry, before the ink begins to drip."

"Don't be so impatient. First I want to read what you've written."

"You don't trust me to write exactly what you said?" Dominique easily conveyed her shock, although she had not forgotten the footnote she intended to add.

Sean swore softly, then shot her a skeptical glance. He read the note through quickly, then signed his first name with deliberate care. Worn out by the effort, he closed his eyes as soon as he had handed her back the pen. "There's no need to address an envelope. I meant it for you."

Unable to decide if she was flattered or appalled, Dominique sat back in her chair and simply stared at him. She had transcribed the love letter without letting herself really feel the words. Not that she would have been jealous of his tender thoughts for another woman, but simply because he infuriated her so. Now she did not know what to believe. She was sorely tempted to tear up the letter and throw it at him, but something stayed her hand.

"You mentioned travel plans?" she asked hesitantly.

Sean opened his eyes and smiled. "Yes. With only one good arm, I'm no use to the army, so you're going to invite me to go home with you. It will be good to see Ian again."

"Take you home!" Dominique shouted so loudly she woke half the room. "No. That's too much to ask."

Sean cocked a brow. "You know better than to cross me, Dominique." He dropped his voice so the other patients could not overhear. "Either you take me home, or Belle is going to spend a very ugly afternoon with Lieutenant Beck."

Not daring to doubt him, a wave of revulsion washed through Dominique, but as she nodded, she wondered if there were a name foul enough to describe a man who would offer a love letter in one breath and such a vile threat in the next.

Eleven

"I will not be that bastard's whore!" Dominique fumed n a desperate whisper. "How can he even imagine that I vould take him home to Williamsburg? What sort of lunacy s that? Not that there aren't enough Loyalists to keep him entertained, but hasn't the very real prospect that I'll kill 1im on the way even occurred to him?"

Belle was equally mystified by Sean's demand. "It's imoossible to say what might be going on in that rodent's mind," she replied, "but you won't have to kill him. Falcon will. You must humor Sean. Make him think you're terrified, and doing his bidding out of fear alone. Then as soon as we leave here, everything will change and he'll become our prisoner."

Dominique had yet to tell Belle about the love letter. It had probably been Sean's insipid idea of humor but she could not bring herself to share it. That she could still harbor a shred of feeling for the man after the demeaning way he had threatened her was pathetic, and she would endeavor to overcome it.

She sank down on her cot and slumped forward. "You were right about Sean. He's the only man who wasn't so eager to win my favors that he would not only fawn all over me, but surrender the last particle of his dignity for a few minutes of my time. I always tried to be gracious, Belle, but the constant adoration became awfully tiresome."

While her sister appeared to be sincerely pained by the memory of the attention she had received, Belle thought she was overlooking an important factor. She sat down opposite her on her own cot. "You flirted outrageously, Dominique, so you ought not to complain when your ploy were effective. What did you expect? If you throw a baited hook into the river, you'll surely catch a fish."

Dominique could not argue with Belle's perceptive comment. As soon as her figure had taken on womanly curves she had been shamelessly eager for attention from men. She had gotten it, too. It had been thrilling at first, but eventually she had grown hungry for something more than sloppy kisses and halting declarations of love.

"Yes," she admitted softly. "I know I have only myself to blame, but still—"

Belle waited, and when Dominique was too troubled to continue, she prompted her. "You were attracted to Sean because he was a challenge. But that was years ago. Now he's the enemy, and a dangerous one at that. Don't tell me you still want him."

Dominique looked up, her glance filled with pain. "That would be stupid, wouldn't it? It's so easy to despise what he is, or his damnable threats, but there's something so compelling about him that I can't help but wish he were a gentleman instead of the loathsome rogue he is."

Belle thought of the way Falcon's thick, ebony hair streamed out in the wind when he urged Nails into a gallop. She was positive she would love Falcon even if he were bald, but she could not deny how much she loved his hair. "It's very difficult to separate a man's personality from his looks, isn't it? Even when Falcon is at his worst, I can't help but think how handsome he is. Wild and stubborn, he is so much a part of me there are times I feel as though there is only one of us, living in two bodies. Do you feel that way about Sean?"

Dominique shook her head, for she was exquisitely aware

of the important differences that separated them. "Perhaps we were simply born at the wrong time," she mused sadly. "If the colonies had not wanted to be independent, no, needed to be free, then perhaps we could have met and fallen in love without either of us having to compromise our ideals."

"If you don't want Sean dead, you better say so now, because if I tell Falcon that you do, he won't live long."

Dominique put her fingers to her temples. "We still have three days, and I've something else for you to tell Falcon." She recounted her conversation with Sergeant Danby. "The troops may have already started marching north, and then it will be plain they're headed for Charlotte, but if not, a few days warning may save some lives, if not many."

Belle nodded. "So we've become spies after all."

Dominique had had several hours to ponder their fate, and fully shared her sister's dismay. "I can't believe how greatly we've changed, or rather, I've changed. You've always been far more serious in your outlook on life. I was the frivolous one. Well, no more. The journey was too hard, and we've seen too much suffering since we arrived for me to ever return home and be content to arrange pretty bouquets all morning and flirt away the afternoons. Assuming any men survive this wretched war to flirt."

"The end of the war may be a year or more away. What are you going to do about tonight?"

Dominique recalled the warmth of Sean's touch and felt only shame. "I'll stay with Sean again. He's too weak to rape me, and he will be for a good long while, so I'll be safe in that respect."

Belle pulled off her kerchief and shook out her hair. "And in others?"

That was the real question. Dominique offered only a sad smile. "A snake fascinates his prey, and that's all Sean O'Keefe is: a handsome viper. I'm going to remind myself of that comparison as often as it takes to order his death without a twinge of regret."

"It's a shame you worked so hard to save him."

"Yes. Isn't it? Mother always insisted it was God who worked the miracles, not the herbs. I just don't understand why God would want a man so totally devoid of character kept alive. Can you?"

"I won't even pretend to understand why good men die, while those with vile natures survive. I would like to believe the world is fair, but it isn't. This war is proof of that."

Dominique rose with a weary stretch. "I need to get back to Sean. After all, the sooner I make him well, the sooner we can leave for home." She ducked out of the tent and walked back to the farmhouse. She had had quite enough for one day, and hoped Sean had already fallen asleep, but he was awake, and waiting for her.

Sean was clutching a bowl of blackberries. "I was afraid you'd gotten lost. From now on, you'll take your meals here with me."

Dominique sat down beside him. "I don't want to leave Belle all alone."

"She'll find other company soon enough." He handed her the bowl. "Some of the men went out to gather berries. I saved these for you."

Dominique loved blackberries, but she did not want to take anything from Sean. "No, please. You eat them." She plucked one off the top and guided it to his mouth. He took it, and licked his lips.

"I've already had some," he claimed. "You must eat a few before I'll take another."

Easily succumbing to that demand, Dominique popped a plump berry into her mouth. It was juicy and sweet, exactly like those growing near home. "I wish we had some cream," she remarked wistfully.

"I asked for some, and was told the farmer's cows had

all been slaughtered for beef. There should be plenty of cream at your house, though, shouldn't there?"

Dominique leaned forward with another berry, and Sean opened his mouth wide. As soon as she had dropped in the berry, he caught her wrist and sucked her index finger into his mouth. She tried to pull away, but he held on in a reckless hint of what he would taste later on. Warm and wet, the sensation was not at all unpleasant, but she refused to provide even a glimpse of her true feelings. She simply stared at him coldly until he finally released her.

"You taste better than the berries," he whispered. "I'd like to drip the juice down between your breasts, and then lick it up."

Appalled by that request, Dominique sat back. She had known other men who were adept at flirting, but none had had Sean's ribald tastes. Or at least they had not taken such obvious pride in declaring them. "When are you going to consider what *I* want? Do you think you could practice being a gentleman for a few days at least? I really believe it would do you good."

"Perhaps, but it wouldn't be nearly as enjoyable. Did you read my letter to Belle?" He saw the answer in Dominique's startled expression and flashed a mocking grin. "I'm so pleased you consider it too precious to share."

"I burned it," Dominique lied.

"You did not," Sean countered, "and we both know why."

Unwilling to play the attentive nurse, Dominique placed the bowl of blackberries back in his hand. "Feed yourself. The exercise will be good for you." She folded her arms across her bosom and looked out the window. The setting sun bathed the scarred fields with burnished gold, but there would be no fall harvest. She wondered how wide a swath of desolation the British had cut, and prayed they would never touch her family's plantation. She was sickened by the thought of Lord Cornwallis using the beautiful Barclay home as his headquarters, as he had Mr. Kershaw's.

Sean studied the play of golden light warming Dominique's sweet features and saw a fierce determination he had previously missed. "Dominique? Why is it so difficult for you to admit that you care for me?"

Dominique did not glance his way. "Eat your berries."

"They're for you, remember?"

"Threats and presents? Do you find that an effective combination with other women?"

Sean toyed briefly with the idea of swearing there had been no other women since he had last seen her, but too many years had passed for her to believe him. There had been a great many women, in fact. Lovely creatures not unlike her and Belle, then later, pretty young widows he had done his utmost to console. Some he had actually missed when he had received orders to move on, but none had lingered in his mind like a haunting perfume the way Dominique had.

"I should have mentioned your voice in that letter," he said. "You speak all the time in the husky tones other women only produce in the throes of passion. It's one of the most enchanting things about you. I would love to hear you sing."

Men often remarked on her voice, but the low, breathless quality was entirely natural. Even as a child, she possessed a woman's voice. "The only time I dare sing is in church when my voice blends with everyone else's. Otherwise, it's simply a disappointment."

"It couldn't be." Sean would have liked to continue the verbal sparring for hours, but he could barely keep his eyes open. "Will you please take this bowl? I don't want to spill the berries when the other men would like them."

That was such a polite request, that Dominique took the bowl and carried it out to the kitchen. Dr. Perry helped himself to a handful the instant she set it on the table. She had expected him to comment on Sean's good progress, but he seemed unconcerned about his patient's health.

"Be careful," he warned. "It's clear you and Colonel O'Keefe are close, but displays of affection are totally inappropriate in this setting. I realize some of my patients would find amorous antics entertaining, but I most definitely would not. In fact, the men are all doing so well here, I believe your talents will be of more use to the men down with fever. Beginning tomorrow, the only time you'll need to be here in the farmhouse is when you brew your herbal remedies."

Dominique had no hope of convincing Sean she was needed elsewhere, and had to refuse a change in assignment. "I'm unwilling to abandon Sean while he's so weak. If he's neglected, we could still lose him."

Stephen Perry thought he had made himself clear. He raised his voice slightly to make his order more emphatic. "You must have misunderstood me, Miss Scott. You'll do as I say here, or I'll have to insist that you and your sister leave."

Dominique smiled to herself. Nothing would please her more than to be ejected from Camden, but again, she knew Sean would never allow it. "I believe Colonel O'Keefe outranks you, Doctor. That means I'll have to stay here where I can look after his needs. Please discuss the matter with him if you like, but we both know what the outcome will be."

Leaving the physician sputtering in astonishment, Dominique returned to the bedroom. Sean's eyes were closed, but he sensed her presence and looked up. "Are you in much pain?" she asked. "I'll fetch you some laudanum if you are."

"You'll be enough."

Dominique sat down and covered a wide yawn. "I doubt it. I'm too tired to do more than sleep."

"So am I. Scoot your cot next to mine again so I can hold your hand." When Dominique didn't obey immediately, Sean was annoyed but chose not to make his request an order. "When we first met, you were such a delightful surprise. I'd come to your family's plantation searching for the scoundrels who were circulating those damnable pamphlets ridiculing the king. Then you came to the door, and I couldn't even remember what had brought me there. You can tell me now. It was your family that was behind the pamphlets, wasn't it?"

Indeed it had been, but Dominique spoke the lie without a pause. "Of course not. We were merely raising tobacco that spring. You have a very suspicious nature, Colonel."

"Sean."

Dominique glanced out the window. He had been given the choice location because of his rank, but she was the one who constantly sought the view. The sun had already set, leaving only a pale pink glow in the west. Without the light, the Wateree River formed a dark border at the edge of the fields. The British troops would follow it up past Wateree Lake, then the Catawba River would lead them on toward Charlotte.

"And you are secretive," Sean finally added.

Dominique turned back toward him. "You know all my secrets, Sean."

She was very beautiful, and in the fading light her expression held the magnificent sadness of a Renaissance madonna. "I know nothing at all," he told her. "You could have fallen in love, married, had children, been widowed. A great deal may have happened to you these past few years."

"I've had neither husband nor children," she confided softly. "My life has simply stood still since the war began. I was eager to change that sorry fact. That's why I'm here."

"No. That's not why you're here at all." Sean's glance was warmly admiring. "You're here to be with me. Now don't make me wait a moment longer. Move your cot close so I can hold you."

Fate had given their journey such a dangerous detour,

Dominique wondered if he could be right. If so, being with him was an apt punishment for the years she had wasted at home doing little more than being pretty. She got up to move the chair aside and repositioned her cot alongside his. When she stretched out on it, he slipped his arm under her shoulders to force her to rest her cheek on his bare chest. She resisted briefly, but the warmth of his skin against hers was so pleasant, she relaxed and draped her arm across him. He was so thin, her fingers fit between his ribs.

She knew she ought to tell him that Dr. Perry wanted her to tend other men, but his reaction was sure to be a poor one, and she did not want to overtax his strength. Sean pulled off her kerchief and wound his fingers in her curls. His touch was gentle, and for the moment, she felt safe in his arms. It was surely a trick, though, and tomorrow he would undoubtedly renew his threats. But for tonight at least, she was content to sleep in his arms.

The next morning, Sean was determined to leave his cot. "If you won't help me, then I'll find one of the surgeons' mates who will."

After waking, Dominique had left him only long enough to clean up as best she could in her tent. The fact that he'd come up with such a stupid idea in the few minutes he had spent alone astounded her. "You've lost too much blood, Sean. You'll surely faint, and if the mate doesn't catch you in time, you might break your one good arm in the fall. Then where would you be?"

Sean's eyes narrowed. "I am not a child and I'll not have you fussing over me like a doting mother."

"Fine. Dr. Perry wants me to tend the men stricken with fever and I'll begin right now."

As she turned away, Sean reached out to grab hold of her skirt. He gave it a good yank to pull her back to him, but then had to struggle to catch his breath. "God, how I hate this," he moaned. He closed his eyes for a moment, and then gave in. "Perhaps you're right and I am too weak to stand, but that doesn't mean I couldn't lie in the back of a wagon and reach Williamsburg safely."

Dominique leaned back against the windowsill as she considered his request. She doubted Falcon would accept another delay in their escape from Camden, and if she and Belle left with Sean, they would have a safe passage past whatever British troops they encountered in the area. If they let Sean live more than an hour to two.

She had awakened several times during the night to find his arm still wrapped around her, She had then seen his need to be near her as pitiful rather than repugnant and had wondered if perhaps his vicious streak weren't masking the fear that he truly would be left a cripple. She chided herself not to make excuses for the snake, and straightened up.

"Your troops brought you here in a ramshackle old wagon that's still in the yard. Belle and I have mounts that can pull it, but it won't be an easy journey, and I'd like you to be stronger before we begin." Knowing he would challenge whatever day she chose, she offered one in hopes of winning with a compromise. "Another week should do it."

Sean actually winced. "No, I can't wait nearly that long."

Dominique was such an accomplished actress, her dismay was completely convincing. "Oh, Sean, really." She shook her head, and then felt his forehead to make certain his fever hadn't returned. "I'll need time to gather what provisions I can, and make certain the wagon won't disintegrate beneath us before we've traveled ten miles. You'll have to request a leave to recuperate in Virginia, and that might not be readily approved. Let's give ourselves three days to prepare, then if you feel up to it, we'll go."

Sean tried to sit up, but was overwhelmed by a sick, rolling dizziness that left him gasping for breath. Suddenly the prospect of being jostled this way and that in the back of a wagon was anything but appealing. "Three days it is then," he agreed, hoping he would feel a whole lot better by then. "Bring me some of the porridge. It's undoubtedly tasteless, but it will at least be filling and my body won't know the difference."

"I'll add a little honey. Would you like that?"

Sean caught her hand and kissed her fingertips. "Yes. Send for Lieutenant Beck. I want to know why they haven't found the bastard who shot me."

Dominique pulled her hand from his and tried not to let him see how frightened she was by his request. "Is that all you want of him?" she asked.

At first puzzled by her question, Sean soon grasped the cause of her apprehension. "Yes," he assured her, but his smile became a self-satisfied smirk. "I'll need him to help me get ready to go. Your secret's safe, for the time being at least."

Dominique wasn't sure if it was the golden glint in his eyes or the new growth of beard, but his resemblance to the Devil had become more pronounced with each passing day. Even so, she could not stifle a sarcastic reply. "You are too generous."

"Yes. I am, but you'll have ample opportunity to repay me."

Dominique knew it was not in the way he intended, but she would definitely see that he got what he deserved.

Two nights later, Belle met Falcon at the edge of the woods. "We're leaving tomorrow morning," she rushed to explain before he could again ask why Dominique wasn't with her. She described how they were going to hitch their prize mares to an old wagon, and ride right out of Camden in full view of everyone. He listened attentively until she mentioned Sean O'Keefe would be their passenger and then she had to clap her hand over his mouth to silence a ringing war whoop.

"Please," she implored him. "Dominique's feelings about Sean are ambivalent at best. One minute she's muttering curses, and in the next weeping as she recounts some sweet gesture he's made. I honestly don't know if they are falling in love or manipulating each other as shamelessly as they did years ago."

Belle paused to give Falcon a quick kiss which he eagerly turned into a lengthy exchange. "Wait," she begged. "There's something else. Cornwallis is preparing to invade North Carolina. Is there some way to warn the people of Charlotte that he's coming?"

Falcon wrapped his arms around Belle's waist and lifted her clear off her feet. "I'm not the only man watching this camp, and the increased activity has already been noted. I never asked you to spy for us, Belle, and I never would, but thank you for the information. Now come with me. I can wait no longer to have you again."

Belle had no desire to play coy, but she was frightened for him. "O'Keefe can't understand why you haven't been caught. He knows only that you ride a sorrel horse, and if you were captured near Camden—"

Falcon stilled her warning with another slow, deep kiss. "I am as elusive as the wind, and the British will never catch me. I'll ride ahead of you in the morning and join you only when it's safe. You'll be able to feel me watching you, though, and know I'm there." He took her hand and led her toward Nails. "Now let's not waste any more of tonight."

Belle waited for him to mount the handsome horse, then he pulled her up behind him. She wrapped her arms around his waist as they rode into the heart of the forest. His hair was tied at his nape and out of her way as she leaned close to whisper. "Promise me you'll leave Nails at home and take another horse when you leave. He's brought you such good luck thus far, but you're being hunted because of him. You mustn't let your pride in him be your undoing."

Falcon considered her warning with the seriousness it deserved, but Nails was a stallion like no other, and not simply because of his gorgeous golden-red hide. His first impulse was to refuse, but Belle was clinging to him so tightly, he could feel her trembling with fear and he could not abide that.

"You refused to become my wife, Belle. How can you worry like one?"

"Wife or not, I can't help but worry about you. Whenever you've been away, I've prayed for you constantly."

That Belle had been devoted to him did not surprise Falcon, but he was ashamed not to have known it long ago. "Do not stop now," he teased. A tap of his heels quickened Nails's pace, and they soon arrived at his camp. He had been away since he had last been with Belle, but he found the small clearing again easily. The ground was softened with a thick carpet of leaves, and a stream that flowed into the Wateree River provided clear, sweet water. It was a fine home for him, but as he slid down from his stallion's back and reached up for Belle, he realized it was no place for her.

"I'll build you as fine a house as Christian built for Liana," he promised as he set her on her feet. "Just as soon as the war is over."

"I'd not even thought of a house." Belle turned and twisted her hair atop her head to keep the long curls out of his way.

Responding to her unspoken invitation, Falcon quickly loosened the laces running up the back of her bodice. "We can't sleep in the forest forever."

When he stepped back, Belle shrugged off her gown, then turned to help him peel off his shirt. She laid her palms on his chest and felt his heart beating far more steadily than her own. "Why not? Then we can see the stars and hear the song of the river, or merely the playful melody of a stream like the one here."

"You are very easy to please," Falcon murmured against her throat.

"No, sir. I am not. You're the only man I've ever allowed to try."

Falcon chuckled with the joy of that thought. She had not bothered to wear petticoats or drawers and once she had stepped out of her chemise, she was nude. He yanked off his moccasins and pants, then ran his fingertips over the smooth swell of her breasts and teased the pale crests into taut buds. "I have pleased you, haven't I, Belle?"

"Always," Belle promised against his lips, and she was so lost in him she didn't see a single star overhead, or hear the musical trill of the stream. She pulled away the thong to free his hair and when he lowered her to the leaves, his sable mane brushed her face and breasts with a gentle tickle. She grabbed great handfuls to hold him, then arched up under him to press the whole length of her body against his.

Falcon slid over her and parted her legs with his knee. Rather than enter with a quick thrust, he dipped into her slowly, gently teasing her with soft, shallow strokes. Then, barely penetrating, he lay still to speak. "I am as much Seneca as white, and to the Seneca you became my wife the first time we were together like this. I would marry you in a hundred Christian ceremonies, but I want you to say yes to becoming my wife this way now."

Belle doubted he would have the strength to withdraw if she refused, but filled with an aching need to have all of him buried deep within her, she had no wish to deny his request. She wound her arms around his neck and ground her hips against his. "Yes," she murmured before luring him into a fevered kiss that put an end to all need for spoken promises. She had always been his, but now he was also hers and her spirits soared as she called him husband in her heart.

That he may have already given her a child was a glorious possibility, but if it had not happened, she prayed that it would now. They would make very handsome children together, but in her mind's eye, she saw them as dark and wild as Falcon. Conceived in a forest, born of love, she could wish no greater legacy for any child.

In that instant, Belle gave herself to Falcon so completely that as rapture fused their bodies into one, their spirits merged as well. It was perhaps the most perfect moment either would ever live, and parting afterward was agony.

While Belle crept back into camp, Dominique lay beside Sean, too distraught over what tomorrow might bring to join him in sleep. She had not sent any message to Falcon with her sister, and she knew it was cowardly to leave Sean's fate in the brave's hands. She could not recall ever feeling so confused. An impulsive person by nature, she had always relied upon intuition to guide her and it was failing her sadly.

She wanted to believe Sean was as torn as she, but feared that was merely wishful thinking. Even confined to a cot, he could be vicious, and yet, more frequently he allowed her a glimpse of a man who was both honest and kind. She knew being so weak had made him badly frightened, and that made his vile demands much easier not only to understand, but excuse.

He was a soldier, after all. What if her prediction proved wrong and he did not recover the use of his arm? He was bright and could support himself in other professions, but would he want to? She thought not. There were men who could flow with life's shifting currents, but she doubted Sean was one of them. He was simply too proud to bend.

He stirred slightly and she sat up, but when he didn't wake she eased back down beside him. She had told him Ian Scott had gone to England, but he had not seemed concerned about it. He would still have friends in Williamsburg, if he lived to get there. The possibility that he would not had been such a simple choice at first, but that night she had not been able to speak the words to Belle.

Tears filled her eyes for she did not know what to do. Sean O'Keefe could be an arrogant tyrant, or the most charming man she had ever met. She did not trust him, and often hated him, but did she really want him dead? Perhaps his only crime was being a British officer, but she knew as Falcon saw it, that was enough. The trouble was, it was not nearly enough for her.

There was no easy answer as to where loyalty to her family and the cause they all held dear should end and purely personal feeling begin but she continued to struggle to find that narrow line. All the while, her hand lay in Sean's, but her heart could not choose sides.

Twelve

Dominique fell into an exhausted sleep shortly before dawn, and soon after, Sean awakened her. Feeling thoroughly wretched in both body and spirit, she sat up slowly. The whole time she had been in Camden, she had been afraid for herself and Belle, but the journey home presented a whole new set of terrors. As she met Sean's taunting gaze, it took every ounce of her courage not to break down and weep uncontrollably.

His head propped on his right elbow, Sean watched with an amused smile as Dominique shoved wayward curls out of her eyes.

"Why were you so restless last night?" he asked. "Had I been able to get up and sleep elsewhere, I surely would have."

Dominique had not realized she had disturbed him. "I'm sorry. It's just the excitement of going home. Had I known I was bothering you, I would have gone to my tent." She stood on trembling legs and shook out her skirt so Sean would not notice her wobbling. "Next time I leave home, I'm going to take more clothes." Her kerchief was on the floor, and she leaned down to pick it up before slipping on her shoes.

"Please do," Sean agreed. "I'm as tired of looking at that wrinkled gown as you must be of wearing it. Go and get the wagon ready. Lieutenant Beck found a suit for me and I'll have one of the surgeons' mates help me dress."

"I don't know what happened to the uniform you were wearing when you were shot, but it was ruined. Perhaps it was burned."

"Well, good riddance. I certainly don't want bloodstained clothing as a souvenir," Sean scoffed. He pulled himself up into a sitting position, but kept his left arm cradled against his chest. He felt strong enough to leave, but just barely. He could not sit up long enough to eat an entire meal, not that he had been served anything worth eating, and he could not walk more than a few shaky steps on his own. He was making progress, however, even if it was dismal. He swallowed hard and refused to give in to the constant fear that he might never be as strong as he had been.

"We've not discussed payment," he mentioned without looking up.

From what Dominique had observed, Sean issued threats with a direct gaze to savor her reaction, but at other times, he displayed an uncharacteristic shyness. "Payment for what?" she asked. "You don't owe me anything."

"I owe you my life, which, as I recall, you were prompt to point out."

The other patients sharing the bedroom were waking with noisy yawns. Dominique had grown fond of them all, and meant to speak to each one before she left rather than merely waving good-bye to them from the doorway. "I came here hoping to save lives. There's no charge for yours."

Sean's head came up. "Are you calling me worthless?"

On another morning, Dominique would have had a clever riposte, but she was too sick at heart for amusing banter and simply shook her head. The color had returned to Sean's cheeks, but the protective way he held his left arm made it plain he was still experiencing considerable pain. "Do you really feel up to leaving today?" she asked fretfully, for *she* surely didn't.

Sean had just given her a fine opportunity to provide one of her stinging insults, and he was puzzled by her failure to do so. It was unlike her to skip a chance to defy him and he was amazed to discover he missed it. "Well, regardless of how little value you may assign my life, I fully expect to reward you for taking me to Williamsburg, but I know better than to pay you before we get there."

He was making yet another joke at her expense, and Dominique still failed to appreciate his humor until she gleaned a sudden insight into just how diabolically clever he truly was. He would have no one to back up his threats once they left Camden, so he had changed tactics and turned on the charm. Brutal one day, amiable the next, she damned him as a two-faced weasel.

"I must see about the wagon," she reminded him, and hurried away before her ravaged emotions betrayed her any further.

Belle was already up and dressed. Filled with the blissful memory of Falcon's embrace, she was eager to be on their way. She greeted Dominique warmly as she entered their tent. "I'm leaving what few herbs we have left with Dr. Perry. He seems rather sad to see us go, and perhaps they will be of some consolation."

Dominique slumped down on her cot. "I didn't sleep more than five minutes last night. Will you mind if I stretch out in the back of the wagon with Sean?"

Belle had already packed her satchel, and now secured the buckles. "There's gossip about the two of you already. Not that we care what anyone says about us here, but I'd rather you sat beside me. Hurry and get ready. It will be hot again today, and I want to travel as far as we possibly can in the cool of the morning."

Dominique nodded, and Belle went up to the farmhouse, but she did not understand how her sister could talk of travel when this would be the last journey Sean would ever take. Wearily, she pushed herself to her feet and fetched water to wash. Setting her mind on each task as it came. she packed her things; after a brief glance at their spare quarters to make certain nothing had been left behind, she slipped out of their tent for the last time. She helped Belle hitch their mares to the wagon and stow their saddles and bridles in the rear, then went with her to bid their patients farewell. She had never succeeded in thinking of them as the enemy, and even now saw only brave lads she could not condemn. She kissed each on the cheek as she said good-bye.

Sean's cot was empty, and she assumed he had been helped outside to wash and dress. She was grateful he had not had to rely on her for the chore, and in the next instant was saddened that he had not. Distracted, she confused two of her patients' names, but caught herself before she made the error aloud.

Dr. Perry waited until the sisters were ready to depart before he drew them into the kitchen. "Rebel bands are roaming the countryside preying on every Loyalist they can find. If the three of you are caught—"

Belle saw Dominique pale, but rebels themselves, they had already survived the only real threat to their safety and if they could ride out of a British camp unharmed, she was confident they would return home safely. "Does the colonel plan to wear his uniform?" she asked.

"He has resigned his commission," the physician replied, "and will be in civilian clothes. Not that that will save you if—"

"Dr. Perry, please," Dominique interrupted. "Our fate will be in God's hands, as it always has been. I know you mean well, but deliberately frightening us is cruel. I have enjoyed working with you, and wish you every success in the future." Disgusted with him, she turned away before he could offer any more unwanted advice, and returned to the bedroom. Sean was seated on the side of his cot.

He was clad in a white shirt, tan vest and breeches, white

stockings, and shoes rather than military boots. His hair was neatly combed and tied back with a black ribbon, but he had not shaved his beard. He looked as though the simple task of getting dressed had exhausted him, and she knew he had had ample help.

She picked up the brown coat that lay beside him. It was well-tailored but plain. She draped it over his shoulders. A cocked hat and battered satchel were his only other possessions. "Why didn't you tell me you'd resigned your commission? I thought you'd merely asked for leave."

"I'm a liability to the army like this," he said, "and I saved Lord Cornwallis the disagreeable task of having to tell me so to my face." He grabbed his hat and plunked it down on his head. "I'll have a pension and I'm far from poor so you needn't worry that I'll embarrass you by begging on the streets of Williamsburg."

"Believe me, that was the farthest thought from my mind." She leaned down to take his right arm and helped him rise. He straightened up, and she was surprised that she had forgotten how tall he was. Easily six feet, his hat added several additional inches. He pulled away, and she knew he was ashamed to need her help. Unwilling to risk letting him fall, she tightened her grip on his arm.

"There's not another man who could walk out of this hospital this soon after being so badly wounded," she whispered. "None will think any less of you for having to lean on me."

"I will," Sean muttered under his breath. "Now get me out to the wagon before I faint!"

Dominique managed that feat, and found Belle and Lieutenant Beck waiting for them. She hoped Beck had come to say good-bye rather than to provide an escort, and was greatly relieved when that proved to be the case. Belle had already lowered the tailboard, and Dominique eased Sean into a sitting position at the rear of the wagon where he could lean back against the side. Believing he would wish to speak with the lieutenant privately, she started back toward the hospital for his satchel, but she overheard Beck apologizing for still not having apprehended the villain who had shot him. As could be expected, Sean responded with a blistering condemnation of his efforts.

"O'Keefe doesn't look nearly as impressive without his fancy uniform," Belle whispered when Dominique joined her at the front of the wagon.

Dominique placed Sean's satchel behind the seat where they had stowed their gear, then ran her hand over Ladybug's rump. "He's only a man, after all, and not a strong one."

The sorrow in Dominique's expression worried Belle, but she spoke through a delighted smile. "Try and look as though you're happy about going home. We don't want anyone to suspect our thoughts aren't on rejoining our families."

Dominique could not have feigned pleasure had her life depended upon it, but she did produce at least a neutral expression that did not alarm any of the men who came up to wish Sean a safe journey. She held her breath, fearful that at this last moment, a friend of Sean's who would recognize them would appear. They would never get away then, but while she and Belle drew many admiring glances, the men were all strangers who merely nodded politely and walked away.

"They're tiring him," Dominique worried aloud. "We ought to go."

Belle had never understood Dominique's concern for a man she claimed to despise, but shared her wish to get underway. "Colonel," she called to him. "It's getting warm and I don't want you to suffer from the heat. Are you ready to go?"

Sean waved to them, and Dominique went back to the rear of the wagon. In civilian clothes, he would easily pass for a merchant, but unlike Belle, she considered him no less appealing than he had been in uniform. "I'll sit with Belle for a while, then I'll come back here with you." Sean swung his feet up out of the way, and she and Lieutenant Beck raised the tailboard and secured it. Wedged into the corner, Sean took hold of the tailboard with his right hand and adjusted his position slightly.

"Are you comfortable?" Dominique asked.

Sean shot her a glance that assured her he was not, but they had already laid a thick layer of straw in the bed of the wagon to cushion his ride and there was nothing more she could do. "We'll stop often, and do our best to find the smoothest roads."

"Colonel O'Keefe is indeed fortunate to have such an attentive nurse," Beck offered, but as usual his hostile glance belied his words.

"Sean is fortunate in all respects," Dominique countered, and quickly brushed by the lieutenant to take her seat next to Belle. Belle clucked to their mares, and with a clattering shudder, the wagon began rolling across the yard. Dominique turned to look back at Sean. He had already lowered his head, and even from several feet away she could tell he was in horrible pain.

"I don't care how this looks," Dominique told Belle. "He's hurting too badly and I'll have to sit with him." Rather than ask Belle to stop the wagon, she just timed her motions to the vehicle's rumbling sway and climbed over the back of the seat. She crawled over to Sean and tapped his thigh. Startled, he glanced up, and she saw the moisture on his cheeks before he could wipe away his tears.

"Let's move to the front of the wagon—you can use my lap as a pillow."

"Wait," Sean begged, but as soon as they had left the camp, he collapsed in her arms.

Dominique laid his coat aside and struggled to pull him forward. It took a bit of doing, but after a moment she had their gear in the front of the wagon as a backrest, and he lay sprawled out on the straw with his head in her lap. She tipped his hat to shade his face and ran her hand down his right arm.

"Is that better?" she asked.

Sean reached up to squeeze her hand, and she knew it was. She also had the answer she had sought all night. She could not stand to see Sean suffer even a moment of pain, and she had not saved his life only to take it later. That insight had solved one problem, but then presented another, for now she would have to convince Falcon that Sean O'Keefe had a right to live.

On horseback, they had wound their way through the forests, but now in the lumbering wagon, they would have to remain on the well-worn roads. Dominique pulled her kerchief down to shade her eyes, but she was too tired to serve as an effective lookout. They would be unlikely to encounter rebel bands this close to Camden, but she doubted they could make it all the way home without being stopped by at least one. The Barclay name would command respect, so that prospect did not trouble her, but there were other men, brigands who used the war as an excuse to prey on either side and on an open road, they would be defenseless.

"We should have brought a pistol at the very least," she told Sean.

He released her hand to raise his hat slightly. "There's one in my bag."

"Wonderful. If we're stopped by men who care little whom they kill, do you think they'll allow us time to unpack it?" She did not wait for him to grant permission, but leaned forward to pull his satchel out beside her and began to rummage through it. He had several shirts, pants neatly folded, socks, toilet articles, and at the very bottom of the bag, a pistol.

"Is it loaded?" she asked before touching it.

"Yes, of course. What good would it be if it weren't?"

Dominique removed it gingerly and slipped it beneath

the straw where it would be within easy reach should the need arise. "Let's keep it out of sight. Anyone who challenges us will focus on you, and with your hands empty, they'll not suspect they're in any danger."

Sean cocked his head to look up at her. "Do you really think you could shoot a man?" he asked.

"If I had to, yes."

"I don't want to miss that. Wake me before you fire."

Dominique jammed Sean's hat down over his eyes rather than promise that she would. She turned to look up at Belle, then thought better of telling her about the pistol when Belle would surely want to have it with her rather than Sean. Dominique regarded the omission as mere caution rather than a betrayal, but it bothered her nonetheless.

Then again, it was difficult to do any serious thinking seated in the back of an old wagon. She was used to riding her mare, or in a fine carriage, and bumping along the rutted road was nearly as uncomfortable for her as it was for Sean. Had she not been overtired, she would never have been able to sleep, but despite her best efforts to keep a close eye on her patient, and the road, she soon dozed off.

Expecting Falcon to appear at any minute, Belle kept scanning the sides of the road, but the sun rose high overhead without any sign he was near. He had said she would sense his presence, but she felt only hot and tired. She was also growing increasingly annoyed with Dominique, who was treating Sean O'Keefe as though he were a precious child when Belle was positive he did not deserve any consideration whatsoever.

Anxious to meet Falcon, she kept the mares moving along at an easy but steady pace. She wiped her forehead on her arm and reached for the jug of water at her side. She had just brought it to her lips when Falcon rode out of the pine forest and came galloping toward them. Bare-chested with his hair flying loose, he looked as savage as any Seneca brave ever born. Even knowing this was the man she called husband, the sight of him charging straight for the wagon unnerved Belle completely.

As Belle yanked the mares to a sudden halt, Dominique was thrown back against their gear with bruising force. Sean was also pitched forward, driving his hat into Dominique's diaphragm and knocking the wind out of her. Violently jolted awake, each made a frantic grab for the other but before either recovered, Falcon leapt from Nails's back into the bed of the wagon. As the brave came toward them knife in hand, Dominique was unable to produce more than an anguished sob, but she leaned forward and crossed her arms over Sean's chest to shield him from harm.

"Get out of my way!" Falcon shouted.

Belle wrapped the reins around the brake handle and leaned over the back of the seat in time to see Sean reach for the pistol. Also dislodged by the abrupt halt, it lay just out of his grasp. "He has a pistol," she screamed. She dived over the back of the seat and lunged for Sean's arm to prevent him from using it on Falcon.

All four of them were in the back of the wagon now, Dominique struggling for breath to beg for Sean's life, Sean desperately trying to defend himself, Belle valiantly trying to protect the man she loved, and Falcon, thoroughly confused, not swinging his knife for fear he would leave a long, bloody gash in one of his cousins. Going after the pistol with a well-placed kick, he sent it out of Sean's reach, and bent down to pick it up.

"Thank you, Belle. Now take Dominique and get out of the wagon," Falcon ordered in a low, controlled tone. "I'll deal with O'Keefe."

Sean tried to sit up, but Dominique tossed his hat aside and tightened her hold on him. "No, Falcon," she gasped. "You'll do no such thing."

Falcon leveled the pistol at the Englishman's chest and smiled as a look of terrified recognition crossed Sean's face. "I see that you remember me. Good. He's mine, Dominique.

Now get out of the wagon. I don't want his blood splattered all over you."

"My God," Sean wailed. "You're Christian's brother." He looked up at Dominique. "You had this all planned, didn't you?"

Ignoring Sean's question, Dominique continued to argue with Falcon. "I won't let you kill him. He's left the army and he's so badly hurt he can barely stand. There can be no honor in killing a wounded man."

Falcon kept the pistol trained on Sean. "You must have heard how Tarleton treated Colonel Buford and his troops in May. How much mercy did they show our wounded?"

Dominique sent a frightened glance toward Belle, who was now hanging onto the back of the seat. They had both heard about the massacre, as indeed all of Virginia had. Colonel Buford had been in command of a regiment of Virginia infantry which had retreated after Charleston had fallen into British hands. Overtaken by Banastre Tarleton's British Legion, Buford had surrendered, but rather than take prisoners, Tarleton's dragoons had slaughtered all the Virginians in a brutal rampage that had left not merely Virginians, but every Patriot aching for revenge.

Recalling the details of the gory battle made Dominique as sick as she had become when she had first heard them. Tarleton's name was now synonymous with senseless, bloody murder. "This isn't Tarleton," she reminded Falcon.

"One murdering English bastard is as good as the next," Falcon replied. "Now get out of the wagon."

Dominique made no move to release Sean, but he reached up to pull her hands away. "Let me go," he complained. "At least let me die on my feet."

"Shut up!" Dominique cried. "No one is going to die here." She had never seen Falcon look so determined, but she had a tight hold on Sean and refused to release him. "I know Sean isn't worth keeping alive, but I don't care. You had your chance to kill him, and failed. I'll not give you another when he's too weak to defend himself. You should be ashamed, Falcon. Have you killed other men who've been in such pathetic condition?"

Belle watched Falcon's dark eyes narrow and feared Dominique had made a grave error in taunting him. He was not only strong, but quick, and could yank Sean out of her sister's arms and slit his throat before Dominique even knew what had happened. When Falcon tossed the pistol over the side of the wagon into the dirt, she knew that was exactly what he intended to do.

"No!" Belle shrieked, Still standing in the bed of the wagon, she pushed away from the seat, and after nearly tripping over Sean's outstretched legs, she rushed toward Falcon and locked her arms around his waist. "Dominique's right," she begged. "He's not worth killing, and even if he were, you ought not to do it like this."

Falcon took a step back to balance Belle's weight and the wood beneath his feet creaked and groaned. "Like what?" he asked her, his gaze never leaving Sean's. "Like the savage that I am?"

Dominique's tears were dripping down onto Sean's face, and he thought it a ghastly coincidence that this was the second time he had nearly died in her arms. He lay very still, praying she and Belle had more influence over their heathen cousin than it had at first appeared. He could recall Christian clearly, but Falcon had been a handsome boy when he had last seen him, not this well-muscled brave with a demon's thirst for blood. The fact that Dominique had known Falcon had shot him made him wonder what other secrets she had kept from him.

He laced his fingers in hers and bit back the pain throbbing in his shoulder. He had escaped death too recently to face it again, but he knew any bargain he offered would only infuriate Falcon all the more and kept still. He had cursed Tarleton as an unprincipled bastard whose fiendish actions had tainted every British officer's name, but knew it would be taken as a pitiful plea for his life if he repeated the denunciation here.

"Falcon, please," Belle begged. "Let him live and I'll never ask anything else of you."

"In the same situation, he would kill me," Falcon swore convincingly.

"No," Sean finally felt compelled to reply. "The war's over for me and even if it weren't, I'd not knowingly kill Dominique's kin."

Falcon was moved by the tears flowing freely down Dominique's face rather than Sean's words. The creamy-smooth prettiness that had once made her so popular was gone, but in its place he saw a beauty and compassion that was far more appealing. Because the war had made equally great changes in him, he felt closer to her now than he ever had.

"Do you believe him?" Falcon asked Dominique.

In truth, she did not, but sensing Sean's life hung on her answer, she nodded. "Yes. I do."

Falcon turned to Belle. "Not another thing ever," he vowed.

Belle swallowed hard. "You have my promise. Thank you." Belle hoped she had not traded away favors she would need desperately later on, but for now, she was content with the bargain. She released her hold on Falcon, and he slid his knife into the beaded sheath on his belt.

Falcon chose the Seneca language to mutter what he truly thought of Sean O'Keefe, then uttered a terse command. "We'll leave the wagon here. It's too slow, and can't be used on the route I want to take. I'll pull it off the road and unhitch your mares. You'll ride behind me, Belle, and O'Keefe can ride Ladybug."

Dominique wiped the tears from her eyes. "Do you feel strong enough to ride, Sean?"

"He rides, or he stays here," Falcon stressed coldly. He kicked open the tailboard and jumped off the end of the wagon. "We have wasted too much time already." He reached up to help Belle down, but quickly released her and scooped up Sean's pistol, then strode around to the front of the wagon with her following close behind.

Dominique gave Sean a gentle nudge to lift his shoulders from her lap, but when he sat up and turned to face her his expression was one of fury rather than gratitude for again saving his life. She raised her hands. "Yell at me later if you must, but Falcon must be obeyed, and quickly." She tried to move past him, but Sean took her wrist in a bruising grip.

He nodded toward Nails. The horse was grazing on the tall grass at the side of the road. "You knew all along who rode that sorrel horse, didn't you?"

Dominique could have quibbled as to the exact moment she had become certain it had been Falcon who had shot him, but drained of emotion, she just didn't care enough to argue such a minor point. "Yes. I did," she admitted flippantly. "You accused me of being secretive. There's your proof, but that scarcely compares to your faults." She jerked her hand free and left the wagon before Falcon started it rolling into the woods.

She had lived with fright as a constant companion for so many days she did not believe she could endure many more. Shaken to the marrow, she had to sit down to rest while Belle and Falcon unhitched the mares. Rather than any sense of triumph at saving Sean, she felt numb. She had done what was right. She had absolutely no doubt of it, but the deed had brought no joy.

When Falcon knelt in front of her, she saw the same deep pools of sorrow in his eyes that she knew had to be reflected in her own, "Thank you for showing mercy to a man I know you despise. I'll find a way to repay you, but right now, I feel sick. Please give me another minute," she begged.

"You have it, but you must stay with us," Falcon warned.

"If O'Keefe falls behind, I'll leave him, but I won't leave you."

At that moment, Dominique doubted she was any stronger than Sean. "Yes, I understand. We'll do our best to keep up with you."

Falcon reached out to caress her cheek. She had lovely cheekbones even if they were freckled. "You've made a poor choice."

"I could have made no other," she confided.

Falcon looked decidedly skeptical, but rather than say so, he just rose and walked away, leaving Dominique to find her own way to live with it.

Thirteen

Sean spent an agonizing day in the saddle, then had to suffer the indignity of having Falcon squat down beside him to observe while Dominique changed the bandage on his shoulder. Unwilling to look at the wound himself, he sat in a dejected slump and watched Belle boil a pan of beans over their campfire. He did not believe he could survive many more such strenuous days, but knew better than to beg Falcon to slow the pace. Dominique was very gentle, her touch soothing as she spread on a freshly made chamomile salve. But now, knowing the extent of her treachery, he fought not to enjoy her attentions.

Sean had not spoken to her all day, and Dominique was relieved rather than insulted because it spared her the ordeal of justifying her actions. She had brought along plenty of linen to fashion fresh bandages, and ripped off a sufficient length to bind his shoulder. "I was afraid your wound might have torn open this morning, but it's healing nicely," she told him.

"You couldn't have been very frightened, or you wouldn't have waited until sundown to look," Sean chided.

Dominique helped Sean ease his shirt back on over his head. "You weren't wearing your coat, so I would have seen the blood the instant it began to seep through your shirt."

Sean nodded grudgingly. She had ridden on his left, but he had not appreciated why. He watched as Falcon got up

4 BESTSELLING HISTORICAL ROMANCES BY YOUR FAVORITE AUTHORS CAN BE YOURS, FREE!

Kensington Choice brings you historical romances by your favorite bestselling authors including Janelle Taylor, Shannon Drake, Bertrice Small, Jo Goodman, and Georgina Gentry, just to name a few! Each book is filled with passion, adventure and the excitement of bygone times!

To introduce you to this great club which is part of Zebra Home Subscription Service, we'd like to send you your first 4 bestselling historical romances, absolutely free! And once you get these 4 free books to savor at home, we'll rush you the next 4 brand-new books at the lowest prices available, as soon as they are published.

The way the club works is that after your initial FREE shipment, you will get our 4 newest bestselling historical romances delivered to your doorstep each month at the preferred subscriber's rate of only $4.20 per book, a savings of up to $8.16 per month (since these titles sell in bookstores for $4.99-$6.99)! All books are sent on a 10-day free examination basis and there is no minimum number of books to buy. (And no charge for shipping.) Plus as a regular subscriber, you'll receive our FREE monthly newsletter, *Zebra/Pinnacle Romance News*, which features author profiles, subscriber benefits, book previews and more!

So start today by returning the FREE BOOK CERTIFICATE provided. We'll send you 4 FREE BOOKS with no further obligation: A FREE gift offering you hours of reading pleasure with no obligation...how can you lose?

*We have 4 FREE BOOKS for you
as your introduction to
KENSINGTON CHOICE!
To get your FREE BOOKS, worth
up to $24.96, mail the card below.*

FREE BOOK CERTIFICATE

Yes! Please send me 4 Kensington Choice (the best of Zebra and Pinnacle Books) Historical Romances without cost or obligation (worth up to $24.96). As a Kensington Choice subscriber, I will then receive 4 brand-new romances to preview each month for 10 days FREE. I can return any books I decide not to keep and owe nothing. The publisher's prices for Kensington Choice romances range from $4.99-$6.99, but as a preferred subscriber I will get these books for only $4.20 per book or $16.80 for all four titles. There is no minimum number of books to buy and I may cancel my subscription at any time, plus there is no additional charge for postage and handling. No matter what I decide to do, my first 4 books are mine to keep, absolutely FREE!

KC0199

Name _____

Address _____ Apt. _____

City _____ State_____ Zip_____

Telephone (_____) _____

Signature _____

(If under 18, parent or guardian must sign)

Subscription subject to acceptance. Terms and prices subject to change.

4 FREE
Historical Romances

are waiting
for you to
claim them!

(worth up to
$24.96)

See details
inside....

KENSINGTON CHOICE
Zebra Home Subscription Service, Inc.
120 Brighton Road
P.O.Box 5214
Clifton, NJ 07015-5214

and approached the fire. The brave walked with such a light step Sean doubted he would make a sound even in boots. Belle slipped her arm around Falcon's waist the instant he reached her, and Sean couldn't hide his disgust.

"What do women find so attractive about the Barclay savages?" he asked.

Dominique set the salve aside and rubbed in what remained on her fingertips. "Are you speaking of women in general, or Liana Scott?"

They were seated beneath a fragrant pine, and now that Dominique was finished with him, Sean leaned back against the broad trunk to rest. She was studying her hands rather than looking at him, and despite his anger with her, he sensed she had been hurt by his choice of topic. He received a brief burst of pleasure from that, quickly followed by sincere remorse.

"I can barely remember her," he confessed, "although she ripped a great hole in my pride. Do you have a handsome savage waiting at home for you?"

"No. There's no one waiting for me."

That wistful comment broke through all that was left of Sean's reserve, and he reached out to take her hand. "That's good, because I doubt I'd survive if he challenged me."

Dominique pulled free of his grasp. "That isn't funny, Sean. Death isn't a suitable topic for humor."

"Especially mine," he added. Clearly exasperated with him, Dominique started to rise, but he again reached out to stop her. "Wait. Why did you do it?" he whispered.

Dominique did not ask for a clarification of the question she had expected all day, but provided only a noncommittal reply. "For precisely the reasons I gave Falcon: it would have been both cowardly and cruel to kill a wounded man."

Sean rubbed his thumb against her palm in a teasing circle. "I agree, and I said the same thing to Tarleton in much stronger terms. He might have called me out had there not been so many other officers who concurred. War is brutal enough without the carnage he caused. I'll not miss the likes of him."

"Why, Sean, I had no idea you possessed such an admirable character."

Sean knew he deserved that, and did not resort to replying in kind. "And yet you've saved my life twice."

"I don't want you to feel obligated to me. Just don't make me regret it," she warned, and this time when she withdrew, he let her go. None of them felt like talking while they ate their meager supper, and Dominique did not need a suggestion from Falcon to go to sleep early. He and Belle cuddled together on the opposite side of the fire from Sean, and she chose a place off to the side to spread out her shawl. She had not missed sleeping on the ground, but here the dirt was padded with a thick layer of pine needles and nearly as comfortable as her cot.

A gentle breeze cooled the forest floor, and content for the moment, she had just closed her eyes when Sean stretched out beside her. "Find your own place to sleep," she scolded.

"Hush, or you'll wake Falcon and Belle."

Dominique had had no choice about sleeping near him in the hospital, and had not intended to continue the practice, but the last of her energy spent, she could not get up and move. When Sean slid his arm under her to pull her close, she resisted only a second or two before relaxing and resting her head on his shoulder. "I'm too tired to argue tonight, but I'll not make a habit of this once we arrive home."

"Of course not," Sean murmured against her hair, "but I don't think Ian would begrudge me a bed."

Dominique would refuse to share Sean's bed, regardless of where he found it, but the only protest that left her lips was a restless sigh that was far more seductive than forbidding.

* * *

Falcon set an exhausting pace, but provided fish and small game in abundance to keep everyone fed. Two days from home, Hunter rode into their camp. When he recognized Sean, Dominique feared they were going to play out the ghastly scene in the back of the wagon all over again, but to his credit, Falcon forcefully defended Sean as a wounded soldier who would cause no harm. Her cousin offered no excuse for their behavior, however, and Hunter's disgust was palpable.

"You willful girls have broken your parents' hearts," he told them. "And for what? To run off and tend wounded Englishmen?" He walked up to Sean and spit in the dirt. "Cross us, and you'll wish you had died in Camden."

Sean still did not have full use of his left arm, but he raised his hands in a placating gesture. "I'm sick of war," he protested, "and the Barclays need have no fear of me. I'll stay in Ian Scott's house, and never set foot on your land."

"Your word is worthless," Hunter shot right back at him.

"Uncle, please," Dominique began, but fell silent under his blistering stare. Hunter turned away to see to his horse, and Falcon followed him. "I'm sorry, Belle," Dominique said. "I'll tell everyone leaving home was my idea. There's no reason for them to be furious with us both."

"We're grown women," Belle countered. "We should not have left in the dead of night, but we had every right to go. Now help me gather more wood. I don't want Hunter to think we can't even build a fire."

Dominique was only too happy to have an excuse to leave their camp and went in the opposite direction from Hunter and Falcon to search for kindling. Sean followed closely, but she did not know what to say to him. He had stayed out of Falcon's way the whole trip, but Falcon's attitude toward him hadn't softened. He may have kept Hunter from killing Sean on sight, but he had made no pretense of liking him.

"I've been so anxious to get home," Dominique confided. "Now I don't understand why when everyone will surely be as furious with us as Hunter."

"You must have remembered how safe you felt there," Sean offered.

Falcon had led them over ancient Indian trails and they had not been sighted by troops or rogue bands supporting either side in the war, but Dominique had never felt secure. "Yes, we were safe at home, and we were not only willful, but stupid in the extreme to leave," she mumbled.

Sean caught her elbow. "You mustn't even think that. I'm not sorry to have found you again even if you feel nothing for me."

They had had few lengthy conversations on the exhausting journey, but Sean had not once reverted to the belligerent bully he had been in Camden. Even suspecting it was merely a convenient ploy, Dominique wanted very badly to believe this was his true personality. When he drew her close, she resisted only slightly, then stepped into his arms. Even then, she dared not remain, and quickly pulled away.

"Hunter is already so angry with me, we don't dare let him find us together."

Each night she had slept cradled in his arms, but their friendship had been quite chaste otherwise. Sean had not felt strong enough to offer more, for one thing, and he did not want her to come to him out of sympathy rather than love. "Everything has changed since we left Camden," he said, "but you've no reason to be ashamed when we've done nothing wrong."

Dominique doubted her family would share his view, but when Sean dipped his head, she could not turn away. Instead, she raised up on her tiptoes to welcome his kiss. He had only one arm to hold her, but she wrapped both of hers around his waist and held on tight. She leaned into his devouring kiss, and for a few glorious moments lost all her fears. His passion was what she had remembered, and she drank it in eagerly until they were both so dizzy they had to stop to catch their breath.

"Everything's wrong." She choked back a sob as she broke away, but Sean refused to release her.

"Not this," he swore, and he kissed her again with the same feverish desire. "I'll do whatever I must to stay at Ian's," he promised, "if only you'll come to me when you can."

Every bit as eager for more as he, Dominique squeezed his hand. "I'll not be able to stay away. Now please help me find some firewood before my uncle starts yelling at me again."

Sean spun her around with the graceful motion he would use to change partners in a dance. "Go on back to camp now, and I'll bring what I can."

Dominique took a step away, then came back for one last hurried kiss. She returned to camp wearing a troubled if innocent expression, but she was sick of deception and longed for the chance to follow her heart without the constant fear every choice she made was wrong.

Simon Farquhar, the ferryman, remembered Hunter but he did not at first recognize Dominique and Belle as the pretty blondes the Indian had been pursuing. Their gowns were wrinkled and stained, their figures gaunt, their faces drawn and strained. That the once attractive pair had picked up a bearded man and another Indian struck him as damn odd, but he earned his living ferrying passengers across the James River, not offering opinions, and didn't comment on their choice of traveling companions.

"Looks like you found your friend's daughters," Simon said as Hunter paid the fare for the group.

Hunter tipped the man handsomely. "Forget that you ever saw them."

Simon doffed his faded hat. "My memory has always

been poor," he promised, but he was curious. Wherever the girls had been, they had obviously had a bad time of it, but they walked on board with a pride he had not noticed on their earlier crossing, so surely they did not feel disgraced. " 'Tis the war," he grumbled to himself. "It's turned everything inside out." But he sure wished he were privy to their secrets.

Hunter had repeatedly positioned himself between Dominique and Sean since the night he had found their camp. He had not upbraided his nieces after his initial outburst, but his disapproval permeated the silence and made them far more uncomfortable than the heat. Belle had Falcon to intercede for her, but Dominique's only ally was Sean, and the others regarded him with contempt.

By the time they reached the ferry, Dominique had had ample opportunity to compose and review the explanation Hunter had refused to hear, but she had yet to create a sufficiently inventive story to save herself and Belle from their parents' scorn. The trouble was, she truly believed they would deserve whatever punishment they received. They had left home filled with foolish romantic notions, and while Belle had achieved her goal of a reconciliation with Falcon, one glimpse of Sean would cause the family to damn Dominique for a good long while.

As usual, Hunter was standing at the ferry rail between Dominique and Sean, and she leaned out to look past the brave to the Englishman. "Whatever possessed you to demand that I bring you home?" she asked.

Sean laughed at the tardiness of her question and just shook his head. "I'd lost too much blood to think clearly, and now that I'm better, it's too late. Don't be frightened for me. I'll be all right."

Dominique preferred to study the rushing current rather than meet her uncle's critical gaze but with home only a few hours away, she could take no more of his dark moods. "I daresay that at first the family couldn't have been thrilled with you, either," she suddenly threw at him. "You of all people ought to be more understanding."

Hunter recoiled slightly, then turned his back to Sean and spoke to Dominique in the same low, threatening snarl he would have used to address his worst enemy. "Do not dredge history for insults or you'll soon find your mother wasn't welcomed, either. What happened to us isn't the issue. That you and Belle endangered your lives, and that of those who had to rescue you, is! Now keep your thoughts to yourself if you've no more wisdom than that."

Sean tapped Hunter on the shoulder. "Don't take that tone with her," he warned.

Hunter raised his hand, but before he could slap Sean with a fierce, backhanded blow, Dominique looped her arms around his elbow. "Stop it!" she screamed. "Stay out of our arguments, Sean. The Barclays have more than enough trouble without you jumping into the midst of it."

"No," Sean swore. "I'll not allow anyone to mistreat you."

Sean and Hunter were near equals in height, but the Indian had a clear advantage in strength. He was fourteen years Sean's senior, but fast as a snake and Dominique had no doubt he could kill Sean in under a dozen blows. That possibility horrified her.

"Thank you," she told Sean, "but I have no need of your protection. Now I think you'd better see to our mounts."

That Sean would challenge him when he could not possibly be strong enough to fight struck Hunter as either very brave, or utterly stupid. Rather than debate the issue with his fists, he dismissed him with a single, rude epithet and crossed the wide deck to the other side. The exchange had taught him something about Dominique he would not soon forget, however. He may have compared her to Melissa in the past, but he would not make that mistake again. Dominique had the courage to defend the man she loved, while Melissa had died without ever admitting that she had once cared for him.

Dominique held her breath until Hunter reached the opposite rail. "Please, don't ever do that again," she begged.

Sean moved close. "Don't ask me to turn away. You'd lose all respect for me if I did."

"Perhaps, but it would spare me the disagreeable chore of tending your grave." Dominique waited a moment to make certain he fully appreciated that risk, then changed the subject. "When we leave the ferry, let's switch mounts. I'll take Belle's mare and you can ride mine on to the Scott plantation and keep her until you have a horse of your own."

"We weren't talking about horses," he chided.

"Please. I can't stand having Hunter yank me one way and you pulling me the other. You promised to wait at Ian's and let me come to you. Don't go back on your word."

Sean didn't speak, but his glance held a promise of an entirely different sort and Dominique knew he would not wait long for the visits she had promised to pay. "I wish that you had stayed mean," she lamented softly, "so that I could hate you, too."

Sean laughed out loud at that, then leaned closer still to whisper, "I wish I hadn't been shot, so that when I found you in Camden, I could have demanded your favors as the price for my silence. I would have reveled in your hatred until it turned to love."

"You would have died of old age before then," Dominique swore.

"Perhaps, but I would have had a glorious life and a great many pretty, blond children."

The ferry reached the bank before Dominique found a suitable retort, but that teasing exchange, despite its vulgar undertones, lifted her spirits to the point that she rode the final miles home without agonizing the whole way as to how she would be greeted once she arrived there. When Falcon rode ahead to announce they were coming, she

looked down at her faded gown and wondered if she would
even be recognized. She turned to Sean.

"You ought to fall back and go on to Ian's after we've
all gone inside the house."

Sean straightened his shoulders, which he did often despite the pain. "I'd not miss this for anything," he replied.
"It's like coming home for me, too."

The way Dominique remembered it, on his last visit
Christian had beaten him so badly his men had had to carry
him away. "We've just assumed that Ian would invite you
to stay with him if he were home. Because he isn't, you
have to ask Liana's permission to reside there awhile."

Clearly perplexed by that suggestion, Sean tossed it back
to Dominique. "I doubt she'll even deign to speak with me,
and we both know Christian will never allow it. Perhaps
you could intercede on my behalf and beg for the use of a
corner in the scullery."

They reached the Barclay plantation before they had settled the issue, but when her family came swarming out,
Dominique had to call upon all her resources to defend
herself for the moment, and left Sean to fend for himself.
Her father yanked her off her mare, his face dark with rage,
and shook her. When he went for Belle, she had already
dismounted and was ready for him, but all he did to her
was push her toward Dominique.

"How could you girls have done this to your mother?"
Byron yelled. "Look at you! My God, I'd not have recognized either of you had Falcon not warned us what to expect." He waved them on toward the porch. "I've seen hogs
with less dirt than you two have on your gowns and your
faces don't look much better. You'll have to soak in tubs
for the rest of the afternoon, but don't you dare come to
supper looking like that."

Arielle came down the steps with her arms outstretched
and eagerly embraced her daughters. "You look very beau-

tiful to me," she exclaimed, "but I will have you looking your best again within the hour."

Belle clung to her mother, but Dominique stepped away and turned back to her father. "I'm sorry for being thoughtless, and causing you so much worry. Going after Falcon was entirely my idea. Please don't blame Belle."

Since the day she learned to talk, Dominique had coaxed, wheedled, and simply been such a charming child Byron had never been able to refuse her anything. There was nothing of the coquette about her now, however, and her calm, steady gaze held no hint of her former sparkle. As alarmed as when she had first disappeared, he followed her over to the steps and lowered his voice.

"What's happened to you, Dominique?"

Dominique saw the fear in her father's eyes and easily guessed what he was imagining. "I've not been raped, or beaten, or mistreated in any way, and neither has Belle. We've simply traipsed across three states and felt every mile." Her father's frown deepened, but she did not know how else to reassure him. Because he had at least ceased shouting, she nodded toward Sean.

"I've brought Sean O'Keefe home with me. He's no longer in the army and hopes to stay at Ian's, if Liana will allow it."

Byron spun on his heel, but with Sean bearded and in civilian clothes, he had not recognized him earlier. "You're not welcome here," he called to him. "And Liana will never give you more than a stall in her father's stable."

"Please tell her that I'm grateful for that," Sean responded. He touched his brim in a casual salute, and with a nod toward Dominique, turned Baby Dee back toward the path along the river.

"Where's he going with your horse?" Byron cried.

"To Ian's stable, I suppose," Dominique replied. "I'll fetch her when he has another."

"No," Byron swore emphatically. "You'll not go anywhere near that bastard for any reason. Now get on inside, and do what you can to make yourselves into ladies again."

"We've never been anything else," Belle argued, but her mother took her hand and lured her inside before her father could say that she certainly did not look like one.

Alanna and Jean were standing just inside the open doorway, and while Alanna's smile was warm, Jean walked out without speaking to his sisters. "I already have water heating," Alanna announced as she followed them up the stairs. "You poor things—not a day has gone by that we haven't all cried, we've missed you so."

Dominique and Belle looked suitably contrite, but while away they had been far too concerned with their survival to weep over those they had left behind.

Dominique chose her coral satin gown and Belle wore lavender muslin when they came downstairs for supper. Christian and Liana, as well as Johanna and David, were there to welcome them home; not having seen the pair earlier, they were all struck by the enormous difference in them. Their once sun-streaked hair was now a paler blond, and their creamy complexions had deepened to a golden tan. Thin rather than merely slender, the effect was surprisingly elegant.

Christian hugged them both. "You look tired, but so beautiful I don't know what to say except please don't ever leave us again."

Liana hung back slightly, and Dominique feared she knew why. "Falcon told you about Sean O'Keefe?" she asked.

Liana slipped her hand in Christian's. "Yes, but from what I gather, your father has plans for him. Until then, he's welcome to stay in my parents' home. After all, he would still be a hero to them and I'll accede to their wishes rather than impose my own."

Dominique was relieved beyond measure. "That's very

gracious of you. Thank you." She noted the anxious glances passing between the others, but at the moment simply did not feel up to defending Sean any further. She took her place beside her father at the dining table, and realized she had not eaten a single meal at a table since she and Belle had left home.

After the blessing, which included a thanksgiving for their safe return, she sat back in her chair and surveyed the table with newly appreciative eyes. "Everything is so pretty: the china, the crystal, the beautiful flowers." She ran her fingertips over the linens. "Just look how white the table-cloth is."

"Are you feeling all right, dear?" Arielle inquired. "You should have heard her exclaiming over the delightful warmth of her bath. You would have thought she had never taken one."

"It's simply good to be home," Belle said, but her smile held special warmth for Falcon. They all raised their glasses in a toast, but he had refused when offered wine. Belle remembered his promise to her; she was touched. He winked at her, and she was not a bit sorry that she had gone after him when she had found so much more than she had hoped.

"Belle," Arielle whispered, "if you keep smiling like that, we're all going to become very suspicious as to the cause."

Falcon laughed and leaned forward to address everyone. "Belle has at last agreed to become my wife," he announced proudly. "I hope we'll have everyone's good wishes."

Dominique found it easy to smile for them, and she was deeply grateful for the distraction that kept the conversation flowing in joyous waves throughout supper. Johanna teased her younger brother, and David and Christian offered advice, but Liana was subdued, and Dominique feared she knew why. Sean had pursued her even after she had wed Christian, and while Dominique knew Liana had cared nothing for him, she knew Liana could not possibly be pleased to have him living so near. Recalling Liana's comment, she touched her father's sleeve.

"What plans do you have for Sean?" she asked.

Byron had just taken a bite of bread and had to swallow before he replied. "Later," he promised.

After existing on a diet of fish and berries on the trail, Dominique had expected to be ravenous once she reached the table, but in truth she had little appetite. They had sent Sean off without a scrap to eat, and while they were enjoying their plantation's usual abundance, she could not help but think of him being hungry and alone. She had not known how badly she would miss him, but it hurt. The meal ended with blackberries drenched in cream, and it was all she could do not to get up and carry her bowl off to the Scott house for him to enjoy.

Byron noted the sharp contrast in his daughters' moods, but did not comment on it. As they left the table, he drew Dominique aside. "Come into my study. I need to speak with you."

Grateful he was not including Belle this time in what she assumed would be another opportunity to criticize her behavior, Dominique followed without protest, but when Falcon joined them, she couldn't hide her surprise. "What's going on?" she asked, her apprehension plain.

Byron slid into his chair behind the desk and gestured for her to be seated. He waited until Falcon had taken the chair beside hers to reveal what was on his mind. "I realize that you and Belle were little more than prisoners in Camden, so I won't blame you regardless of your answer, but whether it was by force or desire, have you been intimate with Sean O'Keefe?"

Dominique had never been so badly embarrassed, and she looked down at her hands rather than meet her father's perceptive gaze. On the surface it was such an easy question, but she sensed it was of far greater importance than the mere state of her virtue. She did not know which answer to give, the truth or a lie that might damn her but protect Sean with a forced marriage.

Byron leaned forward and rested his arms on his desk. "A simple yes or no will do, Dominique. I'll not turn a horsewhip on Sean, or worse, if he's been your lover."

Dominique had to force herself to breathe. "No, we've never made love," she finally admitted, and not at all proudly, either. She wondered if he would ask Falcon the same question about Belle, but he did not.

Byron chose his words with care. "With the exception of Falcon and Belle and Johanna and David, the members of our family have a history of selecting, shall we say, what might appear to some as unsuitable partners. That your own dear mother was Acadian outraged a great many of our friends, and it wasn't until the French took our side against England that I was forgiven for taking a bride from among our enemies. So if you want Sean, I'll not forbid the match, but first, we must be assured of his loyalty."

"That's rather presumptuous," Dominique argued. "He's not offered marriage."

Falcon opened his mouth to comment, but Byron raised a hand to silence him. "If Sean wants to continue seeing you, he will have to," he insisted. "But first, I wish to conduct a test."

Dominique grew even more uneasy. "What sort of test?" she inquired.

Falcon felt free to speak now. "We'd like you to pay Sean a visit tonight. Take him some rations since we neglected to provide any, and then mention in passing how distraught Belle is that I'm leaving tomorrow. You can easily add some remark about how poorly love and war mix, and say I had to rush away to meet a rebel force gathering in Petersburg."

"Is that what you're really doing?" Dominique asked.

"No, but it's an intriguing bit of information, and if Sean wasn't sincere in his vow not to harm your kin, then he'll pass it along to Loyalists who'll warn their troops. The Tuttles' are still staunch supporters of the Crown. Sean knew them well, and with their plantation bordering the Scotts', it will be a short ride. I'm betting on him to make it tonight. You owe it to yourself to discover whether or not he will."

Dominique needed a moment to sort out the implications of Falcon's scheme. "If I mention Petersburg and he shows no interest and doesn't share the information, will you trust him?"

Falcon shrugged. "No, not until the war's over I won't, but I'll take it as an initial sign that his word is good."

"Father? Do you agree with Falcon's plan?"

Byron sat back and steepled his fingers over his chest. "There was a time, and not very long ago, when I considered myself loyal to the Crown, so I can't fault Sean for his beliefs, but I'll not receive him in this house, or give my consent to your marriage, if I can't trust him not to spy on us." He fixed Dominique with a piercing gaze. "Would you really want a man who'd betray us?"

Dominique shook her head. "No, for I'd not be able to love him."

"Then you understand the importance of what we're asking you to do? We need to ascertain his loyalties as much for you as for the rest of us."

"Does it have to be tonight?" Dominique murmured softly.

Byron nodded. "I know you're tired, but Sean will be, too. He'll be less likely to be on his guard and that much more likely to reveal his true nature. I know you can do this, Dominique, and beautifully."

Dominique glanced toward Falcon and envied her sister for falling in love with a man whose loyalties would never be open to question. He had sworn she had made a poor choice in saving Sean, and she prayed she could now prove him wrong. "I'll do it," she agreed, "but Sean's very clever and he may see right through your ruse. If he does, I want your word that you won't continue tormenting him, and me, with repeated tests of this nature."

Byron rose to his feet. "You have my word on it."

Falcon offered his hand to help her rise, and Dominique prayed she had not just gotten into a greater mess than she had made by leaving home. Her next thought was how badly she wanted Sean to protect whatever chance they might have for a lasting love.

Fourteen

Dominique went out to the kitchen and found the basket of provisions for Sean had already been packed before the cook and her helpers had gone to their quarters for the night. There were berries, but no cream, so she filled a small jar from the pitcher in the dairy, and added it to the basket that was already so heavy it was difficult to carry. She had to stop to rest several times on the path running along the bank of the James River, but still managed to arrive at the Scott home while the twilight lit the way.

She had not really expected to find Sean in the stable, and the candles glowing in the parlor led her on into the house. She called to him as she entered the rear door, and he came down the hallway to meet her. The Scott home was similar to her own in design, but that did little to ease her mind and she still felt as though she were trespassing.

"Liana said you're welcome to stay here, but it's obvious you didn't wait for her permission to move in."

Sean took the basket from her and carried it on into the parlor. He set it on the floor in front of the settee, then turned to embrace her. "I feared they'd not let you out of the house for weeks." He kissed her lightly but tenderly, then stepped back to admire her.

"Your gown is as lovely as the sunset, and you, well, you've always been a beauty. I'm sorry I don't have such fine clothes to wear for you."

Although touched by his praise, Dominique was too nervous to engage in flattery. "Thank you, but you needn't worry about your wardrobe, or lack of it. I've never been attracted to a man simply because of his clothes, although you were dashing in your uniform. Now, aren't you hungry?"

"I came in and fell asleep the minute I sat down so I haven't even thought about food. What did you bring?"

"A little of everything, but you mustn't count on me to furnish your meals. I was able to slip away tonight, but it wasn't easy."

"That's all right. I've no wish to be a burden to you." Sean pulled her down beside him on the settee and began to peruse the contents of the basket. "You even remembered cream for the berries," he enthused. "This all looks so good. Are you certain you can't bring me a basket every night? I won't mind eating whatever scraps your family leaves." He unwrapped a piece of cold chicken and took a bite.

Dominique had come to lay a trap, but as she watched Sean struggle to eat with one hand, she felt ashamed. He had already paid a high price for fighting for the British, and she did not want to extract more. "I can only stay a few minutes. I convinced everyone that bringing you something to eat was the most charitable thing to do, but no one thought I ought to offer my company as well."

Sean set the chicken aside and took a bite of apple. "Had you not begged me to stay out of it, I would have objected to the way your father greeted you. I know he must have been worried, but he didn't need to be so gruff."

Dominique smoothed out the folds in her skirt and glanced around the room. The pale green walls reflected the candles' soft glow, but most of the furnishings were draped with muslin, leaving her to assume they were beautiful pieces of highly polished fruitwood. The settee was upholstered in a green and gold striped satin, and comfortable if a bit small for Sean to curl up there and sleep.

Rather than simply toss aside the muslin, he had folded it and laid it on the back. She wondered if that was due to his military training or if he was always so neat. She knew very little about the man and that pained her.

"I expected a lot worse from Father," she finally replied, "and he's already calmed down considerably. Mother wasn't angry with us, but then she's always taken our side whenever we've needed her."

Sean laid the half-eaten apple with the chicken and wiped his hands on the checked napkin peeking out of the basket. "What did she say about me?"

He sounded apprehensive, as though her parents' opinion of him meant a great deal. Instinctively, she longed to reassure him, but would not give him false hopes and was deliberately vague. "She remembered you, but we didn't discuss you."

Finding that impossible to believe, Sean's expression filled with disappointment. "Not at all?"

"Well, perhaps a word or two," Dominique confessed with a touch of her old teasing ways.

"Come here." Sean slipped his right arm around her waist to draw her close, and spread an eager trail of kisses down the silky smoothness of her throat. "I have missed you, and terribly."

Rather than admit she felt exactly the same, Dominique raised her hand to caress his hair. "It's only been a few hours."

Sean inhaled her perfume and moaned with desire. "It seemed a lifetime."

He smothered Dominique's reply with a kiss that sipped her very soul and she clung to him, desperate for the joy of his embrace. She wanted to believe in him, and did not even know how she would cope with her disillusionment if he betrayed them. She leaned back and framed his face with her hands. She had grown accustomed to his beard and rather liked it.

"I must go. They all know I'm here, and if I'm not back soon, my father will undoubtedly come for me. I don't want to risk another confrontation between you two."

Sean leaned forward to nibble her lower lip. "He'll believe you'll come through the door in a minute or two and wait a while longer. I need more, Dominique, so much more of you."

Dominique needed a great deal more, too, but turned her head as he nuzzled her throat and licked her ear. It tickled, and coaxed a throaty giggle from her lips. "No, I must go," she begged. "I left Belle crying because Falcon is leaving before dawn."

She hurried on before she lost her courage. "He swears he has to meet troops forming to move south from Petersburg, but you'd think Belle would be more important to him." She held her breath as Sean kissed her brows, then her cheeks. When he reached her mouth, she slid her tongue over his and drank in his kiss.

Perhaps he had not been listening, but she had spoken the words, and completed her mission. Lost in his affection, she knew she made a very poor spy; but he was all that mattered to her. If she gave herself to him, then he would stay with her all night. She was sorely tempted to insure his silence with passion until she realized he could just as easily pass on the information in the morning. Her heart and head at terrible odds, she gave him a final, fervent kiss and tore herself from his arms.

"I want to stay," she swore, "but not like this when my father might come bursting through the door at any instant. I'll have to wait a few days, perhaps as much as a week, and then slip out of the house after midnight."

Sean placed a loving kiss in her palm. "I'll need the time too," he said. "I want to be strong enough to make everything perfect for you, but it's going to be very difficult to wait." He sucked on her fingertips. "I want to taste all of you."

"Oh, Sean," Dominique moaned. Tears came to her eyes as she left the settee. "I do so want everything to be perfect for us always."

Sean rose and slipped his arm around her waist. He gave her a fond squeeze, and walked her out into the yard. "I'll walk home with you."

"No. You mustn't," Dominique insisted. "Just stay here and enjoy your supper. I'll come back to you just as soon as I can."

"Promise?"

Dominique kissed him again rather than give her word when she was so uncertain of what the future would bring. She took care not to touch his left shoulder. He no longer needed to have the dressing changed daily, but she had enjoyed having the excuse to remove his shirt and touch his bare skin. "God be with you," she whispered as she turned away. She hiked up her gown and ran toward the river with light, dancing steps, but she was barely out of sight of the house when Falcon stepped out of the tall grass to meet her.

"Did you tell him?"

"What do you mean, leaping out at me like that? You scared me to death." Dominique was shaking, but it wasn't because of Falcon's abrupt appearance.

"I'm sorry. Did you tell him I'm leaving for Petersburg, or not?"

"I told him and he didn't seem to have the slightest interest. He didn't ask any questions, or even remark on the cursed war."

"Really? Well, I intend to watch the Scott house for the next couple of hours. Do you want to wait with me?"

Dominique looked out at the river, where the reflection of the stars' shimmering sparkle lent the mystery of the night a romantic mood she would have much preferred to have enjoyed with Sean. Because that was impossible, she wanted to go home, get in bed, pull the covers up over her

head, and forget he had ever been a British officer. She
knew she would never be able to get to sleep not knowing
what he had done, however.

"I'll wait, but I doubt we'll see anything."

Falcon took her hand as they started back up the path.
"For your sake, I hope you're right, but if I'd fallen in love
with a Tory girl, I'd not have forgotten my country."

"There's no comparison between you and Sean,"
Dominique whispered.

"Yes. I know. Look."

They had reached a point from which they could observe
the house and outbuildings without being seen, and there
was already a light in the stable. "Perhaps he just went to
check on Baby Dee," Dominique prayed aloud, but in the
next instant Sean led her mare out into the open. He could
saddle the horse on his own now, if awkwardly, but he had
to lead her to a stump to mount. Dominique did not need
to see any more; heartbroken, she turned back toward home.

"Don't you want to see where he's going?" Falcon called
to her.

"Follow him if you like," she told him. "I already know."
Truly she had no doubt Sean would ride to the Tuttles', and
pass on the news that rebel forces were gathering at Petersburg. She had laced the lie with deep kisses and he had
believed every word. He had accused Liana of ripping a
hole in his pride, but he had just torn her heart right out
of her breast. She would not see him again. She could not,
for it would be far too painful to watch the warm glow of
love turn to an icy hatred in his eyes.

She entered the house and went up the stairs without
going to her father's study to report how swiftly Sean had
taken her bait. She would let Falcon apprise him of the fact,
for she could not bear what would surely be a knowing nod
followed by some murmured platitude meant to diminish
her sense of loss. None of them had trusted Sean to be
anything other than what he had always been: a British of-

'icer. Why had she ever been so arrogant as to believe her
ove would matter more to him than the lives of his coun-
rymen?

She began peeling off her clothes as she entered her
oom. The satin and lace garments were exquisite, but she
flung them aside with a careless toss and pulled on her
oldest nightgown. She yanked the combs from her hair, but
did not stop to brush out her curls before crawling into bed.
As she lay down, she remembered what a nice pillow Sean's
shoulder had made, and could no longer hold back her tears.

The trip home had been long and hard, but the weariness
that overtook her now was deeper than mere physical ex-
haustion. She had waited such a long time for love, and
had tasted it far too briefly. She wanted to blame the war
for the pain scarring her soul, but couldn't when it was so
obvious why Sean had demanded she bring him home. He
had wanted to be near the Barclays because they were such
influential Patriots he would have had ready access to the
Continental Army's every plan.

Sean may have appeared to change, but he was the exact
same man who had threatened her life and Belle's with such
vengeful glee. She tried to recall the stark horror of the
fear he had inflicted, to blot out each instance of joy. Clearly
he had never cared for her, but she was pretty, and her
kisses sweet. He must have enjoyed her affection and all
the while been amused by how easy she had been to de-
ceive.

She was ashamed of how badly she had wanted to stay
with him that night. The love would have been one-sided,
and the consequences perhaps dire. How could she have
been such a fool?

Belle rapped lightly at Dominique's door and then peeked
inside. "Are you already in bed?"

Ashamed to have been caught at the height of her distress, Dominique sat up and hugged her pillow to her
bosom. "I may stay here for weeks. Have you seen Falcon?"

Belle closed the door and came to sit on the end of the bed. "Yes, and he told me about Sean. I'm so sorry."

Dominique wiped her tears on her sleeve. "Yes. So am I, but I knew all along what he was. I was stupid to believe he could ever have been otherwise."

Belle felt for her sister's knee and squeezed it through the covers. "Love doesn't understand the complexities of war. I've no doubt Sean loves you—it shone in his eyes each time he glanced your way."

Dominique would not cling to that hope. "He doesn't even know the meaning of the word, and he could say the same of me. Look how quickly I betrayed him. Would you have told Falcon a lie just to see what he'd do with it?"

Belle looked surprised. "It was no lie. If the British send troops to Petersburg, they'll find Patriots there to meet them."

Aghast at that news, Dominique leaned forward. "You don't mean it! Falcon told me it wasn't true." She ripped off the covers but before she could slide off the bed, Belle moved to block her way.

"They didn't trust you either, Dominique," Belle confided, "but don't tell them you know."

Dominique sucked in her breath. "Who do you mean? Father? Hunter and Falcon?"

Belle nodded. "All of them. We've always been so good, but then we left home and they're no longer able to predict what we'll do. Do you blame them for harboring doubts after what we've put them through? Hunter knew we were in Camden before anyone told him, so obviously he followed us there. He could have been caught. So could Falcon. I think we were very lucky to have been able to work in the hospital when the British might have called us rebel whores and abused us badly. Every time I remember the way Lieutenant Beck looked at us, I feel sick."

Leland Beck had been so easy to dislike that Dominique tried to blur his image with Sean's and despise them both, but the ploy failed miserably. She could still taste Sean's kiss, and wiped her mouth on the back of her hand. "I wish Hunter had had three sons," she said, "so that I might have fallen in love with a cousin, too."

Dominique had such expensive tastes, Belle could not picture her with Christian, Falcon, or any brother the braves might have had. She was simply too elegant for the likes of such overtly masculine men. "You've never been lonely, and I've always envied you the ease with which you chat with men."

"Well, you needn't anymore. It was all a sham. I played at love, and now I'm being severely punished for it. I really do want to go to sleep. I'm so tired, Belle, and there will be no reason to get up in the morning. Are you going to Falcon's room to sleep?"

"Do you think I dare?"

Dominique's smile was sad and sweet. "How can you stay away?"

Belle rose and kissed her sister's damp cheek. "You're right, of course. I don't even want to. Falcon says I'm already his wife, but somehow I don't believe Mother and Father will accept a Seneca custom as fact."

"Then make them accept it, but don't waste a minute that you could be with him."

Because Dominique had learned just how quickly love could end, Belle accepted her advice and went to find Falcon rather than spend a lonely night in her own bed.

Arielle was the only one who truly understood Dominique's despair, and she did not attempt to coax or cajole her daughter from her bed. Having lost her first husband in an Indian raid, she appreciated the grief Dominique could not hide and knew it would pass in its own time. She brought bouquets of fresh flowers to decorate the pretty pink room, brewed soothing herbal teas, and baked tempting pastries laced with chopped pecans. She spent hours at the windowseat with her embroidery, and offered sympathetic comments whenever Dominique cared to speak.

Arielle would have much preferred that Dominique get angry, scream, and break whatever she chose, but Dominique simply slept and withdrew into her pain. When Falcon came to her room three days after her arrival home, Arielle at first did not want to admit him. "Dominique really doesn't feel up to having visitors," she explained, but Falcon looked past his aunt and called to his cousin.

"I'm not a visitor, am I, Dominique? I've something for you, and I want you to know what's happened. Aren't you curious?"

Dominique had been sitting up in bed with an unopened volume of Shakespeare's sonnets clasped tightly in her hands. She glanced toward him, but her eyes were blank, without any sparkle of interest. "Is it anything I truly want to hear?" she asked.

"Yes. I think so." When Dominique nodded, Arielle swung open the door and Falcon strode into the room. He was wearing a new set of buckskins with long, flowing fringe but strangely, did not look out of place in the feminine room.

"Joshua Tuttle passed along your message and nearly two hundred British troops and Loyalist militia marched on Petersburg. We hid in the trees lining the road and surprised them several miles out of town. I don't know which was the most enjoyable, their shocked expressions when we stood and began to fire into their ranks, or the stark terror that lit their eyes when they realized they were surrounded and had no chance of escape.

"We took only a few casualties ourselves, but inflicted heavy losses on them. I overheard more than one Englishman whisper Tarleton's name in dread, but I've never cared for the smell of blood, and the day I serve with a force that will bayonet prisoners is the day I'll gladly slit my own throat. Sean O'Keefe wasn't there, but because he was definitely a part of it, he's been taken prisoner.

"He had no proof he'd resigned his commission, which I've never believed he actually did anyway. Because he's been living among us in plain clothes, there were some of the Patriot forces who wanted to hang him as a spy. He has more courage than most, for he didn't beg and plead for his life while we argued his fate. He seemed almost resigned to it, but out of regard for you, I convinced everyone he belonged in a camp with the other prisoners and that's where he's bound. I brought your mare home. He'd taken good care of her."

Knowing Falcon was surely sparing her the ugliest details, Dominique shuddered at how close Sean had undoubtedly come to being hanged. "You lied to me," she replied coldly. "You told me you were merely testing Sean's loyalties but you'd already planned an ambush when you gave me the message about Petersburg. I'd never have passed it along if I'd known it would endanger his life. You knew that, too, didn't you?"

Falcon had to concede the point. "I'm sorry for that, Dominique, and it won't happen again." He came closer and held out his hand. "I have something for you."

Dominique shrank away. "I doubt it's anything I want."

"Take it anyway," Falcon encouraged her, and when, after a lengthy pause, she opened her hand, he dropped a lock of dark brown hair tied with a bit of thread into her palm. "Sean said he was sorry he had nothing more to send you. He begged me to tell you that you are the only woman he has ever loved. He said he hoped that you'd keep his letter and remember him as fondly as he'll always remember you."

Dominique looked away as she began to cry. Sean had finally spoken of love—when it was too late. It was more than she could bear. She felt certain he had come to Williamsburg to spy, and therefore did deserve to hang, but she could not have borne that.

"Will you see him again?" she asked.

"I will if you want to send him something. I owe you that."

"Yes. You most certainly do. May I borrow your scissors, Mama?"

Arielle brought the delicate pair of embroidery scissors to her, but Dominique's hands were shaking so badly she had to cut a curl for her. She tied it with blue embroidery floss and handed it to Falcon. "Is there anything else, chérie?"

Dominique shook her head. Tears continued to roll down her cheeks and blurred her vision, but she held the lock of Sean's hair all afternoon, then tucked it away with the only love letter he would ever write to her. She knew he would be harshly treated as a prisoner, but having survived being shot, she felt confident he would live until the end of the war. In a way, it was a relief to know he was no longer at the Scotts', but she still felt dead inside and didn't leave her room until the next afternoon when she heard a commotion downstairs.

She stood at the top of the stairs and peered down into the hallway two floors below. She recognized her elder brother's voice as he greeted their parents, and forgetting her own sorrow, raced down the stairs to see him. The fact that she was clad in a nightgown at three in the afternoon didn't concern her until she burst into the parlor and found Beau was not alone. By then it was too late to don more appropriate garb.

"Dominique!" Beau cried as he saw her. He swept her up into his arms and turned in an ecstatic whirl. "I've missed you," he swore as he placed her back on her bare feet, but when he stepped back, he surveyed her with growing alarm. "Have you been ill?"

Dominique looked past him to a handsome young man

with thick black curls and bright green eyes who was observing her with open dismay. "Yes," she said quickly, and turned back toward the door. "But I wanted to welcome you home."

"Wait, don't go. I want you to meet Étienne LeBlanc. I've told him your French is as perfect as Mother's. Won't you at least tell him hello."

"Bonjour, monsieur," Dominique offered with a small curtsy, and fled.

Beau shrugged helplessly. "I'm sorry, Étienne. She truly is the most enchanting creature ever born, but clearly she wasn't at her best."

"She has lovely blond hair," the Frenchman commented, at a loss for anything more complimentary. He had doubted Dominique could actually be as lovely as Beau had described, but he hadn't had time to notice anything other than an unruly mass of fair curls and a wrinkled gown before she had hurried from the room. That she had not wanted to see more of him left him badly disappointed. In the next minute he was introduced to Belle and Falcon, and while he had been warned the Barclay household was a diverse one, he was amazed to find the Indian brave's English was as good as Beau's. He thought Belle was exceptionally pretty, and said so.

While Belle blushed, Falcon took her hand. "Belle is taken, but we'll all thank you if you can make Dominique smile again."

"When has she ever stopped smiling?" Beau asked.

"That's a very long story," Arielle informed him, "and not one I ought to repeat here." A gracious hostess, she made Étienne feel at home and encouraged him to remain with them for supper but he bore such a striking resemblance to a man she had once known that she could not let it pass without comment.

"LeBlanc is a common name—and there was a family of LeBlancs in my hometown, Grand Pré, in Acadia. Where was your father born?" She felt her husband watching her and knew Étienne's answer was important to Byron as well.

"He is also from Acadia, madame, but I do not know where, as he never speaks of his youth. Our family resides in LeHavre, and he is too content to discuss the past. He did not object when I wanted to come to America to fight the British, however, as he damns them to this day for forcing him to leave Acadia."

"As well he should," Byron agreed. "What is his name?"

"Gaetan." Étienne saw a strained look pass between Byron and his wife, and inquired why. "Is it possible that you knew him in Grand Pré?"

"It's possible," Arielle responded, "but as I said, LeBlanc is a common name. What about your mother? Is she Acadian, too?"

"No. She is from Rouen. Her name is Anne-Marie."

"How lovely. That was my mother's name," Arielle said. "How long can you stay?" she asked her son.

"Only one day, while we take on supplies. Anything more is too dangerous. Will you come with me this time, Jean?"

"I'm no sailor," the young man scoffed.

Beau feigned a punch to Jean's shoulder, then hugged his brother. "Good. Then you'll give me no competition for the job of captain of the *Virginia Belle.* Come down to the ship with me now. I've presents for everyone and you can help carry them."

"Don't you mean booty?" Jean asked, but he followed Beau and Étienne out of the parlor.

Arielle sat back in her chair and sighed deeply. "Can Étienne's arrival here be no more than coincidence, Byron?"

"You did know his father then?" Belle inquired.

Arielle thought of Dominique all alone in her room. Étienne might be precisely what her melancholy daughter required to recapture her zest for life, but he could just as asily be a worse companion than Sean O'Keefe. "If I did, t was a very long time ago," she explained absently.

"The man tried to kill me," Byron announced with clear disgust. He moved to his wife's side and caressed her shoulder.

"Oh no!" Belle cried.

Not alarmed, Falcon squeezed her hand. "Obviously, he didn't succeed."

"No, thank God, he didn't," Byron concurred. "But Étienne looks so much like Gaetan, I would have recognized him as his son anywhere. Well, he will soon be gone, so let's not mention the matter again."

Arielle nodded, but she still felt uneasy. The past had a strange way of resurfacing at the most peculiar times, but Étienne had been so respectful and polite she hated to blame him for his father's jealousies. "He seemed to be a very nice young man."

Belle caught the deeper meaning in her mother's comment. "Are you thinking what I'm thinking?" she asked her mother.

"Perhaps. But it is really too soon for Dominique to take an interest in another man."

Falcon laughed out loud at that opinion. "Surely she has wrung the last tear from her tragic encounter with Sean. I'll bet money that she'll join us for supper tonight, and treat our guest with so much charm he won't be able to tell us what he ate."

"Her sorrow has been sincere," Belle argued. "You can't believe that it wasn't."

Falcon started for the door. "Who's to say with Dominique? I'll see what help Beau needs with the presents. Why don't you help your sister get dressed?"

"No. I'm coming with you." Belle caught Falcon's hand as they passed through the doorway, and continued to argue her sister's cause.

Byron drew his wife to her feet and kissed her soundly.

"Do you remember the first time we made love in Acadia? You'd gone to gather herbs after church, and I followed."

Some memories would always remain vivid, and Arielle smiled seductively as she slid her arms around his waist. "How could I ever forget? It was when Beau was conceived."

Byron hugged her more tightly. "Is that the only reason you recall that blissful afternoon?"

Arielle reached up on her tiptoes to whisper in his ear. "Come upstairs with me before supper, and I'll show you precisely what I recall."

Eagerly accepting her invitation, Byron laughed and scooped her up in his arms. He marveled that his slender bride of more than twenty years enchanted him still, and carried her up to their room to refresh their memories before they had to resume their roles as responsible parents at supper.

Alone in her room, Dominique sat at her windowseat and looked down toward the James River. Beau would not leave the beautiful *Virginia Belle* tied up at their docks for more than a day or two; and then he would go back to sea to continue confounding the trade of British merchantmen. How she wished she could sail with him! He would never agree to having a woman on board, nor would her parents allow her to accompany him, but it was a tempting thought.

She watched Beau and Étienne talking on the dock. The sun shone on the Frenchman's thick curls with the same ebony fire that caught Falcon's, but she drew no parallels between the two young men. There had been a time when such an attractive guest would have delighted her, but no more. Now she saw only a man like any other, and he caused not a ripple in the lake of sorrow that still threatened to drown her.

Fifteen

Arielle knew Dominique wasn't coming to supper, and did not delay the meal, but took note of Beau's dismay when his sister's chair remained empty. With Christian, Liana, Liberty, Johanna, and David joining them, the table was crowded and the talk loud and amusing. She observed Étienne and found nothing objectionable about the young man's behavior, but she remained curious about him.

"How did you happen to meet Beau?" she inquired.

Étienne smiled at his hostess. "I came to America with Lafayette in 1777 and fought with him at Brandywine and also at Monmouth. I met Beau in Martinique. He offered me the chance to sail home with him and I took it. I am eager for a chance to fight here."

"You must speak with Falcon," Arielle suggested.

"*Oui*, madame, I intend to."

Belle inquired about France then, and Arielle listened attentively to Étienne's response rather than ask another question herself. She was a woman who relied upon her intuition, and there was nothing alarming about Étienne. His smile was charming, his laugh warm and deep. In the course of the conversation, she learned he was twenty-two, Dominique's age. Three years of war had hardened both his body and spirit, however, and other than his boyish curls there was nothing naïve or youthful about him.

Still, she did not want him living in her house. She caught

a teasing exchange between Falcon and Belle, and at last recalled that Alanna had told him to sleep at Christian's home on his last visit. He had left rather than do so, and in the excitement of having Belle and Dominique home, the order had been forgotten. Of course, he and Belle were engaged now, but in her mind that fact had merely magnified, rather than solved, the original problem.

"What is the matter with Dominique?" Beau asked, abruptly interrupting his mother's train of thought.

Because Étienne would overhear whatever she said, Arielle simply shook her head, but at the close of the meal, Beau drew her aside when the others left for the parlor. Arielle recounted Belle and Dominique's adventure very briefly, but she could see just how badly she had shocked her elder son. "It is absurd, is it not?" she asked. "The one time Dominique truly fell in love, it was with a man she could not have. I imagine he is as heartbroken as she, but fortunately we do not also have to listen to him weep."

Having his little sisters run away astounded Beau, but Dominique in a romance with Sean O'Keefe was unimaginable. "I can't believe any of this actually happened," he complained, "and don't know what to make of it. I really thought Dominique would like Étienne, but she wouldn't even talk to him."

Arielle did not wish to encourage her son's matchmaking, but recalled when Byron had first come to Grand Pré, she had not wanted to speak with him, either. "It's best not to meddle in affairs of the heart. Now, what about you? Will you have time to call on any of the lovely young women here in Williamsburg?"

Beau had a quick answer for her. "No." He looked very much like his father had at his age, and with his fair hair and blue eyes women always regarded him as remarkably handsome, but his life was far too dangerous at present to permit him to court a sweetheart. "Wait until after the war," he promised his mother, "and then I'll call on them all."

"Yes. I imagine you will." They entered the parlor arm in arm, and for an hour or two at least, the war was forgotten in fond memories of home. Beau intended to sleep on board his ship, but before leaving the house, he went upstairs to visit Dominique. He rapped lightly at her door and waited for an invitation to enter.

"I brought you a bottle of perfume," he exclaimed as he approached the bed. "It's the perfect scent for you: all heat and spice."

Intrigued, Dominique lay the sonnets she had yet to read aside, took the elegant crystal bottle, and removed the stopper. "Yes," she agreed. "This is delicious." She set the bottle aside on the nightstand without applying any, however.

Beau sat down on the side of her bed. "You look awful."

"I suppose I do, but I really don't care."

"Well, you should. I finally found you a handsome Frenchman, and I'm afraid you simply frightened him by appearing in your nightgown in the middle of the afternoon."

Dominique shrugged. "I don't care about that, either."

Beau reached out to smooth her tangled curls from her brow. "You're all freckled," he complained, "and your skin was as luscious as cream. What's gotten into you? How could you have run off, or come home with a British officer? Have you lost what little sense you had?"

Dominique batted his hand away. "You go wherever you choose and come home whenever you please with whatever companions suit you, so you've no reason to criticize me. Besides, did you really expect everything to always be the same here?"

"Yes! And it is, except for you." He thought a minute, and then mentioned Belle and Falcon. "I always thought they'd wed, but you, you need someone very special."

"I found someone special," she breathed softly.

She was so thin her eyes appeared enormous, and Beau had never noticed the extraordinary length of her eyelashes.

She had always been such a provocative young woman, and he didn't know what to make of the subdued soul sitting in his sister's bed. "I've missed you, Dominique."

"Thank you. I've missed you, too."

"Good. Then you'll do me a favor." Beau glanced around the petal pink room, and smiled slightly. "It's been months since Étienne has even spoken to a girl. He's rather shy, but if you could just talk with him a minute, it would make him feel welcome here."

Beau was dressed in dark blue with a white shirt and gray vest. He preferred simple styles in fine fabrics as did their father, but wore boots rather than shoes. "You look very much the proper gentleman," she scolded, "so surely you know I ought not to entertain callers here in my bedroom."

"It's still warm. Put on a lace shawl over your nightgown and meet him in the garden."

"No. I'd not be able to think of anything to say."

Beau regarded her with a decidedly skeptical glance. "Dominique, not once in your entire life have you ever been at a loss for words with a man."

Dominique knew she deserved that rebuke for indeed she had seldom been engaged in a conversation she had not led. Thinking back, she felt as though she were remembering another person, not herself at an earlier time. "No. I'm much too tired to entertain him."

"How can you possibly be tired? When were you last out of this bed?"

"I was up only this afternoon. You saw me downstairs."

"Yes, and so did Étienne and he's been pining to see you again ever since. Put on some of that new perfume, and he'll probably faint from the sheer joy of being with you."

Now it was Dominique who grew skeptical. While her brother never discussed his romantic conquests with her, she had no doubt that he had known a great many beautiful women. His experience bore no relation to hers, however,

and she refused to accept his assessment of the situation.
"I don't believe we should take that risk. What if he were
to injure himself in a fall?"

"I think he'd gladly accept a few bruises to lie at the foot
of your bed for a while."

Beau was working very hard to lift her spirits, but an
adoring man was the very last thing Dominique needed.
"You're very sweet, Beau, but no. I don't want to speak
with your friend. Please give him my apologies."

Beau opened his mouth to try another argument, then
thought better of it. "As you wish," he sighed. He kissed
her cheek and then rose to his feet. "You're right, of course.
It was wrong of me to believe nothing would change while
I was away, but I love you so much, I want you to always
stay the same."

"No. The woman I used to be wasn't worth preserving.
Good night, Beau."

"You're very wrong, but I'll not tire you further with an
argument. Good night." Beau left her bedroom and went
straight downstairs where he found Étienne boasting to Falcon of what an excellent shot he was.

"I've seen Étienne shoot," Beau interjected, "and he may
very well match you in talent. Will you excuse us a moment? I need to speak with him privately." As soon as Beau
had drawn his friend aside, he explained his dilemma.

"My sister is heartbroken over a man who was completely unworthy of her affection. Do you suppose you
could speak with her for a few minutes and make her feel
pretty again? I've seen how easily you talk with women,
and it would mean so much to me, to all of us, if you could
just make her smile."

After the fine meal and gracious welcome Étienne had
received from the Barclays, he did not see how he could
refuse, but he tried. "If she is not feeling well, won't she
merely be annoyed if I disturb her?"

"No. She was almost pathetically grateful for my company when I went up to visit with her just now. Come with me out to the garden and we'll pick a few gardenias for you to take to her. She'll have to invite you in to thank you, and then everything will go well."

Fearing he would regret every awkward moment, Étienne nonetheless let himself be led outside. It was a glorious night, warm and bright, and scented by the lush fragrance of summer. He waited while Beau broke off several stems of snowy white gardenias and resigned himself to paying Dominique a visit he would make as brief as possible. He carried the flowers up the stairs with a slow, plodding step and stood aside as Beau knocked on Dominique's door. When she answered, he shook his head.

"I am afraid this will go very badly," he whispered.

"Nonsense. She is adorable. You'll love her." Beau pushed open the door and placed his hand in the middle of Étienne's back to propel him into Dominique's bedroom.

"Bon soir, mademoiselle," Étienne greeted her. He entered her room with his arm outstretched to offer the small bouquet. Wanting to get the wretched visit over with quickly, he hurried to her bedside, but beneath the wild curls he had noted that afternoon, he saw eyes as clear a blue-green as the waters of the Caribbean Sea. Then he noted her long sweep of eyelashes, the gentle arch of her brow, and the delicacy of her nose. Her face was a sweet heart-shape, and her mouth, slightly stained with berry juice, was perfection. Her lower lip had a lush fullness, and the upper a well-defined bow. Why had he seen only her tangled hair, when she was such an exquisite beauty? Then he cursed himself for not rushing up to her room hours ago.

Dominique had seen that same smitten expression on too many male faces to appreciate Étienne's awe. His dark gray suit was far from new, and while he was broad-shouldered, his vest hung loose, emphasizing a thin rather than muscular physique. His hair could do with a trim, but she liked his eyes well enough to produce a slight smile.

"I'm afraid Beau has played a very cruel trick on you," she said in the smooth, husky tone that always drew men near.

"Mon Dieu," Étienne whispered. "You are an angel."

"No. I assure you that despite the sorry way I must look, I'm still very much alive." She reached out to take the flowers and dropped the stems into the pitcher of water on the nightstand. *"Merci.* You've done your good deed, monsieur, and may go."

Étienne had charmed his way into women's beds from the day he had turned sixteen, but he could not think of a single thing to say to Dominique. Her hands were resting in her lap and he reached out to touch her wrist lightly and felt the thrill clear to the soles of his feet. *"Oui,* mademoiselle. You are very much alive."

His hand was tan, his fingers long and slim. His touch was pleasant, but Dominique was more amused than aroused. "You and Beau are our guests tonight, and you ought to hurry back to the party," she advised.

Dazzled by her smile, Étienne tried to remember if she had been tall. The one glimpse he had caught of her in her flowing nightgown had disclosed no hint of her figure, but he thought it likely she would also possess Belle's slender grace. He had always found pretty women an entertaining diversion, but mere amusement would not be nearly enough from her.

"I wish to set America free of British domination," he announced much too loudly for the silent room.

Fearful she would insult him, Dominique used both hands to smother her laugh, but Étienne was so pitifully sincere she was touched. "I'm so sorry. I don't mean to be rude, but this is a poor time, and a most inappropriate place, for a political discussion."

"Oui, mademoiselle." Étienne had never suffered from such a terribly vacant mind; his emotions were in complete turmoil. He was torn between fleeing the room and vowing

never to leave her. Anxious for any excuse to prolong his stay, he seized upon the book at her side. "I could read to you," he offered, "all night if you wish."

His accent was very charming, and Dominique imagined she would enjoy hearing him read, but again, at another time. "You're very kind, monsieur—another night perhaps."

"You did not dine with us, and we were served such delicious food. Are you hungry? Thirsty? Would you like more flowers?"

Dominique shook her head. "What I would like is to be left alone. Good night, Étienne. Sleep well."

Étienne doubted he would be able to sleep at all. He wanted desperately to kiss her, and feared his heart might cease to beat if he forbade himself that joy. He could not find the breath to ask permission and simply leaned down to brush Dominique's lips lightly with his own. Stunned by the exquisitely pleasurable sensation, he could not immediately draw away. Her response was very gentle and sweet, but she returned his kiss. Elated to have had even a small sample of her affection, he straightened up and broke into a wide grin.

"Tomorrow," he promised, "you are going to get out of that bed and spend the day with me."

Shocked that he would be so presumptuous, Dominique watched him swagger out of the room with a confidence he had not once displayed the whole while they had conversed. "What an unusual young man," she remarked absently, but she ran her fingertip over her lips and thought for such a brief kiss, his mouth had felt awfully good. Not as good as Sean's perhaps, but definitely worth a second kiss. She leaned over to inhale the gardenias' exotic fragrance, and thought perhaps she would be able to leave her bed tomorrow. That did not mean she wanted to spend the day with Étienne, but the plantation was large, and it would not be difficult to avoid him.

Étienne had to hold tightly to the handrail to guide himself downstairs, but there was no way he could hide his opinion of Dominique from her brother. "Your sister is precisely the jewel you described," he assured Beau. "But I fear nothing I do will please her."

Beau had never seen Étienne so flustered, and clapped him on the back. "She's not a princess. Treat her as you would any other woman," he advised.

"She is not like any other woman," Étienne complained, "but I will try."

"Yes. I know you will." Beau bade his family good night, and with the befuddled Étienne in tow, returned to his ship.

Falcon and Belle were gathered in the hallway with the others as Christian, with Liberty in his arms, and Liana also left along with Johanna and David. It had been the enjoyable kind of evening Falcon had hoped to have on his last visit home, but as his Aunt Arielle came toward him, he had a sinking feeling he knew precisely what she was going to say. Not wanting to put ideas into her head, however, he waited for her to speak.

"If your mother hasn't already told you to stay at Christian's, then I won't either, Falcon, but please don't make me sorry."

"No, ma'am. You needn't worry about me."

Arielle kissed Belle good night and went on up the stairs but her warning had not been lost on the young lovers. Belle waited until she heard her mother's door close. "Let's go out to the garden and talk," she suggested.

Falcon leaned down to whisper. "If your mother is going to be watching me later tonight, let's go out to the stable and make love."

"Don't be wicked," Belle scolded with a lilting giggle, but she did not want anything to ruin the night that lay ahead, either. When they reached the garden, she threw her arms around Falcon's neck and kissed him soundly. He had not mentioned marriage since he had made her his wife in the forest, and she was loath to bring up the subject herself but she was anxious to make their union a legal one so they did not have to hide their passion for one another.

"How long can you stay home?" she asked instead, and dreading his answer, held her breath as she awaited his reply.

"A few more days," Falcon murmured between hungry kisses. He cupped her breast and teased her nipple with his palm. "I want the war over so I never have to leave you again. It hurts too much, Belle, far too much."

Belle would never forget the fire in his eyes as he had drawn his knife on Sean O'Keefe and sincerely doubted that he gave any thought to her while he was away. He had been gone only briefly to fight outside Petersburg, but she had felt him withdraw into himself even as he had kissed her farewell. She looked up toward the light in her parents' bedroom on the second floor and laced her fingers in Falcon's to still his wandering caress.

"There are a couple of empty stalls in the stable, aren't there?"

"Yes, and they're laid with fresh straw," Falcon whispered enticingly. "It will be almost as nice as the forest."

"We won't be able to see the stars, though," Belle reminded him.

Falcon slid his arm around her waist to guide her along the path. "We'll make our own, Belle, and they'll be just as bright."

They laughed together as they had as children, but the pleasure they had found with each other now was deeper than either had dreamed existed years ago. The stable was warm and dark, but they made it a small corner of paradise and shared all they would ever need of heaven. When they returned to the house after midnight, they parted on the stairs and went to their separate rooms, but were together again in their dreams.

* * *

Dominique awakened the next morning, her chest tight with a nameless fear. It was a horrible sensation and she sat up slowly, believing a forgotten dream must be to blame. She left her bed and crossed to the open window. When she looked out, she saw members of Beau's crew moving about the deck of the *Virginia Belle,* but she lacked their eagerness to greet the day. Beau would not be home long, however, and she did not want him to find her confined to her bed again.

The water in the pitcher on the washstand was fresh and cool, and she splashed her face and patted it dry. Gazing into the mirror she scarcely recognized the thin face that greeted her; her outward appearance had changed as greatly as her inner mood, but that did not trouble her. In fact, she rather liked the more serious expression she now wore and hurried to her wardrobe in hopes of finding something suitably somber among the bright silks and satins.

Way in the back, a pale peach muslin gown caught her eye. It was demure in design, if not solemn in hue, and after donning the layers of lacy lingerie her fashions required, she slipped on the summery gown and was pleased. She brushed out her hair, knotted it atop her head, and added an eyelet cap with a ribbon tie. White stockings and kid slippers completed the outfit, and she was again ever so grateful to have such lovely clothes.

She glanced around her room, and sighting the gardenias, took one and pinned it to her bodice. She had no need of perfume while wearing the fragrant flower, and hoping the tightness in her chest would soon fade, she went downstairs for breakfast. She had not wondered who might share the table, as each member of the family trailed through the dining room at his own pace in the morning, but Beau and Étienne had already eaten and were chatting with her mother and aunt.

"Belle and Falcon have gone fishing," Arielle announced.

"Beau has to prepare to sail, but we thought perhaps you could give Monsieur LeBlanc a tour of the plantation."

"Are you interested in tobacco farming, monsieur?" Dominique inquired. She slid into her usual place beside her father's vacant chair. Étienne was again seated on the opposite side of the table at her mother's right where they could glance easily at each other as they spoke. She never ate more than a few pieces of fruit for breakfast, and began to peel a ripe peach.

"I can not imagine a more fascinating subject," Étienne replied, but he would have been content to discuss whatever topic she chose. Beau winked at him, but he scarcely needed the encouragement.

"It's nearly time for the harvest," Dominique remarked.

Étienne watched Dominique guide a sliver of peach to her mouth. She licked the juice from her lips, and he could barely suppress a moan. "I will enjoy observing that as well."

Confused, Dominique paused before slicing off another bite of fruit. "Beau is seldom home, so I'm afraid you'll undoubtedly miss it."

She did not appear pained by his imminent departure, but Étienne refused to give up his effort to impress her. "I am not sailing with Beau," he explained. "I plan to stay in Virginia and fight with the militia."

Dominique's knife spilled from her hand and clattered to her plate. "Really? Does he know?"

"Yes. I told him yesterday. I can shoot very well, and I will welcome a chance to wear buckskins."

Dominique had already noticed Étienne could do with a new suit of clothes, but buckskins had not been what she had had in mind. "We're all grateful for the assistance France has given us to fight Great Britain. I do hope that you'll return home safe and well."

"Thank you, mademoiselle, I will pray for you as well."

Dominique tried to smile, then found it easier to concentrate her attention on the slippery peach. She recalled Sergeant Danby had offered to pray for her, but she was not certain she was flattered now. She was in perfect health, but feared Étienne might believe her soul was in need of redemption. "You are too kind, monsieur."

Arielle caught Alanna's eye and smiled. "I'm so pleased you're feeling well again, but Étienne has had a long voyage, and you mustn't tire him."

"I'll be exceptionally considerate," Dominique promised her mother. She was relieved when Beau began a description of the beauty of the West Indies, but all too soon he excused himself and went to join their father in the study. She dallied with a few berries, then ate another peach, but finally could delay leaving the table no longer. "Are you ready, monsieur?"

Étienne left his chair in an instant and circled the table to help Dominique from hers. He was dressed as he had been the previous evening, and very neatly groomed even if his attire was worn. "Ladies, you will excuse us?"

"Of course," Arielle assured him, and Alanna murmured a wish for a pleasant outing.

Dominique glanced up at Étienne. His hair was fine, if thickly curled, and his beard so light it lent only a faint shadow beneath his deep tan. She tried to imagine him in buckskins, but failed.

"Let's go out through the garden," she suggested.

"My mother is devoted to her flowers," Étienne confided as they strolled through the well-tended rows of roses, gardenias, and carnations. He bent down to enjoy a deep red rose's perfume, then had to rush to catch up with Dominique. "Do you spend much time here?"

"Sometimes," Dominique replied. "It's a pleasant place to sit and read, or simply think."

"Am I intruding upon your thoughts, mademoiselle?"

He most definitely was, but Dominique smiled and shook her head. "We have a small city on our property, but I'm assuming you'd rather walk along the fields than visit with the blacksmith or cooper."

"Oui." Étienne reached for her hand and was pleased when she did not yank free. "My father is a fisherman as he was in Acadia, and taught me about the sea, so your plantation is a marvel to me."

Startled, Dominique turned to look up at him. "Your father is Acadian?"

"I had forgotten that you were not there when I met your parents, and we spoke of Acadia then. Does it bother you? I see no difference where a Frenchman is born. He is still French, is he not?"

"Yes, of course, but the Acadians were so widely scattered after the expulsion, I've met only a few. It was a surprise, that's all."

"A common link between us that you did not expect?" Étienne wished aloud.

"Yes. I suppose we could view it that way." Dominique led him through the garden out toward the fields which bordered the house. His touch was as gentle as his kiss, not in the least bit confining, and she liked that. Some men held on as though they feared she was about to bolt, but rather than suppress the urge, they encouraged her to flee.

She gestured toward the plants that were nearing six feet in height. The dark green leaves grew long and full in the center of the stalk, but tapered in size toward the top. "The tobacco plants grow for a single season. We start them in seed beds in early spring, then in two to three months transplant them to the fields. They have pretty pink flowers, but when the blooms appear, they're cut or topped off to encourage the growth of larger leaves.

"Harvesting will begin soon. The plants are cut, allowed to wilt, and then cured in special barns where the leaves are air-dried. To improve its flavor, the tobacco is then stored in barrels for two to three years before it's sold. It's an endless process, but then so is fishing for a living."

"Oui." The day was warm, but Étienne was enjoying himself far too much to be uncomfortable. "Would you show me one of the barns?"

"They're empty now, and not all that interesting."

"I want to see one anyway."

Dominique lifted her skirt with her free hand and continued on down the path. "I doubt Falcon will be home much longer. Do you really intend to fight with him in the Carolinas?"

Étienne squeezed her hand. "Did you think I said that merely to impress you?"

Dominique came to an abrupt halt, forcing him to stop with her. "I hope you'd not risk your life to impress any woman. That would be foolhardy in the extreme, Étienne."

She looked sincerely concerned. Pleased beyond measure, Étienne flashed a teasing grin. "I have already fought for three years, Dominique, and I did not even know you existed. Do you like soldiers?"

That question hurt very badly, and while Dominique knew it had not been intentional, she could not hide her pain. "Please. I don't want to talk about other men."

"Neither do I," Étienne assured her. "Now come show me a barn, and then we can walk down by the river."

He had not worn a hat, and the sun reflected off his ebony curls with the same iridescent gleam it gave a raven's wing. His brows and lashes were just as black, accenting his light eyes handsomely. He had such a pleasant smile, but in repose, she saw a glimmer of a darker mood in his expression.

"You've been wounded, haven't you?" she asked.

Étienne spread his arms wide. "Does it show?"

"It's not something I can see," Dominique murmured. "I just know."

A hint of a breeze ruffled the tobacco leaves and the lacy edge of Dominique's frilly cap. Étienne thought her even more beautiful in daylight than she had been in the soft glow of a lamp last night. "I have the scars for proof, should you need it."

"I'll accept your word," Dominique readily conceded, and continued on toward the row of barns. She thought it quite odd to be escorting the battle-scarred descendant of another Acadian around the plantation, but then decided it was exactly the distraction she needed.

"We employ only free men," she explained, "as my family has never condoned slavery. As you can imagine, our views often clashed with our neighbors' even before the war."

"Beau never mentioned your family's customs, but I would not want to own another man. You have every right to be proud."

Dominique dared not comment on pride, when she feared her own was to blame for her current sorrow. "Thank you. What did Beau tell you about us?"

Beau had told him a great many entertaining tales, and Étienne had to sift through his memories for something suitable for her ears. "He said he had an uncle who was a Seneca Indian, which was a surprise, but I was more interested to learn his mother was Acadian. I wondered if she has felt as lost as my father has since being turned out of her home."

They had reached the first barn and the door was open wide, allowing them to enter without breaking stride. Several degrees cooler than the fields, the shady interior was most inviting. "My mother taught us all to speak French as babies, so we've always known Virginia wasn't her home, but I don't believe she's ever been unhappy here."

The sunlight was slanted through the doorway, highlighting the curls that peeked from beneath her cap. The peach tones of her gown were very flattering with her golden tan, and Étienne thought her freckles charming. Alone where no one could observe, he wanted only one thing. He leaned down to kiss her, and wanting more than he had taken last night, slipped his arms around her waist to hold her tight.

Instantly the fear which had marred her waking moments returned in full force, and Dominique put both hands on his chest to shove him away. Then, feeling slightly dizzy, she grabbed for his arm to steady herself. "I think we'd better go," she urged in a breathless whisper.

"Dominique? Are you ill? Oh, of course you are. That's why you were in bed yesterday. Please, let's sit down here until you feel better. Or would you rather I carry you back to the house?"

Badly frightened rather than ill, Dominique shook her head. *What was the matter?* she tormented herself. She had once been so content in a man's company that she could laugh and chat for hours or dance away half the night without ever feeling a bit of fatigue. She was not really tired now, though, but frightened by some unseen peril. Étienne had merely kissed her, as many other men had, and her quivering fright was an absurd reaction.

There was a sprinkling of straw scattered over the dirt floor, topped with ragged bits of last year's crop. Étienne removed his coat and spread it out to provide a place for her to sit. When he gestured with a deep bow, she was grateful for his thoughtfulness.

"Thank you. If I just rest a moment, I'm sure I'll be fine." She arranged her skirt carefully as she knelt down, and then sat surrounded by deep folds of peach muslin.

"You look like the heart of a rose," Étienne exclaimed as he knelt beside her, "all dressed in scalloped petals." He positioned himself at her right where she could lean back against his shoulder. The barn held the pungent aroma of tobacco, but he thought Dominique so sweet, he did not even notice.

"I'm so sorry," Dominique murmured, but despite her lingering anxiety, she found Étienne's shoulder the perfect support. "I'm not in the least bit frail, and I never faint."

"I do hope I have not made you ill," he whispered against her temple.

His accent was as reassuring as her mother's, and Dominique was positive he was not to blame. She was the problem, or perhaps simply love, and for the first time it occurred to her that she might actually die of a broken heart. Her mother had taught her many cures, but there were no herbs to soothe her sorrow. She leaned against Étienne and closed her eyes. It would be so easy to simply let go of life, but as he began to caress her shoulder with light kisses, death lost all its appeal.

Sixteen

Dominique raised her hand to caress Étienne's cheek. "Please stop. I can't be what you want and I'd only disappoint you."

Étienne caught her hand and placed a kiss in her palm. "That would be impossible," he argued. "Why are you so afraid?"

Dominique slipped her hand from his, but remained sheltered against his shoulder. "I'm not afraid of you," she replied hesitantly.

Content simply to hold her for the moment, Étienne waited, hoping she would confess the cause of her reticence to accept his affection. It soon became clear she intended to keep that secret. "Your family is a happy one, is it not?"

That was a much easier question to answer, and Dominique relaxed slightly. "As happy as any family can be with the war causing such great suffering. You may have seen everyone smiling last night, but the war is always on our minds. My father was among the first to speak out for independence, so we've been fighting a long time. If Britain prevails, we'll lose everything: this beautiful plantation, perhaps even our lives."

"It is no wonder you are sad then," Étienne said, "but America will win. Your men are defending their homes and families. The British soldiers are little better than mercenaries."

Dominique turned slightly to look up at him. "And what, pray tell, are you, monsieur?"

Believing he had won her interest, Étienne pushed for more. "Kiss me and I will explain."

Dominique looked away. "I'm not *that* curious." She folded her hands in her lap. She was adept at encouraging men, not discouraging them, but hoped she had conveyed sufficient disinterest to convince him to focus his affections elsewhere.

A persistent man, Étienne nibbled her earlobe. "You are a very beautiful liar, and you are very curious about me."

"I am not," Dominique exclaimed, but as she turned toward him, he leaned down to kiss her. She ducked her head, but he shifted position to catch her neck in the crook of his arm and held her fast. His mouth was warm, his tongue smoothly insistent as he parted her lips, but she was no easy conquest and shoved him so hard he lost his balance. As he tumbled backwards, he pulled her down across his chest.

Étienne laughed at how badly her attempt to escape him had failed. "Do you want to play?" he teased. He slid his hand under Dominique's cap to grab a handful of her hair, and ignoring her muffled protest, kissed her again. She squirmed, pressing the soft fullness of her bosom against his chest and heightening his pleasure to the point where he could not bear to stop. Releasing her hair, he locked his fingers around her wrists, did a quick roll to the left, and forced her down onto his coattails. Captured, her eyes widened, but he wanted only kisses and held her in a light grasp.

"I love passionate women," he declared. "You see? You are exactly what I want."

"But I don't want you!" Dominique cried. "Now get off me, or I'll scream and a dozen men will come running."

Her sultry voice had taken on a steely edge, and when Étienne realized she was not enjoying the amorous play as greatly as he, he was badly disappointed and quickly moved aside. He stood, and leaned down to take Dominique's hands and pull her up beside him. The instant she was on her feet, she pushed his hands away.

"My apologies, mademoiselle. I did not mean to force myself upon you."

Dominique laughed at that ridiculous comment, and shook out her skirt to dislodge the bits of tobacco clinging to every fold. "What do you call it then? Is that the way Frenchmen behave? If so, I'll not even speak to another of your countrymen."

Étienne reached down for his coat and brushed off the tobacco and straw. He stood back as Dominique poked several errant curls up under her cap. Her cheeks were filled with a bright blush, making her even prettier in his eyes, but he took exception to her haughty attitude. "At breakfast, you were grateful for the help of Frenchmen. I am still the same man. Like Lafayette, I believe in the cause of freedom. I also hope that once we have won it for America, Americans will help us win our own independence."

Startled by the seriousness of Étienne's response, Dominique studied him more closely. Rather than handsome, when he was angry, he looked simply dangerous. He was lean, but tough, and much stronger than she had supposed. "You are no gentleman, monsieur, but if you are sincerely committed to our cause, then I'll forgive you, but only this once. If you can't treat me as a lady, I'll not allow you to call."

Étienne's stare turned cold. "I thought you would have a heart worth seeking, but you are no more than a beautiful shell, like a pastry without a delicious filling." He raked her with an insolent glance, and then shook his head. "If it were not the war, you would have another excuse to push me away. Beau called you a treasure, but you are not worth the price of an amusing whore."

Dominique slapped him so hard her handprint was visible

on his cheek as he strode out the door. Nearly blinded by tears, she waited a moment before following, but when she left the barn, she discovered Étienne had gone only a few yards before stopping. Falcon and Belle were rapidly approaching, and Dominique hurried to Étienne's side. "Don't say a thing," she warned.

"He is carrying a rifle. Do you think I am stupid?" Étienne's scowl deepened. "I have no choice but to pretend nothing has happened."

"Nothing has," Dominique hissed through clenched teeth. She raised her hand to return Falcon's wave. "Are you going hunting?" she called to him.

Falcon waited until he and Belle had reached them to speak. "No. I just wanted to see if Étienne is as fine a shot as he claims."

Étienne's cheek still stung, and he turned slightly to hide what he feared would be a telltale mark. "Select a target, and I will gladly hit it."

Eager for a contest, Falcon nodded toward the cottonwood trees at the end of the line of barns. "Rather than put a hole in a barn, let's aim for the trees." He pulled a piece of canvas from his pocket. "I'll tie this to a branch, and give you the first shot."

"I'll not need more than one," Étienne claimed proudly. He held the rifle while Falcon sprinted for the trees and tied the cloth to a low branch. The brave stepped back and adjusted the drape of the fabric to form a target perhaps six inches square. He then came back to the others in an easy lope.

Étienne shoved his coat into Dominique's hands, and too surprised to complain, she took it. He raised the rifle to his shoulder with a relaxed motion, took careful aim, and fired. The report was deafening, but after the puff of smoke had cleared, they could all see the clean hole in the canvas dangling from the tree. "I do not believe that you can do any better," he challenged.

Clearly impressed, Falcon nodded. "You are a good shot. Now I'll show you what I can do." He returned to the tree, untied the fabric, folded it in half, and retied it to create a target half the size of the one he had given Étienne. He ran back, took his weapon from Étienne to reload, and then also drilled a clean hole through the fabric with one quick shot.

"It's unfortunate the British won't hold as still, but I've killed my share," Falcon announced with a pride that sent a shudder through Belle.

"Please," she implored him. "You needn't remind us that you prefer human targets."

"I do as well, mademoiselle," Étienne remarked coolly. He reached for his coat and slung it over his shoulder. "Please excuse me. I wish to speak with Beau."

He moved away with a long, purposeful stride, and Dominique felt certain he intended to tell Beau he had changed his mind about remaining in Virginia. After he had compared her to a whore, she was relieved to see him go, but at the same time, she was sorry he had not taken her at her word when she had first complained she would only disappoint him. She had never enjoyed conflict for its own sake and wished they could have parted as friends. Instead, Étienne had been a demanding, arrogant ass, and she refused to torture herself with a new regret.

When Dominique glanced toward Belle and Falcon, she was embarrassed to find them observing her closely. Fearing she might still be dusted with tobacco, she looked down at her gown, but it looked fine to her. "What's wrong?" she asked. "Do I look strange for some reason?"

"It's not in the way you look," Falcon mused gently. "It's in the peculiar way Étienne behaved. He was obviously furious, and I'll wager your palm is an exact match for the patch of color on his left cheek. I was sure you would tell me if you wanted him marched off the plantation. Was I wrong?"

Étienne had already swung toward the docks and was lost

from view. Dominique had found their whole exchange deeply troubling, but felt no need to share it. "He's an exasperating man, but I didn't need your help to handle him."

"Well, don't hesitate to ask if you do." Falcon took Belle's hand and nodded toward the house. "We caught bass for dinner. Have you already eaten more fish than you can bear?"

Dominique lifted the front of her gown as they started walking toward the house. "Yes, but I don't want to miss dining again with Beau. I fear he's already stayed with us too long."

"He's not been here even a day," Belle argued, "but I imagine he'll sail soon after dinner to clear Hampton Roads tonight and return to sea. Perhaps the next time he returns home, he'll bring along a friend you'll find more appealing."

"I'll beg him not to try," Dominique insisted. "I'm through with men. Oh, not you, of course, Falcon. You're a dear cousin and as close as a brother, but other men no longer interest me."

Falcon rolled his eyes. "Better make a note of the date, Belle, because I doubt Dominique can exist for more than a few days without an admirer or two."

Belle gave Falcon's hand a fierce yank to silence his teasing. "You mustn't make fun of us," she begged. "Neither of us gives our affection casually, and I would never seek another man's company should I ever lose you."

"God forbid!" Falcon shouted.

"Thank you, Belle," Dominique murmured under her breath, for it was comforting to know her sister understood how much she missed Sean. As they entered the house, she had to fight off a numbing dread, but while Beau was in the parlor with Jean, Étienne was not. Nor did the Frenchman appear as they gathered in the dining room, and Dominique took her place, greatly relieved that he would not spoil the meal.

As soon as Byron had ended the blessing, he leaned toward his elder daughter. "Do you have a good reason for reeking of tobacco?" he whispered.

The heat of a bright blush flooded Dominique's cheeks before she realized the peculiar odor could be easily explained without revealing she had been rolling around on the floor of a curing barn with Étienne. She mumbled something about giving Étienne a tour of the fields and barns which seemed to satisfy her father, but she was mortified all the same. She was positive she had not invited Étienne's vigorous attentions, and he had ceased when she had made her disgust clear. She would send her gown to the laundry to be washed that very afternoon to rid it of the lingering scent of tobacco, but she doubted her memories would be as easy to cleanse.

She toyed with her food and spoke only when spoken to, but smiled often at Beau's tales. It was a leisurely meal, and they lingered over dessert, but finally Beau announced he would have to go, and everyone followed him to the docks to wave good-bye. He kissed Dominique, hesitated as though he wished to say something more than a hasty farewell, but settled upon giving her hand a squeeze. Then he boarded his sleek schooner with a haste that made it plain he was eager to get underway. Dominique scanned the faces of the men lined up at the rail. Some had sailed with Beau several years and she wished them a good voyage by name. Others were smiling strangers, so she bid them *adieu* with no more than a wave.

Hoping not to arouse anyone's notice, Dominique searched for Étienne without success. Not that she would have waved to the obnoxious young man, but sighting him would have added the finality she desired. She had learned a valuable lesson from him and would emphatically refuse the next time anyone asked her to entertain a male guest. She did not care if she were perceived as indifferent or rude; it would be far better than inciting the insults Étienne had spewed so freely.

The whole family waited on the dock until the *Virginia Belle* rounded the curve in the river. Dominique covered a yawn and looked forward to a nap—until she turned back toward the house and saw Étienne standing on the path. He was not waiting for her, but for Falcon, and the two young men went off toward the stable, leaving Belle to walk with her to the house.

"Now that we're alone," Belle prompted, "tell me what you really think of Étienne."

"I don't think anything," Dominique sighed. "I just want to go back to bed and stay there for a year or two."

Dominique had encouraged Belle's hopes when she had feared Falcon was lost to her forever, but Belle couldn't find the words to comfort her. Sean O'Keefe had been shunted off to a prison camp, and even if the war were to end tomorrow, both he and Dominique would still feel betrayed by the other and be unlikely to reconcile. She had rather liked Étienne, but clearly Dominique didn't or wouldn't. Belle was sorry that Dominique had not been drawn to the Frenchman, but life had not been easy for her of late. Their mother would say love would come in its own time, but now that she was secure in Falcon's love, she felt very sorry for Dominique, who was all alone.

"I have money to pay for a horse," Étienne confided, "but these animals are much too fine to ride into battle."

Falcon and Étienne had walked through the stable and stopped at Nails's stall. Falcon rubbed his stallion's muzzle and spoke to him softly in the Seneca tongue he swore the horse understood. "I've promised Belle not to take this mount, so I need a new horse, too. I've always fought from cover rather than charging the British, but no horse is too fine for war if men must fight."

"I had not thought of it that way."

Falcon leaned back against the stall door and folded his arms across his chest. "Beau must trust you or he wouldn't have brought you home. I don't make friends as easily as he, and if you disappoint me in any way, I'll leave you right where you stand. You must understand that now."

Insulted, Étienne straightened up and replied in kind. "Your father is Seneca, and they are British allies. Why should I trust you?"

Falcon regarded the Frenchman with a dark, piercing gaze, but didn't intimidate him into looking away. "If what you've seen of the Barclays, and my family, isn't enough to inspire trust, then nothing will. I'm leaving at dawn. I'll have a horse here for you if you want to come with me. If not, follow the road into Williamsburg, buy a mount there, and make your way south on your own."

Étienne had gotten along so well with Beau, he did not understand why everything was going so poorly now. "You shoot very well," he said, "and I've proven that I can, too. Perhaps respect is as important as trust, and I can easily respect a man with your skill with a rifle. All I ask is the chance to fight."

Because the Patriots needed every man willing to bear arms, Falcon nodded. "Fine. We'll leave together then. Do you have a place to sleep tonight?"

None had been offered, and Étienne was much to proud to ask for a bed. "I will sleep here. It is clean and dry."

Falcon had an excellent reason for wanting the stable all to himself that night, but couldn't refuse such a small request. "As you wish. Do you have a hunting shirt, or buckskins?"

Étienne shrugged and spread his arms. "I have little more than what you see, but I do own a fine rifle."

The Frenchman was thinner than he was, but Falcon thought they were near enough in size to wear the same clothes. "I have buckskins you can wear. Come, I'll introduce you to the cook and she'll gather our provisions. I never take much, as the added weight would just slow me down. I hope you'll not mind living off the land."

Étienne wanted to make certain he understood. "Are you talking about fishing and shooting small game, or eating bugs?"

Falcon made a face. "Do the French eat bugs?" he asked.

"No, but—"

"Well, the Seneca don't, either." Falcon led the way to the kitchen and waved as they passed the cooper's shed where barrels for that year's harvest were already being made. "You didn't come to dinner. Do you want to eat with us tonight?"

Étienne knew Dominique would ignore him, and without a smile from her, it would be a wretched meal. "No. Beau was my friend and he is gone."

Falcon paused on the path between the scullery and dairy. "Have you given up on Dominique so soon?"

"My English is not good," he replied.

"What's wrong with her French?"

Étienne had forgotten Dominique spoke his native tongue and realized too late how ridiculous his excuse had sounded. "What I mean is, my English is not good enough to explain what happened to you. She does not like me, and I do not think I like her, either."

Falcon could not believe what he was hearing. "What do you mean, you don't like her? Men always like her, or at least they always have. You do like women, don't you?"

"Of course!" Étienne ran his thumbs down his lapels. "Look at me," he chided. "The Barclays are rich, and what do I have to offer a woman like Dominique except amusing company? She does not want my company, so I have nothing to give her."

"My sister wed a man who wandered up the road seeking work. Who you are will be more important than what you own to Dominique as well. You must be more patient with her. She's been very unhappy. Perhaps what she needs is sympathy rather than to be amused."

Étienne would not delude himself with false hopes. *"Oui.* I know. There was another man, and the war frightens her."

"I have tracked men for days," Falcon confided, "rather than allow a quarry to escape. Do you always give up so easily?"

Étienne looked up toward the house. The brick structure was magnificent, but his own family's home was as modest as the outbuildings here. "I may not be able to track as well as you, but I have never run from a battle. Dominique is not a battle, though. She is a woman who needs more than I can ever give. Do not torture me with questions about her. It is bad enough that I failed to please her for Beau's sake. Let's see to the provisions. I can live a long while on bread and cheese if the cook can spare us some."

Falcon considered Étienne's English exceptionally good, but he was talking in circles rather than reveal what had really happened between him and Dominique. Because Falcon had once believed he had nothing to offer Belle, he did not press him any further, but he thought him a fool for not trying harder. "Dominique is not really herself now," he explained. "The next time we come home, maybe you'll like each other better."

"She could not like me any less," Étienne exclaimed, and he forced himself to think of the journey that lay ahead rather than the maddeningly aloof blonde.

At supper that evening, everyone was rather subdued, for while they had all enjoyed Beau's visit, they knew how dangerous it had been for him. His schooner was far more swift than the British warships patrolling the coast, but he had had a long run of luck, and no one wanted it to end. Although distracted by thoughts of her brother, Belle could not help but notice the light sparkling in Falcon's eyes.

She knew precisely what he was thinking, and wanted to make love again, too. She did not rush her meal, but it was an effort not to bolt from the table when she finished the last bite. When everyone at last left the table, she took Falcon's hand, but he pulled her away from the parlor.

"We're going for a walk down by the river," he announced loudly enough for everyone to hear, then ushered Belle out the front door. They crossed the lawn and hurried down to the path along the shore. "Let's borrow the Scotts' house for tonight," Falcon suggested.

"The whole house, or merely a feather bed?"

Falcon chuckled at her insight. He could not have told her what they had just eaten for supper. He had been too lost in thoughts of what the night would bring. As they crossed onto Scott land, he gave her hand a gentle squeeze.

"I'm sorry for the awful things I said to you the last time I was home. You didn't deserve any of it. I should never have mentioned whores either, because being with them is nothing like being with you, Belle. You needn't worry I'll ever go back to them. I mean to be a faithful husband."

Belle wasn't certain how to respond. "Thank you for saying you're sorry, but I knew you couldn't have been sincere. At least I hoped you weren't. As for your being faithful, I wouldn't accept anything less. You do consider us already married, don't you?"

Falcon stopped and pulled her around to face him. "Well, yes. Don't you?"

There was so much love reflected in his eyes, but Belle wanted to have their union blessed in a church, and have a gold ring on her finger. "If we were truly wed, we'd not have to sneak off to the Scotts' house, would we?"

"We'll have a wedding," he promised, "but they take time to plan and I can't stay home that long, Belle. I've already been here too long."

Belle reached up to kiss him. "I wasn't complaining, Falcon, merely stating fact. I'm very proud of you, and I want everyone to know it."

Falcon looped his arms around her waist and lifted her off her feet in an exuberant hug. "I've always loved you." He kissed her as he lowered her back to her feet. "When I left my room this morning, my parents were standing in their doorway kissing. It wasn't a light kiss, either, but so passionate neither noticed they were being observed. I want us to be like them and always feel as much love for each other as we do tonight."

"I think every day I love you more," Belle replied, and she took his hand to coax him on down the path.

Amused that she was as eager for his loving as he was for hers, Falcon did not lag behind. When they reached the house, he carried her up the back steps and down the long hallway. The house was silent and dark, so he put her down to find a candle, and then took her hand to lead her up the stairs.

"I came over here today," he confided softly. "There are four bedrooms on the second floor, just as we have at home. From the looks of them, the two on the rear belonged to Liana's brothers, while those at the front belonged to her and her parents. Do you want to use her room or theirs?"

Belle remembered the Scotts well. Ian had been tall and red-haired, and his wife a petite brunette. Liana and her brothers had inherited their father's vivid coloring, but only the boys shared his political views. "I think we ought to use Ian's bed. It's more fitting, don't you think?"

"Definitely." Falcon opened the door and led her into the room. The candle's light flickered over the gold walls, and illuminated a four-poster bed made up with fresh linens. "I'd hoped you'd pick this room so I didn't have to make another bed."

"I would have helped you."

"Yes, but I didn't want you to have to."

"Then why did you give me a choice?"

Falcon set the candle on the nightstand and pulled her down across the bed. "I was simply curious to see if your choice would be the same as mine."

"Always," Belle breathed against his throat.

Between deep kisses, their clothes came off in lazy waves and soon lay scattered about the floor. Falcon tossed away Belle's lacy cap and combs to free her curls and she pulled away the thong to loose his hair. Playful, passionate, they teased and satisfied, made love with devotion and dipped into an ageless thrill. Their loving was as natural as their rhythmic breathing, and just as necessary to sustain life. Born to be mates, they remained together long after the time a walk along the shore would have taken, yet neither cared if they were late returning home.

Falcon sifted Belle's glossy curls through his fingers. The candle was burning low, but her hair caught the fading light with a bright sheen. "I have to go," he confessed sadly, "but I can't wait for the day we'll never have to be parted again. You provide all the excitement I'll ever need, and I'll do my very best to see you never grow bored with me."

Belle licked a dark nipple and felt him shiver. She spread a light trail of kisses over his chest, and he wound his fingers in her hair to encourage more. "Tomorrow?" she breathed against his navel.

Falcon sighed sadly. "Yes." He wanted to beg her not to hate him for leaving, but as her kisses swept across the flatness of his belly, he knew she never would. Her mouth was hot, her tongue soft, and her generous kisses brought him to the brink of rapture before he shoved her down onto the feather bed to seek his release deep within her heated core. He held her tenderly as he sought the exquisite joy that now bore her name, and at last understood how love could deepen every day. Even then, he could not leave her, and kept her cradled in his arms where no spoken promise would ever mean as much as what she had already given him.

* * *

Unable to sleep, Étienne went for a walk down by the river. He and his father had sailed up the River Seine, and when he closed his eyes and listened to the tumbling roar of the James River, he could imagine himself in France again. He had missed his home and that night was filled with a painful longing for something more than he had found in America. Ashamed to be lonely, he strolled across the wide lawn and entered the garden. The roses reminded him of his mother, but as he bent down to pick one he heard a soft, plaintive sob.

Not wishing to intrude upon the unhappy individual, he stood very still, and in a moment located the source of the sound. He had noticed the wooden benches when he had passed through the garden earlier in the day. He saw a woman clad in white, her nightgown perhaps, curled up on a bench near the house. She was crying very softly, as though she did not want to be discovered in such a downcast mood, but her sorrow touched him nonetheless.

At first he thought it might be Belle, weeping because Falcon was leaving, but the pair seemed so close, he knew the brave would not leave her to cry alone. He took a single step, and then he did not need to see the young woman any more clearly to know it was Dominique. He knew it would break her parents' hearts to hear her sobbing so dejectedly, but had she wanted their comfort, she would surely have sought it.

Instead, she had left the house and given vent to her tears in the seclusion of the well-tended garden. His first impulse was to go to her and offer the sympathy Falcon had suggested he give, but he lacked faith in the effort to succeed. He did not want to provoke another angry outburst from her, especially when he harbored the lingering suspicion that he had deserved it. He had blamed her for being cold, but why had he expected warmth when she had repeatedly told him she would rather be left alone?

He hated listening to her cry. It tore at his soul and yet he stood transfixed, unable to go to her or to leave to seek his own solace elsewhere. Shadowed by the night, he remembered other young women who had wept over him and wondered what had happened between Dominique and the man she so clearly still loved. Beau had said he was unworthy of her, but Dominique plainly did not share that view. She was mourning the loss of something precious to her, and Étienne felt the depth of her sorrow with every muffled sob.

He heard the rushing river in the distance and the crickets' lively chirp. There was jasmine on the air that he had not noticed during the day. The garden provided a romantic setting, but he felt as though miles, rather than a few yards, separated him from Dominique. He waited in a silent vigil, not even understanding why, but he could not leave the garden until, exhausted by tears, she had gotten up and gone inside.

He picked his rose then and carried it to the stable. Falcon had given him a blanket to spread out on the straw, and he made himself comfortable. He had spent nights in worse quarters, but as he inhaled the rose's heady perfume, he knew he had never been more lonely. A tear slid down his cheek, and he quickly wiped it away. He had come to America to fight, not to fall in love with a fair beauty who loved someone else, but the logic of that thought did not ease his pain and he wished he and Dominique could have wept together.

Seventeen

By the time Falcon and Étienne had traveled together several days, the brave had discovered a great deal about his companion. Étienne was quiet, took excellent care of the bay gelding he had been given, and always did more than his share of the work in making camp. Falcon had had to show Étienne only once how to disguise the charred remains of a fire so their camp site could not be found.

In all, Falcon found Étienne such a good companion that he did not understand why the Frenchman and Dominique had parted on such unfriendly terms. He was well aware that men and women saw things differently, and appreciated different things about each other, but he was still puzzled. He did not know Étienne well, and yet he liked what he saw, and was sorry Dominique had not.

A solitary soul himself, Falcon did not pry into Étienne's past. Instead, he waited until they had grown comfortable in each other's company and then shared a few of his memories from the days his father had first taken him and Christian into the forest.

Unable to produce any amusing stories of his own, Étienne tossed another chunk of wood onto the fire. "It did not ever bother you that your father was, well, different?" he asked.

"That he is Seneca, you mean?" When Étienne gave an embarrassed nod, Falcon laughed. "No. I always considered

him a good deal better than other men, so the difference
didn't trouble me. I believe being part Indian is an advantage, you see, and have never lacked for pride. Christian
can wear suits as easily as buckskins, and no one will comment that he resembles a savage. I've never tried, but if I
trimmed my hair to the length of yours and donned a fancy
velvet suit, I think I could walk through Williamsburg and
receive only admiring glances."

"You are both handsome men," Étienne agreed absently.
They had ridden hard all day, but he wasn't ready to go to
sleep. He had truly enjoyed Falcon's stories, and felt compelled to offer something even if it would not be equally
entertaining. "My father is also different," he revealed
softly. "He could have had a good life in France, but he
never overcame his bitterness with the British for breaking
Queen Anne's promises to respect the Acadians' religion
and lands. Nor could he forgive the French Canadians for
not defending the Acadians when the English demanded
they leave.

"I do not even know why he married my mother. She is
still remarkably pretty, so perhaps she simply caught his
eye, but he has always spent more time at sea than at home.
My mother tends her garden and cares for my three sisters,
but she deserves to have a real husband rather than a man
who longs to be in Acadia instead of in France with her.
He taught me how to sail and fish, but little else of value."

"Is he still living?"

"Yes. If you can count thriving on old hatreds being
alive."

Falcon's home had always been filled with the sound of
happy laughter, and he found it difficult to imagine how
empty Étienne's life must have been. With his father away
at sea, he would have undoubtedly shouldered more responsibility than a young boy should.

"Is your mother kind as well as pretty?" Falcon asked.

Étienne smiled as he thought of her. She had taught him

there was more to life than his father's bleak view. He had been happiest when his father was away, and his mother had read to him and his sisters and joined in their play.

"Yes. She is as sweet as her precious flowers. She will take care to see that my sisters each make a better match than she did and be happy with her grandchildren."

"That's good. What about you? What will it take to make you happy?"

Étienne stared into the flames. Dressed in an old pair of Falcon's buckskins, he was comfortably warm on the autumn night, and beginning to feel sleepy. "I would like to see the same equality in France that the Patriots are fighting for here. I am a good soldier, and perhaps I will one day have the chance to fight in my country."

"I wish you good luck, but this war has gone on too long," Falcon murmured through a lazy yawn, "and so has today. Let's get some sleep. I'll check on the horses."

To please Belle, Falcon had left Nails at home and ridden a dapple-gray gelding named Smoke Ring. Smoke was a fine mount that could carry him all day without tiring, but he was not Nails. Afraid the horse sensed his disappointment, Falcon gave him extra attention and talked with him each night as though he were an old friend.

He would discuss the day's ride and make plans for the next, all the while stroking the gelding's soft, smooth muzzle and finely arched neck. The horse seemed to appreciate the chat, and would snicker softly. "You miss home, don't you, Smoke?" Falcon asked. "What I miss is Belle. I imagine her strolling down by the river about this time in the evening, and thinking of me. At least I hope she is thinking of me as she is never far from my thoughts."

Falcon gave the horse a final pat, then returned to the fire and stretched out on his stomach. Étienne wished him a good night, but sat up a while longer. Falcon could not help but believe Étienne must long for something more than political freedom—a sweetheart as pretty as Belle, perhaps—but respecting his solitude, he did not speak the thought aloud.

While Falcon and Étienne were moving southwest, Lord Cornwallis had captured Charlotte, but with a great many of his force ill, could advance no farther in his effort to subdue the southern colonies. Lieutenant Colonel Patrick Ferguson, the Inspector for Militia in the Southern Provinces, was also bound for Charlotte. Moving west with twelve hundred American-born Loyalists, his mission was to cover Cornwallis's left flank, to defeat rebel militia, and to enlist whatever Loyalist recruits he could find among the residents of the South Carolina Blue Ridge Mountains. Rather than attracting recruits, however, Ferguson, who was noted for being one of Cornwallis's cruelest officers, encountered fierce resistance from armed backwoodsmen.

Unable to summon support from Charlotte, on October 7, 1780, Ferguson took up a defensive position on the slopes of King's Mountain. Digging in on the crest of the steep hill, Ferguson's troops looked down over a rocky slope dotted with towering pines. They felt exhilarated but secure.

Falcon and Étienne had joined the frontiersmen two days earlier. Living on the edge of civilization where Indians were a constant threat, most had shown little interest in the war when it had been waged on the east coast, but now that Cornwallis had sent Ferguson out into the Carolina Piedmont, they had a good reason to fight. Led by Colonels William Campbell, Joseph MacDowell, John Sevier, and Isaac Shelby, they numbered eleven hundred.

"This is going to be too easy," Falcon whispered to Étienne. "We'll move up the hillside from tree to tree and take the mountain before nightfall. You'll see."

Falcon had previously fought with William Campbell, who was Patrick Henry's brother-in-law and led the Virginia Militia. Falcon was clearly looking forward to the battle, while Étienne had to fight the queasiness in his stomach to appear as cool-headed. When the order was given to advance, he copied Falcon's bravado; moving with a lithe grace and using the trees as shields, made his way up the treacherous hillside.

The fire from above was continuous, but so inaccurate that the frontiersmen quickly grew bold. They crawled and lurched up the hill, all the while firing their rifles with the skill they had honed in their youth. Étienne slipped going over a boulder, but Falcon caught him by the belt before he took a tumbling fall all the way back down the mountain. The pair fought on, side by side, coughing in the rain of pine needles and rock chips thrown up by the bullets pelting the earth.

They heard Ferguson's shrill silver whistle and dodged a savage bayonet charge to press on. A white flag appeared on the mountain, but firing continued from both sides. Étienne knelt as he and Falcon used the same tree for cover. He reloaded and had just raised his rifle to his shoulder when a bullet knocked Falcon off his feet.

Étienne grabbed for him, caught the fringe on his pant leg, and hung on. He had to fight to maintain his balance to keep them both from skidding down the steep incline. The bullet had passed through Falcon's right leg just above the knee, and Étienne yanked hard to pull him behind the tree to do what he could for his friend. All around them the bitter fight continued and screams and curses echoed off the trees. Étienne looped his belt around Falcon's leg to stem the flow of blood, but the brave's buckskins were already soaked.

Falcon gritted his teeth, leaned back against the tree, and fought to stay conscious, but he knew the wound was bad. "I won't lose my leg," he swore through clenched teeth.

Étienne was more frightened for Falcon than he was about the outcome of the battle, but he ducked as a bullet whistled by so close it tore a hunk of bark from the tree.

"No. You are very strong." He offered what encouragement he could, but with the firing so intense, he dared not carry Falcon down the hill for fear they both might be shot in the back.

The frontiersmen needed only one hour to overwhelm the Loyalists, but the battle was the bloodiest since Bunker Hill. Colonel Ferguson was killed as he rode his horse on a wild charge down the hill, and his entire force was either killed, wounded, or taken prisoner. As for the backwoodsmen, they lost only twenty-eight men, while sixty-two were wounded.

Despite his agonizing pain, Falcon heard cries of "Tarleton's quarter!" and knew men were being slaughtered who should have been allowed to surrender.

"Stop the killing," he urged Étienne. "Go on. The fight's over. Don't let any more men die."

Amazed that Falcon could think so clearly, Étienne left, but only briefly. He dragged what wounded men he could away from the carnage, but he refused to leave Falcon alone for long. He stood guard over his terrified prisoners and his wounded friend until a physician at last appeared. "Treat this man first," Étienne insisted, pointing to Falcon.

The doctor was a pudgy young man with wispy blond hair, but he had kind eyes and nodded immediately. "Yes. I'm looking after our own first." He slit Falcon's pantleg up the side, then loosed Étienne's belt and handed it to him. "You're very lucky. The bullet missed the artery or we'd have blood spurting with a definite pulse. You see, this is just seeping out all over."

"Well, stop it!" Falcon cried. "It makes no difference if I bleed to death slowly, or fast. I'll be just as dead."

"A good point." The physician did his best to cleanse the entry and exit wounds, then bound them with lint soaked in oil and wrapped the leg with a long piece of linen, "Where are you from?" he asked.

"Virginia."

"Good. There are other Virginians among the wounded and you can all go home together."

His whole leg was throbbing with excruciating pain, and for the first time, Falcon feared he might not make it that far. He reached out for Étienne. "You take me home," he whispered.

Falcon had been a true friend to him, and Étienne could not refuse. "I will," he promised. He knelt beside him and gripped his shoulder. "Belle will take such good care of you, you will be dancing again before the holidays."

Falcon had never cared much for dancing, but tried to smile. "I just want to be able to walk."

The doctor rose, took Étienne's arm, and pointed down the hill. "Wait a while to make certain he does not lose any more blood, and then bring him to the bottom of the hill. I want all the wounded kept together."

Étienne nodded, then, too badly shaken to remain on his feet, he sat down beside Falcon while the physician looked after the Loyalist prisoners. "I have been wounded several times," he explained. "The pain is always bad."

Falcon closed his eyes and concentrated on breathing, but that was such a great understatement, he could not find a clever reply. Nails had always brought him good luck. He had known that, but he would never tell Belle he had been wounded because he had left the stallion at home. She would suffer so badly when he came limping home that he would never cause her more pain, but when he was next called upon to fight, he would ride Nails or simply stay at home.

While Étienne and Falcon waited on the hill, the bodies of the enemy dead were heaped together and covered with logs rather than buried. By the time Falcon felt strong enough to make his way down the hill with Étienne's help, the spoils of the battle were being parceled out. The buck-skin-clad victors took horses, rifles, and even clothing from the defeated Loyalists. By sundown, their mission against Colonel Ferguson done, many left for home.

William Campbell knelt beside Falcon. "I won't ask how you feel because I know it can't be good, but I'll see that you and the other Virginians reach home safely. You're one of the best men we've got, and you must know how much today's victory means. With Ferguson and his men lost, Cornwallis will have to go on the defensive. After the rout at Camden, we needed this victory, and badly."

Falcon nodded as Campbell continued to compliment him and praise their success. Faint from loss of blood, he was glad to be on the winning side, but he was a long way from home, and that was where he wanted to be.

Belle was helping her mother tend her herb garden when she heard Falcon speak her name. Elated that he had returned home, she looked around, expecting to find him coming her way, but he was nowhere in sight. "Did you hear someone call my name just now?" she asked her mother.

Arielle was harvesting the comfrey she had planted last spring. She would dry both the leaves and roots for medicines. She straightened up and scanned the yard. Dominique was standing near Belle, and looked equally perplexed. "No. Could it have been a bird, or the wind?"

There were birds in the nearby cottonwoods, but Belle had never heard any with calls of a single tone which would mimic her name. There was a gentle breeze, but again, it did not have a masculine sound. "No. It was Falcon. He called to me very clearly, as though he had some urgent need." When her mother and sister exchanged a worried glance, Belle was provoked with them both.

"I did hear him. I swear I did. His voice was as clear as yours, Mother. I don't understand why he isn't here."

Arielle set her scissors and basket aside and came to her daughter. "I believe you. Falcon loves you dearly, and no matter how far away he might be, he must surely be thinking of you. Even if his words echoed only in your mind, his thoughts were surely with you."

Having no further interest in the herbs, Belle crossed to the bench at the edge of the garden and sat down. "I don't believe this is a good omen," she murmured fretfully.

Arielle quickly joined Belle on the bench. "Please. Do not worry when there is no need."

"No need?" Belle had already dipped into her mother's store of dried raspberry leaves to brew a tea that eased the nausea she experienced upon waking. She believed she might have become pregnant the first time she had slept with Falcon in August. It was now October. The fact that she and Falcon were not legally wed was a small problem, however.

"Falcon has had time to return to the fighting," she reminded her mother. "When so many others have been killed—"

"Stop it!" Arielle ordered emphatically. "You must not allow that thought to even enter your mind. Falcon is the most skilled of soldiers. He is well, as he always is. Don't doubt that."

Dominique walked over to them, but she did not look nearly as confident as their mother. "Have you ever heard Father's voice when he wasn't near?" she asked.

Arielle gestured helplessly. "No. But I have heard of people hearing the voices of their loved ones when they could not possibly be heard. It could be a very good omen, *chérie.* Falcon may be on his way home again, and thinking of how much he wants to see you. Or perhaps it was merely a vivid memory that touched you suddenly."

Belle shook her head. "I was thinking of how much I still had to learn from you about herbs, not about Falcon. It wasn't a sound I just conjured up. It simply happened as naturally as he speaks to me when he's here. That's why it startled me so not to find him nearby."

Dominique sat down beside Belle. "Let's view this as a

good thing," she proposed. "I wish I had someone thinking of me as often as Falcon must dwell on thoughts of you."

"Half the Virginia militia must dream of you," Belle mused aloud.

"Belle!" Arielle scolded.

Dominique laughed. "No. She's right, Mother. At one time or another, I do believe a great many of the men serving with Virginia's militia have called on me. I should have kept count. Well, no matter. I think it's sweet that you heard Falcon speak your name. Make a note of the date, and when he comes home, ask him what he was doing today. I imagine you'll find he was lost in thoughts of you."

Belle longed to believe that. "I suppose that could be true."

Arielle leaned close to kiss her daughter's cheek. "Of course it is true. Come help me finish in the garden, and we'll go inside and make lemonade."

"No. I think I'll go down to the stable and check on Nails. With Falcon gone, he's undoubtedly feeling neglected." Without waiting for her mother's permission, Belle rose and started off toward the stable.

Arielle turned to watch her go. "I do not like this," she whispered to Dominique. She reached for her daughter's hand. "Say a prayer with me for Falcon. I do not want Belle to lose him when he is so precious to her."

"One soul sharing two bodies, I believe she said." Dominique bowed her head and prayed that her cousin was as well as when she had last seen him. Her thoughts swiftly strayed to Étienne, and she added his name. As she and her mother finished working in the garden, she grew increasingly concerned that Falcon had called to Belle for a reason, and that it could not possibly have been good.

Belle walked through the stable, but Nails's stall was empty and she went on outside to the paddock, where she found the beautiful stallion in a highly agitated state. One of the stableboys was seated on the top rail watching him. "What's gotten into Nails?" she called to him.

The boy scrambled down off the rail and removed his hat. "That I don't know, Miss Belle. He just started kicking up an awful fuss in his stall, so I brought him out here, but he's no happier."

Belle rested her arms on the top rail. She called to Nails and the horse trotted over to her, but then tossed his silky white mane and trotted away. "He misses Falcon as badly as the rest of us."

"That may very well be true, Miss Belle, but what shall we do with him if he won't calm down?"

"If he looks as though he might jump the fence, call Hunter. He'll know how to handle him."

Belle considered going to look for Hunter herself, but if hearing the call of a loved one meant something sinister to the Seneca, she would rather not know it. Apparently calmed by her presence, Nails slowed his restless circling and came back to her. She reached out to pat his neck and recalled the nights she and Falcon had ridden him into the forest outside Camden. She wondered what other secrets the stallion might be privy to.

"I wish you could talk," she told him. "I'm sure your opinions would be unique to say the least, and undoubtedly valuable. As it is, we shall have to be content with no more than a nuzzle and a pat. Leave him out in the paddock for a while," she called to the stableboy. "Perhaps he was simply bored."

"Yes, Miss Belle. I'll do that."

Belle pushed away from the paddock and walked back through the stable. This time she stopped to visit a moment with Ladybug, who was passing the afternoon in lazy contentment. She then went on to the river and sat down on the grassy slope to watch the water surge past in rollicking waves. She missed Falcon more each day, and had even taken to visiting his room in the evening before she went to bed.

There was a bow and arrows he had made as a child lying on the desk. She remembered that each time Hunter had taken him off into the woods to teach him something new, he had come running home to show her what he had learned. He had always been so proud of his skills—and it had been an endless source of wonderful games for her. What a strange pair they must have been, an Indian boy in buckskins and a little blond girl in ribbon and lace.

Belle hugged her knees as she began to cry. She had never known a world without Falcon, and she couldn't bear to think he might have called to her with his dying breath.

Étienne demanded a wagon taken from Ferguson's troops, hitched his bay and Smoke to it, and started off for home the morning after the battle. Along with Falcon, he had three other wounded, but there was little he could offer in the way of care. One man had been shot in the arm, another in the foot, while the third had been slashed by a Loyalist making a bayonet charge. Falcon was the most seriously wounded, but also the one most familiar with the terrain. Étienne relied upon him to set their course.

With three spare horses, Étienne was able to switch teams often, but fording the Catawba River taxed the strength of both man and beast. Wet and weary, they swung wide around Charlotte to avoid British patrols. Then Étienne began angling northeast as they crossed the Pee Dee River, but with better than three hundred miles to cover before they reached Williamsburg, he never drew an easy breath. The man with the injured foot offered what help he could, while the fellow with one good arm did, too, but Étienne watched Falcon and the other man grow progressively weaker.

William Campbell had given them what provisions he

could spare, and Étienne caught fish when he could, but he had a difficult time convincing his ailing companions to eat more than a few bites at each meal. There were days they went without fresh water, and others when Étienne had to get down from the wagon to lead the horses through the swamps. He lost count of the days on the hellish journey, and cried with his passengers when they at last passed into Virginia.

While Belle heard no more voices, she awoke each dawn burdened with a sense of foreboding that kept her from enjoying any part of the day. Rather than accomplish any useful tasks, she wandered the plantation in aimless circles. She could not concentrate on the print in books, nor work on embroidery. She tried fishing, but missed Falcon so badly she never put her hook in the water.

Whenever Dominique, her mother, or her aunt tried to engage her in conversation, her attention would drift to the point that she could not follow along. They all excused her distracted behavior as natural with the man she loved away, but Belle knew it wasn't normal at all. Her intuition told her something was terribly wrong, and sick with dread, she watched the road and waited for the message she was terrified would come.

When Étienne at last drove the wagon into the yard, Belle was the first one out the door. Had Étienne not been smiling, she would never have made it to him, but he quickly turned to show her he had brought Falcon home. "They all need help," he told her, and swung down to the ground. In another minute, he was pushed aside as everyone came pouring out of the house.

Exhausted, he walked around to the side of the house to the well, pulled his shirt off over his head, and after bringing up a bucket of water, drew it aside and poured it over his head and shoulders. The well was covered, and two benches connected the posts supporting the roof. He sat down on one and put his head in his hands. He was so tired he felt sick clear through, but he had gotten everyone to the Barclays' alive, and that meant more to him than he could have ever explained.

Dominique had seen Étienne wander off and did not think of him again until she was certain Falcon was alive. Her cousin was pale and weak, but he was strong enough to hug Belle and that was enough to cheer them all. As for the other three men, they had to be helped from the wagon as well, but asked only to rest on the steps where they could see the James River and then give thanks that they had made it home.

With sad memories of the hospital at Camden suddenly strong, Dominique offered to find Étienne and hurriedly fled. When she rounded the corner of the house and found him seated at the well she first thought he was in tears and hesitated to disturb him. Then she noticed the long scar that sliced across his right shoulder blade. It made him so much more human somehow to know he really had been wounded, and she gathered her courage and approached him.

Étienne looked up, his green eyes bloodshot from the glare of the trail and lack of sleep. "I did my best," he apologized. "I know they're all sick, but at least they're alive."

There was no hint of criticism in Dominique's eyes, only an expression of deep concern. She reached out to caress his damp curls. "And you?"

"I don't think I could have made it another mile." He closed his eyes and sighed softly. "Just let me sit here a few days, and I'll be fine."

Dominique had no intention of granting such a foolish request, but rather than urge him to his feet and coax him inside, she sat down beside him. She was wearing the same pale peach muslin gown she had worn on their ghastly tour of the curing barn, and she hoped he would not remember the gown, or that day. "How did you get the scar on your back?" she asked.

Étienne tilted his head back against the post. "A British soldier tried to run me through with his bayonet, but the blade bounced off the bone. I spun around and, well, you do not want to know exactly what I did, but a soldier ought not to be stabbed in the back."

"No. You're right. That was cowardly. I can't tell you how grateful everyone is to have Falcon home safe with us. Belle hasn't been herself for a couple of weeks. When was Falcon hurt?"

"It was October 7, at King's Mountain. We left for home the next day." He rubbed his hand across his chin, apologized for the stubble, and then shrugged. "Well, none of us looks his best, but at least you know I usually look better than this."

"I think you probably saved my cousin's life so I'll not complain." In truth, she liked him much better now that he had lost his cocky smirk. As for the beard that shadowed his cheeks, it reminded her too much of Sean's. She ran her hand down Étienne's arm and laced her fingers in his.

"Falcon's already been taken to his room. We'll make up beds for the others in the sitting room tonight so they don't have to climb the stairs, and tomorrow we'll see that they reach their homes. You're welcome to use Beau's room for as long as you wish."

She had a delicate hand and long, tapered nails. Her skin was the pale gold of rich cream, and his deeply tanned. Étienne studied the contrast in their skin tones and thought it a sign of how far apart they truly were. "No. I could not use Beau's room," he argued.

"Why not? He'll not be back for months so you'll not be inconveniencing him."

"No. It would not be right."

He was staring off toward the garden, and Dominique did not understand his objection. "Well, if you won't use his room, there's a guest room on the third floor that would be equally comfortable."

"I am too tired to climb the stairs," Étienne offered with his first hint of a smile.

Dominique released his hand and slid her arm around his waist. "Come with me. I'll help you."

Étienne used the post at his left to pull himself to his feet. Dominique rose and stepped close. The sleeve of her gown was whisper-soft against his bare skin, and she smelled delicious, both spicy and sweet. He believed she was being nice to him because of what he had done for Falcon rather than out of any sincere affection for him, but he allowed himself to enjoy it and slipped his arm around her waist.

"I will not faint," he assured her, "but this is nice."

Ignoring his compliment because she feared he would misinterpret any reply, she clucked her tongue softly. "You were too thin to begin with, Étienne. I'll bet you don't even cast a shadow now. Don't you dare leave until you've had enough good meals to gain some weight."

She was fussing over him the way his mother had, and Étienne had not expected that. He longed to lean down and kiss her, but thought he'd better get rid of his beard first. "Did you miss me?" he asked instead.

"Miss you?" Dominique scoffed. "You're thinner but no less conceited, are you, Monsieur LeBlanc? It will undoubtedly surprise you to learn that I have better things to do than pine for you and don't lie and say you've thought of me because I'm sure you haven't."

"Constantly," Étienne swore.

Dominique looked up to scold him, and then was sorry. He was tired and dirty, utterly forlorn, and yet his teasing glance touched her. The war had twisted all their lives, and while she had learned a sad lesson in love from Sean O'Keefe, she did not want to learn anything this dashing Frenchman obviously wanted to teach her.

Eighteen

Falcon was still wearing the same bloodstained pair of buckskin pants he'd had on when he'd been shot. As soon as Byron and Hunter carried him upstairs to his room and laid him on his bed, Arielle pulled off his moccasins. When she saw that his right foot was swollen, her heart lurched. She turned to the men.

"This may take a while, and it's too crowded in here. I'd like Alanna and Belle to help me, but will you two please wait outside?"

Byron recognized the fear in her eyes and nodded toward the door. Hunter hesitated, but then turned away from the bed and Byron followed him out. Arielle took Falcon's hand. "There now, you need not pretend a bravery you do not feel. Cry all you like, and have no fear we will think any the less of you."

"I don't feel well enough to cry," Falcon complained in a hoarse rasp.

"Alanna, will you bring a pitcher of water? I want Falcon to have plenty to drink. He'll also need hot water for a bath, as will the other men."

"Yes. I'll see to it." Alanna leaned down to kiss her son's forehead and frowned as she straightened up. "He's fever-ish."

A consummate *sage-femme,* Arielle displayed no alarm. "That is not surprising, but he will do much better now that he is at home." She waited for Alanna to leave, then peeled back Falcon's pant leg past the bandage. She heard Belle gasp, and did not try and discount her fears. His wound was so badly infected his leg was swollen from hip to toe. It would require all the knowledge and skill she possessed not to simply save his leg, but his life.

Falcon's eyes were closed, but Belle was watching Arielle closely. Arielle raised her finger to her lips to warn her daughter to be still. She removed the filthy bandage and dropped it on the floor. She could see the puckered edges of the entry wound, but did not want to touch it. "Is the bullet still in your leg, or was it removed?" she asked.

Falcon looked up at her, his dark eyes glazed. "It missed the bone and went clear through. At least I didn't get hit in the knee, but I don't want to try and bend it."

"The wound isn't healing well," Arielle told him.

"I know. There isn't an inch of me that doesn't ache. Maybe I just have the fever that's made so many men sick." He squeezed Belle's hand. "I'm sorry. I didn't mean to come home like this."

Belle wiped the tears from her eyes. "You're home. That's all that matters."

Arielle had cared for Falcon since he was small, but he, Christian, and Johanna had always been as healthy as her own three children. Except for the cuts and scrapes all children receive, he had not caused her a minute of worry. Now she felt sick to her soul.

"Belle, I want you to sit with Falcon for a moment while I brew some comfrey tea and make a poultice. I'll have to reopen the wound and encourage the healing to begin again."

Falcon winced. "I don't think I can stand that."

"Let's put you in a hot bath first to soak the whole leg," Belle suggested. She pulled the chair at his desk over to the bed and sat down. "You'll feel much better after that. Then let's ask Uncle Byron for a bottle of his brandy."

The second idea had more appeal, but Falcon had taken a vow. "You know I don't drink."

Belle smoothed his hair off his forehead. Caked with dust from the trail, it had lost its vibrant sheen. "I won't have you screaming, and we don't have any laudanum to numb the pain."

Christian knocked lightly at the door, and then came in. "I know you don't want me in here, so I won't stay, but I had to see my brother." He took one look at Falcon's swollen leg and uttered a curse. "Aunt Arielle gave me such good care when I got shot in the arm no one even knew I'd been wounded. She'll give you the same excellent care, but I wish you'd gotten home sooner."

"So do I." Falcon managed a smile, but it was faint. "Will you look after the other men? We didn't feel well enough to talk much, but I've grown fond of them anyway."

"Of course." Christian drew Arielle aside. "What can I do to help?"

"Help your mother, please. As soon as there's enough hot water, bring it up here with a tub. I want to bathe Falcon before I do anything else." She saw the question in his eyes, but could not promise a cure and hurried him from the room. She paused at the door. "You needn't worry, Falcon. Belle will be the one to help you bathe."

As soon as her mother had closed the door, Belle leaned down to kiss Falcon. "I've been so worried about you. One afternoon I was helping Mother tend her herbs and I heard you call my name. I know you weren't there, but I heard it so clearly, and I've been sick with dread ever since. It was October 7. What were you doing that day?"

Falcon brought her fingertips to his lips. "That was the day I got shot."

"It wasn't merely my imagination then, was it?"

Falcon could barely keep his eyes open. "No. I thought of home, and you. I'm glad you heard me."

Belle began to cry, and Falcon slipped his arm around

her shoulders to draw her head down upon his chest. "We'll be all right, Belle. Your mother can work miracles."

Belle gripped his hand more tightly. "Yes. She can," she assured him, but she was so afraid a miracle might not be enough.

Dominique and Étienne passed her brother, Jean, on the stairs. He was carrying clothes he had borrowed from Beau's room for the injured men, and paused to greet them. "Is it true you were in the battle at King's Mountain?" he asked.

"The story was reported in the *Virginia Gazette,*" Dominique added.

"Yes. We were there. The battle was nearly over when Falcon was hit. I will have to tell you about it later. Now, I am too tired to remember everything you would enjoy hearing."

"Later then," Jean insisted, and he hurried on down the stairs.

Étienne saw the worried look on Dominique's face and tightened his hold on her waist. "The war must sound very exciting to him, but I will tell him the truth about how awful it is. You need have no worries that I will encourage him to enlist in the militia."

"He's only sixteen, but I know there are other young men his age fighting. He's been content to help our father until now, and perhaps seeing Falcon so badly wounded will keep him from thinking of the war simply as an adventure."

"Perhaps I should have stopped to seek treatment for Falcon and the others along the way, but I did not know whom to trust, and Falcon wanted so badly to come home."

They had reached the third floor landing and Dominique nodded toward the end of the hall. "The guest room is on your right. It has a beautiful view of the river." It was also the room where Melissa had died giving birth to Christian, but the Barclays never explained its macabre history to guests. "You'll want a bath, of course."

As they entered the room, Étienne eyed the bed longingly. "All I want is to sleep. If there is water in the pitcher at the washstand, I'll clean up there and bathe later."

Dominique quickly checked the pitcher. "We weren't expecting guests, so I'm afraid it's empty but I'll fill it from the one in my room."

The guest room was painted a pale green, and the pitcher and bowl were white with delicate ivy trim. Dominique picked up the pitcher and carried it across the hall to her room. Étienne followed her to the door and caught a glimpse of the pretty pink room. The color suited her, but he did not know how he felt about spending the night so close to her.

"Where is Beau's room?" he asked as she returned the ivy pitcher to the washstand.

"It's on the second floor, Have you changed your mind? Would you rather be there?"

"Who else has a room there?"

Dominique wondered why he had suddenly become so curious and swept him with a skeptical glance. Unlike Sean O'Keefe, his chest was as smooth as Falcon's, but his pants were slung low on his hips, revealing a trail of dark hair descending from his navel. Her lively imagination provided a vivid glimpse of how he would look nude, and completely losing her train of thought, she looked up abruptly and then recalled what he had asked.

"There are four bedrooms on that floor, too. My parents have one, my aunt and uncle another, and Beau and Falcon have the other two."

Étienne had taken only a couple of steps into the room. He had expected just a cot and washstand, but there was a fine bed, a large wardrobe, a desk with its own chair, and a thickly padded chair near the windows where a guest might sit to read or enjoy the view. There were fine paintings and a beautiful rug with softly muted shades of blue and green. Never having slept in such a splendid room, he was overwhelmed.

"The Barclays treat their guests very well," he said. "I will stay here. Then I won't be in anyone's way."

Dominique did not understand why that concerned him, but did not argue. "You'll need clothes," she offered as she came toward him. "I'll see what we can find for you."

Étienne still held his buckskin shirt in his hand. Dominique's generosity made him feel as though he were a stray dog she had decided to keep for a pet. While it was flattering, it was also a most uncomfortable feeling. "I'll wash these buckskins tomorrow, so I won't need clothes."

"What do you expect to wear while you wash them, Étienne, and while they dry? Just take them off and leave them outside the door before you lie down to nap. I'll see that they're washed and leave clean clothes hanging on your doorknob."

"I do not want to trouble you."

Dominique read an entirely different intention in his gaze. If he had his way, he would give her plenty of trouble, but she was too worried about Falcon to spar with him and hurried around him to the doorway. "Is there anything else you need?"

What Étienne needed was to lose himself in her, but he was too tired to make such an offer, or follow through on it should she accept. *"Merci,"* he called softly. "I am fine."

Dominique closed his door on the way out, but paused on the landing. Her mother and Belle were going to be occupied treating Falcon, which meant the other three men had to be looked after. She found them still huddled on the front steps, arguing with Jean about accepting Beau's clothes.

"Gentlemen, please," she scolded them softly, and instantly had their attention. "Jean, Étienne needs fresh clothing, too." She told him to leave what he had gathered in the sitting room, and what to do for Étienne. Then she smiled at the wounded men.

It was easy to discern the injuries of two with their bandaged arm and foot, but the third fellow was seated where he could lean against a marble column, and was nearly as pale as the stone. She knelt beside him and touched his forehead. He was feverish, and she wanted to get him inside. When her cousin, Johanna, came running up, she asked for her help.

"What's your name?" Dominique asked the soldier.

He tucked his hands in his armpits and began to shiver. "Henry Smith, miss."

"Well, Henry, Johanna is going to help you inside. My mother knows more about herbs than anyone else alive, and we'll see you have a hot bath, slather you with one of her salves, rebandage your wounds, and send you off for home tomorrow feeling a lot better than you do today."

Fascinated by the fetching blonde, Henry nodded. "I feel better already." He looked up at Johanna, who, while a brown-eyed brunette, resembled Dominique slightly. They were both such pretty women, he wondered if they might not be angels. When he asked, Johanna took his arm to help him to his feet.

"You might call us that," she agreed, "for surely we're doing heaven's work."

Dominique waited until Johanna and Henry had disappeared inside to speak to the other men. The one with the bandaged arm was clad in buckskins, the other in a threadbare black suit. "Tell me your names," she encouraged.

"I'm Robert Haywood," the one in buckskins announced, "and this here's Gregory Berry. Neither of us wants your charity, but the Frenchman brought us here anyway."

"You're serving with the militia?" Dominique asked, and the pair nodded. "Then you're fighting for all of us, and if we wish to give you a meal and a change of clothes to thank you for your sacrifice, then you ought not to refuse the gesture."

The men exchanged an uneasy glance, and then hung their heads. "We don't want to be no trouble," Stephen mumbled.

"You're not the first soldiers I've tended," Dominique told them, "and I doubt you'll be the last. Now let's get you inside. Aren't you hungry? When my sister and I traveled up from South Carolina with Falcon we had little other than fish and berries. I'll bet you men haven't had much more. Wouldn't you like some ham and biscuits?"

Robert moaned in eager anticipation. "We didn't mean to be rude, miss."

Dominique got them on their feet, then slipped her arm around Stephen's waist to help him along. "Of course not. You're just tired and sore, aren't you?" She got the pair into the sitting room and sent the cook's daughters, who worked in the house during the day, out to the kitchen to fetch the meal she had promised. Liana came to the door as she was trying to decide how to arrange for baths for everyone.

"How is Falcon?" Liana asked fearfully.

Dominique waited for Johanna to come close. "I haven't seen him since he arrived, but now that he's home, he'll surely make a quick improvement. Let's do what we can for these men so my mother can concentrate on him." With the same excellent organizational ability she had displayed in Camden, Dominique soon had their wounded guests' needs met, but she still did not know what to do about Étienne, who, with a single glance, always seemed to see too much.

Arielle found Byron and Hunter seated on the back steps. She sat down between them, looped her arms through theirs, and laid her head on her husband's shoulder. "I have never been so frightened," she confessed in a trembling voice. "Your son is a strong young man, Hunter, but he is very, very ill. You may wish to summon a physician from town, but I fear he would advise amputation and it is too late to save Falcon's life by taking his leg. He would never agree to it even if it could."

"My God," Byron gasped. "I had no idea he was so severely injured."

"The wound pierced his thigh, which is bad in itself, but it has become infected and the infection has spread. I will do everything I can for him, but I want you both to know it may not be enough."

Hunter slipped his arm from Arielle's and stood to face her. "Does Alanna know how bad this is?"

Arielle shook her head. "I have not told her, but I suspect she must. I have Falcon soaking in a tub now. It will make the wound easier to reopen and clean. I left Belle with him. They have not had nearly enough time together."

"They have had their whole lives," Hunter reminded her. "The Seneca believe evil spirits roam forests, bewitch people, and cause sickness. False Face was a being who was banished by the Great Spirit for boastfulness and condemned to spend eternity curing the sick. The men of our False Face Society carve terrifying masks and wear them for ceremonies which scare away the evil spirits. I'm going to take Christian out to the woods and carve masks so we can perform the ritual for Falcon. It may take us a day or two. Can you give us that much time?"

There were people who laughed at her herbal cures, so Arielle took Hunter's offer seriously. "You must return by sundown tomorrow night at the latest. Even that may be too long."

"I know you'll do all you can to save him." Hunter rested his hand lightly on Arielle's shoulder, and then went inside to tell Alanna where he was bound, and to find Christian.

Byron looked over his shoulder to make certain Hunter

had closed the door. "Falcon was weak, but he was talking to us, and lucid, as we carried him up the stairs. I had no idea he was this sick, and Hunter wants to carve masks?" He shook his head in disbelief.

"Do not forbid him the right to pray in whatever manner he chooses," Arielle begged. "Falcon's life is in God's hands, and he needs every prayer we can send toward heaven."

"Yes. You're right. I shouldn't have made fun of Hunter's beliefs when he never criticizes ours. What shall we do for Belle? Should we send for a priest and insist she and Falcon wed while he can still repeat his vows?"

Arielle relaxed against her husband, but grasped his arm more tightly. "We can not make that suggestion without telling Falcon we are afraid he is dying. No man needs to hear that when he is gravely ill."

Byron patted his wife's hands. "Falcon and Belle are very close, Arielle. It may be a difficult thing to say to him, but it could very well be the best decision for her."

Arielle closed her eyes while she pondered the meaning of Byron's words, but after a moment's reflection, she still could not agree. "Belle would want what is best for Falcon," she assured him, "and she would never accept such a hasty wedding merely to give her his name. If, God forbid, he dies, she can simply call herself his widow and no one will object."

Byron could not help but think of his sister, Melissa, and Christian, the son she had never even seen. "His child might," he insisted.

Appalled by that bitter assumption, Arielle let go of his arm and stood. "Do not even say that," she replied. "I do not ask much from you, Byron, but you must give me this. There will be no questions, and no wedding unless the idea comes from Falcon himself."

Taken aback by the force of his wife's conviction, Byron rose slowly. They had had few serious disagreements over the years, but he sensed this issue could provoke the worst argument yet. With Arielle already carrying so much responsibility for Falcon's recovery, he did not want to burden her with his anger. "You're asking me to put Falcon's welfare above Belle's," he explained calmly. "I don't believe that's wise."

"You must trust me to know what is best for them both." Arielle would not waver and in that belief, and after a few seconds, Byron gave a grudging nod. She rose on her tiptoes to kiss him. "Thank you. You will not be sorry."

Byron waited on the back steps while Arielle reentered the house, but he was not at all certain he had made the best choice. He could at least pray for Falcon, though, and he began that in earnest.

With two of the wounded men happily consuming their meals and the third sipping soup at Johanna's urging, Liana felt her work was done for the moment and went out on the front porch for a breath of air. When Christian joined her, she reached out to take his hand. "How is Falcon doing?" she asked. "I haven't had a chance to go upstairs and see him."

Christian scarcely knew where to begin. "Don't try and see him yet. He's very sick, and—" Overcome with emotion, Christian had to look away.

"Chris?" Liana squeezed his hand. "He is going to be all right, isn't he?"

Christian had to swallow hard before answering, and then it was still difficult for him to speak. By blood, he and Falcon were only half brothers, but Alanna had been the only mother Christian had ever known, and she had never treated them differently. His brother meant the world to him, and the possibility he might lose him filled him with dread.

"I'm going out to the woods with my father to carve masks. He says we need them to perform some Seneca healing ritual. I know it might sound ridiculous to you, but he believes it will help Falcon, and I'm not going to refuse."

"Masks?" Liana repeated numbly. Christian had as much white blood as Seneca, and even in buckskins resembled a frontiersman rather than a savage. That he would suddenly take up what she considered the strange ways of the Seneca appalled her. "Is that what the two of you would do if Liberty or the boys got sick?"

Clearly she thought the idea daft, and Christian did not blame her. "I would ask Aunt Arielle to work her magic first, and then, yes, I just might if I believed it would save them."

"Do you believe it?"

"That doesn't matter," he replied. "While I always thought my father's tales were exciting, Falcon was sincerely drawn to the Seneca tribe. I believe treating him as a Seneca now will help ease his spirit and that ought to help him recover."

Liana felt sick and stepped into Christian's arms. He hugged her tight, but she could feel him trembling and knew he was afraid for his brother. She could not understand how masks could cure anything but she would make no attempt to stop him.

"I'll tell the children how ill their Uncle Falcon is, and we'll all pray for him," she promised. "It would be so awful if we lost him."

Christian would not allow that thought to enter his mind. He stepped back, then kissed her lightly. "I must go now. Help Arielle and Belle all you can."

"Yes. Of course I will." Liana remained on the porch as he started off down the path toward the stable. She truly believed that death was as natural a part of life as birth, but she could not accept the fact that Falcon might not live longer than twenty-two years. He was as dear to her as her own brothers, and forcing herself to be brave for his sake,

she went back inside to do whatever she could to ease his
pain.

Belle squeezed out the sponge and dripped water down
Falcon's chest. He was leaning back, slumped low, his eyes
closed as she scrubbed him clean with the tender touch she
would use to bathe a baby. He had lost so much weight on
the journey home she could see his ribs clearly. She couldn't
bear to look at his leg, and was grateful the soap bubbles
floating on the water kept her from having to. She had
washed his hair first, and like a hank of ebony silk it hung
down over the rolled edge of the big copper tub. She had
not thought to snip off a lock of his hair before now, and
this seemed a poor time to ask for a memento.

"Do you feel any better?" she asked.

Falcon had swallowed two cups of comfrey tea before
getting into the tub, and he was still debating whether or
not he ought to drink some brandy. He felt lazy, or perhaps
merely weak, and murmured a vague response. He was
afraid reopening his wound would hurt worse than getting
shot, and while he wanted to get the ordeal over with, he
was hoping Arielle would not return to his room for hours.

"I wish you could get in here with me," he said.

His smile was sad rather than seductive, but Belle played
along. "I was surprised when Mother allowed me to stay
with you, so let's not abuse the privilege."

Falcon caught her hand. He was so tired, he didn't think
he could stay awake much longer. "Maybe I ought to get
out now. Can you find someone to help me? I don't want
to fall and break my one good leg."

Belle was amazed he felt up to teasing her. "I love you
very, very much."

The wistfulness of her tone broke Falcon's heart, and he
gave her the most loving kiss he could. "I love you more."

When he closed his eyes, Belle rose and hurried to find

help. Her father was the first man she found and he came back upstairs with her. Belle held the towel, and Byron bent down to scoop Falcon out of the tub. She quickly wrapped the towel around his waist so he would be covered when Byron laid him on the bed.

"What do you want to do about the brandy?" Belle asked Falcon.

Falcon could already feel the agonizing pressure as his aunt dragged the tip of a blade over his festering wound, making him gag. "I'm afraid I'm going to be sick whatever I do, but I need something and if brandy is all we have, it will have to do."

Byron was touched by the depth of love mirrored in their eyes. "Is there anything else you need, Falcon, or anyone you'd like to see?"

"No," Falcon whispered. "I don't feel up to entertaining visitors."

Byron had been hoping he would ask for a priest to marry them, but because he had promised his wife not to bring up the subject, he did not. "Your father and Christian have gone to make masks for some ceremony. Perhaps you're familiar with what they intend to do."

"False Face Society masks?" Falcon asked.

"Yes. That's what Hunter called them."

Falcon started to laugh, but caught himself before the effort increased his pain. "That's good. I always wanted to see that."

Belle looked astonished, but Byron sent her a warning glance and she didn't question Hunter's intentions. "I'll bring you the brandy, and I may get good and drunk with you. In fact, Arielle is the only one who has to stay sober." He squeezed Falcon's upper arm, and then, determined to show the same courage as the injured brave, he left to fetch his finest brandy.

Belle picked up another towel to dry Falcon's hair, then sat down beside him again. She took his hand and hoped with all her heart that he would live to see his child born. She could not tell him now that he would be a father next spring, but she painted that picture in her mind. She could see the three of them so clearly, laughing with delight. A son would be a great blessing, or a pretty daughter like Christian's Liberty. When the child had been conceived in such glorious love, she knew he, or she, would be as special as his father.

"I've always been so proud of you," she blurted out suddenly.

Falcon thought the comment odd, but gave her a lopsided grin. He loved her so dearly that for a few moments at least, he didn't feel any pain.

There were woods on the Barclays' land, and with time precious, Hunter dared take Christian no farther. They left their horses to graze and searched for suitable willow and basswood trees. "The mask has to be carved from the living tree," Hunter explained, "and then when it is nearly finished, we'll cut it free of the trunk."

"I'm glad you explained the masks can be ugly," Christian replied, "because other than toy animals for our boys, I've never done much carving."

"Not simply ugly," Hunter countered. "They must be hideous, with the features twisted into fearsome scowls."

"What about big noses, or jutting lips?"

"Yes! Whatever strikes you. Men usually choose images they have seen in dreams, but we have no time to wait for that. We'll cut our horses' tails for hair and use berry juice for stain. Here, this is a good tree." Hunter slapped the willow. "Begin here. Measure your own face so it will fit you, and hurry. There isn't much time."

"Let's build a fire and work all night."

Hunter nodded and continued searching for a nearby tree for his own mask. He had left the land of the Seneca more than thirty years ago, and had little to do with the tribe since, but his childhood memories of the False Face Society were still vivid. They had come to his mother's longhouse whenever someone was sick. If the ailing person were male, once cured, he would then join the society and help to heal the next person to fall ill. Hunter wished now that he could remember whether or not everyone had been saved, but he thought most had.

A slanting ray of bright sunlight fell across the next tree, and taking it as a good omen, he began to whittle away the bark to expose the tender wood underneath. He would start with a crude oval shape, and trust a design to grow in his mind as he worked. "Big eyes," he called to Christian, "and long, drooping tongues. Carve whatever you please."

"Nasty scars and a forest of warts!" Christian shouted back.

"Yes! Let's see which of us can carve the most frightening mask."

Christian was already so frightened that his hands shook as he peeled away the bark. "I'm already afraid," he mumbled under his breath. He and Falcon had fought together when the war had begun, and no man had ever had a finer comrade-at-arms. He had to stop to wipe the tears from his eyes, then decided they did not matter. He did not need to see clearly to carve, and silently repeating the prayers his mother had taught him as a child, he fashioned a grotesque mask to save his brother.

Nineteen

Étienne awakened with a start, and disoriented, needed a moment to remember why he was sleeping in an elegantly furnished bedroom rather than on the ground. His heart was pounding in his chest and as he sat up and pushed the hair out of his eyes he hoped the horrible scream that had jarred him awake had been the last echo of a nightmare and not real. Certain he would never be able to get back to sleep, he pushed himself off the comfortable bed and went to the window.

The sun was low above the river, bathing the water and surrounding countryside in a coppery glow. It was a serene landscape, but it took him a long while to shake off the last tremors of fright. When at last he had, he lit a lamp, carried it over to the washstand, and used the razor the Barklays thoughtfully provided for their male guests. He had not slept long, but still clad in his buckskin pants, hoped to find the clothes Dominique had promised would be hanging on the doorknob. He opened the door, but before he could look for apparel, the sound of heart-wrenching sobs lured him out into the hallway.

Dominique was seated on the top step, her head in her hands, weeping so pathetically he feared someone must have died. He rushed to her side and sat down. "What has happened?" Rather than answer, Dominique just shook her head and continued to cry.

Étienne glanced back toward his open door and saw there were indeed clothes hanging on the doorknob, but with Dominique so terribly unhappy, he did not believe he should excuse himself to dress. At least he was a good deal cleaner than he had been earlier, even if he still lacked a shirt. He slipped his arm around her waist to encourage her to rest her head on his shoulder and she melted against him so easily he cursed himself for not having been more understanding the last time she had been in his arms.

"It is all right, *chérie*. Weep if you must. I will sit here with you all night if you need me."

Étienne's skin was warm, and held the comforting scent of Arielle Barclay's bayberry soap. Dominique was ashamed of herself for breaking down, but she had simply exhausted her strength. "I'm so sorry," she breathed against his bare chest. She was getting him all wet with her tears, but couldn't seem to stop.

Étienne removed her cap, and then her combs to free her hair. He ran his fingers through her curls and massaged her neck lightly. He had never met such a fascinating woman. She had such polished elegance and pride, and yet an occasional rip in that lovely façade revealed the depth of her sorrow. For an instant he wished she might one day weep for him with such intensity, and in the next breath swore he would never cause her such agonizing pain.

He heard the people on the floor below talking in hushed whispers, but could not catch their words. He had brought four ailing men into the house, so he could understand why everyone was so busy, but he still did not understand what had upset Dominique so badly she could not explain. Then a truly horrible possibility occurred to him.

If the tormented scream that had pierced his dreams had been real, then the man who had called out had to have been Falcon. He grabbed Dominique's arms and shook her. "What's happened to Falcon?" he cried. "Have they cut off his leg?"

Étienne looked every bit as terrified as Dominique felt, but she quickly shook her head to reassure him. She wiped her cheeks with her fingertips and tried to catch enough breath to speak, but it was difficult to know what she could tell him that would not merely increase his fright.

"Did you hear him scream? We thought he was too drunk to feel anything, but my mother had to reopen his wound before applying a poultice, and apparently nothing could have blocked such excruciating pain. He passed out, which saved him from feeling most of it, but he's so very sick, he may never awaken."

Étienne searched her face for some glimmer of hope, but saw only despair etched upon her delicate features. He released her and sat back. "This is all my fault," he groaned. "I didn't know what to do for him. If only I had—"

"No one blames you, Étienne." Dominique wrapped her arms across her midriff and leaned forward. "You brought him home and we're grateful."

She did not look grateful, and Étienne doubted anyone else would thank him, either. Filled with remorse, he would have gotten up, walked out of the house, and gone back to North Carolina, but he could not leave without knowing whether Falcon survived. "I have failed you again," he murmured softly.

"What?" Dominique knew she could not possibly have heard what she thought she had. There was nothing between them, so how could he have failed her? Étienne shook his head, refusing to repeat his comment, but she doubted she had misinterpreted his remark. Now he was as thoroughly depressed as she, and she could not bear to think she was simply spreading her pain.

She took his hand and squeezed hard. "Why don't you get dressed and we'll have something to eat."

"I could not eat," Étienne swore.

"I don't feel like eating either but if we don't, we'll be too tired to help later when we might really be needed.

Change your clothes and come downstairs with me. There's soup and freshly baked bread ready, and you can have anything else you'd like."

"This is no time for a dinner party."

Dominique yanked her hand from his. She picked up her combs and cap and quickly restored her hair to its proper modest style. "A party is the very last thing I have planned. I've known Falcon my whole life, and you've known him only a few weeks. Don't you dare mistake my need to keep busy for indifference."

Dominique rose and started down the stairs in a purposeful flutter of peach muslin, leaving Étienne seated in a dejected slump. He rose slowly, and still feeling sick with fear for his friend, ran his hand along the wall as he returned to his room. He grabbed the clean clothes and threw them on the bed. He knew it was important to eat; he had not meant to be short with Dominique, but he did not think he could swallow a spoonful of soup or even a crust of bread.

He was too anxious to stay in his room, however, and began sorting through the clothes. The shirt was of fine linen, and there was a pair of cotton drawers that tied at the knee. The suit was dark grey and the vest white. There were brand new stockings, but no shoes and he did not think the suit would look good with the pair of moccasins Falcon had given him. Forced to compromise, he pulled the shirt on over his head, tucked it into his buckskins, and left the room.

When he walked into the dining room, he found Byron seated at the head of the table, absently tearing a piece of bread into tiny bits. Jean was at his left, scooping up his soup with deep dips. Dominique was at her father's right, staring into an untasted bowl of soup, and the couple he recalled as Falcon's sister and her husband were leaning back in their chairs, apparently finished eating. Dominique looked up at him and gestured to the chair beside her. As soon as he had slid into it, a young woman entered and served him a steaming bowl of vegetable soup from the tureen at the center of the table.

Étienne glanced toward the empty places and wondered if everyone else had had as little appetite as he and simply refused to come for the evening meal. He thought he should apologize for not wearing the suit, but it was obvious his companions were too distracted to care what he wore. The strained silence reminded him too much of home when his father was present, but he took a piece of bread from the plate Dominique passed him and tore off a bite.

"I should be with the other soldiers," he said with sudden insight.

"They're all asleep," Johanna assured him. "They won't miss you."

"And we will," Dominique added softly.

Étienne knew that was a lie, but did not call her on it. The bread was still warm from the oven, and so delicious he ate the whole slice before he recalled he wasn't hungry. He spread butter on a second piece, and then tasted the soup. It was almost as good as his mother's recipe, and he had to force himself not to gulp it down as rapidly as Jean was consuming his.

"Please let me help," he urged Dominique.

Dominique finally picked up her spoon. "There's nothing to do except pray. Are you good at that?"

It had been a long while since Étienne had been to church, but he remembered how to pray. "Yes," he assured her. He noticed the tremor in her hand as she raised the spoon to her lips and wanted to guide it for her but she managed a sip without dribbling hot soup down her bodice. He felt Johanna watching him and tried to smile.

"Falcon has been a good friend to me." Falcon had mentioned Christian more often than his sister, but Étienne still felt as though he knew her. She favored her mother, and he thought her exceptionally pretty. "He mentioned your sons, his nephews. He said they were fine boys."

"Thank you," Johanna replied.

David moved closer to his wife. "I want you to stay here. I'll go home and see they got to bed."

While he had three younger sisters, Étienne had never looked after them and knew nothing about minding small children or he would have volunteered to go instead. He wanted so badly to be useful, but did not know how. David left, and no one else spoke. At least no one had blamed him for the severity of Falcon's illness, but he did not truly feel welcome at the table. He waited until Dominique pushed her bowl aside and then suggested they take a walk.

"Go on," Byron urged. "We'll be up all night, and it would be good for you to get away for a while now if you can."

Dominique paused to kiss her father's cheek. She sensed without having to ask that he was remembering the members of their family whom they had already lost to death, and praying Falcon would not join them. She had not known his brother, Elliott, or sister, Melissa. Her grandfather was also deceased before she was born, and her dear grandmother was gone now, too. The Barclays had enjoyed excellent health for so long, Falcon's horrible wound was doubly terrifying for surely they were due for a loss.

Étienne took Dominique's hand as soon as they had left the house. "Come with me down to the river. It reminds me of home."

Unable to suggest a better alternative, Dominique went along. She knew she ought to encourage him to tell her about his home and family, but doubting she would be able to concentrate on his reply, thought better of it. The gathering dusk steeped the shore in shadows, but she guided him down to the path and without making a conscious choice, began walking toward the Scotts' land.

"I don't mean to be rude," she said. "I know I should make the effort to converse, but I just can't tonight."

"It is all right," Étienne assured her, but then he could

not stifle his frustration. "I seem always to come here at the wrong time."

Again puzzled by his remark, Dominique pressed him to explain. "You came here once with Beau, and now to bring Falcon home. How can you consider either of those occasions 'wrong'?"

Étienne feared he had lost all hope of impressing her, then chided himself for ever harboring such a delusion in the first place. "Perhaps I did not choose the right word," he said. "Soldiers are not always the best tutors for my English."

The evening was cool, but it felt good to Dominique after such a trying day. Étienne's hand held a pleasing warmth, although as before, his touch was light. "We could speak French if you like, but I'm afraid I'd be no more coherent."

"No. I want to practice my English with you so I do not make so many foolish mistakes."

"Your accent is very charming, Étienne, and your English is excellent. You needn't worry about mistakes." When he stopped and took a step ahead to face her, she thought he meant to ask some question about grammar, but instead, he slipped his arms around her waist and pulled her close. As he dipped his head, this struck her as the most inappropriate of times for romance, but she made no attempt to avoid his kiss. Instead, she stood still, and while she gave the ardent young man a cool welcome, it was enough to inspire him to kiss her again.

His kiss was soft, and yet insistent. He traced the shape of her lips with the tip of his tongue, and she opened her mouth without further coaxing. She heard him sigh way in the back of his throat, and almost ashamed that he found kissing her so moving, she relaxed against him. Smooth and sweet, rich and deep, each kiss created a craving for another and she raised her arms to encircle his neck to inspire more. She did not want to think, but simply to feel, and Étienne's generous affection made her feel awfully good indeed.

With right colliding with wrong in Étienne's mind, his thoughts swirled in a painful knot. Dominique was a lady. She was precious to her family, and to him as well, but he did not want to stop their passionate kisses. Aching for more, he grabbed her hand and drew her up the riverbank to a grassy knoll. To the south, tall rushes screened the river. On the north, the windows of her stately home shone brightly in the distance, but he was certain no one would be watching them.

He pulled Dominique down across his lap, then with enticing kisses eased her onto the grass. It still held the day's warmth, but he longed to sample her heat, and pushed her low-cut gown off her shoulders. He nuzzled the curve of her throat, and then the smooth swell of her breasts until he had freed her nipples. It was dark now, but he knew they would be pale like the blush of a peach floating in cream.

Dominique slid her fingers through Étienne's curls and pulled away the tie at his nape. His hair was soft and she grabbed a handful to press his face closer still. His tongue was doing such wonderful things to her breast and she sucked in a breathless gasp. He bit her then, lightly, but causing an exquisite pain that made her moan with desire.

She had never moved past fevered kisses with another man, not even Sean, but she felt no sense of caution with Étienne. He began whispering to her in French, such pretty things, but she could not give him any endearing replies. She was lost in him, and yet not with him at all when her mind refused to make the choice he so clearly wanted. His mouth found hers again, but his hands were never still.

Étienne caressed Dominique's breasts, then slipped his hand under her gown to pinch her knee. He slid his hand up her thigh, then down over her hip to pull her against him. All the while his tongue teased hers with playful jabs and slow curls. Her voluminous skirts were in his way, and he damned her petticoats with a silent curse, but he at last found the ribbon tie on her drawers and pulled it loose. He felt her stiffen, but whispered a hasty reassurance.

"I will not hurt you," he breathed against her lips, then kissed her again as his fingertips brushed across the bare flesh of her stomach. Her skin was so soft, and he spread his fingers wide to feel more. He pressed gently with the heel of his hand, knowing precisely what the effect on her would be.

Étienne spread light kisses down her throat, then laved her breast in tender adoration. Dominique arched her back to lean into him. She shuddered as he shifted position, then dipped into her wetness and coaxed forth a searing heat. His fingertips circled and stroked, delved deeper, then whispered a promise of so much more. She grasped his wrist, but to hold him, not to push him away, and he understood the urgency of her need.

He had to fight back his own desire but he wanted to teach her what love was meant to be before he shared in her joy fully. She was ready for him, dripping a honeyed sweetness he hungered to taste, but this first time he dared not shock her with the boldness of his appetites. Instead he drew her nipple between his teeth and increased the pressure of his fingertips. He heard her breath catch in her throat as the rapture he had created reached its peak, and then with a petal-soft sigh, she went limp in his arms.

After what Falcon had told him about her lost lover, Étienne had not expected her to be a virgin. Now that he knew that she was, he dared not push her further. Instead, he stretched out beside her and cradled her gently in his arms. He had never put a woman's pleasure before his own, but then, he had never been with Dominique before, either. He drew in a deep breath and released it slowly. The stars were magnificent, but in his mind, they did not compare to the woman in his arms.

Arielle had told her daughters that making love created a glorious sensation, but Dominique had not really expected anything more than the joy deep kissing brought. She wanted to fall asleep in Étienne's arms, but feared they had already been away from the house too long. She didn't know what to say to him. Between passionate kisses, he had praised her beauty and grace and complimented her perfume, but as his words came back to her now, there had been no mention of tender feelings for her, no promises of love. It was that alarming omission that made her sit up and hurriedly adjust the fit of her bodice.

Startled that she had left his embrace so soon, Étienne sat up, too. "Dominique? I know I pleased you. What is wrong?"

"Everything," she replied. She stuffed her hair up under her cap, sat up on her knees to secure the bow on her drawers, and then stood. Étienne nearly leapt to his feet, but she would not have left him lying there in the grass. "Turn around," she ordered. "We can't walk in the house with grass all over our backs."

"The last time it was tobacco."

Appalled that he would wish to remind her of that ridiculous encounter, Dominique brushed off his shirt with more force than necessary. He had not asked for any vow of devotion, nor made one of his own, and while her whole body still felt infused with a blissful heat, she could not have said what she thought of him. "Your hair," she suddenly exclaimed. "We've got to find the ribbon."

Étienne knelt and felt around for it but it was black as the night and it took him a moment to find it. He stood to retie his hair. "Are you afraid you will be punished for being with me?"

"I don't even know how to describe what we were doing, but I wasn't actually 'with' you, Étienne. At least, not in the way I think you're afraid my parents might suspect."

"Are you ashamed then?" When Dominique took a moment to consider the question, Étienne had his answer and started off toward her house.

She hurried to catch up with him and took his hand. He tried to pull away, but she was as stubborn as he and tightened her hold. "I'm not ashamed," she swore convincingly. "But I'm not sure what that meant."

"What does it usually mean?"

That he thought she had let other men take such shocking liberties wounded Dominique deeply, but she supposed she deserved the insult when she had not uttered even the softest word of protest No, indeed. She had shamelessly encouraged every bit of Étienne's lavish affection. She could not accuse him of taking advantage of her fears for Falcon, but as they entered the house, she went upstairs to her ailing cousin's bedroom without bidding Étienne good night.

Étienne watched her flounce up the stairs, as aloof as he had ever seen her, and was about to go back outside when Jean appeared. "Do you still wish to hear about the Battle of King's Mountain?" Étienne asked him.

"Yes, sir. I most certainly do." Jean looked Étienne up and down. "I forgot to bring shoes for you," he remarked absently. "Why didn't you say something earlier?"

Étienne shrugged. "I will be here only a few days."

"Well, you need shoes for those few days at least. Let's go look and see what Beau left."

Étienne felt as though he had imposed too much already. "His clothes are not too loose for me, but he is heavier than I am, and I do not believe his shoes will fit me."

"Then come up to my room and we'll look through mine."

Jean started up the stairs and Étienne followed. Most men did not own more than a single pair of shoes, but then most were not nearly as wealthy as the Barclays. A bitterness not unlike his father's perpetual ill-humor surged through him, but he struggled to overcome the envy filling his throat rather than give in to such a petty emotion.

Jean's room was painted the same shade of pale green as the guest room, and as beautifully furnished but contained the boyish clutter Jean never found the time to put away. He crossed to the wardrobe, flung open the doors, and bent down to sort through the half-dozen pairs of shoes. Some had silver buckles and others were plain leather. There were two pairs of boots as well. Jean debated a moment, then pulled out all the shoes.

"Try on any you like," he encouraged.

Étienne hung back. "You make me feel like a beggar."

Offended, Jean's eyes narrowed. "You're a hero, Étienne, a guest. I didn't mean to offend you. If you don't like my shoes, we'll find others."

"They are very handsome shoes—magnificent, in fact." Étienne did not know which was worse, to have Jean offer his shoes so easily, or for him to find it so difficult to be gracious about the loan. He did want to wear the suit so he would be as well dressed as the Barclays, but he was sorry he owned no fine clothes of his own. He had given away the old suit he had worn the first time he had been there, and did not miss it.

"I need my socks," he told Jean, and went to fetch them. He quickly washed his feet, then pulled on the stockings and walked back to Jean's room. He hoped the plain shoes would fit, but they were too small. One of the pairs with silver buckles was nearly as comfortable as his moccasins.

Jean saw Étienne's smile and tossed the other shoes back into the wardrobe. "Consider those yours."

"No. I can not keep them."

"Then leave them here for your next visit," Jean urged. He sat down on the side of his bed and gestured toward the chair at his desk. "Sit down and tell me all about the battle. From what we read in the *Virginia Gazette,* it was completely one-sided."

Étienne turned the chair toward the young man and sat down. "Yes. That is true," he agreed. He did his best to describe the scene as it had actually been rather than to romanticize it, but he saw from the bright glow of interest in Jean's eyes that the young man's imagination was painting a far more exciting picture in his mind.

"There is always great confusion during a battle, and the noise from the gunfire is so loud there is not a second of quiet in which to think. Shooting men is not like hunting deer. The stench of death fills the air, and at King's Mountain the boulders were splattered with blood. Rivulets of gore trickled through the pine needles and dripped all the way down the hill," Étienne emphasized with appropriate disgust.

"A battle is not an adventure that ends in a celebration. It ends instead in a silence broken by screams. Only the lucky ones are killed instantly, Jean. Some wounds are terrible, leaving torn stumps of limbs or wide gashes across faces and chests. The worst are those that rip the belly and spill a man's guts into the dirt. Look at the men who have come here with me. They suffered over every mile, and poor Falcon—his leg has caused him unbearable pain."

The luster had left Jean's eyes, but he was still optimistic about his cousin. "Falcon will be all right."

Étienne admired Jean's confidence, but after hearing Falcon cry out as though the Devil had sunk his claws in him, he could not share it. "I hope you are right, but how can you be so certain?"

Jean shrugged. "My mother can cure anything, even gunshot wounds."

Étienne nodded and sincerely hoped Jean was right. Finally recalling his promise, he rose to his feet. "You must excuse me," he said. "I want to be alone now to pray."

"For Falcon?"

"Oui," Étienne replied, but as he left the room, he thought he ought to say a prayer for himself as well. He was going to need a few angels on his side if he were ever going to touch Dominique's heart. Knowing she would be plunged into despair should they lose Falcon, he went to his room and got down on his knees to pray for his friend. Falcon

would have to survive, or Étienne would have no hope of
love. Then thinking such reasoning too selfish, he concentrated upon Falcon alone. Falcon was a good man and a
fine friend, and Étienne's prayers flowed easily from his
heart.

When Dominique entered Falcon's room, she found her
mother pacing nervously. Alanna was seated in the rocking
chair she had brought over from her room, while Belle sat
at the brave's bedside. "Why don't you get into bed with
him, Belle?" Dominique suggested. "Your closeness will
be a comfort to Falcon, won't it, Mother?"

Arielle was surprised by her daughter's idea, as she had
always felt people preferred to be alone when they were
gravely ill. She studied Dominique's expression and was
pleased by a newfound maturity. Like Falcon, Belle was a
creature of the river and forest, and more at home outside
than in, but Dominique was very different. She had always
had great charm, and a gift for touching people. Arielle saw
it now for the rare talent it might become.

"You are right," she agreed softly. "Belle, you can snug-
gle up closely without touching Falcon's leg, and I do believe your presence will be a comfort to him."

Falcon had been sleeping soundly, perhaps too soundly,
since Arielle had reopened his wound, and she did not want
his spirit to slip away in his dreams. The comfrey poultice
would draw out the poisons making him so sick, but the
herb required more time than he might have. "You do not
mind, do you, Alanna?"

"No. Not at all." Alanna continued to rock slowly in the
chair where she had once rocked her babies. Her hands
were folded tightly in her lap. She looked up as Johanna
joined them, but her smile was faint. "Are the soldiers comfortable?"

"They'll not wake before morning. What can I do here?"

"Will you bring us a kettle of water and we'll set it on the fire to make some tea for ourselves," Arielle said.

"Then we'll need five cups." Johanna left to see to the errand, and Belle, having been given permission to join Falcon on the bed, went around to the other side to climb up. She had never expected her mother and aunt to allow her to sleep with him, but being closer to him was a comfort to her as well. She plumped the pillow and curled up on her side next to him.

She closed her eyes and sent him a loving prayer, but as she took his hand, he seemed to be even more feverish than he had been after his bath. She sat up again. "Mother, come touch him. He's awfully warm."

Arielle crossed to the bed in an instant and placed her palm on Falcon's forehead. "Yes. His fever has worsened." She peeled back the sheet covering him. "Bring the pitcher and we will take turns bathing his skin with cool water. That will help to break the fever."

"We ought to try and wake him," Dominique added. "He needs to drink more comfrey, or white willow tea."

Belle called Falcon's name in an urgent plea, but the brave failed to respond. She slapped his face lightly, but he gave no sign he felt her touch. "Mother?" she asked fearfully.

Alanna had come to the bed, and along with Arielle, Belle, and Dominique, gazed lovingly at her son. "If we can keep him cool until Hunter and Christian return, then perhaps—"

She did not need to finish the sentence. The women joined hands for a moment and prayed that if Arielle's medicine failed to save Falcon, the Seneca's magic could.

Twenty

Hunter rubbed the dark stain into his mask. Because they had chosen the willow and basswood trees to carve in the afternoon, tradition dictated the masks had to be black. He had incised deep furrows across the brow and radiating out from the crooked nose to stream over the swollen cheeks. The eyes were small and mean. The mouth was puckered and twisted into a grimace. It was easily one of the ugliest masks he had ever seen, and yet he thought Christian's design equally awful.

Christian had sculpted huge, bulging eyes and a thin nose that jutted outward like a twig. The upper lip was small and tight, while the lower drooped open. A wickedly pointed tongue flicked out of the anguished mouth. He was seated near his father, also working on the stain.

"You must keep your mask hidden," Hunter warned. "It must be wrapped and laid facedown or it will lose its power to heal. When we finish here, we'll rub a little fat and tobacco on our masks' lips. That will keep its spirit content."

During the night, Hunter had taught Christian what song to sing as they performed the ritual, and the young man had kept humming it softly while he worked. The first blush of dawn had just kissed the horizon, but Hunter felt no fatigue despite having worked all night. He got up to add more wood to their fire.

"I didn't take you home with me often," he remarked

sadly. "I hope the False Face Society does not sound foolish to you."

Hunter was not glancing his way, but Christian knew his answer was important to him. "Nothing about the Seneca has ever sounded foolish to me, Father, except, of course, for their stubborn loyalty to King George III. That was a grave error. I will take very good care of this mask, and some day teach my children about it. They are all too young now, but—"

"No. They're not," Hunter cautioned. "When the False Face Society visits a longhouse to cure someone, the whole family is present. When we get home, we'll gather everyone who wants to watch. They all love Falcon, and want him well. We needn't give lessons on how to make the masks, but we can show everyone how they are used."

Christian heard the pride in his father's voice and nodded. "I'm glad you already had a turtle shell rattle as I'd not have wanted to make one of those, too."

Hunter sighed softly. "I have not taught you nearly enough."

Christian could not agree. "You have taught me far more than most men teach their sons, and all of it valuable. I hope that I can teach my boys half as much. As for Liberty, she already knows more than a little girl should."

"Just like her mother."

"Yes. She favors Liana in all ways." Christian held his mask up and peered through it. It had taken a long while to bore out the holes for the eyes, but he could see well through them. "Are you ready to cut the horses' tails?" he asked.

"Almost." Hunter rubbed stain down into the deep creases at the corners of the mouth, and then was ready. His stallion's white tail would make good hair, and after carefully laying the mask aside, he rose and drew his knife. "It will grow back, so hack off as much as you want," he advised his son.

Christian's mount was a spirited black stallion that did not take kindly to his master's need for part of his tail. He danced sideways and kicked, and it wasn't until Hunter spoke to the horse sternly that he finally stood still for such an indignity. Hunter had no problems with his sorrel mount, and with a good-sized hank of white hair, he sat down to gouge tiny holes around the top half of his mask with the tip of his knife.

"Let's hurry," he urged. "Arielle asked us to be home by sundown, but I'm anxious to get back before then. We'll need to cut two slender limbs for staves—then we'll be ready to go."

Christian felt equally uneasy about being away too long and worked with renewed zeal to attach the hair quickly. "The war is coming back to Virginia, and it won't be confined to Portsmouth this time. I'll fight again, and willingly, but if I'm wounded, I want you and Falcon to wear these masks for me."

"I'll help Falcon make his own," Hunter promised, "but I hope it will never be used." He threaded several strands of horsehair through the first hole, knotted it, and went on to the next. He refused to reflect upon the possibility that Falcon might not live to perform the curing ritual for another man. "I will fight again, too," he swore. "Virginia has given me too much for me to stay in the fields."

"Good," Christian said, for he did not know a finer man to be by his side in battle. "The British will have no chance against us. They'll be cut to pieces as they were at King's Mountain."

"And fed to the crows," Hunter added.

Christian chuckled at that grisly image and began to thread the gleaming black horsehair onto his mask. He was pleased with it, despite the hasty carving. From what his father had said, they had strayed from two important traditions. They had not been inspired by dreams, nor taken three days to burn an offering of tobacco to ask the trees' forgiveness before taking a piece of its wood. He hoped those omissions did not doom their effort, and got up to toss a pinch of tobacco on the fire to appease the spirits of the trees as best he could. Then, as Alanna had taught him, he also asked for God's blessing.

After midnight, Liana had joined the others tending Falcon, allowing Johanna to lie down in Dominique's room for a brief nap, but despite the women's exhaustive efforts, the injured brave's condition continued to deteriorate. Sweat poured off his body and soaked the bedclothes, and no amount of cool water eased his torment. Unconscious, he gave an occasional moan, but never opened his eyes.

Jean came to the door at midmorning. "Hunter and Christian are back. They said anyone who wishes to observe may. I thought I should ask you first."

Arielle came to the door to speak to her son. She dared not tell him that she feared all anyone could do now was bid Falcon a loving good-bye, and instead opened the door wide. "It is a large room. Everyone is welcome."

Belle and Dominique were on the far side of the bed as the rest of the family began to file in. David brought his sons and they ran to Johanna. Liberty tame in, holding her three-year-old brother's hand, and Jean carried Christian's year-old baby boy. Byron entered and leaned against the wall, followed by Étienne, who caught Dominique's eye and then moved aside. Many of the servants lined up in the hallway, but respectful of the situation, they remained outside.

Dominique reached for Belle's hand and held on tight. They heard male voices intoning a rhythmic chant, accompanied by a rattling sound, pebbles bouncing inside Hunter's turtle-shell rattle, but they could not identify it until he came into view. Even after being warned the Seneca ritual required masks, none of them had expected such ghastly faces and when Hunter and Christian entered, there was a collective gasp; frightened, Christian's youngest son began a high-pitched wail. Liana quickly plucked him from Jean's arms and carried him to the window to distract him.

The braves tapped their staves on the floor in a brisk, thumping cadence and made straight for the fireplace. The fire had gone out before dawn and the ashes were cold. Each scooped up a handful, and with Hunter leading, they circled the room, sang, and sprinkled ashes on the heads of everyone gathered there. To continue the ritual, Christian returned to the fireplace and built a new fire. When it was burning brightly, he and his father moved to the bed.

Their deep voices filled the room with the sacred chant of the Seneca, punctuated by the turtle-shell rattle. Hunter shook ashes along the length of Falcon's leg, then, taking care not to inflict more pain, rubbed them into his skin very gently. He sprinkled more ashes on the poultice, and this time blew them away. He again shook his rattle over his son and never breaking the rhythm of the ancient chant, led Christian from the room.

Dominique was so tired she wasn't sure what she had just witnessed, but she did not consider the ritual nearly as strange as the masks Hunter and Christian had worn to perform it. She had actually found the sonorous chant comforting and hoped Falcon had heard it, too. He appeared to be breathing easier, which was an enormous relief, even if there was no other visible sign of improvement. She smiled at her family lining the room. From their weary and confused expressions, she doubted they had understood any more than she.

"I think we can go now," she suggested softly, and with nods of agreement, everyone except Belle began to shuffle out slowly. When Dominique sent her sister a questioning glance, Belle shook her head. "I just need a moment's rest, then I'll be back," Dominique promised, but as she went out the door, Étienne took her hand.

"You have not slept at all, have you?" he asked.

"There was no time."

"There is time now," he urged, and with a slight tug, encouraged her to come with him up the stairs. "You are very good with others, Dominique, but who takes care of you?"

"I don't need anyone," she insisted, but she did not object when he followed her through her door. Her bed looked so wonderfully inviting, she did not even take the time to undress before she lay down and curled up on her side.

Étienne came to the bed to remove her slippers and sat down to rub her feet. "Your feet are as pretty as the rest of you."

"Hmm." As usual, Étienne had a magical touch, and after a few minutes of his gentle attentions her feet were no longer sore. Dominique knew it was improper for him to be in her room, and that she should send him away, but she could not seem to find the energy to do so.

Étienne waited for a word of encouragement or appreciation, then realized from Dominique's easy breathing that she had fallen asleep. He ran his fingertips up her calf, and remembered how good the rest of her had felt. He leaned against the post at his back and tried to decide what to do. Someone had to drive the injured men home, and he was the logical choice, but he had not gotten much sleep last night either.

He kicked off his shoes, removed his borrowed vest, and still clad in his shirt, gray pants, and stockings, curled up behind Dominique. He dropped his right arm over her waist to catch her hand, and snuggled close. He longed to make her love him with a passion that would bind them together for all time, but thus far, he had had scant success with that. He closed his eyes and wished they were again down by the river so he might have another chance to convince her to accept still more of his affection. For the moment, just holding her close was nice. She might not care all that much for him, but he felt certain she must like how he made her feel.

It was a beginning.

After leaving Falcon's room, Arielle and Byron sat down in the parlor for a few minutes, where each hoped Hunter's ceremony had given Falcon's body the time it needed to heal. They were both so tired, the fact they were now relying on a primitive ritual did not even strike them as odd. "I need to change my clothes, and then I must return to Falcon's room," Arielle said to her husband.

"Let's just go to bed," Byron encouraged. "You said yourself you've done all you could."

"Yes, that is true, but——"

Byron helped her to her feet. "Come on. I insist. Belle and Dominique will know where to find you should you be needed."

Her sense of responsibility clashing with her fatigue, Arielle did not give in until she realized that she must. "Let us pray that I am not called." She covered a wide yawn, but as they reached the landing, she veered toward Falcon's room. "I just want to check on him," she whispered, and Byron went on into their room.

Arielle looked in on Falcon and found Belle asleep beside him. She tiptoed over to them, then, pleased that Falcon was resting so peacefully, saw no reason to disturb her daughter. She went on up to Dominique's room and rapped lightly at the door. When she did not respond, Arielle thought she might be elsewhere, but peeked in.

A single glance made it apparent Dominique had fallen asleep the instant her head had touched her pillow, but Arielle could not believe her daughter would have invited Étienne LeBlanc to join her. She approached the bed, meaning to send him out of the room at once, but asleep, with his dark curls spilled over his forehead, he resembled his father so closely that she was taken aback.

Dominique had been up here in her room when Arielle had told Belle and Falcon that she might have known Étienne's father, so Dominique had no reason to fear the young Frenchman. Were it not for harsh memories of Gaetan LeBlanc, Arielle would have thought them a handsome pair. After the awful way Sean O'Keefe had behaved, she hated to reveal Gaetan's history and perhaps prejudice her daughter against a young man who had already proven himself to be responsible.

Because the day had been extraordinary, and fatigue made any serious contemplation impossible, rather than awaken Étienne and send him to his own room, Arielle turned and left the pair to enjoy what she assumed would be an entirely innocent nap. She could not manage anything else herself, and was grateful that Byron was sound asleep when she joined him in their bed.

Étienne had felt Arielle's presence, and without having to open his eyes, had recognized her by her perfume. He had hoped she would be too tired to be provoked with him, and was relieved that had proved to be the case. He had to laugh to himself then because with such a lovely daughter, Arielle ought not to be so trusting.

Hunter, Alanna, Christian, Liana, Johanna, David, and the children were gathered on the front steps. Hunter and Christian had left their masks upstairs, but the roles they had played were not as easily laid aside, Neither man spoke as the others expressed their hopes for Falcon's recovery. The eldest at five years, Liberty was the only child who really understood just how dire her uncle's situation was. While her brothers and cousins played on the steps, she stared at Hunter with a level gaze he could not ignore.

"What is it, Liberty?" he finally had to ask. "Did our masks frighten you, too?"

"I'm not one of the babies," the little red-haired girl replied proudly.

Hunter caught her mother's eye. "Was she ever a baby?" he asked.

Liana shook her head. "She was small, but never a baby. Liberty was born wise."

"She has a good name then," Hunter said. He reached out his hand and Liberty came to him and leaned against his knee. She was an affectionate child and was frequently in her grandfather's arms.

"Well, Miss Liberty," Hunter encouraged, "tell me what you think."

Liberty cocked her head, but her gaze was steady. "I think Falcon is going to be angry he missed seeing you dance."

Hunter laughed, but the rest of his family was still too frightened to appreciate the humor in Liberty's comment. "I hope he is furious," Hunter told her. "Then I'll know he's well."

Liberty played with the fringe on his sleeve, then glanced over at her father. "Falcon's going to be mad at you, too."

"I certainly hope so," Christian swore. "In fact, I'll be real disappointed if he isn't."

"Do you want to go home, too?" David asked Johanna.

"I don't know. Do we dare?" She searched her parents' faces for a hopeful sign but they both looked very tired. Johanna waited until she could not be overheard. "I'm still terrified we're going to lose Falcon."

Alanna reached out to take her daughter's hand. Alanna had lost her whole family in an Indian raid when she was small, but once she had recovered from the horror of that day, they had continued to live on in her heart and mind. "No one is ever really lost, sweetheart, as long as someone who loved them remains alive. Happy memories last forever."

Johanna was close to tears, but refused to give in to them. She rose and shook out her skirt. "I'm going up to stay with Belle and Falcon. Why don't you get some rest?"

"Perhaps later." Alanna took her husband's hand as soon as they were alone. "Thank you," she whispered.

"Do not thank me yet," Hunter warned.

Alanna rested her head on his shoulder. "No. I want to thank you now for trying as best you could to save our son."

Hunter could have done no less, but choked on tears, he could not refuse her gratitude.

The sun had set before Dominique awakened from her nap; horrified to have slept so long, she left her bed and hurriedly lit a lamp. She went to the washstand and splashed water on her face, then, needing a change of clothes, stripped and washed her whole body clean. Praying that Falcon's condition had improved, she donned fresh lingerie, a rose silk gown, and restyled her hair atop her head.

It wasn't until she returned to the bed for her slippers that she noticed the light dusting of ashes on the second pillow. There was a smudge on her own, but she had awakened in nearly the same position as she had fallen asleep. Puzzled, it took a moment for her to recall that Étienne had followed her into the room. That he would have lain down beside her, which he obviously had, annoyed her no end.

She cursed herself for giving him the mistaken impression that she would welcome his company, and shoved her feet into her shoes. She would deal with Étienne later. Right now, she had to see Falcon. When she reached his room, the door was slightly ajar, and her spirits soared when she heard soft conversation rather than weeping coming from inside. She knocked as she entered, but stopped just inside the door.

Falcon was sitting up in bed, and Belle was feeding him

a bowl of soup. Hunter and Alanna were standing at the foot of the bed; her father was seated in the rocking chair while her mother was at the fireplace brewing a pot of tea. They all turned toward her and smiled.

"I didn't mean to sleep so long," Dominique apologized as she came toward the bed. "It's so good to see you awake again, Falcon. I've really missed you."

Falcon responded with a sheepish smile and swallowed another spoonful of soup. He had to lean back against his pillow to rest a minute, but his eyes had lost their fevered glaze. Bare-chested, he was much too thin, but Dominique thought he looked wonderful. When she came up to the bed, Belle moved aside so she could kiss his cheek. His skin felt cool; elated, she had a difficult time containing her tears.

There was no way to tell what had worked the miracle— her mother's herbs, the whole family's prayers, or Hunter and Christian's Seneca incantations—but clearly Falcon had had one. "I hope that your whole life is as blessed as it has been today," Dominique told him.

"I've always been lucky," Falcon claimed. "Isn't that right, Belle?"

"Yes. That's true." Belle laughed as she fed him more soup. "Of course, I'm so happy to see you smiling I would agree with anything you said."

"It is true," Falcon swore.

"Can I bring you anything else?" Dominique asked.

Falcon thought a moment. "Blackberries?"

Dominique started for the door. "I'll bring some cream," she assured him. She raised her skirt and hastened down the stairs. There was no one in the parlor, and she was surprised to find Jean seated in the dining room. A big bowl of blackberries had been set out for supper, and she spooned some into a small bowl and poured on cream.

"Have you seen Étienne?" she asked as casually as she could.

Jean had been reading and looked up from his book. "He's gone."

Startled, Dominique nearly slopped cream over the table-cloth but caught herself before she spilled the first drop. "Gone?" she repeated calmly, but her heart was caught in her throat. "Where?"

"He left this afternoon to drive the wounded men home. Henry Smith was from Richmond, and Haywood and Berry from somewhere just a few miles closer. But why should you care where Étienne's gone? Will you miss him?"

Dominique sent her brother a withering glance. With Richmond fifty miles to the northwest, by her reckoning Étienne might be gone nearly two weeks. Unless, of course, he left the old wagon he had arrived in in Richmond and came home on horseback. This wasn't his home, though, and maybe he wasn't coming back. She was surprised at just how painful that possibility was.

"Don't be silly, Jean," she chided. "He's Falcon's friend rather than mine."

"I know, but he left the minute he knew Falcon was going to be all right."

Dominique had the berries and cream, which was all that had brought her downstairs, but she couldn't leave the dining room without knowing what to expect. Adept at projecting an innocent gaze, she smiled at her brother. "Is he coming back here?"

Jean laughed. "Of course he's coming back. He's in love with you. Couldn't you tell by the way he nearly drooled when he looked at you?"

"All men do that," Dominique murmured under her breath, but as she turned away, she nurtured the warming burst of pleasure Jean's teasing opinion had brought. It wasn't until later, when she went out into the garden to enjoy the evening, that she began to wonder if Étienne's feelings for her might not simply be another of the infatuations she had inspired in her admirers over the years.

If so, she would not encourage it with another shamelessly passionate interlude. Had that only been last night? she asked herself, and once she realized that it had been, Étienne's departure took on the appearance of flight. Had the man feared she might demand he offer marriage and run away before she could? *How dare he presume so much?*

At the very least he could have told her good-bye, but no. He had waited to be certain Falcon was all right, and then had fled. There was no other way to describe what he had done, and Dominique was so insulted she did not know what to think. She had been too preoccupied when she got dressed to examine her breasts, but it would not surprise her if his tooth marks were clearly incised on them both.

What had possessed her to behave in such a wanton fashion, and with Étienne, of all people? Thank God he had not done more than he had before abandoning her, but it still hurt that he had not even wanted to tell her farewell. She sat alone for a long while, trying to be grateful that Falcon was so much better rather than dwelling on her own shame, but it was difficult. The very least the man could have done was write her a note. Hoping that he might have left a message she had missed in her haste to dress; she returned to her room, but there was no envelope bearing her name.

Discouraged, and still tired despite her long nap, she removed the pretty rose gown, and then, gathering her courage, carried a lamp over to her dresser. She could see more easily in this mirror than in the smaller one above the washstand, and with trembling hands, she loosed the tie on her chemise. She leaned forward and eased the soft linen garment down over her nipples.

To her absolute horror, she found Étienne's ardent bites had left bright red crescents on her pale skin. She traced them with her fingertips and shivered as her whole body was flooded with the delicious sensation she would rather forget. A knock at the door jarred her so severely that she got her fingers twisted in the ribbon and created a horrible knot as she tried to retie her chemise. She rushed to open her door a crack, but when she found Belle, she reached out to draw her inside.

"I'm so thrilled for you," Dominique exclaimed happily. "Falcon will grow stronger each day now."

"Yes. That's what I'm hoping, too. Mother won't let me sleep with him tonight, but I wanted to tell you good night before I went to my room."

Dominique sat down on the side of her bed. "I'm tired, too, but too excited to sleep now. Aren't you?"

Belle joined her on the bed. "Yes. Étienne is still apologizing for not taking better care of Falcon. He told us Lafayette was shot in the leg at Brandywine Creek and recovered so quickly he hoped for the same happy result with Falcon."

"I imagine Lafayette had a surgeon's attentions," Dominique responded.

"Yes. I suppose, but we gave Falcon better care than any surgeon could have. Did you see Étienne before he left?"

Dominique strove to hide her excitement. "No. I was asleep. Did he give you a message for me?"

Belle heard more in that question than Dominique realized. "No, but obviously he should have. He'll be back soon. Perhaps then you two will have the chance to become better acquainted."

Dominique pretended a rapt interest in the lace edge of her petticoat. As she saw it, she and Étienne had already become too intimately involved. "I just don't know quite what to make of him. He has immense charm, but he can be exasperating in the extreme. Today, he actually suggested I needed someone to take care of me. Isn't that preposterous?"

"You do!" Belle cried. "Étienne is even brighter than I thought. Be honest with yourself for a minute. Don't you like him a little bit, if not a lot?"

Dominique shook her head slowly, for she feared what she liked about Étienne was the affection that flowed so easily from his fingertips and lips. Had she ever showed such a damning weakness for another man, she would surely have wed and given birth to half a dozen babies by now. She and Étienne would make very beautiful babies together, and then, badly embarrassed by her traitorous imagination, she attempted to banish the thought.

Belle studied the lively play of emotions crossing her sister's face, and saw the secret Dominique was clearly fighting to hide. "With all the attention you've always received, you never really cared for anyone until you met Sean. I'll always be sorry that ended badly, but even if Étienne did come along much too soon afterward, don't let him slip away like all the others if you really want him. Do you remember telling me you'd sleep with a man you loved even if he were drunk and make certain he adored you by dawn?"

"I can't believe how stupid I was last summer," Dominique complained, "but we were talking about Falcon, whom you love dearly. Now, I'd not resort to such a desperate trick with any man. It's pathetic. Love is a gift, not a treasure to be won through feminine wiles."

Belle could not believe she was listening to Dominique, who had rebuffed so many devoted young men after using the very same feminine wiles she was disparaging. She reached out to tip Dominique's chin up so she could no longer avoid meeting her gaze. "Étienne is the perfect man for you. He has your elegance and charm, and he's fought our war simply because he believes in freedom rather than for any personal gain. Give him the chance you've denied so many other men."

Positive she had already given him way too much, Dominique slid off the bed. "I'm sorry, but I'm tired after all. Let's talk another time."

Recognizing Dominique's stubborn streak, Belle kissed

her good night on her way out, then tiptoed back down the
stairs to see Falcon again. He was asleep, and knowing how
badly he needed his rest she did not wake him, but she
could not wait for the night when she no longer had to
sleep alone.

Étienne could not believe how hard the ground felt after
sleeping in one of the Barclays feather beds. He struggled
to find a comfortable portion of earth not sprinkled with
rocks, but sleep would not come. Accepting the misery, he
propped his head on his hands and gazed up at the stars.
His injured companions were already snoring lightly, and
he was grateful to the Barclays for the supplies that would
see them all the way to Richmond.

He knew he had been right to begin the trip as soon as
Falcon had begun to improve, but just a few hours ago he
had not expected to miss Dominique so terribly. The intense
physical cravings she aroused were easily satisfied, but even
after he had done it, he still wanted her in his arms. He
doubted the Barclays would ever accept him as her husband,
and he knew his father would never accept her as his wife,
but that did not ease the exquisite longing that kept him
awake far into the night.

He had come to America filled with righteous ideals, but
all he would take home was a broken heart.

Twenty-one

Falcon was too active a young man to enjoy being bed-ridden, so as soon as he felt strong enough to try, he wanted to get up. Horrified by how close they had come to losing him, Belle transmitted her fears to her mother. Arielle read-ily understood Falcon's impatience, as well as her daughter's apprehensions, but she made her decision based on what was best for Falcon alone.

"Your leg is still healing," Arielle stressed. "If you get out of bed, all you will do is put yourself right back into it, and for far longer than if you had stayed put. Do you want to be confined to this room until next spring?"

Falcon bunched the sheets in tight fists. "I'll grant you that my leg still hurts, but not nearly as badly as it did when I came home. I know you're worried about me, and I appreciate your concern, but if I don't start using my leg soon, I'm afraid it will get stiff or become so weak it will be useless."

Arielle's stare grew cold. "If you were to get up and put any weight on your leg, the pain would make you pass out for a second time. You may not recall the first time that happened, but I do not want to hear you scream ever again. Stop thinking only about yourself, Falcon. Belle and the rest of us deserve your consideration as well."

Arielle left the room, and fearful of how badly Falcon would react to her mother's refusal, Belle moved away from the bed toward the window, the tobacco had been harvested, and the barren fields fit her mood. They also reminded her of the farmland around Camden, South Carolina, and she rubbed her arms to ward off an anxious shiver.

She had read to Falcon for hours at a time, and requested his favorite meals. She had been as amusing a companion as she could possibly be on mornings when she could barely hide her queasiness. After pouring so much time and effort into Falcon's recovery, she felt utterly drained and near tears as she slumped down on the windowseat.

Falcon was angry with everyone who was conspiring to keep him in his bed, and that included Belle. It had been a week since he had had a fever, and while his aunt applied a fresh comfrey poultice each morning, he doubted he still needed them. He threw back the covers and wiggled his toes. Those on his right foot were as agile as those on his left, and it caused him only a slight twinge of pain.

"I don't expect to get up and run," he exclaimed. "I just want to get out of this damn bed and stand a few minutes. How can that possibly be of any harm?"

Belle had called her mother to answer that question, but obviously Falcon wasn't going to accept Arielle's opinion. She tried to recall if he had inquired about her health even once since arriving home, but he hadn't. She understood that being ill he was far from himself, but still, it pained her to have to listen to nothing but complaints when it was so difficult to keep her own spirits high.

Wearily, she got to her feet. "I need to go out for a little bit," she called to him as she crossed the room. "I'll be back before time for your dinner."

Astonished that Belle would abandon him with nothing to do, Falcon opened his mouth to object, but she swept out the door with an alarming haste and he was left to deal with his frustrations on his own. He had never enjoyed remaining seated for as long as reading required, so he did not have that habit. He did like to draw, but he did not feel like fiddling with it now. He supposed he could fashion arrows, but he would have to ask his father or Christian to fetch him some straight branches and feathers first. All he truly wanted was to get up, and nothing less would satisfy him. He wondered if his father would help him, or perhaps Christian.

Then, too anxious to wait for the necessary assistance, he began to ease himself over. Just shifting his position hurt, but his leg had ached for so long he was used to it now. The problem was, he would have to scoot all the way across the bed to get out on the other side to put his left foot down first and shift his weight to his left leg. That took a great deal of effort. He could lift himself up off the bed with his arms, but moving his legs over was still a terrible chore.

He was sweating profusely by the time he slid his left leg over the side of the bed. He was dressed in cotton drawers, which he did not usually wear under his buckskins, but they would at least keep him covered while he walked as far as he could. He took hold of the bedpost, turned slightly so his right leg remained resting on the bed, and gradually eased himself up on his left. He was shaky and slightly nauseous from just moving across the bed, but hanging onto the post gave him the sense of balance he needed to feel secure.

His elation was brief, however; dizzy, he swayed slightly, then sat down, but he felt as though he had really accomplished something for the first time since he had been shot. He tried standing again, and when his left knee wobbled, he dared not swing his injured leg off the bed, but instead sat down and gave up the effort to walk for the day. It was enough to know he could stand, if not without strain on his good leg. He moved back into the middle of the bed and worn out, lay down to take a nap.

Belle returned with a bouquet of chrysanthemums, and after a respite from the strain of caring for him, she was in a more optimistic mood. Falcon watched her adjust the flowers in the crystal vase and then patted the bed to encourage her to come and sit down beside him. When she joined him he took her hand.

"We've been awfully good," he told her.

"About what?"

Falcon regarded her charming innocence with a sly grin. "About sleeping in our own rooms. I'm stuck here, but I want you to come back after everyone's gone to sleep and spend the night here with me."

Belle had waited in vain for him to set a wedding date, and when he knew she did not like fooling her parents, she could not understand why he was so reticent to make her his wife. Uncertain what to say, she looked away. "I'd rather not."

"Belle!" Falcon cried. "Don't you miss me as badly as I miss you?"

"Miss you? I'm with you every minute of the day, Falcon."

Falcon lowered his voice to a seductive whisper. "You know what I mean. I miss being with you, Belle. I can make love to you without tearing up my leg." He tilted his head back against the headboard and looked utterly forlorn. "God. Don't make me beg you to stay with me."

Belle could not refuse that plaintive plea and squeezed his hand. "All right, but please don't expect me to sleep with you every night."

"You belong with me, Belle, not upstairs alone."

Belle met his defiant gaze with forced calm, but no more willing to beg than he was, she refused to insist upon a wedding as a condition for joining him. She left to fetch his dinner, but was a distracted companion the rest of the day. When she bade him good night that evening, she spent some time with her parents in the parlor, then looked in on Dominique, who was compiling a list of every male caller she had ever had.

"Whatever possessed you to begin such a project?" Belle asked. "I thought you found keeping diaries too tedious."

Dominique was seated at her desk sorting through mementos she had kept over the years. There were faded party invitations, and cards with sweet messages that had been enclosed with gifts. "Yes. I'm afraid I do—that's why the years are such a blur in my mind. Williamsburg was so much fun before the war, and I should have kept a better record of all the fabulous parties. Now all I have are a few frayed ribbons and notes from men whose faces I can't recall. It's terribly sad, don't you think?"

Belle looped her arm around a bedpost and sat down at the foot of the bed. "I'm sure you remember all the really important things."

Dominique picked up a handful of cards and let them slip slowly through her fingers. "That's just it, Belle. I can remember fittings for lovely gowns and attending some truly fabulous parties, but none of it seems important now. We make bayberry candles every year and their scent is delicious, but after they burn down, they're gone. Parties are no more substantial than pretty candles."

Now Belle understood her sister's concern. "You're looking for something that will last. Mother believes you have a talent for healing. That's a remarkable gift."

Dominique shrugged. "I'm no better at it than you."

Belle had not seen Dominique so depressed since Sean had been taken captive. She hated to see her sister so sad, and yet knew the love she had to offer just wasn't enough. Dominique had not mentioned Étienne even once in the time he had been gone, and Belle doubted this was the time to remind her.

"It's this awful war," Belle murmured regretfully. "It has everyone unsettled. No one can live out his dreams until it's over." She left the bed and paused for a moment to scan the souvenirs that littered the top of her sister's desk. "I didn't realize you'd dated everything. Doesn't that make it easier to organize?"

Dominique picked up a card. "This is from September of 1777, but who was Bruce Nesbitt? I can't recall a single thing about him. I don't know if we met at a party, or if he was visiting someone we knew. Can you remember him?"

Belle repeated the name and shrugged. "I'm sorry. I can't place him either. Why don't you just put all that away and begin keeping a diary tonight?"

"I've nothing to write about tonight."

"Well, just start with your thoughts then. What's important to you now? If it's no longer being the most popular dance partner, then what is it? Perhaps describing your dreams will help you achieve them."

Belle gave her sister's shoulder a fond squeeze, then went to her own room. She was too restless to sleep, but afraid if she lay down for a nap she might sleep too long and not be able to join Falcon as she had promised. *As he had insisted she promise,* she thought to herself. She sat down to brush out her hair, then put away her clothes and donned her nightgown, but she felt more like crying than awaiting their rendezvous with the appropriate joy.

She knew precisely what the trouble was, too. Falcon was simply bored. That's why he had insisted she visit his room, and she was so hurt she did not know if she could hide it. "Why should I have to?" she worried aloud. She got into bed and sat hugging her knees until the house was perfectly still. The last time she and Falcon had been together, he had taken her to the Scott house, and she tried to recapture the loving warmth she had felt for him then, but as she tiptoed down the stairs, she was only partly successful.

She let herself into Falcon's room and added a log to the fire before approaching the bed. She had thought he might be asleep, but he raised the covers to welcome her to his bed. She slid in beside him, then leaned over him to kiss him and he nearly crushed her in his arms.

"God, how I've missed you," Falcon moaned.

The fire on the hearth lit the bedroom with an amber glow, but Belle's curls veiled her expression and Falcon had no hint of her distress. He felt only her sweetness, and responded with an enthusiasm which quickly taxed his small store of strength. He kissed Belle once again, and then tugged on her ruffled gown. "Get rid of this," he urged.

Belle sat up to pull it off over her head, then let it slip to the floor. Only two months pregnant, there was no change in her lissome figure, and she had no fears Falcon would discover her secret as yet. She leaned over him again, and the tips of her breasts grazed his chest. She felt him shiver with delight, and with his next kiss, all of her doubts melted away. He was right—this was where she belonged. Her qualms dissolved by his eager kisses, she gloried in it as greatly as he.

Falcon ran his hands down her spine and over the smooth swell of her buttocks. He did not want to rush her, but he needed her so badly he soon grasped her waist to pull her across him. She knew what to do, and rose up to draw him inside her. Wet with wanting him, she sank down on him slowly, then swayed, rose, and fell with a taunting rhythm that flooded them both with an ecstatic heat.

When her erotic play had coaxed the rapture to its peak, Falcon drew her down into his arms and muffled his cries in her hair. He held her clasped in a tight embrace and felt her heart beating wildly against his chest. He knew he would soon want her again, but unlike the nights they had spent together in the past, he lacked the strength now to follow through.

"I love the way your skin feels next to mine," he whispered in her ear. "It's softer than satin or silk. It's a shame we ever have to wear clothes." Belle started to move aside, ut Falcon tightened his hold on her. "No. Stay with me, ust like this."

"That's all I've ever wanted," Belle replied. They fell asleep wrapped in each other's arms, and neither awakened until the rooster began to crow to greet the dawn.

Belle sat up to shove the hair out of her eyes, mirrored Falcon's startled expression, and scrambled out of his bed. Not surprisingly, the nausea that plagued her upon waking struck in full force, but she fought not to give into it in front of him. She yanked her gown on over her head, but before she could race for the door, Falcon leaned over to catch hold of her sleeve.

"Kiss me again," he ordered.

Belle could not have kissed him had her life depended upon it, and breaking free, she rushed to the door with her hand clamped securely over her mouth.

"Belle?" Falcon stared after her, at first thinking she was merely afraid her mother would find them together, but after a moment's reflection he realized it hadn't been fear he had seen in her eyes, but something quite different. She had looked sick, and Belle was never ill. He lay back down on his pillows and flung his arm over his eyes.

What he saw then was that he had demanded so much of her time he had simply worn her out and not once thanked her for all the loving attention. He had expected it, demanded it, and even this morning asked for more rather than thanking her for staying with him. He was thoroughly ashamed of himself but his remorse swiftly turned to dismay when he realized what he might really have seen. He felt sick himself then.

Had he been able to, he would have pursued Belle up the stairs, but he doubted he could make it as far as the door. He swore with disgust, knowing he would just have to wait until she returned with his breakfast. *And then what would he say?* He had thought they were as close as any man and woman could possibly be, so if Belle were pregnant, why hadn't she told him? When had she known? It had been two months since the first time they had made love, and even if it had happened then, she couldn't have known long. Still, if she did know, why hadn't she told him?

Nearly two hours had passed before Belle returned with his breakfast tray, and he had not gone back to sleep. Jean was the one who helped him whenever he needed to use the chamber pot, but the two of them never got into lengthy conversations during those occasions. That morning, however, Falcon was unusually reserved. He waited for Belle, not knowing how he would ask the question he must, and yet so anxious to do so, the wait was agony.

When Belle at last appeared, dressed in blue and looking as pretty as she always did, he waited until she had laid the breakfast tray across his lap, and then grabbed her wrist so she could not flee the room again. "Why didn't you tell me?" he asked.

Belle had hoped he had not guessed the reason she had fled his room earlier, but because he had she would not lie. She sat down beside him on the bed. "You have enough problems, Falcon, without my adding to them."

Falcon watched tears fill her lovely blue eyes. "You are my wife, Belle. If we have made a child together, we ought to be celebrating. Did you really think I was so selfish that I wouldn't be glad?"

He looked furious rather than pleased, and Belle wasn't surprised. "You may call me your wife, and we may feel married in our hearts, but that is not the same as being legally wed and you know it. I wouldn't force you to marry me last summer, Falcon, and I won't force you into it now."

Falcon released her hand only long enough to set the tray aside, then he pulled her down into his arms. "You promised to forget what happened last summer," he reminded her, "but I was hurt when you wouldn't marry me, Belle.

hadn't even realized I wanted a wife until you turned me down, and then I just ached with wanting you."

Belle sat back to look up at him. "And that's why you left home so soon?"

Falcon nodded. "I hadn't forgotten you wanted to get married in church. I just wanted to be able to walk. I should have mentioned that, too, shouldn't I?"

Belle nodded, then snuggled down against him again. "I don't care if you can walk or not, but if you have to be carried into church, you're going to look awfully unwilling."

Falcon laughed and hugged her close to his heart. "No one who sees the width of my smile is going to think me unwilling, Belle." He held her a moment longer, and then released her with one last squeeze. "Will you please ask your father to come in to see me when he finishes his breakfast? I know he'll give us permission to marry, but I want to do this right."

Belle slid off the bed and smoothed out her skirt. "You won't tell him?"

"That he'll be a grandfather? No. Not yet, not until you're ready."

"Thank you."

As she turned away, Falcon called her back. "You don't feel you have to marry me, do you? I want to be your first choice."

Belle leaned down to give him a kiss that removed all his doubts. "Oh Falcon, there's never been anyone for me but you." She watched his smile slide into a wicked grin and shook her head. "That smile would be most inappropriate when you ask my father for my hand."

Falcon wiped his mouth and made an effort to look serious. "How is this?"

"Too stern." She kissed him to coax another smile from him. "There, that's as perfect as you are."

Falcon knew he was a long way from perfect in all re-

spects, but any man who had a wife who was blind to his
faults was blessed indeed. "You are the perfect one, Belle,
and I hope we have a pretty little girl who looks just like
you."

Belle smiled as she left to summon her father, but she
wanted a son who would make her as proud as she had
always been of Falcon.

Falcon ate his breakfast, then suffered through Arielle's
attentions to his leg. He leaned over to watch her rebandage
his wound. "It's healing well now, isn't it?"

"Yes. It most certainly is," she assured him, "but that is
because you have not put any weight on it. All we can
observe is the surface, Falcon. The wound has to heal deep
inside your leg, too."

Falcon leaned back against his pillows. He did not care
what his aunt advised. He was going to try standing again
today, and every day until he could walk as smoothly as he
had before he had been shot. "I understand."

"I'm so pleased that you do." She withdrew, and a few
minutes later Byron appeared.

"How are you today?" he asked.

Falcon shrugged. "I'm much better, but sick of being in
bed. I don't want to discuss my health, though. I want your
permission to marry Belle. I know I announced that she
had said yes, but I want your blessing before we begin planning the wedding."

Falcon still looked pale and he had yet to regain the
weight he had lost, but his forceful declaration gave clear
evidence he would not be an invalid long. "Of course you
have my blessing, but I'd like you to wait until you're well.
There's no reason to rush the ceremony, is there?"

His uncle was giving him an opportunity to confide in
him, but Falcon would not break his promise to Belle. "Yes.
There's a good reason," he exclaimed. "I want her too badly
to continue sleeping alone."

Byron laughed at his nephew's candor, but then shook

his head. "This is no time to begin a honeymoon. Belle would never complain about having to wait on you, but you can't expect her to keep you entertained all day and all night as well. Think of her for a minute, Falcon. Wait until you can take care of her to make her your wife."

His aunt had admonished him to do the same thing, and Falcon nodded obediently. "I don't plan to stay in this bed a second longer than I have to," he swore. "I want you and Aunt Arielle to help us decide on a date, because Belle will want to have a new dress made, and I'll make certain I can walk down the aisle."

Byron folded his hands behind his back and rocked back on his heels. He had debated the future of the country in the Continental Congress with more success than he anticipated having with Falcon. It was not unreasonable to ask that the brave be fit before he wed Belle, but Byron sensed that would be a futile demand and gave in.

"All right. We'll begin making the wedding plans but I think we should have a private ceremony for the family rather than attempt any kind of a lavish celebration in the midst of the war. Belle has never cared much for fancy parties, and I know you haven't, either, but I don't want either of you to be insulted if we don't invite half the town."

"Christian and Liana didn't have a big wedding, and neither did Johanna and David," Falcon reminded him. "It wouldn't be right for us to have more than they did, and Belle and I don't need it. We just want it to be legal so no one can ever say she isn't my wife."

Byron had once had his doubts about Falcon, but they were gone now. He and Belle were as perfect a pair as he and Arielle were and he knew every day they spent together would be happy. "What are you going to do when you get well?" he asked. "Fight with the militia again?"

"Is Cornwallis still moving north?"

"No. Your victory at King's Mountain has kept him in Charlotte for the moment."

"He won't stay there," Falcon predicted darkly. "He can't."

Byron knew better than to forbid Falcon to return to the war when his own actions in support of independence had cost the lives of so many other men's sons. "If the war spreads to Virginia, we'll all fight," he promised. "Now get the rest you need, and let Belle and her mother prepare for the wedding."

Falcon smiled as though he intended to obey, but as soon as Byron had closed the door on his way out, the brave began inching across the bed. If he got up, even for a few seconds, each time he was left alone, he was confident he would regain his strength far more rapidly than if he remained in bed. He grabbed the bedpost and eased his left leg out of the bed. When he pulled himself upright, he was still shaky, but a tad better than he had been yesterday, he thought.

He sat down on the edge of the bed and slowly eased his injured leg off the bed, too. When that simple act sent horrible pains shooting up his leg, he forced back his tears and made himself endure it. After all, a bullet had passed through his leg so part of the muscle was gone, but it would grow back in time. The problem was, he did not have a month or two to recuperate.

Belle came through the door and stopped instantly. "My God, what are you doing?" She rushed to him then, and saw how badly he was hurting. "You've got to get right back in bed," she scolded. "I don't want you to get sick again."

Falcon let her help him get back into bed, but it was a humiliating ordeal. "Your father wants me fit for the wedding. I didn't want to tell him we didn't have any time to lose."

Belle sat down on the side of the bed and took his hand. She knew what her parents expected of her, but she had no regrets about losing her virginity before her wedding night, nor of being pregnant, either. She just did not like feeling squeezed between the way she had been raised to behave and the choice she had made.

"If we have a six- or seven-pound babe next spring, no one is going to believe he was born early. I shouldn't have asked you to keep it a secret, but I'd no idea Father would have any conditions."

Belle looked so miserably unhappy, Falcon could not bear it. He reached out to pull her into his arms and rubbed her back lightly. "I want us to have a proper wedding, Belle. Now don't worry. By the time you have your dress made, I'll be able to walk. Étienne will be back soon, and I'll have him help me exercise."

Belle rested in Falcon's arms. She wasn't ashamed, but she wished she could believe as he did that they were already married. Liana's family had abandoned her on the Barclays' doorstep when she had fallen in love with Christian, but Belle would not have to give up anything to wed Falcon.

She sat back and wiped the tears from her eyes. "I don't know what's wrong with me, but everything makes me cry these days."

Falcon took her hands and kissed her palms. "It's the baby, Belle. Liana and Johanna get upset easily when they're pregnant, too. Don't you remember that? I won't give you any other reason to cry. Now let's take turns reading to each other today. You shouldn't have to do all the work."

"Reading isn't like work," Belle insisted.

"Maybe not, but we'll take turns all the same. Now bring me the book, stretch out here on the bed, and I'll read to you for a change."

Belle got up to get the copy of Henry Fielding's *Tom Jones* and brought it back to him. The young man's adventures were entertaining, but as she curled up beside Falcon, she did not think the fictional tale could rival their own.

* * *

Dominique had slipped into her father's study to consult his maps, but no matter how often she redid her calculations, Richmond remained maddeningly far away. Then she would become angry with herself for being anxious to see Étienne again after the cavalier fashion in which he had deserted her. At Belle's urging, she had begun a diary, but the entries were confused ramblings that made no sense at all upon a second reading.

Dominique could recall once flirting so easily, but she no longer possessed that talent, or perhaps, curse. Anticipating Étienne's return, she had attempted to practice provocative conversations in her mind in order to control her own emotions as well as manipulate his, but the romantic instincts which had once served her so well now failed to provide the necessary material. She could not think of a single amusing phrase or teasing jest with which to greet him, and she did not want to confront him with angry rebukes and reveal just how badly hurt she had been by his failure to bid her farewell.

Nothing made any sense when she thought of Étienne and more often than not she would simply end up with her stomach tied in knots and her hands shaking as though she had never spoken a single word to a handsome young man. That she could have been reduced to such an awful state by a man who cared nothing for her was heartbreaking, and the only way she could get out of bed each morning was to think first of how much Belle needed her to help with the wedding.

Still in possession of her organizational ability, if little else, she went out to the garden to survey the flowers. They would be able to decorate the house with chrysanthemums and roses, but she wished they had had the abundance from which to choose that existed each spring. When Étienne walked up behind her on the garden path and tapped her on the shoulder, she was so badly startled she whirled around and shrieked.

"Mon Dieu!" she cried. "Did you intend to frighten me out of my wits?"

The lovely blush that flooded her cheeks was so pretty, Étienne almost hated to apologize. "I meant only to bid you a good afternoon. Should I have whistled as I approached?"

Dominique had to sit down to catch her breath, and then was grateful he had given her such a good excuse for being unable to engage in clever repartee. She raised her hand to plead for a moment. "Whistling would have been crude," she advised when she could, "but you could have called out my name."

Étienne had taken the time to wash up outside the laundry and put on a clean shirt, so he was badly disappointed that his efforts to impress Dominique had not succeeded. He had not expected her to throw herself into his arms, but he would have appreciated a smile. They were doomed—he knew that now—and he would not sacrifice any more of his pride begging for a kind word.

"How is Falcon?" he asked.

Just looking at Étienne hurt, and Dominique wished he had asked after her health first. Obviously he did not care if she had been desperately ill the whole time he had been away. "He is much better, thank you. How are you?"

"Me?" Étienne was amazed she had thought to ask.

"I'm so tired I would like to lie down and sleep for a week. Is there a chance I might use the guest room again?"

"We never turn anyone away," Dominique replied, her chest tightening with a painful ache.

Étienne assumed that meant yes. "I will not trouble your family long—a day or two and I will be on my way."

Dominique nodded. Tears clogged her throat and she could not even inquire as to where he intended to go next, then decided it was none of her business anyway. She tried to recall when she had last been the vivacious young woman no man could resist, but the memory was so faint she could not attach a date to it. She heard Étienne mumble something about looking in on Falcon, but remained in the garden while he went inside. Her tears came easily then, but it was too late to say how much she had missed him.

Twenty-two

Belle was just leaving Falcon's bedroom as Étienne reached the top of the stairs. "Étienne!" she cried. "It's so good to see you. Falcon will be delighted you're back." She opened the brave's door and ushered Étienne inside.

Belle was gone before Étienne could thank her for welcoming him with such giddy enthusiasm. It was a sad disappointment that Dominique had not been equally thrilled. As he approached his friend's bed, he was pleased to find him looking so much improved. "You look wonderful!" he exclaimed.

Embarrassed, Falcon shrugged off the compliment. "I didn't expect you back so soon. You must have had an easy journey, or a very hard and fast one."

"There was no reason to stay in Richmond," Étienne replied, unwilling to admit to Falcon's second guess. Not that he had any reason to be in Williamsburg, either, he did not add.

"That's good, because I need you here." Falcon described his wedding plans. "I know I might limp, but I have to get up and walk just as quickly as I can. My aunt tells me it's too soon to get out of bed, but I don't care. Will you help me?"

"Of course. What can I do?"

"Just stop by every morning and afternoon so Belle will have some time to prepare for the wedding. I can already stand, but only on my good leg and not for long. I'll do all the work. I just want you here to catch me if I fall. This has to be our secret, Étienne. If Arielle finds out what I'm doing, she'll tie me to the bed."

Étienne nodded. "I understand. She's worried about you, but it is your leg, after all."

"Exactly. I hope you didn't have other plans."

He had not bothered to make any until he had seen Dominique, and now that oversight struck him as foolish and he quickly provided a reasonable prospect. "I had hoped to rejoin the Virginia militia, but they can wait until after your wedding." Despite his best efforts to suppress the thought that he had just been given a reason to remain with the Barclays and enjoy a bit more of Dominique's company, Étienne's floundering hopes soared. He took it as a good omen and vowed not to waste a single moment of his time there.

"Do you want to practice now?" he asked.

"This is as good a time as any," Falcon agreed. He could now scoot across the bed without exhausting himself, but waited for Étienne to come around to the side before he pulled himself up. "This is all I've done for the last few days, but it's getting easier each time. Just standing up makes my whole leg throb, so I've been afraid to put any weight on it yet."

"Shift your weight gradually," Étienne suggested. "Just rest a little on your toes."

Falcon touched the carpet with his toes and a fierce jolt of pain tore up his leg with near-blinding force. He bit his lip to keep from crying out, then slumped back down on the bed. It took him a moment to catch his breath. "I don't think I can stand to do that again today."

Étienne knelt in front of Falcon and took his right foot in his hands. He rubbed his thumbs along the sole. "Does this hurt?"

"No."

"Good." Working gently, Étienne moved his hands to Falcon's calf muscle. "How about this?"

Falcon winced. "Yes, and it hurts like hell to bend my knee."

"Get back up on the bed," Étienne ordered. "My mother used to rub my feet when I was small. My father liked to have her rub his shoulders. You have not been walking for nearly a month. It is no wonder your muscles are sore. If I rub your leg a bit before you try and walk, it will not be so difficult for you."

"Just don't touch my thigh."

Étienne raised his hands. "Never."

Falcon took a deep breath and relaxed against his pillows. "It really is good to have you back. How can I repay you for all you've done for me?"

Étienne looked down at his buckskins and scuffed moccasins. "I could use a new suit to wear to your wedding, and new shoes of my own."

"You'll have them, but that's a small thing. I owe you my life. There must be something else you want."

Étienne noted Falcon's sly grin and realized he already knew what he longed to possess. Fearing it was hopeless, he still decided he had nothing to lose by asking. "I want Dominique. Can you arrange that as easily as shoes and a new suit of clothes?"

Falcon nodded. "Possibly. Belle will help us work on it."

Étienne leaned against the post at the foot of the bed and crossed his arms over his chest. "Beau described Dominique as an exceptional beauty, which she most definitely is, as is Belle, but he suggested I pretend to resist her charms if I wished to impress her. Unfortunately, she has not flirted with me, so how am I to resist the charms she has not displayed? I am afraid I am only wasting my time, and annoying her. We argue every time we are together."

His friend's anguish was so painful to observe, Falcon gave the problem serious thought and then leaned forward.

"Invite Dominique on a picnic. Take her down by the river and just talk to her. You're a fisherman's son. Catch a few fish. Belle and I always enjoyed doing that."

Étienne straightened up. "Does Dominique like to fish?"

"She knows how, but she's not had a chance to fish just for fun. None of her callers ever thought to take her with them, but there's beautiful scenery along the river, and if you did no more than sit together and enjoy the view, you would surely impress her."

Étienne did not understand how, but the fall weather was still warm enough for a picnic, and wanting to be alone with Dominique no matter what the excuse, he agreed to give it a try. "Perhaps you could influence her to accept my invitation."

"Of course. You're our guest. She'll be obliged to entertain you. Just don't give her a reason to slap you again."

"I know better now," Étienne promised, but he was not absolutely convinced that he truly did.

Because both of Arielle's daughters were more slender than they had been when they'd had their last gowns made, she decided to check their measurements before sending for the seamstress. When she discovered Belle's waistline had not decreased like Dominique's but was an inch and a quarter larger, she measured her again and then made a note of the figure. She could think of only one reason a young woman might lose weight but expand in the waist, but chose not to confront her. She had been pregnant with Beau when she had wed Byron, so had good reason to be an understanding mother.

"Your father was rather vague about the date," Arielle remarked. "But let's not rely upon Falcon's progress to schedule such an important event. If we have the wedding here rather than in town, we can help him down the stairs, and in two weeks he should be able to stand long enough to repeat his vows. Would you like that?"

Because her clothing was all looser now, Belle had not noticed the increase in her waist measurement until her mother had written it down. She had then prayed Arielle would not realize there was such a difference. Although elated to be able to have the wedding in just two weeks' time, she tried to appear merely pleased.

"Yes. That's more than enough time to complete our gowns, but I don't want anything too elaborate. It would be unseemly now."

"The war will be over one day," Arielle reminded her, "but your memories of your wedding will last a lifetime. You shall have the most beautiful dress in all of Williamsburg, and Dominique's will be lovely as well."

Dominique had already pulled on her gown and adjusted the lace at the sleeves. "I only wore my pale blue gown once," she proposed. "Why don't I wear it again? No one in the family will remember it, and it will save us the expense."

Dominique had become so practical since her return from South Carolina that Arielle was continually amazed. "I do remember that dress. Try it on to make certain it still looks new before you make your decision. If you want to wear it again, you may, but there is no need to worry about the cost of a new gown."

"Well, perhaps it is high time that we began to worry," Dominique replied. "There will be enough flowers in the garden to fill the house, and as always plenty of delicious food, but we ought to hire musicians."

"I doubt Falcon will be able to dance," Belle said, "but that doesn't mean everyone else shouldn't. Do you suppose Étienne knows how to dance?"

Afraid her distress would show in her expression, Dominique strolled over to the window before replying. "He told me he'd only be with us a couple of days."

Falcon had repeated his conversation with Étienne, and although eager to help the Frenchman, Belle attempted to sound nonchalant. "Well, he's changed his mind," she informed her sister.

Dominique listened with growing alarm as Belle described Étienne's desire to remain with them until the wedding. "How very thoughtful of him," she replied.

"Yes," Belle enthused. She donned her gown and stood still while her mother laced up the bodice. "We do owe him a great deal. Falcon doesn't want him to feel obligated to help him, though. He would like him to be treated as a guest. Do you suppose you might invite him out for a picnic tomorrow?"

Unaware of her daughter's intentions," Arielle raised her brows. "The last time you girls went for a picnic, you were gone for weeks."

Dominique's mouth had suddenly gone dry, and she sounded hoarse when she spoke. "There's so much to do with your wedding in just two weeks. I doubt I'll have the time."

"Make the time," Belle encouraged. "You've not had a bit of fun lately, and you've told me yourself you find Étienne charming."

At last perceiving Belle's intentions, Arielle also encouraged her daughter. "We've always entertained our guests with whatever amusements we could, but I fear we are dreadfully out of practice. I imagine if given the opportunity, Étienne could tell you some exciting stories. He served with Lafayette, and perhaps was with him at Valley Forge."

Dominique's mouth fell agape. "He knows the Marquis de Lafayette?"

"Yes. Didn't he tell you?" Arielle frowned slightly, then thought it an advantage that the young man had not bragged to Dominique about his exploits. "He appears to be modest, which is another point in his favor."

Dominique felt trapped. After the calamitous tour of the

tobacco fields, in which Étienne had had the audacity to compare her unfavorably to a whore, she had vowed never to entertain another guest. He was, of course, the same guest, and that awful morning now seemed a long while ago.

"I fear I'm not nearly as good at entertaining our guests as I used to be," she admitted unhappily. "I doubt I can summon the necessary enthusiasm anymore."

Arielle caressed her daughter's cheek. "Étienne does not strike me as the type who would be drawn to superficial charm so you need not worry. Just go and have a pleasant picnic and talk with him. Speak French. Peel apples in a single strip. Just be happy again, *chérie*. You deserve to be."

Dominique was not certain she could even remember how that felt, but after rushing up to her room directly after supper to avoid having to speak with Étienne, she marshalled the necessary courage to accompany him on a picnic the following day. After all, what could possibly happen under the sunny autumn skies? she asked herself, but when he took her hand as they left the house, she began to fear that she knew.

"Falcon told me the fishing was good upriver, but I did not really believe that you would want to fish," Étienne said.

Grateful that he recognized her tastes were nothing like Belle's even if Falcon didn't, Dominique began to relax. "Thank you. I would rather do almost anything than fish."

Étienne laughed at her unintentional humor. "Then I will assume that you like being with me better than fishing."

Dominique felt breathless although he was thoughtfully gauging the length of his step to hers. She had always loved parties, but she could remember the girls who had hidden in the shadowed corners and merely watched the others dance. She had never understood what it meant to be shy until last summer when her whole life had been turned inside out and nothing she had ever done had made any sense since then.

"I used to be such an amusing companion," she confided suddenly, "but now I think I was merely too foolish to understand there is more to life than knowing the latest dance."

Dominique had given Étienne a timid smile when they had set out that morning. He had expected to have to coax her into going on a picnic, but she had been waiting for him, all prepared. He would have to thank Falcon and Belle for that, but for the moment he was concerned only with Dominique. He could feel her drawing away from him although her hand still lay in his. He did not want to rush her again, but it was so difficult to contain his own emotions, he did not know if he could adequately assess hers.

"You are the very best of companions," he argued. "You have told me what is in your heart, and I have behaved very badly. You have every right to be sad, and I should never have compared you to a woman who must be paid for her favors. That was not just insulting, it was mean and I never asked your forgiveness. Will you forgive me now?"

Dominique had to move in front of him for a moment as the path narrowed around a poplar, but when they could again walk hand in hand, she thanked him. "Yes. Of course, I will. I think we were both at fault that day."

"No. Absolutely not. I should never have spoken so crossly to you, and then later, I fear I did something even worse."

Dominique could not imagine what he meant. "I didn't even see you later. Well, perhaps for a moment at the docks, but surely you can't be referring to that."

Étienne recalled that instant clearly. After waving goodbye to Beau, Dominique had turned with a graceful swirl. As she had glanced toward her home, their eyes had met briefly. Her expression had been one of shocked surprise, tinged with what he had assumed was disappointment, but he had been too angry with her to care.

"No. It happened later. I went out for a walk that night, and saw you weeping in the garden. I knew you were not crying for me, but I should have gone to you and offered the comfort I had failed to provide that morning."

The day was warm and clear, and Étienne had suddenly become so thoughtful that Dominique scarcely recognized him as the brash young man who had previously confused her at every turn. She recalled how miserably unhappy she had been that night and shared the reason. "I'd never fallen in love," she admitted softly, "and when I did, it was with a man whose motives I never should have trusted. That it ended badly was my fault as much as his, but it was tragic all the same."

Her lovely voice was husky with the remembered heartbreak, and no longer able to ignore her sorrow, Étienne drew her to a halt. "This is a pretty place. Let's stop here."

An ancient oak shaded the path, and off to the side, a wide stretch of grass beckoned invitingly. Dominique didn't care where they ate their lunch, and readily agreed. She helped him spread out the blanket, but the minute she sat down, Étienne knelt beside her and pulled her into his arms.

"I have never met anyone as sad as you, *chérie*. If you want to cry forever, I will be content to hold you."

He was wearing a clean pair of buckskins, and as Dominique rested her cheek against his shoulder, his invitation held an irresistible appeal. She had not meant to burden him with her pain, but touched by his sympathetic response, her tears dripped down the fringe adorning his sleeve and onto the grass at his elbow. He rubbed her back, and in a moment, pulled her down across his lap to cradle her in his arms more easily. She reached into her pocket for a handkerchief, but it was soon soaked and she held it in trembling hands.

Étienne removed her cap and tossed away her combs. She

was dressed in an aqua gown that matched her eyes. He bent his head to kiss her damp cheek, and then gazed out at the river while he waited for her to shed however many tears it took to mend her broken heart. He would have stayed with her until nightfall and then carried her home, but Dominique had already experienced too much grief and soon exhausted this new bout of tears.

She cuddled against him, and, as always, felt at home in his embrace. Even after she had regained her composure, she hesitated to move and end such a perfect moment. Étienne had always been physically appealing, but she was ashamed not to know more than that he was the son of an Acadian who believed in freedom and spoke with a delicious accent. He was unlike anyone she had ever known, and yet, as he looked down at her, she saw her future reflected in his eyes.

With the same graceful ease she had charmed so many other men, she slid her arm around his neck to invite a kiss; and his response was immediate, and wildly enthusiastic. Thrilled with his fervor, she laughed and coaxed him down onto the blanket. She loved his thick curls and light eyes and the way he held her as though she were precious. She slid her hands under his shirt and ran her fingertips along the scar crossing his shoulder.

Responding to her enticing touch, Étienne yanked his shirt off over his head and tossed it aside, and Dominique welcomed him back into her arms. His devouring kisses made her hungry for more, and when he turned her in his arms to unlace the back of her gown, she melted into him rather than pulling away. She caught a glimpse of cloudless sky and a canopy of leaves, then saw only Étienne as he freed her breasts and licked her nipples into taut buds he again grazed with his teeth.

Dominique tore away the ribbon confining his curls and leaned into his glorious kisses until her whole body ached for more. She pushed him down on the blanket then and leaned over him. She raked his hair off his forehead, then kissed his well-shaped brows, dark lashes, and ears before dipping her tongue into his mouth. His taste was sweet, and she slid her hand over his chest to pinch his leathery nipple. She felt him flinch and having discovered his flesh was as sensitive as hers, she did it again, harder. She longed to know his body as well as her own, and when he began peeling off her clothes in great grabbing handfuls she arched her back to help him and laughed again with a deep, throaty giggle.

Étienne had never expected Dominique's sorrow to erupt into passion, but once it had, he was beyond caring who might come along the path and find them in each other's arms. He craved her with an aching need that drove him past reason to the shores of rapture and he wanted all that she could possibly give. He splayed his fingers out over her ribs, then cupped her breasts before again pressing his face close to suckle.

Moving lower, he flicked his tongue into her navel, then trailed kisses across the seductive hollow of her belly. He nuzzled the triangle of pale blond curls and, lost in her lithe body's own delectable fragrance, wrapped his arm around her leg and sank lower to drink in her taste. He split her open with the tip of his tongue, then tickled the slippery bud at the top of her cleft to inflame her desire until it matched his own.

The enchanting sensations Étienne coaxed forth were no longer unexpected even if the method he had chosen was, but drowning in his exotic affection, Dominique was more exhilarated than shocked. He moved with such natural grace, his gestures so deeply adoring, that she doubted she would ever have enough of his abundant affection. Lured past any remaining defenses, her surrender was again spontaneous, and this time, complete.

Étienne moved up over Dominique then, and hastily shoving his buckskins aside, he began to tease her with the whole length of his swollen shaft. He tilted her hips, then yanked the blanket aside to leave no trace of their first coupling. Adjusting her body to his, he probed, gently stroking her, then dipping into her with brief, shallow thrusts. She was so wet he slid into her easily but her body still held back, and desperate to sink to her depths, he lunged forward and swallowed her cry as he felt her tender flesh tear.

He lay still, and knowing he had taken what no other man ever could take again, he rose up slightly to look down at her. His breathing was ragged, but hers was no more controlled, and when she smiled, the love that filled her eyes warmed him clear to his soul. He gave her a bruising kiss and began to move. Each time he neared his limit he slowed to let the urgency subside until he could control it again, and again.

She was so tight and hot, he longed to stay hard forever, but finally she rolled her hips to pull him down into her and he was lost. He clung to her as his climax surged forth and her blissful inner contractions caressed him until he had nothing more to give. Exhausted by the sheer splendor of loving her, he moved aside, grabbed the blanket to cover them, and held her so tight it took him a moment to realize she probably could not breathe. He relaxed his grasp, but only slightly, and kissed her temple.

"I have never told another woman that I loved her, but I love you, Dominique," he swore with convincing ardor. *"Je vous aime. Voulez-vous m'épouser?"*

Dominique lay snuggled in his arms, too sated by pleasure to do more than respond with a grateful sigh. She was going to have to tell her mother—after the wedding, of course—that her description of making love provided barely a hint of the joy she had found in Étienne's arms. She had never been more certain of anything in her life, but love him she did.

Étienne hoped that he had interpreted Dominique's response correctly as an affirmative, but he could readily understand why she could not speak. Had he not felt compelled to declare his love, he could not have drawn the breath to speak, either. He did not know if he wanted to shout or cry, so he simply held her and wished that he did not ever have to let her go.

"I would not mind dying now, if I could take you to heaven with me, Étienne."

Her breath washed over his chest with a seductive heat, and captivated anew by the incredibly responsive young woman, Étienne rose on his elbow. He combed her tangled curls out of her eyes and sighed with the first genuine contentment he had ever known. "Do not talk to me of death, when life has taken so long to finally become this good."

Intrigued by the glint of tears in his eyes, Dominique reached up to caress his cheek. "I tried so hard to drive you away. I'm glad you were too stubborn to go."

Étienne kissed her palm, then laced his fingers in hers. "I do love you, *chérie*. You must never doubt that."

With his body pressed against the length of hers, she would have been warm even without the blanket, but his comment filled her with a sudden chill. "Why would I doubt it?" she asked. "Have you forgotten to tell me something? Oh Étienne, you don't have a wife and children in France, do you?"

Étienne laughed at the ridiculousness of that thought, but he did have another confession he knew he ought to make. At the same time, he was loath to do it, and risk losing her. Torn between the honesty he knew true love required and the discretion that would protect him, he chose to remain silent and leaned over to kiss her. "You will be my first and only wife, and I have never fathered a child."

"You are hiding something, though. I can feel it." Frightened, Dominique sat up and began gathering her scattered lingerie. "I know so little about you, Étienne. I want you to tell me everything this afternoon. Will you promise me that?"

"I will promise you anything." He leaned over to lick the pale crest of her breast and it hardened beneath his lips. As he sat up, he saw the marks of his teeth on her pale flesh and was horrified. "You are so fair—I did not realize loving bites would hurt you."

"You haven't hurt me," she assured him, "but I don't want mere promises, Étienne. If you promise me something, you must follow through."

"Yes. I understand."

He looked away as he reached for his buckskins and again Dominique sensed something was very wrong and was frightened. The first time he had kissed her, her response had been fright, and she had been confused and ashamed. Now she wondered if it hadn't been a premonition she ought not to have ignored. He went down to the river to wash; still unsettled when he returned, she also took advantage of the water to cleanse away the evidence of their passion. She waited until they were both fully dressed, then faced him squarely.

She had so many images of him in her mind: his startled expression when she had run into the parlor to greet Beau; the way his thick, black curls caught the sun. She remembered his defiant stance when he had raised the rifle to his shoulder in the shooting match with Falcon, and how exhausted he had been when he had brought her cousin home from King's Mountain. Each glimpse of him was precious now, but even with the sweetness of his touch still lingering on her skin, she knew something was wrong.

She had to swallow hard to find her voice. "I do love you," she swore, "but if there's something you haven't told me that you should, please do it now."

Her eyes were a more beautiful blue than the sky, and having won her heart, Étienne would not risk losing such a prize. "My life has not been easy, but I have committed no crimes. If I return to France, I will not be arrested on the docks. I have never seduced another man's wife, nor cheated anyone."

Dominique nodded thoughtfully as Étienne recited an impressive litany of offenses he had not been a party to, but her suspicions remained unresolved. Then she began to fear she was merely attempting to find a new way to discourage him, and was ashamed of herself. "I'm sorry. I know you're a fine man, and I didn't mean to offend you. It's only that love is so new to me, and I feel unsure of myself."

Relieved beyond measure that she had ceased interrogating him, Étienne pulled her into his arms. "You need never be unsure of me," he vowed. "I love you with all my heart and soul. Now let's have something to eat so we can say we really did have a picnic, and I will tell you more about myself."

He pulled a bottle of wine from the basket, and two pewter mugs. "I sailed to America with Lafayette on *La Victoire,* but I was only a sailor, not one of his officers. I wanted to fight with him, though, and did. When he was given a brigade of Virginians to command, I liked them and thought Virginia must be a fine place to live." He stopped to smile at her, adding, "And it is. When Lafayette returned to France, I stayed here. I sailed with a couple of privateers, and met Beau in Martinique. When he asked if I would like to come to Virginia, I did."

Dominique took the mug he handed her, and while she was surprised the basket contained wine rather than cider, she took a long sip. "Were you with Lafayette at Valley Forge?" she asked.

"Oui. I was with him when he chased off the Hessians."

He was smiling as though it had been a great adventure. She remembered reading about it in the *Gazette.* "Is that what you remember about Valley Forge, not the cold, or being hungry?"

Étienne unwrapped a platter of ham. "It is always better

to remember the good things, Dominique, rather than the
bad."

Dominique considered that for a moment, and then nodded. "Do you really want to go back to France?" she asked
in a fearful whisper.

She had not bothered to replace her cap, and her curls
framed her face with an innocent charm that delighted him.
"I will make you a promise right now, Dominique. I will
not go home to France without you." He winked at her and
raised his mug in a silent toast.

"I would like to see France," Dominique assured him,
"but even with you, I'm afraid I would miss my family
terribly. Don't you miss yours?" Étienne frowned slightly,
and when he began to rummage through the basket for the
bread and cheese, Dominique had her answer.

"I know not all families get along as well as ours does,"
she said. "Were your parents opposed to your coming to
America?"

"No." Étienne ripped off a hunk of bread from the loaf,
then broke it in half to share with Dominique. "My father
despises the British and wished only that he had a dozen
sons to send to fight them."

"Yes. I don't imagine any of the Acadians admire the British, but when my mother fell in love with my father, she
forgave him for being English—although I do believe it took
a long while for the good people of Williamsburg to forgive
her for being French. Now that Lafayette is regarded as a
great hero, being French is no longer a problem."

"I am so relieved to hear you say that."

Dominique laughed, and their conversation drifted off
into teasing banter. They did not make love again, although
they wanted to, but now allowing their passion for each
other free rein in the open countryside struck them as too
dangerous. As they gathered up the remains of the picnic
and replaced them in the basket, Dominique rested her hand
lightly on Étienne's sleeve.

"You've asked me to marry you, and I've said yes, but this is Belle's time to be a bride and I don't want to take anything away from her. Will you please wait until after she and Falcon are wed to speak to my father?"

"On one condition," Étienne stated firmly.

Dominique's eyes widened in surprise. "And what might that be, monsieur?"

That afternoon, Étienne had finally seen the charm that had captivated so many other young men, but he had had so much more than any of them, and that fact made him bold. "That I do not have to wait that long to make love to you again."

Dominique leaned close to kiss him. "Do you think I could bear to ask that of you?"

Étienne shrugged. "Well, I hope not."

"We will have to be discreet, and because my bedroom is right above my parents, we dare not use it tonight."

"And the guest room?"

"You're right above my aunt and uncle, and Hunter can hear a leaf fall in the forest, so we'd never fool him if we used your bed. We'll have to sneak out of the house, or will that be too awful?"

"It would only be awful if you did not want to meet me."

He picked up the basket and Dominique slipped her arm through his as they started back down the path. "I can not even imagine that happening."

Étienne could, but he kept still.

Arielle was seated at the windowseat in the parlor and when she saw Dominique and Étienne coming up the path arm in arm, she called to her husband. "Byron, come here, please. I want you to see this. I was hoping Étienne would lift Dominique's spirits, but he seems to have done much better than that."

Alarmed, Byron walked over to the window. He watched

his daughter dip her head and then look up at the young man in one of her classic coquettish poses. He uttered a low moan. "He looks far too much like his father to suit me," he murmured darkly. "What if his turning up here wasn't merely coincidence?"

Arielle took her husband's hand. "What are you thinking?"

Étienne and Dominique paused, and unaware that they were being observed, exchanged a lengthy kiss that sent Byron's temper up a notch. "I think that even after more than twenty years, if Gaetan and I were to see each other on the street, he would try to kill me again. What if he sent Étienne to harm us in whatever way he could?"

"There is nothing hostile about him, Byron. He has not given us any cause to doubt his sincerity, and we can not condemn him just because he is Gaetan's son."

"What if he is diabolically clever?"

Arielle closed her eyes. Her husband was not given to making wild accusations and in this case, she readily understood his fears. "What are you going to do?" she asked in a breathless whisper.

Byron bent down to kiss her, and then turned away. "I'm going to invite him in for tea and ask him just what his intentions are."

"And you think he'll blurt them out?"

"No. I think he'll lie, and both of us will see it. If that happens, I don't care how good a friend he's been to Falcon, he'll be off the plantation within the hour."

Arielle nodded, but she could not bear to think how badly Dominique would be hurt if Étienne, like Sean O'Keefe, had only come there to betray them.

Twenty-three

Byron stepped out into the hallway to greet Dominique and Étienne. "Come join us for tea," he invited with a disarming smile.

Étienne left the basket by the door and followed Dominique into the parlor. He went first to Arielle to greet her. "Good afternoon, madame." He bent to kiss her hand, and then waited for Dominique to take her place on the settee before he chose the chair at her right. The Barclays had always been hospitable, and he returned their smiles easily, but he was still so excited to have made love with Dominique that he could barely sit still.

"How was your picnic?" Byron asked.

"Very nice," Dominique replied with the confidence she had regained only that afternoon. "It's such a pretty day—we had a lovely time." She smiled at Étienne, who nodded in agreement. "It's a shame Falcon and Belle can't get out, too. I wish we could have all gone together."

"Falcon will be better soon," Étienne assured her.

The Barclays still paused in the afternoon for tea, although since the dispute with England had begun, they no longer drank the imported beverage. Arielle kept them supplied with herbal varieties; it was peppermint that day, served with delicate vanilla cookies sprinkled with pecans. She was a gracious hostess, but preoccupied, and waited for her husband to lead the conversation.

Byron made a few comments about the upcoming wedding and then spoke directly to Étienne. "The night you arrived with Beau, we spoke only briefly about the possibility of our having known your father in Grand Pré. Now that we know each other better, I'd like you to tell us what he said about Arielle and me."

Confused by her father's question, Dominique turned to Étienne and watched the color drain from his face while he struggled not to drop the fragile porcelain cup. "You told me your father was from Acadia," she prompted him. "Why didn't you tell me he was also from Grand Pré?"

Étienne set his cup on the table by his side and sat forward. He felt as though Byron had just dropped a noose around his neck, but he strove to remain calm. "I told you that my father did not speak of Acadia," he replied.

"I know that's what you told us," Byron shot right back at him, "but we'd prefer the truth this time."

Dominique had no idea what was going on, but she did not appreciate the tone her father had taken with Étienne. "Father, please. You're being very rude."

Byron responded as though he were shocked by her comment. "Am I? I suggest you listen carefully and then decide whether or not I've forgotten my manners. I was speaking to you, Étienne. Shall I repeat my question?"

Feeling at a terrible disadvantage, Étienne rose to his feet and took a step away from Dominique. "My father is an angry and bitter man," he announced defensively, "and I have not communicated with him in three years."

Alanna came to the doorway, saw what was clearly a confrontation, and turned away, but Byron called out to invite her to join them. "Please give us the benefit of your wisdom, Alanna. This is a family matter, after all."

Alanna sent Arielle a questioning glance, and only after receiving an encouraging nod did she enter, but she took a chair near the window rather than intrude. She accepted a cup of tea from Arielle, but immediately set it aside. "Is there a problem?" she asked.

"You might say that," Byron answered. "You will recall that Arielle and I had a difficult time leaving Acadia."

"Yes. I do remember," Alanna said. "The Acadians being transported on your ship seized control from the captain and held you prisoner for a time. What made you think of that after all these years?"

Byron gestured toward their guest. "Having the son of an Acadian in our midst prompted all sorts of intriguing memories. Tell us the version you heard of that shipboard revolt, Étienne," Byron encouraged. "I'm certain your father must remember things differently than we do."

Étienne swept Dominique with a fearful glance. "I am nothing like my father," he swore. "You must not blame me for his mistakes."

"Of course not," she replied. She looked toward her mother, who was studying the swirling design in the rug. Her Aunt Alanna was staring wide-eyed at Étienne, while her father wore a smugly satisfied grin as though he had just sold his tobacco crop at a record price. Not liking the odds, she left the settee, went to Étienne's side, and looped her arm through his. He patted her hand and she felt him trembling.

"Could we possibly begin at the beginning?" Dominique inquired. "You appear to be blaming Étienne for something his father did in Acadia, which is absurd. If I'm the only one here who doesn't know precisely what it was, I can't defend him as readily as I'd like."

Byron gave Étienne a chance to speak, but when the young man remained silent, he provided his own version of the story. "Gaetan LeBlanc was in love with your mother. She had refused his proposal before I arrived in Grand Pré, but he was not a man who could accept her decision in a gentlemanly manner. In fact, he was a firebrand who fought everyone who crossed him, and when we left Acadia on the same ship, he led the men who overpowered the crew, tried to beat me to death, and made a hostage of your mother. She and I escaped, but even after all these years, I find it difficult to believe Gaetan LeBlanc's son could have walked into our home by chance."

Although stunned by her father's ghastly statement, Dominique knew without having to ask that this was the secret she had sensed but that Étienne had refused to reveal. At first, she did not understand why a fight his father had had with hers should matter, even if it had nearly been a fight to the death over her mother. It had occurred before either she or Étienne had been born so surely it did not concern them. Then she looked up at Étienne and saw the dread in his eyes. If he felt so guilty, then there had to be a reason, and she was far too bright not to perceive the cause.

She released him and took a step away. "You told me your father hated the British. Clearly he also hated my father at one time. Does he hate us still? Is that the real reason you came to America, Étienne? Was it simply to harm the Barclays rather than fight for America's independence?"

"No!" Étienne shouted emphatically. "I came only to fight, not to seek revenge on my father's old enemies."

His anguished expression was convincingly sincere, but then Sean O'Keefe had been credible, too. Dominique wanted to believe Étienne with a desperation she could not hide. "But you knew my father's name, didn't you? And that the Barclays were from Virginia?"

There had been a great deal Étienne had not told her, but he would not lie. "I recognized the name when I met Beau, but it was merely curiosity that brought me here, not a sinister wish to harm any of you. Please believe me, Dominique. Please."

Dominique heard her mother sobbing softly and wondered if she were crying for everything she had lost in Acadia, or because she was terrified Gaetan LeBlanc might have several other sons he would send to America to find them. She had trusted Sean, and been hurt so badly; now the trust she had placed in Étienne was being sorely tested. But if he were no more than a cunning liar, then how could his kisses have tasted so sweet?

Her heart told her to trust him, but her head advised the caution she had cast aside that afternoon. If she made the wrong choice, he might murder them all in their beds. She also knew she was too dazed from his loving to think clearly on any issue concerning him. She took a deep breath, but it made her decision no easier.

"I want to believe you," she assured him, "but you should have told me that our parents knew each other long before this."

Étienne gestured helplessly. "You can see for yourself how easy it is to misunderstand my motives. When you have all been so kind, I did not want to take the risk of turning you against me."

"So you lied," Byron interjected accusingly.

Étienne did not respond to him, but to Dominique. "Not to you," he swore.

As he reached for her hand, she felt not simply his warmth, but an ecstatic rush that she recognized as the power of love. She had been raised with abundant love, and taught to value it above all else. She had her answer, and trusted her heart to decide what was best.

"I don't believe we should make any decisions based on what happened so long ago," Dominique told her father. "Had Étienne wanted to hurt us, he would have slit Falcon's throat and left his body at the side of the road rather than bring him home."

"That could easily have been a deliberate ploy to win our trust," Byron argued. "Besides, Falcon is only a Barclay on his mother's side, and killing him would never have satisfied Gaetan's thirst for revenge. You don't know the man, sweetheart, but I was surprised when he didn't follow us home after we escaped from his camp in New Brunswick."

"No," Dominique agreed. "I don't know him, but it sounds as though he fought for what he wanted as savagely as you would." Although her father objected to that comparison with a fiery oath, Dominique refused to retract it. "I only know Étienne, and he's a fine man. I'm not willing to turn him away because of a feud you once had with his father. I can understand why you might not want him staying in our house, but Christian will surely take him in after all he's done for Falcon."

"I can find my own lodgings," Étienne protested. He brought Dominique's hand to his lips. "I love you with all my heart, but I can not ask you to choose between me and your family. No man should ask that. I will not desert Falcon while he is ill, but I won't see you when I visit him, and I will leave right after the wedding."

The sorrow in his eyes mirrored her own, and as he left the room, Dominique felt as though her heart had been wrenched from her chest. Étienne had sacrificed his own desires rather than force her to abandon her family, but that did not mean she had to meekly allow him to do it. He had not asked for her hand when her father would surely have laughed in his face, but she did not think he should have walked out on her, either. She could not even imagine what it must have been like to grow up in a house with a man who was consumed with hatred, but Étienne had already proved he knew how to love. She could do no less.

Byron went to his daughter's side and slipped his arm around her shoulders. "I should have confronted him the night he arrived, and I hope you'll forget you ever knew him."

Dominique glanced away as though the strain of Étienne's parting had hurt her deeply. She did not reply, but forgetting him was the very last thing she intended to do.

* * *

Étienne stood outside Falcon's door until he regained control of his emotions, but his expression was still tormented as he entered his friend's room. Belle and Falcon had again been reading *Tom Jones*. Belle marked their place and left the bed to come toward him. Étienne tried to find a smile for her, but failed.

"Oh, dear," Belle greeted him. "We hoped that you and Dominique would have a good time together. What happened?"

Belle resembled Dominique so closely that Étienne now found looking at her an excruciating reminder of what he had lost and he had to turn away. He felt sick and was sorry he had come upstairs. "It was the best afternoon of my life," he confided, "but when we came home, Byron asked me to leave. He and my father were enemies in Acadia, and he does not trust me."

Falcon began to swear, then for Belle's sake caught himself before he completed the colorful curse. "When you came home with Beau, Uncle Byron told us a Gaetan Le-Blanc had tried to kill him years ago. I don't understand why he waited from that day to this to object to your presence here."

Étienne noted the confusion in their faces and was mystified as well. "Do you mean you have known the whole time just whose son I am?"

"Every man acquires a few enemies," Belle exclaimed, "and because of my father's political views, he probably has more than most. I'm sure he tried not to be prejudiced against you, but perhaps he's become fearful of what might develop between you and Dominique."

"With good reason," Étienne muttered under his breath. "I told him I would still come to see you, Falcon, but I can't stay today. I need to gather my belongings and find another place to live."

Belle sent Falcon a quizzical glance and he nodded. "Just move over to the Scotts', south of here," she suggested. "The house belongs to Liana's family and we keep an eye on it. There are linens on the bed in the master bedroom, and you'll be comfortable there. We'll have food for you here when you come to visit Falcon. Don't be discouraged, Étienne. We'll convince my father he's being unreasonable about you."

Overwhelmed first by the vehemence of Byron's objection to him, and now by Falcon and Belle's support, Étienne didn't know what to believe. "Why would you take my side against your father?"

"Because he's wrong!" Belle exclaimed. "If you had had evil intentions, I doubt you would have walked in and given a name my parents would recognize. It would have been stupid to put them on their guard, and anyone can see you're very bright."

Étienne was sorry he had not brought up that point himself. "I wish you had been downstairs just now," he replied. "Unfortunately, Dominique knew none of this, and she is hurt because I did not tell her our fathers were enemies before Byron did."

Belle rolled her eyes. "Oh, Lord."

"Oui. I will see you tomorrow, Falcon. Now, I just want to go."

Readily understanding his friend's plight, Falcon excused him, but as soon as the Frenchman had left the room, he pulled Belle into his arms. "I'm so glad we don't have such problems anymore. Poor Dominique. Do you suppose she'll refuse to leave her room until the wedding?"

"I hope not." Belle clung to him, and sighed dejectedly. "Dominique used to be so strong, I can't bear to think she might be as miserably unhappy as she was over Sean."

Falcon leaned back against his pillows. "Perhaps if we hadn't pushed Étienne and Dominique together, your father wouldn't have thrown him out." He was quiet a long moment, and then kissed Belle's temple. "I know that I promised to build you a house as fine as the one Christian built for Liana, but if we stay here, we will always be in your father's shadow. When the war finally ends, maybe we ought to clear our own land, and begin our lives together somewhere new."

Belle had always thought they would remain at home, but she needed only a moment's reflection to understand his concern. "Do you have a place in mind?"

Falcon nodded. "The Seneca used to hunt in the Ohio Valley. It's a beautiful place, Belle, and we could have a fine life there. We'd not have to answer to anyone, or be thought of as the Seneca branch of the Barclays."

Belle rested her forehead against his while she considered his plan and could find no reason to object. "There's not only my father to think about, but Beau as well. One day this will be his home, and it will be awfully crowded no matter how many houses we build."

"You'll come with me, then?"

"Of course, but you must promise that you won't make me chase you through the wilderness ever again."

Falcon pulled her down on the bed, and while their loving play went no further than deeply adoring kisses, they were content. When Belle left him, she expected to find Dominique in her room, at best in a melancholy mood, at worst, weeping uncontrollably, but her sister's room was empty. Perplexed, Belle went looking for her and at last found her out in the herb garden.

"Are you all right?" Belle called to her.

Dominique looked up, and there was no trace of tears in her gaze. "Yes. Why wouldn't I be?"

Astonished to find Dominique so calm, Belle recounted Étienne's anguished tale. "Falcon and I fear we're at fault for encouraging his interest in you. He's heartbroken that Father sent him away. I didn't realize that you didn't care for him at all."

Dominique snipped a sprig of rosemary and twirled it under her nose to enjoy its pungent scent. "Did Étienne really describe our picnic as 'the best afternoon of my life'?"

Exasperated with her older sister, Belle put her hands on her hips. "Damn it all, Dominique. I thought you'd stopped playing with men's affections."

Dominique tried not to smile, but failed to suppress the joy of her own memories. "Please believe me. I'm not trifling with Étienne. Do you know where he's gone?"

Belle recalled how miserable the Frenchman had looked, and couldn't bear to think Dominique might simply toy with him. "Do you really care?" she asked.

Dominique feared she may have deserved Belle's sarcastic question a great many times in the past, but not now. She dropped the rosemary into her basket and spoke from her heart. Her voice was flavored with the sweetness she had showed Étienne. "Yes. I care very much. Now tell me, so I don't have to waste any time finding him."

Belle saw too much of the old Dominique in the bright gleam in her sister's eyes to suit her, and remained apprehensive about her motives. "He's staying at the Scotts', but please don't go over there just to torment him, Dominique. He really loves you."

"Yes. I know."

"He told you?"

"Yes. In both English and French." Dominique drew Belle to the end of the garden where their privacy would be assured. "I realize I must seem as fickle as I used to be, but please believe me when I say that isn't the case. I adore Étienne and have no intention of giving him up just because Father has forbidden him to call."

Fearing she had misjudged her sister, Belle sucked in a startled gasp. "Oh, no, Dominique. What sort of plot are you hatching now?"

"I do not hatch plots," Dominique protested, "and even

if I did, the last one brought you and Falcon together so you ought not to complain."

Belle could not easily dismiss the grave peril of nearly becoming British prisoners, but Dominique was correct in one respect. "That is true, but—"

"Just listen," Dominique insisted. "I want Mother and Father to believe I'm still pining for Sean and that Étienne was no more than a momentary diversion. Please tell Falcon the truth. I intend to tell Étienne, but not until after your wedding. I don't want anyone to know I'm still seeing him.

"Please help me with this, Belle. I can't bear to have Étienne suffer for something his father did. If Father were to guess that I love him, then he would take steps to keep us apart. But if he believes I don't care, then I'll be free to come and go as I please. I'm not asking you to lie or make excuses for me. Just don't mention Étienne at all."

Belle didn't know which was worse, lying to their parents again, or knowing that Dominique had become her old manipulative self.

Étienne had not been hungry after the awful scene at the Barclays' so he had not missed supper. He had explored the Scott residence and found the empty house reminded him far too much of the one he had been forced to leave. Too sick at heart to search for another home that night, however, he decided to remain.

The bed Belle had offered was comfortable, but when he had lost the only woman he had ever wanted for his wife, he found it impossible to sleep. He lay stretched across the bed, staring up into the darkness and not caring if he saw the dawn. When he heard the back door open, his first thought was that Byron had either sent someone after him or come himself, and he grabbed his knife and waited on the landing. When he heard Dominique whisper his name, he dropped the weapon on the hall table and ran down the stairs.

"Mon Dieu!" he cried. "What are you doing here?"

"I know it's after two, but I took the chance you'd find it as impossible to sleep as I have."

"Dominique," he sighed, and gathered her into his arms. He hugged her, then pulled her down beside him on the stairs. "I did not think you would ever come to me."

Dominique leaned across him and ran her hand up his inner thigh. His buckskins were very soft and her touch whisper-light. "Refusing to ask me to choose between my family and you was a wonderfully noble gesture, Étienne, but I already made my choice yesterday afternoon. Didn't you understand that?"

Étienne tried to still her hand, but she continued to knead his thigh with a knowing touch. His breath caught in his throat. "What are you saying?"

Dominique bit his lower lip, then kissed him. "That after I'd given myself to you, you can not give me back to my father." She raked the tip of her thumbnail across his crotch. He was already hard, and pleased she had such a potent affect upon him, she used her fingertips to stroke him lightly. "You asked me to marry you, and I'm going to insist that you keep your word."

Étienne could scarcely breathe, let alone think, with Dominique demanding he honor a promise that he wanted so badly to keep. When she reached for his belt buckle, he knew this was one argument he was never going to win. Then she slid her hand inside his buckskins and he had to lean back against the stairs. With his elbows braced on one step and his head resting on the one above, he was as comfortable as he had been on the grass.

Étienne's grateful moan inspired Dominique to grow even more bold. Her hair was loose, and she let it fall across his bare belly as she dipped her head. He slid his hands through her curls, his garbled French now unintelligible, but his gesture was unmistakable and she swirled her tongue around the crown of his shaft. She had not expected it to be as soft as her breast when he was so hard. Her hands were small, and she could not wrap her fingers all the way around him.

She mimicked the motion he had used inside her while she continued to tease him with her mouth and tongue. "Did you really believe I would let you walk away?"

What Étienne could not believe was how glorious her heated kisses felt. Her mouth was a magical pool that lapped at his very soul and when he could stand no more, he knew he could never carry her upstairs to the bed, and instead pulled her down onto the floor. She was clad in a nightgown that he swept aside easily, entering her with a single, driving thrust; then he had to use all the willpower he possessed not to release his climax in that instant.

He grabbed thick handfuls of her hair and forced himself to speak. "Witch! Do you want to make a slave of me?"

Dominique raised up to lick his lips. "No. Only a husband." She drew him down into a slow, deep kiss, and then ground her hips against his to entice him into an ageless dance. He was what she had always hoped love would be, and even on a plank floor, she felt close to paradise. She kept him locked in her embrace until neither of them wanted, or could stand, more.

"I love you," she breathed against his ear.

Étienne could remember being desperately unhappy only an hour ago, but with Dominique in his arms, he could not recall why. "We ought to go upstairs."

Too relaxed to move, Dominique couldn't agree. "I like it here."

Étienne nuzzled her throat. "I should have waited. It was too soon, and I hurt you again."

"It does not compare to the threat of losing you."

He covered her face with tender kisses. "I will not earn enough with the militia to buy your slippers," he revealed.

"I must own a dozen pairs. I won't need any new ones for years."

He licked her ears. "And your pretty gowns?" he asked. "It will take me more than a year to save enough to buy one."

"I've plenty of those, too." Dominique slid her hand up his arm, then across his shoulder. "I don't need fancy clothes to be happy, Étienne. I need only you."

While Étienne felt her love in her every touch, he could not quite accept his good fortune. "Beau is never going to believe this."

"I don't care whether he does or not. We'll have time to make plans later. For now, just hold me, and everything will be all right."

Also too content to move, Étienne was quiet for a long while, and then propped his head on his elbow. "I want you to know the truth."

Dominique raked her nails across his belly, and then moved her hand lower for a bold caress. "I can feel the truth," she swore.

Étienne caught her hand, and this time held her fast. "Listen to me!" he begged. "When I told my father I was sailing with Lafayette; he gave me your father's name, but it was your mother he wanted killed."

"Oh, my God," Dominique gasped. She felt sick, and escaped his embrace to sit up. She reached for her nightgown to cover her breasts even though their bodies were heavily veiled by shadows. "What made you change your mind? Or do you still plan to do it?" That he might also kill her was her next thought, but if she could not trust her heart, she did not care to live.

Étienne longed to hold her, but waited for her to return to him willingly. "I begged you not to blame me for my father's crimes. I have no quarrel with your parents, and they have nothing to fear from me, but I want you to know everything. I would love to show you France, but I do not dare take you home while my father is alive."

Ashamed for doubting him if only for an instant, Dominique reached up to touch his silken curls. "And you can't stay here with me when my parents refuse to accept you, so we'll have to find someplace new, my love."

Étienne wanted to believe her, but couldn't. "How can you give up everything when you have so much?"

Dominique answered his question with a searing kiss. "I left home last summer because my life was so empty I couldn't bear it. This time, I'll leave because you have made my life so full. If my parents can't accept you, then their love comes at too high a price. As for everything my family's wealth provides, they are only things, after all, and don't compare to you."

Still not quite able to believe he had won the heart of such a dear young woman, Étienne carried Dominique up the stairs. He made love to her again in Ian Scott's feather bed, and while he did not make the promise aloud, he vowed for as long as he lived to make her proud to be his wife. As for Dominique, leaving him before dawn was the most difficult thing she had ever done.

She held Étienne's face in her hands and begged him to understand. "I can't come back here. The risk is simply too great that I'll be caught, and you'll be the one to suffer. I intend to give my parents a choice after the wedding. They can either allow us to wed that same afternoon, or I'll leave with you and not return."

"Dominique—"

"No. You must agree. I'll want you every minute, but I also want Belle and Falcon to wed without any anger or sorrow about us to spoil their happiness. If my parents are half as good as I believe them to be, then they'll put aside their old hatreds and welcome you as a son."

Étienne knew just how far he would get should he ask

his father to regard Dominique as a daughter, and felt utterly defeated. "I don't want you to be hurt."

Dominique kissed him tenderly. "Then you will not even think of leaving Williamsburg without me," she insisted. "We'll make such handsome children together, Étienne, but I don't want to have to raise the first alone."

The idea that they might have already made a child was staggering, but Étienne hoped that they had. "I wanted what was best for you," he explained. "Now I understand what is best for you is to be with me."

"Thank you. I'll see you at the wedding."

Étienne walked her almost all the way home, then stood down by the river until he was certain she was in the house safely. He waited for a lamp to be lit or any sign someone had noted her absence, but all was still in the beautiful house. He walked back to Ian Scott's, and now considered it a fine place to live, but he did not think he could survive two weeks without making love to Dominique.

Twenty-four

Étienne went for long walks along the James River at dawn and fished to catch his breakfast. He chopped wood to replenish the Scotts' woodpile and swept the dust from the floors of their impressive home. He visited Falcon in the middle of the day so Belle could dine with her parents and not worry about leaving Falcon alone. Étienne had his friend up and walking by the end of the week, but he missed Dominique so badly he could barely stand it. Coming to her home and not seeing her was excruciating torture, but he meant to honor his promise.

Sweat dripping down his face, Falcon returned to his bed and waited for Étienne's gentle attentions to work the soreness from his muscles. He did not need to inquire what was wrong with his morose companion, however, for he knew. "It's only one more week, Étienne, not an eternity."

"I do not have your faith," Étienne murmured. "Try bending your knee."

Falcon braced for the pain, but it wasn't nearly as bad as it had been a few minutes earlier. "Thanks. I'd probably still be stuck in this bed if it weren't for you. I'll get up again later and take a few more steps."

Étienne shook his head. "You must not risk a fall."

"Don't worry. I'll hang onto the bedpost." Falcon had described the Ohio Valley and his plans to live there, but thus far, Étienne had been too distracted to offer any plans of his own. "You don't trust her, do you?"

Caught off guard, Étienne grew defensive. "Don't trust who?"

Feeling more relaxed, Falcon propped his hands behind his head. "Dominique, of course. Who else? You'll be getting married on Saturday, too. Your suit is being tailored, and you'll have everything else you require. You ought to buy her ring yourself, though. Do you have any money?"

"Some." Étienne swallowed hard and began to pace beside Falcon's bed. "I know I should have a ring, but if Dominique changes her mind, it would be a sad keepsake."

"Look at you!" Falcon exclaimed. "You're almost as handsome as me, and nearly as clever. Why would she change her mind?"

Étienne laughed easily at Falcon's joke, for it was not his appearance or intelligence that troubled him. He went to the window and looked out. Falcon's room faced the fields, and for as far as his eye could see, this was Barclay land. That Étienne owned nothing except his good name, which Byron refused to accept, still troubled him. "Is there really good land in the Ohio Valley?" he asked.

"Yes. That's why the French fought so hard to keep it. You and Dominique ought to come with us, Étienne. We get along well together, and Belle and Dominique would have each other as best friends. Did you hope to return to sea and leave Dominique languishing in port for months at a time?"

Étienne laughed at the ridiculousness of that thought. "Dominique is not the type to languish," he replied.

Falcon nodded to concede the point. "No. She would undoubtedly begin selling herbal remedies, or designing fine gowns, or open an academy for girls, but she would not be unfaithful to you. Why don't you trust her?"

Étienne could have explained in French, but it was a difficult concept to relate in English to a man who never held any doubts. "Perhaps it is because my father could not win her mother's love. It may not be our fate to be together, either."

"My God! Where do you get your ideas?" Falcon cried. "Sit down and I'll tell you a couple of love stories that are so tangled you won't believe your ears." He definitely had Étienne's attention then, and when the Frenchman was comfortably seated, Falcon began with his own parents' tale. "Did you realize that while Christian and I are brothers, his mother was my Uncle Byron's sister, while my mother is Byron's cousin? If you feel out of place here, can you imagine my father, a Seneca brave right out of the woods, walking into this mansion and taking not one beautiful Barclay woman, but two?"

Étienne's mouth fell agape. "I had no idea."

"The Seneca view the world differently than white men do," Falcon explained. "A Seneca brave owns nothing other than his buckskins, moccasins, and his hunting implements. The women own everything else—the fields where they grow their food, and the longhouses in which whole families live. It's the women who select the chief, and remove him if his decisions don't benefit the tribe. When a man marries, he goes to live in his wife's house, with her family. They believe it is a fine way to organize things, so my father has never cared that this was not his house or his land. He is complete in himself, Étienne, which is a good way for a man to think."

Étienne did not have to ponder that idea to appreciate its value. "So we could go to the Ohio Valley, build houses for our wives, clear land for them, and then hunt and fish and simply be men?"

Falcon responded with a ready grin. "The Seneca way has always held great appeal for me, and I can see that it does for you, too. Now let me tell you about the rest of this fine family."

More than an hour passed before Étienne understood

what trials the Barclays had overcome to become the harmonious family he had met. What amused him most was that Christian could call Ian Scott father, and yet had pursued Ian's daughter and made her his wife. He liked that enormously. *"Audacity* is the right word, is it not?" he asked.

Falcon nodded. "If we had a family crest, that would definitely be in the motto. You belong with us, Étienne. Bring Dominique to the Ohio Valley, and we'll begin a dynasty that will put the Barclays of Virginia to shame."

It had been the wild streak in Falcon that Étienne had first admired, and striking out on their own was incredibly appealing. He nodded, and decided no matter what Dominique had asked, he had been alone too long. He was smiling as he left, and the autumn sky was suddenly a brighter blue. He had kept the horse Falcon had given him and rode him into Williamsburg that afternoon to buy Dominique a wedding ring. Falcon had told him where to go and what size to purchase, and he bought the prettiest one he could afford.

That night he slept fitfully, and no longer content to bide his time, left his bed after midnight and went back to the Barclays'. He slipped in the back door as silently as he had at noon, and wearing moccasins, made no sound on the stairs. It wasn't until he placed his hand on Dominique's doorknob that it occurred to him she might have locked her door, but it swung open easily and he closed it silently behind him.

She was sleeping too soundly to hear him, and he kicked off his moccasins, dropped his buckskins, and climbed into her bed. He drew her into his arms and nuzzled her throat. She sighed sweetly and opened her eyes. Pale moonlight lit the room, but neither needed to see the other clearly to taste the love flavoring their first kiss.

"I could not stay away," Étienne whispered. He parted her legs with his knee and moved over her. "We will have to be very quiet." He brushed her lips with his own, then eased into her with a shallow thrust and withdrew.

Dominique's breath caught in her throat, and she wrapped her arms around his shoulders. "Devil," she murmured against his cheek. He smothered a laugh in her hair and this time slid into her with a light, fluttering stroke and again withdrew. He kept up the teasing assault on her senses until she moved her hands down over his hips to lure him deep. He sank into her and lay still, stretching her with his heat, not moving and yet filling her with a radiant joy.

Étienne kissed Dominique with the fevered intensity he dared not display in a more forceful manner when it would surely rock the bed and wake the whole house. When he had to move, he slid back on her creamy wetness and pushed forward again. "I did not want you to forget that you are mine," he swore softly.

The weight of his body was a glorious reminder of that, but Dominique had no such need. She wrapped her legs over his thighs to hold him tight, and he moved up to create a more perfect alignment and increased their pleasure tenfold. Dominique breathed deeply as their rapture soared to a shattering crest, but Étienne refused to allow her bliss to fade.

With deep kisses and shallow thrusts, he kept her hovering on the edge of ecstasy until she begged for another release. He buried himself deep within her then, and, lost in his own surrender, felt a starry swirl entwine their hearts and bind them anew. He knew making a paradise of her bed was a primitive way to keep her love, but he thought it undoubtedly the best one.

It wasn't until Étienne had to leave that he realized how great a mistake spending the night in Dominique's bed had been, for that single taste of bliss was not going to be nearly enough to see him through their final week apart.

* * *

When Dominique awoke with the new day, she feared her smile was going to be much too wide. When she had displayed no more than a brief regret over Étienne, her parents had ceased mentioning his name and she was certain she had convinced them she had forgotten him as quickly as her other beaus. She could never have really forgotten him, however, and now that he had entered her bedroom with the same stealth that had claimed her heart, she longed to be with him always, and in all ways.

That afternoon she slipped out after tea, strolled through the garden, and enjoyed a lazy walk along the shore until she was out of sight of the house. Then she hiked up her skirts and ran the whole way to the Scotts'. She found Étienne in the barn, tending his horse, and had to grab for the stall door as she fought to catch her breath.

"You are wicked!" she exclaimed. "How dare you sneak into my bedroom at night? Have you no regard for my reputation, monsieur?"

Étienne responded with a low, courtly bow. "It is because I value your reputation so highly that I call on you only after midnight."

Dominique fell into his arms and he welcomed her with the same enthusiasm she had shown him before dawn. When he released her, she hugged him one last time before stepping back. "We have guests coming for the wedding. Some may arrive early and stay more than one night. I'll have to share Belle's room, and I don't want you joining the wrong woman in my bed."

Étienne looked aghast at that possibility. "Neither do I! Must I stay away?"

"This time you absolutely must, Étienne." His disappointment was so touching she slid her arms around his waist and rose on her toes to kiss him. "We have a few minutes together now. Let's not waste them."

Étienne scooped her up in his arms and nearly scorched her lips with a searing kiss, and for what time he had, he

made her stay memorable. When she left, he waited at the
barn door as she walked down to the river. Finally satisfied
that she would still want him come Saturday, he allowed
himself to dream of the life they would have in the Ohio
Valley.

On Saturday morning, Dominique and her mother went
out to the garden to cut the flowers for the wedding. The
day was clear and crisp, and carrying armloads of white
chrysanthemums and beautiful white roses, they returned
to the house in high spirits. Arielle had the crystal vases
on the dining room table ready to fill.

"I think you are much better at this than I am," Arielle
complimented.

Dominique sliced off a chrysanthemum stem and dropped
it into a tall vase. "Only because I've had you for my
teacher," she assured her mother.

Arielle was delighted by her daughter's smile. "I can not
tell you how pleased I am to see you happy once again. I
could not have planned such a perfect wedding for Belle
and Falcon without your help, and I know one day love will
come for you."

"It would be most welcome today," Dominique replied,
thrilled to know that it would.

Arielle assumed her daughter was teasing. Amused, she
laughed with her. "Falcon has invited friends from the militia. Are there any whom you have yet to meet?"

"I don't believe so, but I'll look forward to seeing them
again." Dominique directed her mother's attention to the
candles and away from herself, but she was so excited it
was difficult not to confide that her dream of love had already come true. The wedding would take place in the afternoon, followed by a lovely supper and dancing. It would
take all day to have everything as perfect as Belle deserved,
but Dominique enjoyed every minute.

When she at last went upstairs to her room to bathe and dress for the ceremony, she found a note on her bed. She had not realized Étienne had been there to see Falcon, but this time he had left her a note. It was a simple *Je vous aime,* signed with an E, and yet worth a dozen love letters from other men. When she dressed, she tucked it inside her bodice for luck, but she was already convinced the evening would go her way.

Dominique's ice blue gown was as exquisite as she had remembered, and with her hair styled atop her head in a cascade of pretty curls, and pearl jewelry, she was as lovely as she had ever been. She went to help Belle and found her primping in front of her mirror. Her wedding gown was of a luxurious iridescent white satin, and so feminine and sweet, there was no trace of the adventuresome little girl who had won Falcon's heart as a child.

When Belle turned toward her, Dominique greeted her in an ecstatic rush. "You have never looked more beautiful, Belle," she enthused. "Falcon will surely remember how gorgeous you are for the rest of his life." She came forward to adjust a single curl, then pronounced her little sister a vision of perfection.

"How can you be so calm?" Belle asked.

Dominique had waited for that day with a longing she knew she would never be able to explain. Rather than feeling nervous about the outcome, however, she was elated. "This is going to be such a glorious wedding and I'm thrilled for you, but you're the bride, so why shouldn't I be calm?"

Arielle came to the door dressed in pale yellow satin. She glanced at her two lovely daughters, and overcome with emotion, had to wipe a tear from her eye. "I want you to stay here with Belle, Dominique, and I will let you know when all the guests have arrived. I had thought holding the wedding here would be easier for Falcon, but I failed to realize just how many people your father would invite."

"It's warm. The guests can spill out into the garden and it will be a wonderful party," Dominique assured her.

Trusting Dominique's opinion, Arielle gave both her girls a kiss and then swept out of the room. Belle still could not quite believe she was the elegant blonde in the mirror. "I do hope Falcon recognizes me," she joked.

"Of course he will. You and I will be the only ones here with freckles, and he'll be sure to remember you're slightly taller."

They had had a great many whispered conversations during the last two weeks, but Belle still could not believe Dominique meant to leave with Étienne if their parents would not accept him. She knew she would have made the same choice for Falcon, but she had never been able to predict what Dominique might do. "Are you still convinced Étienne is the man for you?" she asked hesitantly.

Dominique drew in a deep breath and unabashedly beamed with pride. "He is my heart and soul, Belle, but we'll not create a disturbance at your party." She went to the door and peeked out. "I can hear the musicians tuning their instruments. I can hardly wait to dance."

Belle followed her to the door and as the string quartet's lyric melody began to float up the stairwell, she finally realized that she was actually getting married today. She had absolutely no doubts, but that did not mean the ceremony would not be a strain. "Please stand close to me so I don't faint," she begged.

Dominique took her sister's hand, and when it was time for the wedding to begin, the guests crowding the parlor swore Virginia had never produced two more beautiful young women. Christian stood with Falcon. It was the only time anyone could recall ever seeing Falcon in a suit, but he looked as splendid as his elder brother in black velvet with black stockings. The ruffled cuffs and stocks of their white linen shirts contrasted sharply with their deeply tanned skin, but the pair appeared to be unaware of how dashing they looked in formal attire.

Étienne's elegant black suit matched theirs, as did his dark stockings and silver buckled shoes, but he waited until the ceremony was about to begin before he entered. Rather than take one of the few remaining chairs, he moved to the back of the parlor, then prayed he would have no reason to wish he were closer to the door. When the other guests sent inquisitive glances his way, he nodded and smiled as though he had as much right to be there as they. He recognized Falcon's friends from the militia, and felt more comfortable.

The musicians began a new tune and Dominique entered carrying a bouquet of white roses trailing long satin streamers. She moved to the right of the priest, while Christian and Falcon were on the cleric's left. She turned toward the room and looked directly at Étienne. Her expression was one of such loving joy that he did not care who followed her gaze.

Belle came in on her father's arm and the ceremony continued amid complimentary murmurs from the guests. Étienne counted the seconds as the priest read the ceremony and hoped it would not last longer than Falcon's endurance. He listened carefully to the exchange of vows and slipped his hand into his pocket to make certain he still had Dominique's ring. When the couple was at last pronounced husband and wife, he relaxed against the wall, but was still apprehensive about what the evening might bring.

As soon as the guests began to congratulate Falcon and Belle, Dominique slipped away and joined Étienne. She leaned close to whisper, "You look magnificent, monsieur. I hope you're here to see me."

Étienne had been rather surprised himself when he had donned the handsome apparel Falcon had provided. After having worn buckskins, it was a chore to have to wear so many layers of fabric, but he had to admit the effect was well worth the effort. "Do you think I will be mistaken for a gentleman?" he asked.

"Most definitely, but it will be no mistake." Dominique could have simply looked at him for hours, but all too soon her father appeared at her side.

"Do not presume upon my generosity another minute, Monsieur LeBlanc. You've attended Falcon's wedding, and now I must ask you to leave."

Among the guests, there were several men who had signed the Declaration of Independence, and Dominique could not help but believe her father had unwittingly raised her to defy all forms of oppressive authority. She did not want to engage him in a debate on liberty now, however, and looped her arm through Étienne's so those standing nearby would think the three of them were chatting amiably, but there was no mistaking the forcefulness of her tone. "We wish to speak with you later, Father, but now you should attend to your guests."

Not used to receiving orders from his daughters, Byron took immediate exception to Dominique's request. "That is precisely what I am doing, sweetheart. I am arranging to have one less," he hissed through clenched teeth.

"This is a wonderful party," Étienne announced loudly enough for everyone to hear. "You must be very proud of your daughter and new son-in-law."

One of Falcon's friends from the militia echoed that sentiment, and those who had already been served wine began proposing toasts to the bride and groom. Étienne stood quietly, daring Byron to throw him out, and while he could see the anger in Byron's eyes, he finally walked away rather than act on it. "I am sorry to have put your father in a hostile mood," Étienne swore under his breath.

"I sincerely doubt that, but come with me. Let's have some wine so we can offer a few toasts of our own."

Étienne followed Dominique's lead, but he made certain he knew where Byron was the whole time since Falcon was too busy to watch his back and he did not want any new scars. He had never been to such an elaborate party, but with Dominique smiling proudly by his side, he found it easy to respond to introductions graciously, and when Byron did not confront him again, he took it as a good sign.

Byron, however, was not enjoying the evening nearly as much as his guests. He drew Arielle aside and asked her advice. "Dominique knows I won't make a scene at Belle's wedding, but seeing her wrap herself around Étienne in such a disgusting fashion is making me ill."

"She is merely holding his arm," Arielle pointed out, "but you are right. She knows we do not approve of him, and that her behavior will surely upset us."

"Then why is she doing it?"

Arielle leaned close and whispered, "I can think of only one reason, and that is love."

Byron winced. "Christ! I would sooner have Sean O'Keefe here in his uniform!"

"Yes. Dominique has acquired somewhat unusual tastes in men, but everyone in Grand Pré said the same of me and in not nearly such polite terms. Could you not regard Étienne as one of my people, rather than as Gaetan's son?"

Appalled that she had taken Dominique's side against him, Byron brushed his wife's hands from his arm and walked away without offering a reply, and Arielle knew Dominique was not the only one who had gone too far that night. She would not allow her dismay to show in her expression and passed among their guests wearing a delighted smile, but now she had far more on her mind than keeping them entertained. She received effusive compliments on the food, and the musicians played such lovely music the dancing lasted far into the night, but the whole while she knew the party was merely a prelude to what could easily become the worst fight she and her beloved husband had ever had.

Because Falcon was not well enough to travel, he and Belle were remaining there for the night, but while he knew the guests would at least expect them to bid everyone good night and go upstairs, he did not want Étienne to have to contend with Byron on his own. He had spent the greater part of the evening seated, but taking Belle by the hand, he walked across the room to stand with Étienne and Dominique. "Let's have the second wedding while everyone is still here," he suggested.

"That's a lovely idea," Dominique agreed, "but it may not be easy to arrange." She looked up at Étienne and was delighted to find the confidence he had displayed all evening still reflected in his smile. She waved to Jean, and when he responded she asked him to summon their parents. Inspired by her gesture, Falcon caught Christian's eye and he and Liana joined them.

Byron and Arielle approached from different sides of the room, but stood together. Byron was even less cordial than he had been earlier. "If you have anything to say other than good night, Monsieur LeBlanc, I've no wish to hear it."

"That is a pity," Étienne responded, "for I have a fascinating subject to discuss. Dominique has agreed to become my bride, and with your permission, we would also like to get married tonight."

Stunned by the Frenchman's announcement, Byron turned to Arielle. "Did you know about this?"

Although hurt by his accusing tone, Arielle raised her chin proudly. "No. I had absolutely no idea Dominique was even interested in Étienne."

Intending to yank Dominique away, Byron reached out to grab her arm, but Étienne stepped in front of her to block the move. "I would like your answer, sir," he challenged.

"Do I have to say it again?" Byron sneered. He kept his voice low, and what the guests observed was merely a gathering of the family in a quiet conversation. "Get out of my house and don't ever come back."

Falcon braced his weight against the back of a chair, but

spoke firmly. "If you have a quarrel with Étienne, then you have one with me."

Christian moved forward to support his brother. "If you have a quarrel with either Étienne or Falcon, then you have one with me as well."

Too perceptive a man to be fooled by hushed voices coming from the scene in the corner, Hunter approached in time to hear the last exchange. He saw how tightly Dominique was clinging to Étienne's hand and understood everything in an instant. "My sons know what is right, and so do I. I will take Dominique's side."

Dominique had always sensed Hunter did not really approve of her, but she saw a new, loving acceptance in his eyes that night. "Thank you, Uncle. I want to wed Étienne, and because Father has refused to give his consent, we'll have to go."

Byron laughed out loud at that threat. "And just how far do you think you'll get?"

"They need go no farther than my parents' home," Liana offered. "In fact, let's take the priest and invite everyone who wishes to join us for the ceremony to follow us there."

Dominique had not thought past having to march out the front door, but was delighted by Liana's suggestion. "What do you think?" she asked Étienne.

"I think it is a fine idea."

Byron felt someone at his elbow and found Johanna and David had joined them. He had once advised her not to risk her heart on a young man who would soon go on his way but she had fallen in love with David anyway, and he had stayed to become her husband. Alanna had appeared to take Hunter's hand, and he recalled what a shy creature she had been before the brave had entered her life.

Feeling badly outnumbered, Byron slipped his arm around his own dear wife's waist and remembered how insulted his parents had been by his choice. He had never regretted marrying Arielle, and knew she would be a delight to the end of his days. His anger dissolved by the warmth of the love surrounding him, he sighed softly. "Is this what you truly want, sweetheart?"

Dominique spoke to Étienne rather than her father. "With all my heart."

Byron attempted to accept her choice with grace. "Then there's no reason to traipse off to the Scotts'. You two will be married right here where you belong, but I swear if you ever give my daughter a second of grief, Étienne, I'll see you're on board the next vessel sailing for France."

Étienne extended his hand. "You have my word. I will give Dominique the very best of lives. It is what she has already given me."

Reluctantly, Byron shook Étienne's hand, and in the next instant Dominique threw her arms around her father's neck to hug him, and her joy made everything right. When she released Byron, he turned to Jean. "Beau will probably bring home a princess from the south seas, but will you please try to find a bride from among our friends?"

"I'm only sixteen! I don't need a wife."

Jean's protest was drowned out by his family's laughter. English, Seneca, French, they had been drawn from different cultures and different lands but together they had created something beautiful and new. Dominique and Étienne's wedding was celebrated with the same joy as Belle and Falcon's, and while the guests may have been astonished by the impromptu ceremony, no one doubted the radiant love in the couple's eyes or their chances for a blissful future.

NOTE TO READERS

I hope that you have enjoyed sharing Belle and Dominique's passionate adventures with Falcon and Étienne. Love is always a powerful force, and especially so in perilous times. America has a fascinating history, and it has been a joy to bring it to life through characters who display the diverse influences of the English, Seneca, and French. Thank you for again celebrating love's ageless thrill with me. I welcome your comments. Please write to me c/o Zebra Books. Include a legal-size self-addressed stamped envelope for an autographed bookmark and newsletter. Or you can E-mail me at: phoebeconn@earthlink.com.

ROMANCE FROM JO BEVERLY

DANGEROUS JOY   (0-8217-5129-8, $5.99)

FORBIDDEN   (0-8217-4488-7, $4.99)

THE SHATTERED ROSE   (0-8217-5310-X, $5.99)

TEMPTING FORTUNE   (0-8217-4858-0, $4.99)

ROMANCE FROM JANELLE TAYLOR

ANYTHING FOR LOVE   (0-8217-4992-7, $5.99)

DESTINY MINE   (0-8217-5185-9, $5.99)

CHASE THE WIND   (0-8217-4740-1, $5.99)

MIDNIGHT SECRETS   (0-8217-5280-4, $5.99)

MOONBEAMS AND MAGIC (0-8217-0184-4, $5.99)

SWEET SAVAGE HEART   (0-8217-5276-6, $5.99)

ROMANCE FROM FERN MICHAELS

DEAR EMILY   (0-8217-4952-8, $5.99)

WISH LIST   (0-8217-5228-6, $6.99)

AND IN HARDCOVER:

VEGAS RICH   (1-57566-057-1, $25.00)